The One You Fight For

RONI LOREN

sourcebooks
casablanca

*To those who have lost someone they
love to violence, may you find peace and
a path to your happily ever after.*

Published by Sourcebooks Casablanca, an imprint of Sourcebooks, Inc.
P.O. Box 4410, Naperville, Illinois 60567-4410
(630) 961-3900
Fax: (630) 961-2168
sourcebooks.com

Printed and bound in Canada.
MBP 10 9 8 7 6 5 4 3 2 1

Doug lifted his gaze at that, as if just noticing she was still there. "Right. That's...interesting."

Yep. He hadn't heard a word she'd said. *Awesome.* But she wasn't surprised. She hadn't conducted a formal study, but she'd collected enough anecdotal evidence to know that she sucked at this whole dating thing. People wanted to talk about breezy stuff on dates—what Netflix shows they were bingeing, what hobbies they had, which cities they wanted to visit one day. She didn't have time to have favorite TV shows or quirky hobbies or to take vacations to exotic places. She had research, developing her program, and teaching. She barely had time to sleep, much less be recreationally well-rounded.

Why had she subjected herself to a date again? She could've been home and in her comfy clothes by now. Instead, she was here in uncomfortable shoes and even less comfortable conversation. Maybe she'd agreed to this because she liked the *idea* of dating someone. When she came home late at night, lugging a pile of research and student papers with her, she sometimes imagined what it would be like to have someone to call or have dinner with, or more than have dinner with. That was probably what had landed her on this blind date—the *idea* of these mythical things. But in actual practice, dating was just straight-up painful.

She took a long sip of wine as her date glanced at his phone *again.* "Do you need to check that?"

"Huh?" Doug glanced up guiltily. "Oh, no. It's fine. Well, maybe I should check in case it's work."

Taryn shrugged, expecting the answer. She had a degree in reading people, but Doug's behavior didn't require a doctorate to decipher. "Knock yourself out."

At least she could tell her friend Kincaid that she'd given this a shot. Kincaid had set her up on this date because *Girl, I worry about you. You need to get out of that research lab and live a little. Doug is smart and a sly kind of cute, like an eighties teen movie villain.*

Taryn had pictured a young James Spader, which had gotten her to reluctantly agree to this, but Doug would never have been able to pull off feathered hair and a white suit. Also, she suspected he had a mild case of narcissistic personality disorder—which was probably why he'd shut down when she'd started talking about sociopaths. They were in the same psychological family. He was probably insulted.

Or maybe she should learn to shut up about the research part of her job and just tell people about the more straightforward part—that she taught psychology at a university. When people asked about what she did for a living, they usually were just being polite and didn't actually want to hear the details. She liked details—telling them and hearing them. People's life stories were endlessly fascinating to her. She collected them like other people collected photographs of interesting places. What made someone tick, what led them to their career, what made them who they were. But even she'd had trouble finding something interesting about Doug the financial planner.

Date experiment conducted. Experiment failed. Oh well. This outcome would've matched her hypothesis anyway. Blind dates had a high crash-and-burn rate. She wouldn't have gone on this one if Kincaid hadn't looked so damn sincere and concerned about Taryn's lack of a social life. Her friend didn't want her to be lonely, and

Taryn loved her for at least trying. However, now she was ready to get home, get in her pajama pants, and compile the final data for her presentation.

Taryn checked her watch, and when she saw that Doug was still scrolling through something on his phone, she pulled her own phone from her purse. Two missed calls and a text alert filled her screen. Two from her mother. One from her dad.

Shit. Taryn got that queasy pinch in her gut, and she almost fumbled the phone, trying to quickly open the messages. She'd silenced her phone and had forgotten her nightly check-in text to her mother. Which meant red alert at her parents' house if her mom was having one of her bad days. She quickly texted both of them back, feeling like a guilty teenager instead of a grown woman.

To her mom: I'm sorry. I'm fine. Got caught up at work. All is well.

She didn't mention the blind date because that could potentially set off a whole other slew of panicked questions. *Who is he? Are you in a safe, public place? What do you know about this guy?*

To her dad: Sorry. Out with a friend and had phone on silent. Is Mom okay?

Her dad quickly responded: She'll be fine. Enjoy your night. Thanks for getting back to us, sweetie.

Taryn lifted her glasses and rubbed the bridge of her nose, guilt flooding her. How could she have forgotten? Was it really so hard to remember one text? She'd probably sent her mom into a tailspin and ruined both her and her father's nights. *Ugh.*

"Everything all right?" Doug asked, startling Taryn. She glanced up as the waiter dropped the check between them. "Um, yeah. Just a missed call." She dropped her phone into her purse and reached for her wallet. They were definitely going dutch on this date. "Well, we should probably—"

"Do you want to come by my place for a drink?" Doug asked, interrupting her and dropping a sleek, black credit card on top of the bill. It didn't even have numbers on the front.

The waiter swept in like a stealth bomber and took the card.

Taryn blinked. "Wait, what?"

Doug drained the rest of his wine and smiled. "My place. I don't live too far from here, and it's still early."

The chagrined smile he gave her said everything she needed to know. He was suggesting they sleep together. Even though they'd bored each other. Even though they had about as much in common as a grasshopper and a skyscraper. And he'd said it as if it were a totally normal thing to suggest.

She tilted her head. "So even though we clearly don't have anything in common and this date has been pretty boring, you're inviting me to go to your place?"

Now it was Doug's turn to blink like an owl. His smile faltered. "Wow, you don't pull punches, do you, doc?"

She had a tendency to blurt things out and speak her mind, but she wasn't going to apologize for it. "Am I reading the situation wrong?"

He chuckled and adjusted his tie. "No, you're not. I like your honesty. The date hasn't gone as well as either of us had probably hoped, but I think we're just two very busy people who have a hard time talking about anything but work. But"—he shrugged—"that also means we're two people who could probably stand to blow off a little steam without worrying about who's going to call whom tomorrow. You're attractive and smart. Physically, we'd probably work out just fine. It could still turn out to be a good night."

Taryn considered him. That was the first thing he'd said all night that made some sense—or at least had a shred of logic to it. Maybe Kincaid hadn't been totally off base with this match. When Doug dropped the smooth-talking, *I'm Mr. Important* act, he was almost likable. Almost.

But it'd been longer than Taryn cared to acknowledge since she'd slept with anyone, and if she was going to break that dry spell, she wanted to make it count. She'd had *It's convenient and we like each other well enough* sex before. It'd always been vaguely unsatisfying during and then awkward after. She'd sworn to herself after the last uninspired hookup that she'd wait for some kind of *Oh my God, I must get this guy naked* spark. So far, she'd only gotten that watching the occasional movie with a hot actor in it.

She tried to imagine tugging off Doug's tie and unbuttoning his shirt, running her hands over his chest, letting him touch her. Her internal interest meter swung to the far left, to the icy tundra zone. *Nope.*

She pulled her purse onto her lap and gave Doug a polite smile as the waiter dropped the receipt and card back on the table. "I appreciate the offer, but I've got a lot of work left to do tonight." *And probably a James Spader movie to watch.*

"You sure?" he asked, looking genuinely disappointed.

She stood and smoothed the wrinkles from her skirt. "Yeah. Thanks so much for dinner, though."

"Here. Let me walk you out."

She let him lead her with a loose hand on her lower back through the restaurant and out into the muggy spring air. A few cars whizzed by on the damp downtown street, but otherwise, this part of Austin was pretty chill on a Friday night—only a couple of restaurants and after-work-type bars were open, mostly frequented by the locals living in the condos along this stretch. The tourists had more exciting places to be. She'd always liked this part of town.

She turned to Doug and put out her hand to shake his. "Thanks again. It was nice to meet you. I'll be sure to call you when I decide to invest in some mutual funds."

His face lit up. "Oh great. Here, let me give you my card."

She didn't have money for mutual funds, but she accepted the card and tucked it into her purse like a peace offering. "Thanks."

"And if I run across any sociopaths, I'll send them your way…" He cringed. "Wait, that was supposed to be a joke, but now that I say it out loud…"

She smirked, amused. "It sounds like a threat."

His cheeks dotted with red in the glow of the street-light. "I didn't mean it that way. Sorry, after what you've been… That was kind of horrible. Sorry."

Her stance on Doug softened a little more at his obvious embarrassment. Maybe he wasn't so much a narcissist as a guy trying to be smooth and confident when he was just as awkward at this as she was. Plus, once people knew who she was and her history, they inevitably put their foot in their mouth about it and forgot everything else about her. It was like some weird disease.

She'd gotten used to it. Her past either freaked people out or morbidly fascinated them. She wasn't sure which was worse—pity or rubbernecking. Flip a coin. At least Doug had made it through the whole date without asking her about the Long Acre High shooting. He got points for that. "It's fine. I know that's not what you meant."

His shoulders sagged in relief, and he met her gaze. "I really do think it's remarkable what you're doing. I'm not sure I'd be able to bounce back after something like that. I definitely wouldn't be able to dive into research about school shootings. I'd probably never want to think about it again. I'd be a total ostrich."

She laughed, picturing Doug sticking his head in the sand in full suit and tie. "Ostriching is a valid reaction." She slipped her purse strap over her shoulder. "That might've been the route I would've taken if I remembered that night like my friends do. But my mind has blocked most of it out."

His brown eyes widened. "Seriously?"

She nodded, though she got that familiar uncomfortable twist in her stomach at the oft-repeated lie. "I lost my sister. I remember that part. But I have no solid details of the rest of the event."

"Wow, that must be kind of scary." He tugged on his tie as if it'd gotten too tight. "I'm not sure I'd like knowing there are memories I can't access. Doesn't that make it hard to, like, move on?"

Move on. Was that a thing people really did after something ripped your entire world in two? Move forward, maybe, but moving on seemed like a ridiculous expectation. That was like saying *Why don't you move on from your personality and get an entirely new one?* Taryn lifted a shoulder. "I don't have to remember that night to know how important it is to make sure those kinds of tragedies don't happen again, you know? I've got all the information I need."

Doug tucked his hands in his pockets, his gaze serious as he nodded. "Now I feel kind of shitty that I was so checked out at dinner. I'd like to see you again, do better, really get to know you instead of being so distracted by work. You think I can have a do-over?"

Taryn smiled, though it felt a little brittle. *Now* she'd captured his interest. She was beginning to worry that the only thing others found interesting about her was her tragic history. That was goddamned depressing. "How about as friends next time? No pressure to impress."

Doug looked down at his feet and laughed lightly before meeting her gaze again. "Sounds like a plan."

Taryn stepped forward and gave Doug a quick hug, deflated about how the night had gone and ready to get home. "Have a good night."

They walked in opposite directions to get back to their cars, and she didn't bother looking back to wave. Her steps were purposeful on the sidewalk, but her mind sifted back through the date, replaying the conversation, *analyzing*.

Damn, she *had* been boring. She spent so much time with her colleagues, who thought the minutiae of research were top-level entertainment, and her students, who were forced to pay attention to what she said, that she'd forgotten how dry all that stuff could be to someone outside of that world.

Ugh.

Taryn pulled out her phone and texted Kincaid.

> **Taryn:** Thanks for the setup.

It only took a few seconds for her friend to respond.

> **Kincaid:** Uh-oh, ur texting me before midnight. That can't be good. Did I miss the mark?
>
> **Taryn:** Not ur fault. Apparently, I'm boring.
>
> **Kincaid:** WHAT? Did he say that? B/c I will kick Doug's ass.
>
> **Taryn:** No. I'm saying it. I bored him.
>
> **Kincaid:** It's not ur job to entertain a dude.
>
> **Taryn:** Correction—I bored myself. He was just along for the snore-worthy ride. I'm BORING.
>
> **Kincaid:** *hugs* You're not boring. You're brilliant.
>
> **Taryn:** The two aren't mutually exclusive. Can be both.

The phone rang in her hand. Taryn passed her parked car and kept walking, needing a bit of fresh air before the drive home. "Hello?"

"Stop calling yourself boring," Kincaid said without preamble.

Taryn stepped over a wad of gum stuck to the sidewalk. "I'm just calling it like I see it."

"No. You're not seeing it clearly. You're just in a rut, honey," Kincaid said, her sassy country-girl accent coloring each word with concern. "Don't be so hard on yourself. It can happen to the best of us."

"Oh, please. When in your life have you ever been boring?" Taryn asked with an eye roll her friend couldn't see. Kincaid was the definition of the life of the party. She could probably turn a seminar on time-shares into a hot ticket.

"It's happened. I swear," she said dramatically. "I had a stretch where I worked so much that I was in bed with a guy and found myself telling him how the cornices on his windows would raise the value of his house."

Taryn laughed. "Oh no."

"Yes, you better believe I took myself on a vacation two weeks later," Kincaid said with a huff. "If I'm thinking about cornices when I have a naked man literally on top of me, it's a code red. That needed the Bahamas."

"I don't have time to go to the Bahamas." She didn't have time to get a pedicure, much less take a trip to an island that served umbrella drinks.

"I know, but maybe you just need to take a break or shake things up a little," Kincaid suggested. "Try some new things. Meet some new people. Hell, move to the city. I could get you a good deal on a condo. I know an agent who works the area near the university."

"Move to the city?"

"Sure, why not? You're young and single. You can move where you want."

Taryn's eyes drifted to the loft apartments in the building on the other side of the street. The big plate-glass windows shone bright with interior lights at this hour, different versions of home being displayed in each—a modern minimalist look with bizarre artwork on white walls and a couple sitting at a dinner table, another apartment with a collection of African masks above the couch in a funky display, and yet another with a cat perched in the window and a woman drinking coffee or tea in a chair nearby.

Move to the city? Not that the thought didn't sound glamorous. Taryn had always been captivated by the idea of living downtown in some big city. The buzz of life all around her. Restaurants and shops just a quick walk away. It was so far from her reality in Long Acre, three streets over from her parents in a boring ranch-style rental house, that she couldn't even wrap her head around it.

Even though she worked in Austin, she'd never lived anywhere else but the small town an hour outside of the city. Growing up, she'd had dreams of going to college in New York, of traveling, of seeing all the things the world had to offer. But after the shooting and her mom's decline, those options had become so far out of reach as to be laughable. Now, even the simple lofts in downtown Austin seemed downright exotic.

"That's not even a remote possibility," she said to her real-estate-agent friend.

"Fine, but maybe try to loosen the border restrictions on your life a little. I know you have a lot on your plate, but sometimes you just need to go out, do something crazy…examine some cornices from beneath a sexy guy."

Taryn snorted. "There will be no cornices tonight."

"Doug's loss. But look, I'll see you on Sunday at the charity run. We'll do some brainstorming," Kincaid said resolutely.

"We're also supposed to start training for the

university's 10K run that you agreed to do with me. We need to figure out a schedule," Taryn reminded her.

"Hold up. Did I actually agree to that?" Kincaid asked, her voice getting higher-pitched at the end. "Like with a yes?"

"Yes."

"Was I sober? Because I don't think it counts if I wasn't."

"Stone cold," Taryn said, shaking her head. "Don't try to back out of it now. You said you were, and I quote, 'eating like a bear preparing for hibernation and needed to get your ass off the couch.'"

"I would never say such a thing, but we'll talk about it after the 'Let's find excitement' brainstorming. That's more important. I am not friends with boring people, so I know there's a wildly fascinating woman on the other end of this phone. We just need to bring her out a little. Because I could give a shit if some dude finds you interesting, but Lord, if you're boring yourself, it's intervention time, sugar."

Taryn smiled and leaned against a light post. "I'm not sure there are interventions for this but thanks."

"Yep. And sure there are. I'm on it. See you on Sunday."

Taryn exchanged goodbyes with her friend and pushed away from the light post, feeling a little better and trying to decide which was the best way back to her car. She should probably circle the block. She'd just given Kincaid a speech about preparing for a run but hadn't exercised beyond walking back and forth across the classroom in ages. She started walking and reassessing the rest of her night. Maybe tonight she *would* take a break, skip the statistics compiling, and just go straight to the James Spader movie.

Taryn turned the corner and, after half a block, passed a small bar with an open door. Her steps slowed. The sidewalk sign outside the door advertised open mic night at the Tipsy Hound, and the initial guitar chords of an old Green Day song she used to love drifted out to her, mixed with the clink of beer bottles and muffled conversation. Unable to stop herself, Taryn paused to listen and leaned into the doorway to peek inside.

The bar was tiny and only half full, but the skinny guy onstage commanded the room with a single spotlight, bright-purple hair, his acoustic guitar, and a song about walking lonely roads and empty streets. Taryn listened to the opening verse of the song, her fingers curving against her purse strap as if holding the neck of a guitar, her muscle memory playing chords along with him. "Boulevard of Broken Dreams" had been one of the songs she'd secretly taught herself to play on the guitar in high school. It had contained the proper amount of angst. Taryn mouthed the lyrics.

"Want to come in?" an upbeat male voice asked from the dark interior.

Taryn startled and squinted as a guy with a backward baseball cap and long, red hair stepped into the light of the doorway. He had an apron tied at his waist and a pen behind his ear, but somehow she got the sense he was in charge.

"No cover charge," he added. "And if you want to perform, the audience favorite wins fifty bucks and a free beer."

"*Perform?*" she asked, unable to hide the incredulity in her voice.

He shrugged. "Sure. I mean, you were singing." He nodded toward her shoulder and wiggled his fingers. "And air-guitaring."

Had she been? "Um, no, thank you. I mean, I can't."

"Sure you can. Anyone can," he said with an easy smile. "That's the beauty of open mic night."

She shook her head, her shoulders tightening. "No. I don't have a guitar or anything and—"

"We have a loaner up there." He cocked his head toward the stage. "You play?"

Taryn's gaze jumped to the stage. *Did she play?* No. Not in over a decade.

But this weird urge to say *Yes, I do and sure I'll play* zipped through her like a firecracker. *What in the hell was that?* Maybe the combination of wine and her conversation with Kincaid had been too much. It was making her think insane thoughts. Taryn stepped back and lifted her palm. "No, I haven't played since I was in high school. I better be getting home."

"Aww, come on. I know that look. You want to." He swept a hand toward the stage where the guy was finishing his song. "Take a shot. I bet you'll remember more than you think. Plus, Mo's the last of the night, and I could stand to sell a few more beers. Give it a whirl. It's technically nineties night so anything from that decade is welcome, but, as you can see, even if you pick something off theme, you're fine. Boos and hecklers aren't allowed here." He tapped his name tag, which had *Kaleb* typed in blue letters and a logo with a droopy bloodhound on it. "The Tipsy Hound needs to be true to its mascot. People are friendly here. And drunk. But mostly friendly."

Taryn swallowed past the dryness in her throat, and her heart thumped faster than the rhythm of the music. Was this what Kincaid was talking about? Stepping over the borders of her normal life and walking into completely unknown territory? Taryn had played guitar all through high school, but she'd never performed in front of anyone outside of church. Her parents never would've approved of the songs she played or the ones she wrote in the privacy of her room because they thought music was a distraction.

"Okay," she heard herself say.

Okay??? Her stomach dropped, her mouth betraying her and saying the opposite of what she'd intended to say.

"Great!" Kaleb said. "All right, what's your name? I'll do an intro when Mo's done."

"Uh…" *What am I doing? What the hell am I doing?* "James." She cringed inwardly at the fake name. James Spader really needed to get out of her head. "With a *z*."

With a z? What the hell? Like that made it less weird?

But the guy didn't flinch. "Unisex. I like it. Cool." He waved a hand. "Come with me. I'm Kaleb, by the way, owner and operator."

She needed to turn around. There was no way she was actually doing this. But her feet moved forward as if an invisible hand was pulling her puppet strings. Her hands were sweating, and she couldn't catch her breath. She felt disconnected from her body in a way that was disconcerting. Still, she kept moving.

The stage got closer.

The other song ended. Kaleb smiled at her.

Holy shit. She was doing this.

chapter
TWO

I CAN'T DO THIS. DON'T DO THIS. RUN! THE COMMANDS RAN through Taryn's brain like scared mice, but her feet stayed rooted to the floor beside the stage. A smattering of applause followed Mo's performance, and then Kaleb hurried up the few steps to the small, battered stage.

"Tonight, we've got one more for you," he said into the microphone. "A newcomer who's probably a little scared of y'all, so give her some love and order another drink in her honor. Please welcome Jamez with a z!"

Taryn was going to throw up. Literally, all the shrimp she'd eaten at dinner to stave off the boredom were going to make a reappearance right there onstage. But Kaleb was already handing her the well-worn but freshly strung acoustic guitar. He pulled a pick from his pocket. "Stage is all yours."

Her feet felt like they'd been dipped in cement, but she took the instrument and walked to the stool. A few people clapped. Ice cubes clinked against glasses. Taryn couldn't look at anyone. She sat on the stool, crossed her ankles, and stared down at the guitar, half wondering how it'd appeared in her hands. Maybe she'd fallen on the sidewalk outside the restaurant, hit her head, and this was some sort of concussion dream.

She had no idea what song to play. No idea if she could still play at all. And the single spotlight felt like it was burning her skin and exposing every damn insecurity she had.

She cleared her throat, and the microphone amplified the sound, making her jump. She licked her lips. "I'm sorry. I haven't done this in a really long time."

Someone from the back whistled their encouragement.

Don't freak out. Don't freak out. She was totally freaking out. Taryn fitted her hand to the neck of the guitar and tried to focus. *Nineties songs.* She needed a song she knew by heart and that wasn't too complicated on the guitar. She scrolled through her mental playlist and landed on one that used to fill her angsty teenage heart with all the feels. She took a breath and dared a glance upward, not knowing who she was in this moment, but in too deep to bail now. She didn't make commitments she didn't keep. She lined her fingers up for a G chord and tested it. The sound was pure and well-tuned and vibrated through her with familiarity. That gave her a small bit of comfort. Guitars never changed, even if she had.

No more delaying.

She forced herself to look out at the audience and put her mouth closer to the mic. "My sister used to like this one. I hope y'all do, too."

Taryn took another deep breath and forced her hands to move as she played the opening chords to "What's

Up?" by 4 Non Blondes. She was trembling all over as if an electric current were moving through her. Looking at the few faces at the table closest to the stage was too much, and she missed the cue to start singing. She closed her eyes and went through the opening chords again, willing herself to just get the words out. A few verses and this temporary bout of insanity would be over.

Finally, her voice pushed past the dam of nerves in her throat and filled the small space of the bar. She sang the first lines about time passing and still not making it up the big hill of hope. Her voice felt rusty and trembled a little, and her fingertips were tender against the strings, but she kept going, eyes squeezed shut, the lyrics racing up from the vault in her mind to the surface.

Songs from her childhood were like that—old friends who never quite left her, even when she'd forgotten they existed. The words came back as though they'd just been waiting in line to be sung. She sang louder and steadier as she went, and before she knew it, she'd reached the climax of the song and was belting the tough high notes, her voice coming out gritty against her throat.

Taryn was lost for a moment, transported back to her bedroom that shared a wall with her younger sister's. When Taryn played and sang, Nia would slap her hands against their shared wall at the end of each song, her own version of a crowd demanding more. Her sister who always listened to Taryn sing. Her sister who, no matter how mad she got over whatever siblings got mad about, never revealed to their parents Taryn's secret plan to be a songwriter. Her sister who believed in her.

The memory hit Taryn like a gut punch, and the song left her just as quickly. Her eyes popped open, her chest tight and her skin burning hot. She didn't know where she'd ended the song but the words were gone. In the silence, she felt frozen. But before the next blink, the small crowd erupted in applause with a few whoops for good measure. The sounds were foreign to her ears and too much to handle. The room spun in her vision.

She quickly got to her feet, almost knocking the stool over in her haste, and set the guitar in the stand. She hurried toward the side of the stage in her uncomfortable heels and down the steps, brushing past Kaleb, who was trying to get her attention. She needed to get out of there. *Right. The hell. Now.*

"I think it's pretty obvious who our winner is tonight," Kaleb called out from somewhere behind her. "Jamez with a z, come on back up here!"

Taryn bumped hard into the edge of a table in the dark and yelped. She reached out and grabbed the back of a chair to keep herself upright but stumbled anyway, her ankle turning and her shoe slipping off.

"Hey, easy there," said a deep voice. A hand cupped her elbow, steadying her. "You okay?"

No. "I need to get out of here."

The man released her but stayed near. She couldn't see anything but his broad outline in the dark. "But you won. There's money—"

"I need my shoe." She could hear the hysterical note in her voice but couldn't help it. The bar felt too small, the memories too smothering. "Where's *my shoe*?"

"Hey, it's all right. Head on outside for some air," he said, his voice strong but soothing, like a cop trying to talk someone off a ledge. "I'll find your shoe and bring it out to you, all right?"

The offer was a godsend. "Thank you."

She zeroed in on the door and hobbled toward the light, ignoring the repeated calls from the stage for her to come up and collect her prize. She stumbled outside and took a deep breath. She pressed her back to the side of the building and tilted her head against it, trying to regain control of her body.

A minute or two later, footsteps sounded to her left, and the calming voice was back. "There you go. You're okay. Just catch your breath," the man said. "I have your shoe, and I told them you're not coming back in. You can take as long as you need."

Taryn rolled her lips inward and gave a little nod, but didn't open her eyes. "Thank you."

The man didn't say anything else, giving her space, but she could sense his presence, smell the mountain spring of his laundry detergent and the faint tang of beer. She probably looked like a lunatic. She should've stuck with boring.

Finally, after a few more breaths, she opened her eyes and turned her head to thank the stranger, but the words got lodged in her throat like dry bread. The guy was broad-shouldered and as solid as the wall she was leaning against, his muscular body not at all concealed by the forest-green T-shirt he was wearing. Her gaze flicked upward, finding dirty-blond hair pulled back into a man bun and light eyes that looked gray in the moonlight. Some weird zip of familiarity went through her, like déjà vu, and a sick awareness twisted her stomach. She knew those eyes.

But that wasn't possible. Those eyes belonged to a dead teenager, a killer. Her mind was playing tricks.

The guy handed her the high-heeled shoe she'd lost and a crisp fifty-dollar bill. "Your prize winnings."

Taryn took the items with a shaking hand. Her brain was having some sort of attack. Singing that particular song had triggered something, opened a door. Memories were trying to surface and were blending with reality. Memories she had no interest in handling right at this moment. She forced herself to focus on the handsome stranger, pick out the features that *did not* look like Joseph Miller. The strong jaw covered in scruff, the full bottom lip, the faint scar through one eyebrow, the slightly crooked nose. Plus, Joseph hadn't been sexy. This guy had sex appeal in spades.

She swallowed past the panic. *Not him. Not him.* "Thank you. I'm sorry."

He frowned. "What are you apologizing for?"

She blinked, her thoughts scattering like dropped pennies. "I don't know."

"Nothing to apologize for. Stage fright happens to a lot of people," he said, his voice as smooth as river rock. "Do you want me to grab you some water? Or a shot of something stronger?"

She managed a smile at that. "Tempting. But I have to drive. I'll be all right. I have a bottle of water in my car. I just… It's been a long time since I've been onstage."

He leaned a shoulder against the wall, looking like an After ad for the newest gym equipment. "How long?"

She smirked and slipped her shoe back on. "Um, never."

He chuckled, the sound warm and rich, and crossed his arms, making his shirt even tighter and more distracting. "That'll do it. I used to compete in…swim competitions, and I'd get sick right before every time."

A swimmer. Well, that explained the ridiculous body. Taryn dragged her attention down to the money he'd handed her. "I can't believe I just got paid for that. I literally ran offstage. The other competitors must've really sucked."

His lips lifted at one corner. "You're kidding, right?"

"What?"

He pushed off the wall. "I mean, I'm not going to lie and say the competition was stiff, but you have to know you can sing your face off, right? You earned that fair and square."

She shook her head and pushed her out-of-control hair away from her face. The humidity was making the curls grow bigger by the minute. "This is nuts. I was supposed to be watching a James Spader movie."

He tipped his head to the side. "Huh?"

She waved a hand. "Nothing. It's just been a weird night." Another off-the-reservation idea hit her. Right now, she was Jamez with a z, not Taryn who had to get home and tally study results. "Hey, I didn't catch your name."

"Lucas."

She extended her arm for a handshake, and his big, warm hand wrapped around hers, making her feel small and delicate—a decidedly unfamiliar feeling. The guy was just so…solid. The physical spark she hadn't been feeling with Doug hit her like a goddamned bonfire with Lucas, sending heat straight up her arm. She held on to his hand for a moment too long. "You were really nice to hunt down my shoe. Let me buy you a decaf or something. There's a place down the…"

Lucas's lips parted to respond, but her phone's shrill ring shattered the space between them.

Taryn frowned and looked down. "I'm sorry. Let me…" She dug around in her purse for her phone. She read the screen and heaved a sigh. "I have to take this one."

Lucas nodded. She moved a few steps away and turned her back. "Hi, Momma."

"Hey, baby, it's so good to hear your voice," her mother said warmly.

"Same here," Taryn said, keeping her voice down and trying not to sound annoyed at the interruption.

Her mom was quiet a moment. "Where are you? I hear cars."

Taryn's shoulders relaxed a little. At least her mom sounded calm. Maybe she was having a good night. "I'm just finishing up some errands in the city. I'm about to drive back home."

"Taryn, you really shouldn't be out this late. The roads are wet, and I heard robberies are on the rise downtown," her mother said, forever coming up with something to worry about.

"I'm safe, Momma. I promise. I have my Mace and my mad ninja moves."

"Okay," her mother said, sounding unconvinced and missing the joke. "Call me when you get home and let me know you got there safely."

Taryn closed her eyes, rubbing the center of her forehead and taking a deep breath. "It's going to be late. I'll wake you up."

"No, you won't. I won't be able to sleep until I know you're safe," her mom said, a tense tone in her voice. "I had a nightmare this afternoon. Your car went off the road and hit a tree. And, Taryn, if I lose—"

"Momma, it's fine. I'm sorry. I'll call, all right?"

Taryn tried to keep her voice light and hide the dread that filled her every time conversations took this turn. Nothing like hearing all the ways your mother imagined you dying. "Is Dad home?"

"Yes. He dozed off on the couch watching one of those military shows he likes so much," her mom said, sounding a little perturbed and more like the mother Taryn knew before everything changed.

"Daddy's sleeping?" If her mother was having a bad day, she didn't doubt it. Her father was probably exhausted, and her mother was probably alone now and working herself into an anxiety attack with all her dark thoughts. Taryn checked her watch, inevitability settling onto her shoulders. "Hey, why don't I stop by before I go home tonight? I'll make you my famous green tea."

"Oh, what a good idea. That sounds perfect, baby." Her mother's tone perked up. "I'll see you soon. Be careful."

Be careful. Of course.

She always was.

But when Taryn turned around to tell Lucas she'd have to get his number and give him a rain check on the coffee, the sidewalk behind her was empty.

Maybe he'd gone back inside for something, but what good would it do to hunt him down? Tonight had been weird and terrifying and exhilarating and strange.

It had also not been her real life.

Taryn turned and left *Jamez with a z* to die a quick death on the sidewalk. Back to Long Acre. Back to work. Back to reality.

chapter
THREE

SHAW MILLER MADE HIS COFFEE ORDER AT THE counter of the bustling shop and dug a few bills from his wallet. It still felt weird using cash for everything. He could feel the gaze and smile of the cashier on him as he plucked out the money, but he chose not to look up. He would need at least two cups of coffee and a different personality before he was in the mood for small talk.

The pretty redhead took the money and kept her gaze on him. "Hey, have we met before? I don't think I've seen you in here, but you look familiar for some reason."

He glanced up briefly and tried to appear nonchalant, even though the words sent his gut twisting into a knot. "I don't think so, but I've been told I have one of those faces."

"Maybe so. Or maybe I was just wishing I'd met you before." She gave him a sly grin.

The flirtation bounced off him like hail against a windshield. He shoved two bucks in the tip jar. "Where do I wait for my coffee?"

Her smile faltered at his flat tone, but she cocked her head to the right. "Over there. Lance will set you right up. And here…" She slid a loyalty card across the counter. "Next time we'll be even faster because we'll already know your order."

He pocketed the card and mentally scratched this coffee shop off his list of places to frequent. "Thanks."

"Anytime, darlin'."

As soon as he had his coffee in hand, Shaw hurried out of the mocha-scented shop and into the humid morning with a chill snaking up his spine. *You look familiar.* His long strides ate up the sidewalk as he headed to work, and he couldn't help checking over his shoulder to see if anyone was following—an old habit he couldn't seem to break.

Rivers, Shaw's best friend and the one who'd coaxed him back to this town, would tell him he was overreacting. Rivers had assured Shaw that his fears about returning to Austin were overblown. Shaw had changed his name, his look, and had cut the traceable ties to his old life as much as anyone could in the world of the internet. He'd covered all the bases. But the woman at the coffee shop had, for a moment, looked at him as though she'd recognized him for real, and that had sent ice through his veins.

Shaw *wanted* to dismiss it as his own paranoia. The woman had probably just said it as flirtation. It wouldn't be the first time he'd thought someone was looking at him askance, only to be reading too much into it. Last night at the bar, he'd even had a brief snap of fear that the sexy singer who'd lost her shoe had looked at him with some hint of familiarity at first. But based on the fact that Jamez with a z had been about to ask him to coffee, he knew he'd been wrong.

Of course, that hadn't meant he could accept her invitation—as much as he'd been tempted by it—but it did prove he was prone to thinking the worst. Being stalked by the press for so many years made him see motives in everyone and feel like he was constantly on a stage or under surveillance.

When he unlocked the back door of the soon-to-be-open Gym Xtreme, the steamy, chlorine-scented air hit him in the face like dragon breath. He grimaced and finished the rest of his coffee before tossing it in a trash can in the hallway. Rivers wasn't in the office, so Shaw headed to the front of the building. As he entered the main part of the gym, his footsteps echoed in the cavernous warehouse space as if he were in a horror movie, but fear was the last thing he felt when he stopped and looked around.

Sunlight streamed in from the skylights he and Rivers had gotten installed, but the main lights weren't on. Dust motes danced in the air, and the reflection off the pools painted blue patterns on the far wall. Despite the stuffy atmosphere and too-warm temperature, the tension in Shaw's shoulders eased. He closed his eyes and took a deep breath. A quiet gym was like entering his version of church. It was the only place where his mind went still.

A clink of metal sounded off to his left, and Shaw stepped around a row of equipment. Rivers was a few feet away, balancing on a ladder as he adjusted something on a set of still rings in the gymnastic area, his dark hair slicked back from either sweat or a dip in the pool.

"How'd it go at the permits office?" Rivers asked, not looking away from his task but apparently hearing Shaw's footsteps. "I hope it's more fun than the DMV."

Shaw snorted as he walked over. "It made the DMV look like a rave, but we're all squared away. I's dotted, t's crossed, ridiculous fees paid."

"Great."

Shaw pulled his shirt away from his chest, the material starting to cling. "What happened to the AC? It feels like a sauna in here and smells like chemicals and used gym socks. Are you trying to save money on the electric bill?"

Rivers sniffed. "No, I'm not choosing this misery. The system froze up. I already had a guy out to look at it. He said to turn off the units for a few hours so they can thaw and to consider adding another one to cover this much square footage. He said once we have people in here, it will only get hotter quicker, and in the summer, we'll be completely screwed."

"Fantastic. More expenses," Shaw groused. The gym was bleeding money, and Shaw was having a hard time finding ways to stanch the wound. He'd helped Rivers plan this project down to the penny, but the old building had issues they hadn't anticipated, the equipment had been pricier to build than the original estimates, and the insurance was through the roof. If they didn't have a stellar opening month, they were going to drown before they ever made their first lap around the pool.

"I know. It sucks." Rivers glanced down at him. "But it is what it is. We can't have people passing out from the heat."

"At this rate, we're not going to have people at all because we're never going to open."

"It'll all work out." Rivers smiled, unperturbed, which tended to be his natural state, and returned to checking the still rings, yanking on them. "The smell is because I got all the pools treated again. The chemical balance was off. Now they're clean and ready to catch all the people who will fall off our badass challenges."

Shaw smirked and stepped under the rings. "I'm not sure I would market them that way. *Come to the gym that is sure to crush your spirits!*"

Rivers snorted. "Breaking spirits to rebuild them, Shaw." Rivers put a hand to his chest, a dramatic look on his face. "We're doing spiritual work here. The people need us."

"Yeah, okay, Reverend McGowan." Shaw eyed the other side of the high-ceilinged space of what would hopefully become Austin's premier extreme gym. The side he and Rivers were on had more traditional exercise equipment along with a full setup for gymnastics. Those basics were vital, but the other side was what made the place unique. There were crazy-hard obstacles that tested strength and balance—a huge curved ramp to run up, rock-climbing walls with nearly impossible angles, rolling cylinder bridges, trapeze-style challenges, and two deep swimming pools and foam pits that would catch people if they fell off the obstacles.

He and Rivers had come up with the idea after drinking too much beer one night and watching too many episodes of *Ninja Warrior Challenge* when Rivers had come into town to visit him. Shaw had thought his best friend was joking. They'd had crazy conversations like that before when they'd been college roommates. Rivers was an inventor by nature and a big talker. But then a month later, Rivers had shown up on Shaw's doorstep in Chicago with a stack of paperwork. Rivers had leased out the warehouse in Austin, quit his engineering job, and had developed a business plan—a plan that included Shaw moving back to the town he'd sworn he'd never return to and running the gym with him.

Shaw had refused. His life plan was to lie low and never do anything that would have the press sniffing his way again. So what if he was miserable and unable to find decent work because of the reputation that followed him around like a plague? But when Rivers had laid out the plan—Shaw changing his legal name, the business being listed under Rivers even though they'd split the profits, and Shaw getting to handle the business's finances while also being a trainer—Shaw hadn't been able to walk away.

Besides the much-needed job, his friend had been offering him a taste of freedom he wasn't sure he deserved but that sounded like a dream. A fresh start. A job that would let him be in an environment he loved. His best friend—hell, his only friend—living in the same building instead of across the country. The only sticking point was that it was in Austin, just down the road from the place of his nightmares, where everything in his world had been ripped away and burned to ashes. Where he wasn't just hated and feared in a general sense, but in very, very specific and personal sense.

He deserved that hate.

Shaw had come anyway, even when he knew it would be temporary. Everything in his life was. Putting down roots anywhere had always invoked trouble. He'd lost the right to roots. Secretly, Shaw had vowed to devote one year to this project. He'd take some online business classes to finish up the degree he'd had to abandon all those years ago and work as a trainer at the gym. He'd help Rivers get the business off the ground, build himself a little nest egg, buy an RV to travel the country, and then leave Rivers to run the gym. He hadn't told Rivers about his planned time limit, but he'd cross that bridge when necessary.

The close call in the coffee shop today had only confirmed the necessity of that plan. It'd probably been a false alarm this time, but it wouldn't be every time. He just hoped he could make it the full year so he could save up enough for the RV and some living expenses. The clock was already ticking. Someone would eventually recognize him. Someone would call the press. The cycle would start over.

"We're still on track to open next week?" Shaw asked, examining his friend's work on the rings.

"Yep." Rivers climbed down from the ladder and wiped his damp face with his T-shirt. "Well, open to the public at least. I signed us up for a charity event tomorrow morning."

"A what?"

"You're coming. Don't try to get out of it. If we get a lot of interest, I may open for a sneak preview on Monday and give a few tours and initial workouts. I don't want to lose good leads if we get them. The event looks very Austin quirky, so I have a feeling it will get some press, which we desperately need."

"A charity event with *press*?" Shaw's stomach sank. "No way. You know I can't be anywhere near a goddamned camera."

Rivers made a dismissive sound. "You won't be. I've already thought this through. It's a costume run. Runners will be chased by people in costumes, like a zombie run, but vendors can dress up, too. We'll make sure you have a good disguise. You'll just be there to help me man an information table and give out flyers for the gym. As far as anyone knows, Lucas Shaw is just a trainer here. They have no reason to pay attention to you."

Shaw let out a breath, the name Lucas still sounding weird in his ear. He'd chosen to keep the Shaw part of his real name, Shaw Miller, because if he or Rivers slipped up and used the name Shaw, there would be an easy explanation. But getting used to an entirely new first name was going to take a while.

"I hate the idea of any press being involved," he groused.

"I know. But this is too good an opportunity to pass up," Rivers said.

Shaw couldn't deny that fact, and he did trust Rivers not to purposely expose him to anything that would blow his cover. He should be relieved Rivers had handled things and created a great promotional opportunity, but the thought of charities and press still made him itchy. "Fine."

"Excellent." Rivers gripped his shoulder. "And don't worry, man. I told you I was willing to be the face of this thing, and I meant it. I'm not going to expose you to any of that. Plus, I have such a pretty face."

Shaw snorted.

"But if we want this business to be successful, we have to jump on opportunities like this, get people excited and spreading the word," he explained. "There needs to be some sizzle and pop."

Shaw gave him a droll look. "Sizzle and pop?"

"Yes. Don't make fun of my very technical marketing terms." Rivers nodded toward the equipment. "Now get up on these rings and tell me if they're going to break and kill someone."

Shaw smirked. "Nice. I've been demoted to guinea pig now?"

Rivers stepped back with an unrepentant grin. "*Oink, oink.*"

Shaw pulled his T-shirt over his head and tossed it at Rivers's face. "Guinea pigs don't oink, dumb-ass."

Rivers caught the T-shirt before it hit him and flipped it over his shoulder. He folded his arms and waited. "Show me what you've got, big man."

Shaw shook his head and dug a rubber band out of his pocket to pull his hair back. He didn't have any chalk for his hands or ring grips, and cargo shorts weren't ideal for flexibility, but he was just testing the things out, not doing a routine. He did a few quick shoulder and back stretches to make sure he was loose enough before reaching up. Rivers had set the rings lower than Olympic height so Shaw was able to jump up and grab them without assistance.

The rings felt achingly familiar in his hands as he hung from them, the scattered thoughts of the morning settling into singular focus as he adjusted his grip and made sure the apparatus wasn't going to fall apart on him. Once he felt confident the rings would support him, he lifted his weight, his arms working to keep the rings as still as possible, and raised himself up until his hips were even with the rings and his arms were taut. After a few seconds, he exhaled and spread his arms out to form a T with his body, an Iron Cross.

The strength and focus required to keep his body and the rings steady in that pose were like the rush of a drug, every part of him working toward the same goal. Shaw's muscles quivered with the effort, and he lifted himself again, tilting forward and swinging his legs behind and upward to invert the cross. He glued his gaze to a spot on the floor and tried to hold the upside-down position for as many seconds as his body would allow him. *One, two, three…*

"Damn," Rivers said. "It kills me a little that we can't market you. *Former Olympic-level gymnast will personally train you on feats of strength!* A photo of this alone would sell a shit ton of memberships. Hell, I could probably fill up our rosters with all my single friends…gay or straight. We could oil you up and let them pay to ogle."

That made Shaw choke on a laugh, and it broke his concentration. His muscles gave up the good fight, and he swung down out of the inversion. He dropped to his feet on the mat beneath with a muted thump, out of breath, his muscles burning from the effort. "Stop flirting, McGowan."

Rivers scoffed and tossed his shirt back at him. "As if you'd be so lucky. You're not my type."

Shaw caught the T-shirt and tugged it back on with a grin, not insulted in the least. "Too straight, huh?"

"Straight?" Rivers crossed his arms and lifted a brow. "Oh, you actually still have an orientation? I thought yours was *monk*."

Shaw's mouth flattened. "The rings work. We won't kill anyone."

He tried to move past his friend, but Rivers put a hand on his arm, halting him. "Come on, don't be like that. I'm not trying to be an asshole."

"You're not doing a very good job of it."

Rivers didn't relent. "I'm just trying to wake you up a little. You've been here for months, and I have yet to see you do anything but go to your apartment and back here. Every time I ask you to come out with me and my friends, you have an excuse."

Shaw had, in fact, gone to a bar last night, but Rivers wouldn't count the Tipsy Hound even if Shaw told him. He'd gone in because he really wanted a drink, and the place was dark with loud music. Not a place to socialize. But somehow he'd ended up outside with a pretty woman, treading into way-too-dangerous waters.

The liquor had loosened his good sense, and he'd found himself drawn to the woman who'd sung her guts out and then run offstage, and not drawn to her for the obvious reasons. The woman was a knockout with her cloud of dark curls, black-rimmed glasses, and a pink blouse that had exposed just a hint of smooth brown skin at the open collar. She was all curves and quirky sophistication. Rivers would say *nerdy hot*. But Shaw didn't think *hot* needed any kind of qualifier.

Despite all that, the thing that had drawn him to her was the way she'd sung onstage. She hadn't opened her eyes the whole time, but once she'd gotten started, it was as if she'd opened a vein and let it bleed onto the floor in front of them. Her voice hadn't been classically pretty. It'd been powerful and raw, with sandpaper rubbing the high notes. He'd felt each note of her song like she'd shoved the music directly into his chest, sending a shot of adrenaline straight into his system. He'd been sweating a little by the end. So when she'd stumbled by him, he couldn't stop himself from reaching out. He'd wanted to help her, but more than that, he wanted to know why she was running.

But he should've minded his own business. In those brief moments outside the bar, she'd nudged a part of him he'd thought he'd long ago cut the wires to—the part that said he should smile at her, flirt, and get her story. The part that said he could want the normal things a man could want.

What a fucking lie that was.

"I don't do clubs," he said to Rivers, shutting down the memory of last night, of him walking away from her like a coward who couldn't even manage to tell her good night.

"Fine, go to a movie then. A bar. Whatever. You don't need to do the monk thing anymore. I get why you shut yourself off from the social scene, but this is a big town. You have a new name. You don't look like the guy from those old news stories anymore. Go out, have fun, take a roll in someone's bed."

"Riv," Shaw warned.

His friend raised his palms. "All I'm saying is don't rule out a simple hookup. It's unhealthy not to get laid at least every now and then." He gave Shaw an up-and-down look. "I don't know if it's wise to test out that use-it-or-lose-it theory, you know? What if you actually *can* lose it?"

Shaw's fingers curled into his palms. "I'm going to make some calls to price out adding another AC unit."

"Shaw."

Shaw ignored him and shouldered past him. *Use it or lose it*. Right. Like his damn dick was going to fall off if he didn't have sex. Ridiculous.

The thought sent a shudder through him anyway. He tried to shake off his irritation as he made his way to the office. Rivers meant well. The guy thought he was helping, but these types of discussions were off the table. Rivers didn't get it.

Shaw had tried that road and had ended up getting serious with someone. The one woman he'd dated after the Long Acre shooting had acted as his confidant, had gotten him to open up about all the shit he was going through. Then, when things had gone bad between them, Shaw had made a dumb mistake, physically attacking a reporter who'd been goading him about the relationship. Shaw had gotten arrested, and the woman had gone to the press to confirm everyone's worst assumptions.

An unnamed source close to the shooter's brother, former Olympic hopeful Shaw Miller, says he's drinking too much, angry, and a loner. Studies show that mental health issues run in families. Joseph Miller, the mastermind behind the Long Acre shooting, was reportedly suffering from...

After reading the stories, Shaw had thrown his laptop against the wall and broken it into pieces. He hadn't read a news story about himself or touched another woman since.

Sex was amazing. He missed it at a level so primal, he couldn't describe it. But no matter how good it could be, it wasn't worth risking feeling that exposed again, that...violated.

Rivers didn't get it. He couldn't.

No one could know how it felt to be stripped down and no longer seen as an actual person but only as a news headline, a sensational sound bite to be sold and collectively hated. To be shamed. A name to be thrown around the dinner table and judged.

Mass murderer's brother.

Fallen Olympic hopeful.

Shaw Miller was now just a name on endless web pages. A cautionary tale. A common enemy.

He didn't get to meet a pretty woman at a bar and ask her out. He didn't get to want the things normal people wanted. That life had been stolen the day his brother had ended all those others.

Maybe he should feel angrier about that loss.

He would.

If he didn't know that he deserved to pay every bit of that steep price.

chapter
FOUR

TARYN USED HER KEY TO GET INTO HER PARENTS' house early Saturday evening, repeating her motions from the night before when she'd stopped by and found both her parents asleep in the living room. Her father had awoken at the noise of her heels on the wood floors and had told her to leave her mother be, that he'd take care of getting her to bed, and to stop by for dinner tomorrow instead to visit.

Like usual, he hadn't asked if Taryn had other plans. Like usual, she hadn't had any plans besides work. She'd spent the day compiling her stats and polishing a presentation. Now she was starved and hoping it would be a low-key evening with her parents.

She made her way into the kitchen, following the scent of Cajun spices. "Smells like dinner."

"Hey, *cher*, I didn't hear you come in." Her father was at his spot in front of the mini deep fryer, his fingertips covered in batter and his thinning blond hair held back from his face with his cooking bandanna. "You're early. Got all your work squared away?"

She smiled at her father's familiar endearment. Though he'd lived in Texas for decades now, he'd never quite lost his Cajun accent from the small town in South Louisiana where he'd grown up. His *cher* came out like *sha*, and it sounded like home to her ear. She set her purse down and gave her father a hug as he lifted his messy hands out to his sides so as not to batter her like the fish. "I'm almost done, but my brain went on strike, demanding I feed it."

"Ah, that happens," he said, stepping back from the hug. "It just needs a heaping plate of fried catfish. Lucky for you, that's just what we got on the menu."

Taryn stepped over to the counter where the little fryer was bubbling away and took a whiff. "Awesome. Momma's not going to fuss at you for making the kitchen smell like fish?"

Her father's smile faltered a little bit. "I'm not sure she's going to join us for dinner tonight. She's had a rough day and said she'd probably go to bed early."

Taryn's skin prickled, the words setting off her sensors. How many times had she heard him say something to that effect over the years? Her military father could make everything sound small and manageable. A panic attack was bad nerves. Depression was feeling a little blue. Wars were skirmishes or conflicts. He thought if a person didn't make a big deal out of things, they wouldn't be. "A rough day? How rough?"

He rinsed his hands and then used tongs to poke at the fish. "It was about that film you were in last year."

"What about it?" Taryn sat at the table, the muscles in her neck tightening. Last year, she, her friends, and some of the other survivors of the shooting had taken part in a documentary, one that would raise money for charity. It had been one of the hardest things Taryn had ever done, but she didn't regret it because it'd brought her friends Liv, Kincaid, and Rebecca back into her life. But she had no idea what that had to do with her mother.

Her dad looked back over his shoulder, deep lines in his suntanned forehead. "Your mom was interviewed for it, too."

"*What?*" Taryn's fists curled. "Daddy, you know she's not in a place to do that kind of thing. There are so many triggers…"

"She didn't want me to tell you because she knew you'd say that, but she told me she thought it would help with closure," he explained. "I went with her, and she actually did pretty well. She didn't want to be on camera, but she shared our story. She cried, of course. Who wouldn't?"

Taryn hadn't. She'd had to do that interview with steel running through her veins. She'd seen what letting all that grief and emotion in could do to a person. She saw it take down her previously tough, brilliant mother and eat away at her like a cancer. But Taryn's interview had also been brief since she'd told them she had few memories from that night. "But what does that have to do with today? That stopped filming a long time ago."

He turned back to the fryer and pulled out a piece of golden fried fish bubbling with oil to lay it on a paper-towel-lined dish. "They sent her an early copy today. She watched some of it before I got home. I found her in Nia's room."

"Oh no. Was she—"

He turned to her. "No, it was okay. She was sitting with

one of Nia's sweaters in her hands. She fussed at me for checking on her. Told me she has the right to a bad day."

Relief moved through her. "That's good. If she got annoyed with you."

"Right."

If her mom had gotten mad, that meant she was probably all right. The bad times were when her anxiety and grief got so intense that the past and present blurred for her, flooding her with all the horrible memories or worse, putting her in a state of reality-altering denial. In the year after the shooting, her mom would go in Nia's room and fix it up like her little sister would be coming home later.

She hadn't had one of those episodes in a long time. Her medications seemed to be working, but thoughts of those episodes still sent dread cramping Taryn's stomach. She could deal with her mother's extreme protectiveness and her anxiety. But she'd been terrified seeing her strong, smart mother disappear into a confused mess.

Before the shooting, her mom had been the bread-winner of the family, a journalism professor and writer. She'd spent her early years before kids traveling the world as a reporter. That was how she'd met Taryn's father. He'd been deployed to a location she was covering. She'd seen war-torn countries and countless tragedies and had faced down intimidating and difficult people without faltering. But losing her youngest daughter had been her unraveling. The once never-let-them-see-you-sweat journalist had dissolved into grief, losing more pieces of herself with each passing day.

Taryn had watched it all like a slow-motion horror

movie. Her sister gone. Her friends killed. Her family
falling apart around her. Taryn had been dissolving, too,
but when she'd gotten hysterical at Nia's funeral, her
father had hugged her and pulled her aside. She'd never
seen her dad look so old and desperate. *You have to be
strong*, cher. *Your mom needs you. I need you. You're all
we have now. We can't lose you, too. We need to keep
each other together.*

At the time, she hadn't known all he'd seen with her
mother in those first few days after the shooting, but
she'd felt his terror. In that moment, a new chilling fear
had filled her, one that had changed her from little girl to
woman in an instant. Her daddy, the strong military man
who had told her all her life that he would protect her,
was lost and terrified. He couldn't help her. He couldn't
protect her from any of this. They were all hanging on the
edge of the cliff, and *he'd* asked *her* to find some rope.

Her father handed her a plate. "Why don't you bring
her some dinner? I'm sure seeing you would cheer her up."

"Sure." Taryn took the plate of fish, hearing the
message loud and clear. *Go check on her. I'm worried.*
She grabbed a can of soda from the fridge and headed
toward the stairs. When she turned the corner, the light
from Nia's room shone on the polished wood floor of
the hallway.

Taryn took a deep breath, steeling herself for
whatever awaited, and headed to the room, passing
all the family photos that lined the walls—photos of
a *Before* family that didn't exist anymore. She peeked
inside. Even though she'd seen the room a thousand
times, the sight of the perfectly preserved museum that
was her sister's teenage bedroom still hit Taryn like a

swift kick to the chest. Photos pinned haphazardly to a bulletin board along with flyers advertising the different theater productions Nia had been in. Mr. Jingle Pants, the stuffed gingerbread man her sister had slept with since she was four, was propped against the bright-purple throw pillows on the bed. And her prized collection of makeup was organized neatly on her vanity table, hot-pink polish dried into the sides of the bottle, last used on prom night.

Taryn's throat felt swollen shut. She swallowed hard and glanced to the left where she'd found what she'd seen so many times before—her mother sitting in a chair and looking out the window. Her hands were folded in her lap, and there was a distant look on her face, her brown skin smooth and lax.

"Hey, Momma," Taryn said quietly, hoping not to startle her.

Her mother turned her head and smiled at Taryn. "Hey, baby. Sorry I missed you last night. I guess I was more tired than I thought."

Relief loosened some of Taryn's muscles. Her mother looked sad, but clear-eyed and calm. "No problem. I'm glad you got some rest." She held up the plate. "Daddy said you weren't up to having dinner, but I thought you might want some to nibble on."

Her mom *tsk*ed. "I appreciate that, honey, but don't bring that in here. The whole place will smell like fish. Nia hates fish. Leave it on the table out there, and I'll get some in a little while."

Taryn's stomach dropped. "*Hated*, Momma, not *hates*."

Her mother's lips pressed together, a sharpness coming into her gaze. "I'm sure she still hates it in heaven, too, and wouldn't appreciate us stinking up her room with it."

"Right," Taryn said and set the food and soda on the table in the hallway before stepping inside the bedroom. "So how are you doing?"

"I'm fine," her mom said, tone clipped. "Did your father send you up here to check on me? I told him not to worry. It's just been a tough day."

Taryn sat on the edge of the bed, almost afraid to put her weight on it and disturb anything. Her mother liked everything in the room to be kept just right. "Yes, I'm sure Daddy sent me up here to check on you, but I also just wanted to see you. He told me you saw the documentary."

Her mom smoothed a hand along the arm of the rocking chair and nodded. "They did a good job with it." She glanced at Taryn. "You did well, too."

Taryn looked down at her lap. "Thanks. I don't think I'll ever watch it. You probably shouldn't have either. It's not good for you to—"

"Can you believe they interviewed that Miller woman?" her mother asked, vitriol in her voice. "How dare she even set foot on those grounds again? What her son did…" Her mother made a disgusted sound in the back of her throat. "And you should've heard the things she said. Acting like she had nothing to do with how her kid turned out. Like it was just a bad roll of the dice."

"Momma…"

"That's such bull," she spat out. "You know it, baby. You do all that research. There were things those parents could've done. She just doesn't want anyone pointing fingers. She got out of those lawsuits with that excuse. Bad genetics, my rear end." Her fingers balled. "It just makes me so *angry*. She raised a killer, maybe two, based on the stories I heard about the brother a few years ago. Don't act like a victim. How about taking some responsibility? Makes me want to sue her myself."

Taryn blew out a breath, stood, and put a hand on her mom's shoulder. "This is why you shouldn't watch things like that."

She turned to Taryn, brown eyes ablaze, and put her hand over her daughter's. "You're going to show her, and everyone else. When you get your program in schools, people are going to see the difference it makes. This could've been prevented. We didn't have to lose Nia or all those other children. The world needs to know that."

Taryn gave a little nod. "I know, Momma. I'm almost there. The program is ready to go. I present to the school board on Thursday."

"Thank you, Jesus," her mother said softly. "That's my brilliant girl. I knew you'd do it."

Taryn looked up, finding her mom fully focused on her. The effect was like sunlight warming her skin. After so many years of seeing her mom struggle, she cherished these moments when her mom was totally present with her. Seeing her get angry was better than seeing her wallow in despair and anxiety.

Taryn put her other hand on top of their clasped ones. "I told you I would. I just need the school board to say yes now. One of the members all but assured me it would get approved."

Tears filled her mother's eyes. "Your sister would be so proud of you, baby."

Taryn's throat felt stuffed with cotton so she simply nodded.

Her mother put a hand on Taryn's face, her palm cool against her cheek. "How about we go downstairs and have some dinner with your dad? It's not very nice of us to make him cook and then let him eat alone."

Taryn smiled. "What you really mean is that you're afraid he's going to eat all the fish and forget to leave some for us."

"Exactly."

Taryn helped her mother out of the chair and glanced at the wall covered with theater bills—the wall she'd shared with her sister. The wall Nia had tapped on when Taryn sang and played guitar. She could still picture herself and her sister sitting in this room and talking about nothing and everything. It was as though she was looking at a scene out of someone else's life. Maybe she was. That life had died along with Nia.

Later that night, Taryn took a long sip of coffee, her belly still full from dinner with her parents, and stared at the wall of her home office. Over the last couple of years, she'd covered the blank wall opposite her desk with floor-to-ceiling cork and had turned it into a massive bulletin board. On it, small black-and-white photos of school shooters were spread out like a map, red strings connecting them to different points on her diagram. It was her masterpiece—and also the most depressing office artwork ever.

Her eyes were getting blurry with the need for sleep, but she lifted her glasses to rub them and wake herself up. *Only a little longer.* After her talk with her mom, she was determined to get this school-board presentation perfect.

On the wall, she'd separated the shooters into four main groups—the psychopaths, the psychotic, the suicidal, and the traumatized. Then she'd pinned different elements around the board to connect strings to data points such as whether the shooter worked alone or with someone, whether they told someone their plan, if there were signs that were missed, if they were bullied, if they'd committed previous crimes. She'd gone through all the published research, the family histories, and the police reports, examining hundreds of characteristics and conducting a meta-analysis that had taken most of her adult life to assemble. But she'd done what she'd set out to do. She'd isolated common factors and identified the areas that could potentially be impacted most for prevention.

She was finally ready to use what she'd found to help. To change things. She simultaneously wanted to cheer and rip all the ugliness off the wall because she was so damn tired of looking at those faces and statistics.

But she kept her hands at her sides. She wasn't done with this wall yet. She wouldn't be until her program was rolled out in schools and making some kind of difference. Research was just information. It was useless without action.

In a time capsule letter she'd written after graduation with her friends, she'd promised to dedicate her life to action. Action for those who hadn't survived, action for her sister, and action for her family. Back then, Taryn had been obsessed with answering the question *why?* Now, she was standing before a wall filled with years of work, and the reality of it settled over her. There were a thousand answers to the question. She hadn't known that at seventeen when she'd made the promise, but she'd realized it pretty quickly once she'd gotten into her studies. So much influenced a person that there could be no $x + y = school\ shooter$. That didn't mean there was nothing to be done. She had a plan and felt confident it would make an impact.

If she could get people to believe in it.

She needed to get a group of local schools on board to allocate some funds and pilot the program to prove the method first. Taryn turned her back to the corkboard wall and sat in front of her computer again. Her eyes were burning from being up late last night, and she had to get up early in the morning, but she needed to put together a few more PowerPoint slides. She stretched her neck from side to side, giving herself an internal pep talk like she used to do when she ran track and her lungs started burning and her muscles wanted to cramp. *Just one more lap. Almost to the finish line.*

There would be time for sleep later. Once she had the pilot program in place, she could finally take a breath for the first time since everything had happened. Give her mom something tangible to hold on to, get some rest, and maybe take Kincaid up on working a little more fun into her life.

Maybe.

But for now...she put her fingers on the keyboard.

Just one more lap.

chapter

FIVE

"OH, NO, NO, NO. THIS IS ALL WRONG." KINCAID SHOOK her head, purple-streaked blond ponytail swinging and glittery unicorn horn sparkling in the morning sunlight as she looked Taryn up and down. She stepped around the sign-in table to get closer. "You said you were coming as Belle from *Beauty and the Beast*."

Taryn groaned, her head pounding despite the double-shot espresso she'd downed on the way there. "The costume shop only had the yellow ball gown, and I wanted the peasant-girl outfit from when she's reading the book. I can't run in a ball gown. I figured I'd try another shop yesterday, but then I was working on my school-board presentation and I lost track of time."

Kincaid gave a put-upon sigh and placed her hands on Taryn's shoulders. "Overworked professor is not an approved costume. I love you, but you look like hell."

"Aww, don't you say the sweetest things," Taryn said, trying for lighthearted sarcasm but sounding grumpy instead. "I didn't think I needed full-face makeup for a charity run."

Kincaid frowned, her hazel eyes narrowing as she examined Taryn's face. "This has nothing to do with makeup, and you know it. Did you pull another all-nighter?"

"No. I got about four hours, I think." She'd woken up with her cheek against her keyboard. She hoped the imprint of it had finally faded, but the crick in her neck sure hadn't.

Kincaid let out a heavy sigh and released Taryn's shoulders. "Girl, we need to have a talk after this race. Your fun diet needs to start ASAP."

"Yeah, about that," Taryn started. "I don't think I can spare—"

But Kincaid was already two conversations ahead of her. "Hey, you want me to see what they have in the costume tent? A lot of people brought extras so people could borrow them."

"No, it's fine." The thought of getting into some elaborate costume seemed overwhelming at the moment. "I'll just get a set of flags to tie around my waist and be one of the chased. Have you seen Rebecca yet?" She craned her neck to see over the milling crowd of costumed runners and search for her friend and the organizer of this charity race. "Do you know where she needs my help?"

"I saw her first thing this morning when she and Wes were setting everything up, but they left a while ago to get their costumes on," Kincaid said. "She left me in charge. I've been doing costume approvals and handing out racing tags. I'm not sure what she wanted you to do, but she should be back any minute."

Taryn lifted her brows. "Costume approvals?"

"Yep. Rebecca wants to ensure this is not a triggering event since it's benefiting victims of violent crime. No blood. No fake weapons. No scary monsters or Jasons or Michael Myerses. I thought it'd be an easy job, but you'd be surprised what people consider an acceptable costume. Like some dude thought a zombie would be okay." Kincaid's eyes rolled upward as if looking at the unicorn horn atop her head. "I mean, seriously, you're literally the *walking dead*. There is fake blood dripping out of your eyes and mouth. What mental checklist did you go through to make that okay, buddy?"

Taryn smiled, her bad mood no match for Kincaid's endless chatter. "I'm sure you've hated being in charge."

"Right? I was made for this. Costumes and being the head honcho? Best combination ever." Kincaid clapped her hands together. "Oh my God, here come Rebecca and Wes. And *ugh*. They did a couple's costumes and look freaking adorable."

Taryn grinned as Rebecca headed their way with her man in tow. "Which means we need to hate them on the spot."

"Obviously," Kincaid said. "Them's the rules."

Rebecca and Wes had gone with the Lucy and Ricky Ricardo combo. Rebecca's red hair was curled and pinned, and she had on a black-and-white polka-dot dress. The outfit was not one to run in, but Rebecca had an old leg injury from the shooting and wouldn't be running. Wes had greased his blond hair into a pompadour and sprayed it black. But the thing that made it so cute was how the two of them looked together. Rebecca was so relaxed, leaning into Wes and laughing about something. He was smiling at her like no other woman existed on earth.

The sight made Taryn's chest warm. It hadn't been that long ago that Rebecca had been crying in Taryn's office, confessing heartbreaking things about the night of the shooting and sharing the struggles she'd had since. Rebecca had looked so tired and downtrodden. Now it was as if Taryn's very serious lawyer friend had shed a few layers of skin, and this new, shiny version had emerged from beneath.

The couple reached them and everyone exchanged greetings and hugs. Rebecca gave Taryn a squeeze. "Where's your costume, missy?"

"Dr. Landry has issues with ball gowns," Kincaid offered as she reached out and knocked on Wes's stiff hair as if she were knocking on a door. "Good Lord, what'd you put in here? Cement?"

No one flinched at Kincaid feeling up Rebecca's husband's hair. She was a toucher.

Wes smiled proudly. "Temporary hair dye and Brylcreem. That stuff is amazing. I'm thinking of making this my new look."

Rebecca gave him the side eye. "Don't get any ideas, Ricky. I like you blond, and I think that hair gel will be a fire hazard in the food truck."

Wes chuckled and leaned over to kiss Bec on the cheek. "Yes, ma'am."

"You guys make me completely nauseous. I love it," Kincaid said happily. "Where's our other duo?"

"Finn and Liv stopped at the restrooms." Rebecca glanced over her shoulder. "Oh, here they come."

A couple wearing tight-fitting costumes with capes

trailing behind them came into view from behind a gaggle of Smurfs that were waiting in line for tags. "Batman and Wonder Woman," Taryn said when her other friends walked up. "Nice!"

"Thanks." Liv pushed her dark hair away from her face, a look of frustration pursing her lips and a gleam of sweat on her forehead. "But please remind me next time to pee before I get into my costume. Ever try to get out of this much spandex in a port-a-potty?"

"All the time," Wes said seriously.

Rebecca gently shoved him in the arm. "Oh, Ricky."

Liv smirked at the other couple. "Well, I'll take some tips for next time. I'm afraid to look. Did I dip my cape?"

Finn laughed next to her, a deep sound filled with warmth, and tugged off his Batman mask to check her costume. "You're all dry, Livvy. I thought I was going to have to do my first rescue, though. The curse words coming out of that bathroom were not safe for a family-friendly event."

Liv snorted and put her hands on her hips. "Wonder Woman needs no rescuer, Bat Boy."

Taryn rolled her lips inward and pointed. "Maybe not, but Wonder Woman does have toilet paper attached to her shoe."

"Oh hell," Liv said, shaking it off. "So anyway, all that is to say sorry I'm running a little behind. We're ready to be sent out on our missions now."

Rebecca pulled a paper square from the inner pocket of Wes's jacket and unfolded the neatly typed to-do list. "I think we have most everything covered. Kincaid's been helping with check-in and costume approval, but that should be close to done. Wes, if you could make sure we have water bottles set out at each checkpoint, that'd be great. Liv and Finn, could y'all help hand out flags to the runners and show them how to hook them around their waists?"

"Yep, sounds good," Finn said.

"Taryn, if you could help Kincaid finish up and then, if you two don't mind, do a walk by the vendors' tables to make sure they don't need anything. They paid a fee to advertise here, and a lot of them made an extra donation on top of that, so I want them to feel like they're well taken care of."

"Got it," Taryn said.

"Then when the race starts, everyone just have fun and grab some flags," Rebecca said.

Kincaid rubbed her hands together. "I'm so ready for that part. Everyone is going down!"

Taryn lifted her palms. "The unicorn is on the hunt! Let all be warned."

Kincaid nodded seriously. "Yep. You should be worried, doc. You're going to have flags. This unicorn eats flags for breakfast."

"I ran track, sister," Taryn said, jogging in place and trying to get her energy up despite her lack of sleep. "You've got no shot."

"Hey, I was on the dance team," Kincaid said, affronted. "I have moves."

Taryn made a bring-it-on motion with her hands. "We'll see, twinkle toes."

The couples said their goodbyes and headed off to their tasks. Taryn turned to Kincaid to see what she needed her to do first, but before she could get a word out, Kincaid shrieked and clutched her hands to her chest.

The noise startled Taryn and made her jump. "What the hell?"

"Christmas on a cracker. What the hell is right," Kincaid said, staring at something behind Taryn.

Taryn turned, but Kincaid was already stalking forward in the direction of a very tall, very brightly colored clown. *Oh crap.* She'd known Kincaid long enough to know what was about to happen. Taryn hurried behind her, ready to intercept, but Kincaid was already talking.

"Excuse me. Excuse me, you with the red nose!" Kincaid said, snapping her fingers.

The unsuspecting clown turned her way, putting a hand to his chest and blinking in confusion. "Me?"

"Yes, you." Kincaid stopped in front of him, half a foot shorter, but miles taller in attitude. "I'm sorry, but in what universe would you consider this a non-scary costume? The instructions were clear."

The clown shrank back. "I'm a circus clown," he said, lifting his big glove-covered hands. "Kids like the circus."

"No-o," Kincaid said, dragging out the word into two syllables. "Kids tolerate the scary-ass clowns at the circus to see the cute animals and eat cotton candy. Have you never seen *It*? Or *Poltergeist*? Or *The Strangers*?"

"Well, technically, *The Strangers* didn't have cl—" Taryn started.

"Clowns are super high on the scary meter," Kincaid went on. "They're like right below the porcelain dolls they sell on home shopping channels."

"Porcelain—" the guy said in bewilderment.

Kincaid lifted a palm, an angry unicorn stomping her

hooves. "We appreciate you participating in this charity run, but for the love of all that is good and holy, please go to the costume tent and choose a different costume or get some flags and be a runner."

The clown looked down at his floppy shoes. "Okay. I'm real sorry, ma'am."

Taryn winced and stepped forward. "Sir, we really are happy you're participating. I'm sorry for the confusion. Next time we'll be more clear on which costumes could be triggers."

Kincaid gave her a look and a little eye roll that the clown couldn't see. The clown gave Taryn a small smile, which did end up looking kind of creepy, and then loped off toward the costume tent. Kincaid huffed. "See? I told you. Can you believe some people? I mean, clearly that was the most terrifying costume ever made. How can people not realize that?"

Taryn bit her lip, trying not to laugh. "Porcelain dolls on home shopping channels?"

They were walking toward the vendor area now, and Kincaid gave her a look that seemed to say *obviously*. "Unblinking eyes are freaky. I'm sorry. My grandmother used to have a whole curio case of the little demons. I think they steal the souls of the dead and trap them in there."

"Of course you do."

"What?" Kincaid asked, glancing her way. "What is that tone?"

"Nothing. You're my favorite friend," Taryn said solemnly.

Kincaid groaned and shoved her in the shoulder. "Hush, sleepy professor. Let's go get you another coffee, and then we'll go make nice with the vendors. I have a surprise for you."

"I hate surprises."

"You'll like this one."

A little while later, Taryn followed behind Kincaid, her friend's unicorn tail swishing with purpose and her smile bright as she greeted the different vendors. Taryn sipped her coffee and joined in the conversation when needed, but since Kincaid was much better at chitchat and schmoozing than Taryn could ever hope to be, she let her friend do her thing. But when they moved toward the vendor on the far end of the row, Kincaid sent Taryn a conspiratorial look over her shoulder. "You'll like this next one."

Taryn tossed her cup in a nearby trash can and lifted her brows. "What do you mean?"

"You'll see." Kincaid smiled and cocked her head for Taryn to follow her.

When they reached the end of the row, two guys were sitting behind a fold-out table draped with a banner, but Taryn couldn't tell what they were advertising because her attention was stuck on the men: a cute guy in a fedora dressed as Indiana Jones and a broad-shouldered blond with aviator sunglasses and a flight suit—Iceman from *Top Gun*.

Well, hello.

Indiana stood up quickly, almost knocking off his fedora, and grinned widely when he saw Kincaid. "Hey, there's my favorite unicorn."

Taryn didn't have time to register that Kincaid already knew Indiana because Iceman's head swiveled toward Taryn, pinning her with a look. She almost stumbled backward, something about the guy's focused attention making her breath catch for a moment. His lips parted as if he were going to say something, but then he snapped them back together and looked down at the table where brightly colored flyers were spread. That was when she saw the familiar man bun.

Her belly flipped. *Oh shit*.

The guy from the bar. Lucas.

"Rivers," Kincaid said to the dark-haired guy with delight and grabbed Taryn's elbow. "This is the friend I was telling you about."

Taryn dragged her attention away from Iceman—no, Lucas—and managed to smile at Rivers. "Um, hi?"

"Hi," Rivers said, putting out his hand and shaking hers firmly. "Kincaid was telling us all about you. Said you're going to be her partner in crime at the gym."

Taryn took a second to process what he'd said, her peripheral attention on Lucas and his obvious discomfort. "Partner in crime?"

Rivers tilted his head. "Yeah. At our adventure gym. Gym Xtreme."

"Gym X-what?" Taryn asked, all the words bumping into one another and not lining up right.

Kincaid made a happy little sound and turned to Taryn. "Xtreme. This is your surprise," she announced. "I was checking out the tables earlier, and Rivers here gave me quite the pitch. You should see the pictures of the place. There are curved walls and balance beams and trapeze things and foam pits!"

Taryn finally looked at Kincaid, whose face was full of expectant excitement. "*Foam pits?*"

"Yes! To fall in. Pools, too. Because the obstacles are

really tough. It's like that TV show—the warrior ninja thingy. But it looks like so much fun, and this will be way better than that 10K training we were supposed to do," Kincaid said, talking fast now. "And way less *boring*."

Taryn blinked at the emphasis Kincaid had put on the last word, and everything finally clicked. *Oh*. This was Kincaid's fun diet. She wanted to sign Taryn up for some crazy-ass gym. God help her for having friends with good intentions. "Look, I don't know…"

"Oh, come on, Taryn," Kincaid pleaded. "Don't say no yet."

"Taryn?" Lucas said, finally acknowledging their presence. He pulled his aviators off and frowned her way.

"Yes," Kincaid said with a smile. "Taryn, this is Lucas. He'll be one of the trainers."

But Lucas was still looking at her. "The other night, you said your name was Jamez."

Kincaid's head whipped around, her wide-eyed gaze colliding with Taryn's. "The other night?"

Taryn winced and gave a little nod. "We've already met. I ran into Lucas at a bar I stopped in Friday night."

Kincaid's eyes got even bigger. She looked downright thrilled at this new development and was for sure going to ask a million questions, but she held them for now. "Well then. I guess you've already met your trainer." She turned to Lucas. "Her middle name is Jamie. So sometimes we call her Jamez."

Total lie. Her middle name was Mariah. But in that moment, Taryn loved Kincaid with a depth of friendship she almost couldn't put into words. Kincaid was pushy and bossy and sometimes overwhelming. She was also a woman who would cover for her friends, no questions asked, because she believed without a doubt that if one of her friends was lying, they had a good reason.

"Good to see you again," Taryn said, managing to sound calm. "But I'm not sure about this whole training thing, Kincaid. This looks a little above my pay grade."

"Oh, don't be intimidated," Rivers said, handing Taryn a flyer. "We have a program for beginners, and we lead you through everything at your own pace. It's challenging stuff but not impossible. The hands-on training is really what makes us stand out above the others."

Hands-on training. With Lucas. Who looked like sin wrapped in hotness dipped in *oh my God* in that flight suit. The thought sent warm tingles over her skin, but Lucas was also the guy who'd bailed as quickly as he could when she'd turned her back to answer a phone call. And he hadn't exactly looked happy to see her today.

"I'll give it some thought," Taryn said to Rivers, hedging. "I'm a college professor and my schedule is so crazy right now that I'm not sure I could fit in something this involved."

Rivers smiled, undeterred. "Well, first workout is free. So all I ask is that you ladies give it a shot. If it's not for you, nothing lost."

Kincaid put her arm around Taryn's shoulders. "I'll work on her. I've been told I'm quite persuasive."

"Oh, is that what we're calling it?" Taryn said with a smirk.

Lucas started to laugh and then covered it with a cough, pulling his face into a serious look again.

Kincaid gave Taryn a wink. "We better head back to the starting line and get ready for the race. You boys running?"

"Nah, we're going to hand out flyers to the crowd," Rivers said. "I think this one is going to be more fun to watch from the sidelines anyway."

Kincaid put her hands on her hips. "Chickens." She dipped her head. "Be honest. You fear the unicorn."

"Hell yeah, we do," Rivers said. "That horn is pointy."

"No costume for you, Jamez?" Lucas asked, his voice low, like it was just for her ears.

She met his stare. "Nope. I'll be bait today."

Lucas's gaze skimmed over her at that, and Taryn felt every bit of it like a stroke to her skin. "Be careful out there."

"She's not worried," Kincaid said. "She was a track star. She'll probably outrun us all."

"'Was' being the operative word. In high school. That was a long time ago," Taryn said. "Now I just run numbers in research studies, but my goal is to not embarrass myself."

"Solid plan," Lucas agreed.

"We'll be cheering for y'all," Rivers added.

"Thanks," Taryn said, and they exchanged quick goodbyes before Kincaid hooked arms with her and dragged her toward the starting line.

To Kincaid's credit, she waited until they were at least a few yards away from the guys before she pounced. "*Jamez?* What happened Friday night? I talked to you Friday night! You said nothing."

Taryn shrugged. "It was after."

"You must tell me everything," Kincaid demanded gleefully. "Right now. Tell me what happened with the American Gladiator. Please say it was sordid."

Taryn lifted a brow. "*So* sordid. You told me to think

outside the box, and I just went for it. I saw Lucas from across the room, and we couldn't resist each other. I told him I had one night to give and that we shouldn't exchange real names. There was kissing in the dark and body shots on the bar and then hot, sweaty sex against a wall in the alley."

Kincaid gasped. "*Really?*"

"Oh my God. No!" Taryn laughed. "Do you know how dirty alleys are? And have you met me?" She turned to her friend and put her hand out. "Hi, I'm Taryn, the forensic psychologist who studies murderers and would never go anywhere alone with a strange man from a bar."

"I hate you," Kincaid said with a pout. "I thought you'd had some kind of epiphany and had just gone for a wild and crazy night. That guy"—she jerked her thumb behind her—"would so be worth a one-night stand with no names exchanged. He's probably got those abs you could bounce quarters off of."

Taryn's mind went there for a moment—Lucas without a shirt, quarters bouncing—but the thought overwhelmed, and she quickly dragged her focus back before she got too warm. She frowned. "Do you think the quarters would actually bounce? The physics of that seems off."

Kincaid grinned. "Well, you should totally test that theory! Like immediately. He was checking you out. You should—"

"Slow your roll, girlfriend," Taryn said before Kincaid went completely off the rails with this fantasy date. "I asked him out for coffee that night, and he turned me down, all right? It's a no-go." She folded the flyer Rivers had handed her and tucked it in her pocket.

"As is this gym idea. I love that you're looking for fun things for me to do. You're sweet. But I don't have time for that kind of commitment. Maybe once I get this pilot program rolling, we can figure something out. But I'm just too buried right now."

"But on Friday you said—"

"Friday was a temporary moment of insanity after a bad date," Taryn interjected, her lack of sleep making her words come out sharper than she intended. "I was signing checks I couldn't cash."

Kincaid's mouth curved downward. "But, honey, you need a break more than anyone I know. This"—she waved her hand, indicating Taryn's general person—"is not healthy. You really do look run down."

"I'm fine."

"T—"

"I'm *fine*. I promise. You don't have to worry about me, okay?" She reached out and gave Kincaid's hand a squeeze of thanks. "Now come on, we've got some running to do."

But as Taryn headed to the starting line, she felt like she was running from more than people in crazy costumes. And she didn't feel like she could run fast enough.

chapter
SIX

SHAW TRIED TO IGNORE THE LASER-FOCUSED STARE RIVERS was shooting his way as the two women walked off. He slipped his aviators back on and let his eyes follow Jamez/Taryn the college professor as she walked off with her friend, but he couldn't fully enjoy the sight of her curvy body and those strong, smooth legs. He frowned.

She looked so different from Friday night when he'd first seen her onstage. She'd obviously been intimidated that night, not used to being onstage, but she'd also been alive with an almost raw energy and a passion that had infused every lyric. Today, none of that energy had been there, and she'd seemed like a different person. He recognized today's look because he'd been there. Not just tired but hollowed out. Running on empty.

He'd almost told her to sit down, relax, and watch the race with them, but he couldn't do that. He'd walked away for a reason Friday night, and that reason hadn't changed. But damn, he'd wanted to reach out, pull her aside, and ask her why she looked so utterly exhausted.

"You went to *a bar* on Friday night and *met a woman*?" Rivers asked, incredulity dripping from his words. "Who the hell are you and what have you done with my friend? No, I don't care. Leave him wherever you've chained him up. This new guy is an improvement."

Shaw sniffed derisively and casually flipped Rivers the bird. "It's not what you're thinking. I had a beer. She lost her shoe near my table. I helped her find it. End of story."

"So you *saved her in her time of need* and now you may be training her? This is breaking news, dude."

Shaw sent him a sharp look, though it was probably lost behind the aviators. "I will *not* be training her. She said herself that she doesn't have time. And…Friday night, she looked at me like she might've recognized something about me. I can't risk her figuring out who I am. Even if she did come to the gym, I couldn't be her trainer."

Rivers groaned. "You're being paranoid. She was sneaking glances at you the whole time they were standing here. Ever thought that maybe she was looking at you funny because she likes what she sees?"

Shaw couldn't let his mind go there. He couldn't let himself take a step down that path. Couldn't let himself picture asking the pretty woman with the guitar out for a drink and some conversation. It would be a game of lies. *Tell me about your family. Where'd you grow up? Have any siblings? What'd you do for a living before the gym?* He gathered a stack of flyers and shoved his chair back. "The race is about to start. Let's go stand on the sidelines and watch."

"Shaw—"

"It's Lucas," he said firmly. "Let's go."

Rivers grunted but shifted his chair back, almost flipping it over into the grass, and followed Shaw toward the racecourse. They handed out flyers along the way as they ventured closer to the middle section where ropes lined the path. The organizers had laid out obstacles and hosed down areas to make them muddy. There were low walls for people to climb over, large metal tubes for tunnels, a shallow pond, and various natural hills that would make the run a fun, albeit messy, challenge. Shaw almost wished he'd signed up to run, but he'd rather be working to get people interested in the gym. This really was an ideal crowd to advertise to—people who liked a little adventure with their exercise.

Plus, he couldn't do the run and risk being on camera. One of the local news stations had been lurking around all morning, interviewing people and taking shots of the course. They'd now set up near the finish line, so he made sure to find a spot far from that area.

"This looks like that zombie run we saw on TV," he said when Rivers stopped next to him at the ropes.

"Yeah, but no zombies at this one. Or anything scary."

Shaw glanced his way. "No?"

Rivers didn't look at him, but his jaw flexed. "Yeah. It's a charity run to benefit victims of violent crimes. Costumes that could trigger stress or anxiety are banned."

Shaw's stomach wrenched. "This is for crime victims?"

Rivers's throat bobbed, revealing that he knew exactly how Shaw would feel about that. "Yeah. Great cause."

Of course it was. It was a fantastic cause. One Shaw would have happily given money to—anonymously—and then stayed the hell away from, had he known. He was ready to bail right now. They'd done what they'd come to do. But before he could step back, the starting countdown for the runners sounded over a loudspeaker, and the people behind him surged forward, crowding him against the ropes to get a view. There was no starter pistol, but when the word *go* was announced, the crowd erupted in cheers.

Shaw was trapped where he was for the moment and gritted his teeth, turning back to the race. In the distance, the crowd of uncostumed runners had started racing down the course. They'd get a head start before the chasers were released. Jamez/Taryn was somewhere in that crowd, and Shaw found himself looking for her. It was too hard to tell from that distance, but after a few minutes, the runners were getting closer and he caught sight of her pink bandanna and glasses. She was moving pretty fast and looked to be right behind the first set of runners. Mud puddles splashed around her as she charged forward.

Another announcement was made, and the costumed group was released. The crowd cheered again, and the runners started looking over their shoulders, which meant a few tripped and landed in the mud. Taryn was still running hard, her white shirt already splattered with dirt. A few yards behind her, a guy dressed like a Super Mario brother was hot on her trail. Shaw found himself yelling for her to run faster, to watch out behind her, to lose him at the pond. But if she heard Shaw, she didn't look his way. As she got closer, he could see determination on her face, legs pumping forward, and her chest heaving with breaths. The woman was on a mission.

He murmured *Come on, come on, come on* under his breath as she created a little distance between her and her pursuer. She'd made some progress, but when she got to the edge of the muddy pond, she put one foot in the shallow water and then fell to her knees hard.

Shaw flinched as if he'd been the one who'd fallen, and gripped the rope in front of him. "Come on, Taryn, get up. You're okay."

But she wasn't. She didn't get up. One of her hands plunged into the water to brace herself and the other went to her chest. Super Mario snapped off one of her flags, which were now floating in the water, and kept running. But Taryn didn't move. Her shoulders were heaving too hard, and Shaw's stomach dropped.

"Something's wrong," he said over the noise of the crowd.

"What?" Rivers asked, his attention on a different part of the course.

Taryn fell forward onto her elbows, and Shaw didn't hesitate. His body seemed to know what to do before his brain caught up. He ducked under the rope line and took off at full speed, dodging princesses and superheroes and all manner of characters as he made his way to her. His blood rushed in his ears, and he scanned the landscape for a medic.

He didn't see any obvious help before reaching her. When he got to the edge of the pond, he dropped to his knees. "Jamez, Jamez."

She didn't respond at first.

"*Taryn.*"

She looked his way, panic pinching her features.

"Tell me what's wrong. Are you hurt?" he demanded.

She squeezed her eyes shut and clutched the neck of her T-shirt. "Chest. Hurts. Can't breathe."

Shit. "Okay, I've got you. Stay calm for me. I'm going to get you up. We'll get you help." His voice came out calmer than he was feeling as he took her arm and helped her to her feet, but his mind was already laying out a plan. He'd seen the ambulance parked near the start/finish line. He just needed to get her there. He tried to help her step out of the pond, but she faltered. Before he could think too hard about it, he bent and lifted her off her feet, dirty water dripping off her legs and shorts.

Her eyes went round, but she didn't have the breath to protest.

"I'm going to get you to the medics. Just try to slow your breathing. You're probably hyperventilating or having an asthma attack or something," he said as he jogged toward the sideline and out of the way of the runners, carrying Taryn and trying not to jostle her more than necessary. He wanted it to just be hyperventilation. Real chest pains were far scarier to contemplate. But either way, time was of the essence.

"My friends," Taryn gasped.

"I'll find them for you later," he said between breaths as he ran.

If people noticed Iceman from *Top Gun* carrying a woman to the finish line, no one came to help. Maybe they just thought it was part of the event. He reached the ambulance, panting and sweating.

A man and woman in EMT outfits were leaning against the ambulance, chatting, but as soon as they saw Shaw, they both hopped into action.

"What's wrong?" the woman asked, rushing forward.

"She collapsed on the course. Chest pains. Trouble breathing," Shaw said.

The woman nodded, no nonsense. "Let's get her inside."

Shaw followed her to the back of the ambulance, climbed in, and set Taryn down on the stretcher inside the vehicle. Both the EMTs went to work immediately, and Shaw stepped back, giving them space. Taryn's eyes met his, fear there, but then they put an oxygen mask over her mouth and ordered her to lie down.

The male EMT spoke into the walkie-talkie on his shoulder and then looked at Shaw. "We're going to take her to Austin Memorial. Follow us there."

Shaw tensed. "But I..." *Don't know her. Need to find her friend. Have no business following.* All the words were right there on his tongue, but instead, he found himself nodding. "Okay."

He hopped out the back of the ambulance and pulled his phone from his pocket. He had three missed calls from Rivers, who answered on the second ring. "Where are you? I saw what happened but lost you in the crowd. Is she okay?"

"They're taking her to Austin Memorial. I'm going to follow," Shaw said. "Find her friend and send her that way. I don't want Taryn to be by herself."

"Yeah, absolutely. Go. I'll find the unicorn," Rivers said, going instantly into mission mode.

"Thanks."

Shaw ran to his SUV and caught up to the ambulance as it was leaving the park. The red lights flashed in his vision, and sweat dripped down his back. He didn't know this woman, but he found himself sending up pleas to the universe for her to be okay.

Forty-five minutes later, Shaw was sitting with his

hands clasped between his knees in a blue-tinted waiting room with a noisy vending machine. A nurse stopped in front of him, his white shoes interrupting Shaw's view of the gray floor. "Lucas Shaw."

Shaw looked up.

The middle-aged man gave Shaw a kind half smile, dutifully ignoring Shaw's ridiculous costume. "You can come in and see your friend. She's doing okay now."

Shaw stiffened. He'd been hoping Taryn's friend would be here by now, but Rivers had texted that they'd gotten stuck in traffic. Shaw cleared his throat. "Um, okay."

He followed the nurse down the hallway and into a small room near the back corner of the building. Taryn was inside, awake, her bandanna gone and her fingers clasped in her lap on top of the blue hospital blanket. When she looked up and Shaw stepped inside, surprise crossed her face.

"I brought your friend for a visit," the nurse said cheerfully. "The doctor should be back soon to give you discharge instructions and then you can go."

Taryn wet her lips and gave the nurse a wan smile. "Thanks."

The nurse checked something on a monitor and then left them alone in the room, awkwardness filling the space in his absence.

Shaw folded his arms across his chest and swallowed past the dryness in his throat. "Uh, your friend...the unicorn should be here any minute. Rivers found her and let her know what was going on."

Taryn winced. "God, poor Kincaid. She's going to be in a panic. Does she know I'm okay?"

"Yeah, I texted Rivers. He's riding here with her since I took the car."

Taryn sighed and rubbed the bridge of her nose beneath her glasses. "Thank you. And not just for that. Thanks for doing this, for helping. I'm so sorry."

Shaw shrugged and stayed by the door. "Nothing to be sorry for. You needed help. The doc said everything's all right?"

She shifted on the pillows, looking more than a little uncomfortable. "Yeah, I feel pretty stupid right now. I thought…I thought I was having a heart attack or something." She looked down at the covers and picked at a stray thread in the blanket. "Turns out it's just mild dehydration and exhaustion."

"Exhaustion?"

She smoothed the blanket. "Yeah, apparently it's a bad idea to pull an all-nighter going over research, skip breakfast because you're running late, and then attempt to break land speed records at a race the next morning when you're completely out of shape."

"You're not out of shape," he said without thinking.

Her attention snapped to him.

"I mean…" he said, backpedaling. "Well, I saw you running before you fell. If you were completely out of shape, you never would've been able to do that. But yeah, that doesn't sound like a good pre-race plan. I didn't realize exhaustion could cause chest pains. They checked your heart?"

"Yeah, everything looks okay." Her mouth tilted wryly. "According to the esteemed professionals of this fine establishment, the chest pains were just *straight-up stress*." She made a disgusted sound in the back of her throat. "So yeah, I made a complete spectacle of myself, ruined your day, and freaked out my friends, all because I'm apparently a little stressed and didn't sleep enough."

Shaw relaxed his stance and stepped fully inside the room. "You didn't ruin my day. I'm glad you're all right."

"You keep seeing me at my very worst," she said, sitting up higher in the bed. "I'm usually not this much of a disaster."

"Maybe I'm bad luck," he said, not entirely joking.

She laughed. "Yes, this is clearly all your fault. Good thing you turned me down for coffee. Who knows what would've happened?"

"I didn't turn you down," he said before he'd thought out the implication of the words.

Her brows lifted. "No, you're right. You just…disappeared before I got to hear the no."

He blew out a breath and leaned against the wall. "I'm sorry. That was a crap thing to do. I guess I just didn't know what to say."

She smiled a warm, easy smile. "I'm a big girl, Lucas. I would've been able to handle a no. It's not a big deal."

"I didn't want to say no," he said almost under his breath.

Taryn was quiet for a moment. "Oh?"

Hell. How'd he get himself in this conversation? "Yeah, I…I don't date. Things in my life are too busy right now with the new business to fit anything else in, so I didn't want to…give a false impression." *You know, like a fake name and a bogus life history.* "But I also didn't want to say no, so I left. I'm sorry. I know that was lame."

Taryn leaned back against her pillow, relief crossing

her features. "It's fine. Believe me, I'm well versed in the too-busy-to-have-a-life school. I'm right there with you. When I got off the phone that night, I was turning around to tell you I needed to offer a rain check if you said yes."

He chuckled. "The coffee that truly wasn't meant to be."

"Maybe we could have one in a completely non-date capacity at some point. I have a lot to thank you for, it seems. I might even get you a pastry. If gym owners actually allow themselves such decadence."

Decadence. He could think of a lot of decadent things to do with Taryn, and none had anything to do with baked goods. But he forced himself *not* to remember how good she'd looked in those running shorts and that thin T-shirt earlier today, not to notice how beautiful she was, even worn out, wearing a hospital gown, and without makeup, not to picture how sexy she'd been onstage when she sang. This was not the time, the place, or the woman. Plus, what kind of guy checked a girl out while she was in the hospital?

A dickhead. That's who.

He cleared his throat. "I am not opposed to the occasional treat."

"Cool, maybe we—"

But before she could get the words out, the door burst open behind him, and a crowd of people tumbled in, led by the unicorn and followed by superheroes and old TV stars. Taryn's real cavalry had arrived. Shaw stepped back, trying to melt into the wall and disappear. And after a few minutes, he did just that, slipping into the hallway and not looking back. He had no place here.

This is not for you.
She is not for you.

chapter
SEVEN

TARYN SIPPED THE LARGE MILKSHAKE KINCAID HAD picked up for her on the drive home from the hospital and tried to keep her expression neutral as she and her friends made their way back to Long Acre. Kincaid was driving, and Liv and Rebecca had dispatched the guys to return Taryn's car to her house since no one wanted her to drive yet. Her friends had then piled into the back seat, insisting on seeing her home as well.

Taryn was thankful for the support, but she was struggling to keep it all together in front of her friends. The doctor had discharged her with firm instructions to work on her stress levels. At first, she'd been outright dismissive of the doctor's advice—*Oh, stress, everyone has it, right?* But the doctor was having none of it. She'd told Taryn straight up, *This can kill you. Your body is giving you a warning. If you don't take the warning, next time it will move to crisis phase to get your attention.* Her friends had been in the room, and she'd seen their reactions to the doctor's words, the deep concern.

That was when the reality of it all had settled in for Taryn. The chest pains she'd felt on that course had been real. At first, she'd thought maybe she was having some sort of panic attack because people were chasing her and maybe that had triggered something. But she'd experienced anxiety before. This had been different—a terrifying tightness in her chest, bone-deep dread. For a few terrifying seconds, she'd thought she was having a heart attack and that she was dying.

A very specific fear had overtaken her. *I can't do this to my parents.* That had scared her more than anything. The idea of someone breaking the news to her mom and dad that they'd lost another child. Then a fresh panic washed over her with a new thought. *I'm not done yet. I haven't* started *yet.*

She didn't know what to do with that. The sense that even though she was thirty-one, she hadn't *started.* Started what, she wasn't sure. Maybe it was because she hadn't gotten her program in schools yet. She'd made it her life's work, and it could've ended before she ever got the program off the ground. That might've been where the panic had come from, but the more she thought about it, the more that didn't feel quite right. The dread had felt more all-encompassing—a desperate, smothering sense of loss of what could've been—and it was freaking her the hell out.

She didn't have time for an existential crisis. She had work to do.

"You should call in and take the week off," Liv said from the back seat, breaking Taryn from her thoughts. "The doctor wrote an excuse for you. You should jump on that. Get some rest. Binge Netflix. Go on a little getaway. Something."

Taryn frowned and glanced at Liv in the rearview mirror, catching her dark-eyed gaze. "I can't. The school-board presentation is Thursday night, and I have classes to teach. I'd need to give my department more notice than that. I'm okay. I just need a good night's sleep, and I'll be fine."

"*Fine?*" Kincaid said, the word full of sharp edges. "I'm about to outlaw that word from your vocabulary." She gripped the wheel tighter and returned her gaze to the road, the muscle in her jaw working. "You're *not* fine. You heard the doctor. This could *kill* you."

"Kincaid, it's not—" Taryn started.

"No, don't even." Kincaid's voice was tight, as if there was a hand around her throat pinching off the air. "Do you know how terrified I was when Rivers told me you'd collapsed?" Her long lashes blinked rapidly, her sparkly blue unicorn eyeliner smudging more. "My heart dropped right out of my chest. My mind went to… bad places."

Taryn swallowed her protest, hating that she'd put that fear into her friend. "I'm sorry. You're right. I didn't mean to scare you."

"Well, you did," Kincaid said, her chin jutting out like a child trying not to cry.

"You scared all of us," Rebecca said gently from the back seat. "And believe me, I know what it's like to have so much on your plate that taking a break can seem impossible. I've been there. But your body *is* telling you something. I don't want to freak you out, but there was a lawyer when I first started at the firm who was really successful and seemed to be healthy and have it all together. He collapsed one night when he was working late, died of a heart attack at thirty-seven. His assistant found him the next morning."

Taryn's stomach flipped over. "God, how horrible."

"It was, and it was the first time I realized youth didn't give people a pass on those things," she continued. "I'm not saying you're in the same boat as him. The doc said your heart looks good, but the hours you're pulling and the stress you're dealing with *are* doing damage."

Taryn absorbed the warning and leaned her head back against the seat. "I know working this much isn't good for me, but I'm almost there. I don't keep this schedule all the time. It's just this last year that's been hairy. If I can get through this school-board presentation and get the program piloting in a few schools, I can take a break and recuperate."

"That's the thing, though," Rebecca said, leaning forward between the seats. "I've told myself that story, too, but there's always another thing after whatever you're stressing about is over. For me, there was always another difficult court case. For you, once you get past the school board, you're going to have to roll out the program. Then you're going to have to work out kinks in the program. Then it will need additional funding."

"Exactly," Liv said. "The stress doesn't really go away. It just takes on different faces. You need to find ways to give yourself pockets of time to relax, recharge, and have fun during all that so you can manage it."

"I know," Taryn conceded. "You're right."

"Yes, we are. Which is why..." Kincaid said, giving her another pointed look. "Even if you can't take time off, you're at least doing this Gym Xtreme thing with me. Starting this week. No excuses. I'm pulling rank."

Taryn lifted a brow. "Rank?"

"I'm a month older than you," Kincaid declared. "And relentless. You do not want this girl stalking you all week. Because I will."

"Ha. She's not kidding," Liv said. "I've seen her in that mode."

Taryn lifted her glasses to rub her eyes, weary. She didn't have time to start a gym program. She didn't have time for anything that wasn't already on her schedule. "Does it have to be this week? I have—"

"This week," Kincaid said. "I'm serious. You can find an hour here or there. Lucas has some openings on his schedule."

Taryn adjusted her glasses and peeked over at Kincaid. "Lucas?"

Kincaid smirked and gave a knowing nod. "Yes, your *Top Gun* rescuer has some room this week. You're the lucky winner of that time slot."

Taryn opened her mouth to protest again, but then she remembered Lucas standing in her hospital room, looking tousled and worried and damn hot. He'd told her he didn't date, which was fine, but maybe it wouldn't be *so* bad to spend a little time getting sweaty with him in a different way. *Maybe* she could find an hour this week. Plus, based on how poorly she'd run at the race, she could probably use some kind of physical activity. The former track star inside her was embarrassed at how out of shape she'd become.

She could hit a few check boxes with one pen with this plan—help her friends stop worrying, get back in shape, and hang out with a hot guy—all without having to interfere with her work too much. "Okay," she said finally. "I'm in. I'll try the crazy gym."

Kincaid's determined expression turned bright and sunny again, her friend's normal state returning. "Yay!"

"Awesome," Liv said, reaching out and squeezing Taryn's shoulder. "I'm glad. Y'all let us know how it goes because that shit looks scary. Have you looked at the website?"

"No," Taryn said, glancing back warily.

"Don't," Rebecca chimed in. "Better to focus on the fact that the trainers are, like, holy-crap hot."

Taryn laughed, some of the pressure on her chest lifting. "Y'all saw them?"

"Yeah, the dark-haired one came to the hospital to pick up the guy who helped you," Rebecca said. "Wes teased me about my head being on a swivel when they passed."

Taryn smirked. "He wasn't offended?"

Rebecca snorted. "My husband knows he's pretty and that he's got me completely hooked. He's got no worries."

"He's got no worries regardless. Rivers, the one dressed as Indiana Jones, is gay," Kincaid said, taking the exit for Long Acre. "And Lucas has his eye on one lady right now, and she's sitting in the front seat."

Taryn shook her head. "That better not be what this whole thing is about, Kincaid, because you're wrong. He's a nice guy, and yes, easy to look at, but he's not interested in me that way. He's already turned me down. He said he's got too much going on with opening the gym. So I'm willing to go and work out with you, but you have to promise me you're not going to try to play matchmaker again. That's not what this is about. This is about getting some exercise and stress relief."

Kincaid made a dismissive sound. "Sex with a hot guy can be great stress relief."

"Amen," Liv said with a laugh. "I'm on that fitness plan and fully endorse it."

"Hallelujah," Rebecca added, lifting her palm in praise.

"Hush, you two, with your hot men and all your sex. It's not nice to gloat." Taryn poked Kincaid in the arm. "And you, Miss Thing, have to promise this is exercise only or I'm not going. That's my hard limit. This is not 'get Taryn a date,' part two."

"What if it's just 'get Taryn laid' and not dating per se?"

"Kincaid!"

"Fine." Kincaid didn't look pleased, but she relented. "Your loss. Just exercise."

Taryn narrowed her eyes at her friend. "Okay, then it's a deal."

Kincaid tapped the steering wheel as if she were stamping a contract. "Excellent. They're opening for a sneak-preview week for special guests only, and I got us in. We start on Tuesday. I've already signed us up and paid our deposits."

"You what?" Taryn said, exasperated. "You didn't even know I would agree."

Kincaid reached out and patted Taryn on the knee. "Oh, honey, you're cute."

"No one resists the unicorn," Liv said with a wry smile in the rearview mirror. "Don't even try."

Kincaid neighed like a horse and dipped her head,

even though she'd tossed her unicorn horn in the trunk, and the other women laughed.

Taryn rolled her eyes, but inside, warmth spread through her chest. Her friends were being lighthearted with her, but she got the message loud and clear. *We care. We're here. And we're not going to let you get away with not taking care of yourself. Get it together, girl.*

Now she just had to figure out if she actually could.

Early Tuesday morning, Shaw bounced on the balls of his feet, getting his blood pumping and his muscles warmed up. He'd already gone through a series of stretches, but he needed to make sure he was fully limbered up. Yesterday's unofficial grand opening had done a number on him. The buzz from the charity race had worked, and they'd had a steady stream of sneak-preview invitees coming by for demonstrations, tours, and intro workouts.

Shaw had given countless demos on the obstacle courses for their potential customers to prove the challenges weren't impossible and then had coached a number of newbies on how to safely get started. Even though he'd worked hard to get his body back in top condition over the last year, the obstacles were no joke. He'd fallen into the pool twice when he'd lost his grip, the foam pits half a dozen times, and he'd tumbled down a ramp on another challenge. His muscles had protested when he'd rolled over in bed this morning, begging for a few more hours of rest or a hot tub.

He'd forced himself up at dawn, though. The morning workout was nonnegotiable. Both the doctor and therapist had told him after he'd gotten arrested that anger was like a hungry monster living inside him, and he had to keep it tamed. *Intermittent explosive disorder*. Three words scrawled onto his permanent medical record that he couldn't erase—or even deny after how he'd acted. The main doctor had said it was probably a genetic predisposition, that he would need to stay on psychiatric medication to keep it in check. Shaw had tried that for a while. But the meds had just made him feel sick and…numb. He'd already watched his dad get lost in pills, seeking that numbness. Shaw had accepted that something was broken inside him, but he didn't want to live life feeling like a hollow shell.

So he'd visited another doctor, one who wasn't sold on Shaw's treatment plan and who was open to alternatives. She'd told Shaw physical activity and stress management techniques could be as effective as medication in some people with anger problems. In other words, if there was a beast inside Shaw, he could exhaust the motherfucker and keep it leashed. Exertion had become his medicine.

Shafts of early-morning sunshine angled through the gym skylights and reflected off the pools, making the walls look as if they were in motion. Soon, the place would, hopefully, be filled with more potential members, but for now, it was all his. He leaned over and turned a knob on the wall, dialing up the volume of the music as he faced down the tumbling floor in front of him. Pearl Jam's "Not for You" screamed through the speakers. A concert for one.

Shaw stretched his arms and shoulders one last time and eyed the expanse of blue floor in front of him.

Floor exercise had never been his favorite event, but there was nothing like good, hard tumbling first thing in the morning to get his mind in the right place. Well... there was one other good, hard activity that could have a similar relaxing effect, but that wasn't an option these days unless it was by his own hand. Flipping through the air would have to do.

He stood at the corner of the floor, centered his focus, and then took off in a run. In one fluid motion, he went to the floor, his palms landing against the mat, and propelled himself into the tumbling pass. The world blurred around him as his body went through a routine that had been burned into his muscle memory. It wasn't as elaborate as the one that had qualified him for the World Championships—an event he'd had to drop out of after Long Acre. His body was over a decade older and the risk of injury higher, but it was still a challenging pass that took all of his concentration. His feet landed at the far corner of the floor mat, and his momentum carried him into taking a big step back.

Stick the landing. The berating voice was familiar. His old coach still lived inside Shaw's head. He took a rib-expanding breath and made another pass, ending with a full twisting layout. This time, he made it to the corner, and his feet only bobbled the landing with a tiny step. *Better.* Though he used to be able to make the layout a double with no bobble at all.

His muscles complained with the effort, the aches from yesterday making themselves known, but Shaw wasn't near stopping. The harder he practiced, the more those pains would ease and his thoughts would quiet. He could start his day in that place of peaceful exhaustion.

The song hit its angry, cathartic peak, the gritty vocals echoing around him, and Shaw fell into the rhythm of the music. *Run and tumble. Stick the landing.* Sweat dripped down his back, and his breath came in shorter bursts. Any stress he'd been feeling when he'd awoken this morning faded into the background.

He'd have to stop soon. Rivers was probably in the office by now and readying the place to open the doors. Shaw would need to shower and get prepared for work, but he couldn't resist a few more passes. He pushed his body to find a little more.

When he stuck the landing cold on the last pass, something loosened in his gut. There it was, that little high that came with hitting his limit. *Mission accomplished.* He rode that buzz and reached for the towel he'd left nearby. He wiped the stinging sweat from his eyes and then pulled the rubber band from his soaked hair to scrub the towel over his head, missing the ease of his former short haircut, even though Rivers regularly reminded him that the military cut hadn't been doing him any favors. *You're ruining a good face with a buzz cut. Give a woman something to hold on to.* Rivers hadn't yet gotten it through his head that there would be no woman.

"Looks like you could use some water." A female voice behind Shaw cut through the opening of the next song and his thoughts like a blade.

He stilled, startled for a moment, and then spun around. He'd expected a stranger, maybe a new hire. Rivers had brought on a small team of part-timers who were training this week. But the familiar face that greeted Shaw had his ribs cinching. Big brown eyes and a face he'd thought about way too much since leaving the hospital Sunday night.

What was Taryn doing here? Shaw turned down the music, trying to piece the puzzle together and not show his reaction on his face. "Uh, hey. I'm sorry. I didn't see you there. I thought we were still closed."

"You are." Taryn's gaze dipped to his bare chest. He'd only thrown on a pair of running shorts since they were easy to tumble in, but for some reason, he felt bare naked standing there. He liked the way she was looking at him a little too much. He draped the towel over his shoulder, and her attention quickly jumped back to his face. "I'm sorry. I didn't mean to interrupt. Rivers said it was okay to come out here."

She looked so out of place in her tan slacks, pale-green top, and heels. All cool sophistication in the thick, chlorine-scented air of the gym. Smart. Lush. Beautiful. His hands flexed at his sides, the lyrics to the song he'd been blasting whispering through his head. *Not for you.*

"I hope that's all right," she said tentatively.

He realized he'd been staring and silent and dragged his focus back to where it needed to be. "Um, of course. How are you doing? You look better."

She smiled. "I hope so. Hospital blue really isn't my color."

He winced. "I mean…"

She shook her head. "It's fine. I know what you mean. And yes, I'm feeling a lot better. I got some rest and only worked a half day yesterday."

"That's good to hear."

Taryn held out a bottle of water, her movements a

little stiff, almost awkward. "Rivers gave me this, but you probably need it more than I do." She nodded at the mat. "That was…something."

So she'd seen him tumbling. *Shit*. He never did that stuff in front of anyone but Rivers anymore. The risk of people putting two and two together was too high. He searched Taryn's face, looking for any hint of recognition, but her expression was simply curious. He accepted the water and took a long swig. Wiping his mouth with the back of his hand, he finally said, "Thanks. Just getting the blood pumping before I get started today."

"That'll do it. I love that song."

He took another gulp of the water. "You should add it to your set list when you do your next big show at the Tipsy Hound."

She laughed in a self-conscious way that was so endearing it made a smile jump to his face as well. She shook her head. "Um, so that won't be happening. There's no encore show, and I'm not sure I could pull off that kind of vocal anyway."

He narrowed his eyes. After hearing her sing, he had no doubt she could pull off some Eddie Vedder and nail the emotion of it, too, but he let it go. "So, is there something I can help you with?"

"Right. Reason I'm here. I should've probably led with that." She rubbed her lips together, smoothing the pink gloss there. "My very loving yet pushy friend Kincaid has signed me up for sessions here. They start today, and I have another scheduled on Friday. With you."

A record scratch sounded in his head. "Wait, what?"

She wrinkled her nose. "Yeah, I figured you didn't know. I think she set it up with Rivers. I'm supposed to come in tonight after work."

Shaw swallowed. *Hell.* In every other universe, this would've been a boon. An attractive woman wanting hands-on training from him? *Yes, please.* Sign him up. But he already felt like this was barreling into dangerous territory. He liked Taryn a little too much. Had thought about her a little too often the past few days. Had thought about how sexy she'd been when she was singing, then how down-to-earth she'd been when they'd talked. How she'd looked at him like she wanted him. She was temptation personified, and that was the last thing he needed. "Right. Okay."

She gave him a chagrined smile. "So, I'm here because I kinda sorta asked you out twice, and both times, you bailed right after. And I just wanted to let you know that I'm not, like, stalking you or anything."

He stared at her for a long moment and then burst into a laugh. "*What?*"

She crossed her arms and cocked her hip as if affronted, but a small smile peeked through. "It wasn't until after I agreed to do this with Kincaid that I realized how it might look to you."

He coughed over the last of his laugh. "How it might look. Like you were a stalker. Like that is a thing I would actually think about you."

Now she was in full grin. "Well, you could! I don't know. I'm just here to state for the record that I am not a woman who throws herself at some guy. I'm simply coming here for a workout and some stress relief. No ulterior motives."

He nodded in mock seriousness. "So you haven't tattooed my name on your shoulder or anything yet?"

"Of course not," she said, smile falling, eyes wide and solemn. "Only your initials."

She delivered it with such a serious tone that it took him a second to get it. When it clicked, another laugh, a sound he'd almost forgotten, rumbled out of him and shook his shoulders. "Well, that's a relief."

Her smile returned. "But seriously, you're okay being my trainer?"

No. Absolutely not. Danger! Danger! "Of course. As long as your doctor has cleared you to exercise."

She gave him a thumbs-up. "All clear. Apparently getting sweaty is the best prescription for what happened to me on Sunday."

"Getting sweaty is…" His mind wandered off leash, and dirty pictures unfolded in front of him—Taryn's smooth skin glistening with exertion, his hands tracing paths along her curves, slipping off clothes, tasting the salt on her skin, feeling her heat wrap around him. He cleared his throat, trying to shove the images into a deep closet in his mind. "Yeah, it's good stuff. Sweating's good."

She adjusted her glasses, still smiling, but something unreadable flickering in her eyes. "Great. Well then, I guess I'll see you tonight."

"Yep. See you then," he said, managing to keep his voice casual. "Looking forward to it."

She gave him one last glance and then headed back toward the hallway that led to the offices and the entrance. He let his gaze follow her all the way out—every damn swish of her hips, every click of her heels. As soon as she was out of view, he took the ice-cold water and dumped it right over his head, hissing at the sting.

Just a pretty woman. Just a pretty woman.

He could handle this.

This was nothing more than hormones and being hard up and pure physical reactions. Nothing he couldn't wrangle. He'd tamed a lot worse demons.

By the time Taryn walked in tonight, he'd have these reactions on lockdown. He slicked his hair back and groaned. But first, maybe a really long shower.

chapter
EIGHT

"YOU ARE *NOT* DOING THIS TO ME, KINCAID," TARYN said into the speakerphone as she turned the steering wheel, driving off the half-flooded road and into the parking lot behind the gym. Hard rain spattered her window with a relentless drumbeat. "You're screwing with me."

Kincaid made a pained sound. "God, I wish I was. I'm not messing with you, I swear. I am so sorry. Today has been a total nightmare. This house sale was supposed to close yesterday, and then today has been issue after issue. I can't leave yet, and even if I did, I'm all the way out in Wilder, and it's storming here. I just saw a group of stray dogs joining up two by two and looking for an ark. You're going to have to do the first session without me."

"No way. I'm going to go home and get some work done," Taryn said, irritated after fighting traffic and torrential rain to get to the gym and now finding out that Kincaid was bailing.

"No, please, don't," Kincaid begged. "I feel terrible. I promise this isn't one of my schemes. I have my gym bag in the car and was looking forward to tonight. Please don't cancel because of me. They kept the gym open late just for us, and you need this. We were going to be training with separate people anyway. This won't be that different."

Taryn blew out a breath and tipped her head back against the car seat. "You swear this isn't some trick?"

"Cross my heart," Kincaid said, sincerity in her voice. "This is important to me. I want you to have some fun and wanted to be there for it. I promise I'll be there for the next session. This was just a freak thing. Please go."

Taryn pressed the ignition button, cutting off the engine, and listened to the rain. She really didn't feel like working out. She also didn't feel like fighting more rush-hour traffic and a downpour on the hour-long drive home to Long Acre. At least if she stayed a while at the gym, traffic and hopefully the storm would die out, letting some of the drains catch up and clear the roads. "Fine. I'm here already, so I'll go in for a short session. But if this is horrible, you owe me all the chips and queso I want."

"Deal. But I don't think it's going to be bad. Just do what you can and have fun. Hold on. Hey, Harold, don't let them sign that yet. I'll be right there." There were voices in the background as Kincaid dealt with her clients. "Taryn, I've got to go, honey, but let me know how everything went later. Don't pull any muscles or break any bones."

"Encouraging," Taryn said wryly, but Kincaid was already gone.

Taryn ended the phone call and looked toward the glass doors of the gym, the light from the building the only bright spot under the dark clouds and rain. As she stared, trying to psych herself up for this, the light shifted and a silhouette filled the space—broad and tall. She was beginning to recognize that outline. Her belly tightened, nerves and something else making her tense. She'd visited the gym earlier today to squash any awkwardness that could arise with Lucas, but her body hadn't gotten the message that she wasn't supposed to react this way around him.

Just a workout. That was all this was.

Before she could finish her pep talk and get her ass out of the car, the main door swung open and the silhouette turned into a full 3-D form as Lucas jogged out into the puddles with a large, black umbrella. Taryn grabbed her bag and quickly opened her car door.

"Hey, there," he called over the thrum of the rain. "Let's get you inside."

Taryn stepped out into the now inch-high water in the parking lot and ducked under the umbrella, clutching her bag to her chest. Lucas huddled close to her and they hurried to the door, but a hard gust of wind hit them and the umbrella flipped inside out.

Water poured down on them both, and they broke into a run. When they reached the overhang, a thick streak of lightning zipped through the sky, illuminating the dark parking lot, and the accompanying clap of thunder made Taryn yelp.

"Shit," Lucas said, yanking open the door. "That sounded like it hit close. Get inside."

He guided her in first with a hand on her lower back and then slipped in behind her, tossing the useless umbrella onto the floor by the door. The cool air of the gym chilled Taryn's wet skin, and she shivered.

Lucas scrubbed a hand through his hair, sending droplets flying, and his shoes squished when he moved. "You all right?"

Taryn had managed to keep her head under the failed umbrella but the rest of her was a loss. Lucas was even worse off, his shirt soaked through. She swiped water off her arms. "Yeah, I'm fine. I'm sorry you got drenched. You didn't have to come out and get me."

"I wasn't sure if you had an umbrella. If you made it all the way here in this rain to work out, you've earned curbside service," he said, pulling his shirt away from his skin as if to check its status. "But my umbrella was a fail."

She laughed. "You think? We look like we fell into the pool."

"Maybe that's where we should start the workout, then," he said with a chagrined smile. "I've already gotten you wet."

Gotten you wet. The second the words were out, she could feel her face heating. God, she was like a teenager around this guy, her mind turning everything into double entendres. "Um, I didn't bring a swimsuit."

Lucas cleared his throat. "Maybe not, then." He rubbed his palms on his workout pants, even though they were soaked, too. "How about you get changed and then we'll do some warm-up exercises to get the chill out and your muscles limbered up?"

"Right. Sounds good. Where are the locker rooms?" Taryn picked up her bag.

He pointed. "Down that hall on the left. And before we get started, I just want to let you know that when Kincaid called and said she couldn't make it, Rivers went home. He figured you were going to cancel, too."

Taryn looked up. "Oh?"

Lucas crossed his arms and nodded, looking a little uncomfortable. "Yeah, so it's just us here. Rivers only lives a few blocks away, so if you don't feel comfortable, he's happy to come back, and I won't be offended. Or we can reschedule. I want you to have whatever you need."

Taryn considered him, trying to tap into her gut feelings, something she'd learned to trust. Her mother would tell her to get the hell out of there because she didn't know this guy and no one could hear her scream. That was where her mom's mind would instantly go. But Taryn didn't feel that fear with Lucas. He could've skipped telling her this if he had bad intentions. He also would probably be trying to do a better job of reassuring her. Plus, she'd asked the guy out twice. He wasn't exactly eager to get her alone. "It's okay. I don't want Rivers to have to come out in this rain. Plus, Kincaid knows I'm here, so if you kill me, she'll know it was you and hunt you down. I expect she'd make it a painful and slow death."

She'd meant it as a joke, but Lucas frowned. "You're safe with me."

The stark sincerity in the words hit her right in her gut. Something in his eyes said he truly was worried she'd see him as some kind of threat, even though he'd shown her nothing but kindness since he'd helped her find her shoe the other night. Maybe he was used to people being intimidated by him because he was so fit. She nodded. "I believe you."

The tension in his face softened. "Thanks. I'll meet you on the main floor, okay? Take your time, and be ready to sweat."

She shivered again. "That actually sounds pleasant compared to rain-soaked and freezing."

His lips lifted at one corner. "We'll see if you're still saying that after the workout."

She laughed. "I'll probably just be cursing you and the horse you rode in on."

"Probably," he said brightly.

She groaned and headed toward the ladies' locker room. Once inside, she quickly took off her glasses, put in her contacts, and tied back her hair with a bandanna. Then she changed into her workout clothes, the new items feeling foreign and far too clingy. She'd planned on wearing her old sweatpants and loose T-shirts for these sessions, but when she'd mentioned that to Kincaid, her friend had vetoed that idea immediately. *If we're really going to subject ourselves to falling into swimming pools, you don't want to be drowned by your ugly, floppy pants and old T-shirt. We need to look cute as we embarrass ourselves.*

Taryn had dutifully bought two new workout outfits on her lunch break yesterday, still debating whether she'd actually wear them. The last thing she wanted to do was wear Lycra after not having worked out in years. But when Rivers had emailed her last night with the information for the training sessions, the safety rules had been attached. *No loose clothing allowed on obstacle courses and the equipment.* Because it posed a safety risk. Having a sweatshirt get hooked on something as you fell was a good way to hang yourself, apparently.

So now Taryn was wearing clothes that clung to her as if she'd applied them with superglue and feeling completely out of her comfort zone. Before leaving the locker room, she snatched her hoodie and pulled it over her head. She could claim it was because she was cold. Plus, she probably wouldn't be doing obstacles right away. They were just going to warm up.

Lucas was waiting for her when she stepped inside the main part of the gym. The skylights flashed with the lightning outside, and the rain battered the roof, making it sound like they were inside a huge barrel. Lucas had changed into different clothes—a snug, black T-shirt and a pair of gray track pants. She worked hard not to stare.

Definitely failed.

Lucas smiled, clipboard in hand. "All ready to go?"

She shrugged. "As ready as I'll ever be."

He didn't seem deterred by her lack of enthusiasm as he looked down at the clipboard. "All right. Let's walk or jog a few laps around the track to get warmed up and then we'll try The Wall."

He said the last two words as if they were capitalized and should be followed by *of Doom*.

"Wait, hold up." Taryn lifted a finger and pointed to the giant curved wall off to the left behind Lucas. "Surely you don't mean that wall over there."

He glanced over his shoulder. "The very one."

"You've got jokes, Lucas."

He gave her an amused glance. "No jokes. You're trying that wall tonight."

Yeah, and ice-skating in hell would follow that event. "You're nuts."

"Maybe." He grinned and set aside his clipboard. "I said you're safe with me. I never said I'd be easy on you." He clapped his hands. "Now get moving, songbird."

"Songbird?"

"Yep." He started running in place. "A talented singer. But also a lady who's doing a lot of crowing right now."

She lifted a brow, affronted. "Did you just call me a crow? Don't make me throw my shoe at you again."

He jogged away. "You'll have to catch me first."

Well, that did it. She hadn't been a runner in a long time, but that old competitive spirit from track fired up at the challenge. She jogged after him toward the narrow indoor track and poked him in the arm when she caught up. "I'm out of practice, but not slow."

"Getting cocky already, songbird," he said, keeping pace with her.

She picked up her speed a little to pass him and put her arms out to flap them like wings. "*Caw-caw*."

His deep laugh was a balm to the nerves she'd felt coming in here tonight. This wasn't so bad. Lucas was easy to be around, and it actually felt good to be moving. She jogged ahead but didn't push it too hard, still wary of what had happened at the race, and soon Lucas caught up and kept a steady pace with her.

"I want you to stay at the level of effort where you can talk but it's a bit of a challenge to hold a conversation," he said, his feet pounding the track next to her. "And never be afraid to ask for a break. I'll push you because that's what you're coming here for, but I need to be able to trust you to tell me when it's too much."

"I'll tell you," she promised. "I'm not known for keeping my mouth shut."

"Good. Now let's sweat."

Half an hour later, Taryn was warm from the inside

out and dripping with sweat. Lucas looked like he was barely glistening. She hated him a little in that moment.

He handed her a bottle of water and a towel and then took a towel for himself. He wrapped it around his neck and nodded at her. "That was good work. Feeling okay?"

"I'm feeling out of shape." She took a long sip of the water. "But okay."

"Out of practice. That's all," he said, his tone reassuring. "But that's why you're here. Today will be the worst day. The only place to go from this point is up."

"Right."

"And by up, I mean up that wall." He cocked his head toward the ridiculous obstacle.

She dried her face with the towel and groaned. "Still with the wall?"

"I keep promises," he said, a wicked gleam in his eye. "You and I have a date with that wall."

"I thought you didn't date," she teased.

"I make an exception for Wally. We're in a steady relationship. And we're about to invite you in."

"That sounds dirty." She tossed the towel aside and set her water bottle on the floor next to it. "And is it a requirement for all trainers to be sadists? Do they screen for that? Because I feel like you're enjoying this a little too much."

A dimple appeared in his left cheek. "Yes, it's the third class in trainer school…How to Make Your Clients Hate You Before They Love You."

"Uh-huh. Gotta be honest. Not loving you so much right now."

"You're not supposed to." He turned. "Let's get started."

She frowned, his tone sounding different from the playful one he'd been using, but she followed him to the obstacle course area anyway.

Taryn put her hands on her hips and stared at the giant curved wall in front of her. The thing had to be twelve feet tall, and the rope she was supposed to capture near the top seemed to be miles away. It might as well have been hanging off the side of a ten-story building. "Shouldn't I have, like, a skateboard or something to get up this thing? A rocket booster?"

Lucas picked up his clipboard from where he'd set it down before their run and then dug around in a gym bag near his feet. He handed her a set of kneepads. "Nope. But don't freak out. Day one, I just need to see where you are so I can track your progress. It's a benchmark. I expect you to suck at this one."

"Well gee, thanks, Coach," she said as she strapped on the knee pads. "Good speech. Very motivating. You should do a TED Talk."

He smirked, blue eyes crinkling. "Would you rather I lie to you?"

She groaned and bounced on her toes, trying to rev herself up like she used to do before a race. "No, but a little positivity wouldn't hurt."

"Okay." He swung his arm out. "The mat at the bottom is soft, and you're wearing knee pads, so it probably won't hurt that much when you fall."

She gave him a droll look. "Are you supposed to want to hit your trainer?"

He set the clipboard aside and crossed his arms over that broad chest, looking like a Greek god with a mean streak. "You should take off the sweatshirt.

The bulk is going to make it even harder to build momentum."

"Right." She wet her lips and, after a moment of panicked hesitation, nervously tugged off the shirt. When she dropped it to the side, leaving her in what amounted to a skintight tank top and leggings, she felt more than a little exposed, and the cold air was probably making things even more visible, but she tried to keep her expression neutral. This was a gym. These were gym clothes. Lucas's gaze darted down her body and then quickly shifted to a spot over her shoulder.

He cleared his throat. "I'm ready when you are."

The Wall. That was where her focus needed to be. Taryn let her gaze travel up the intimidating curve of the obstacle, and sweat broke out on her lip. She squatted down to make sure the knots on her shoelaces were tight and then stood and checked the waistband on the new workout leggings to make sure they weren't going to give up on her when she tried to get up this damn wall.

Shaw lifted a brow, a little of the humor back. "You're stalling."

Taryn narrowed her eyes. "That is my right."

He nodded, conceding the point. "If you're too scared…"

Scared. She flexed her jaw and eyeballed the ramp again. Well, that did it. She was a lot of things, but she wasn't a coward. It was a wall. So what if she fell? What was the worst that could happen? A hurt ego? A sore butt? Her pants ripping? Her bones breaking into a million—*nope, not going to think about that*. She squared her body toward the wall.

She took a deep breath, braced a foot behind her as

though she was waiting for the starter pistol of a race, and then took off with as much power as she could. She made it two strides up the wall, her arms outstretched for the rope that was far out of reach, and then gravity took over and dragged her backward. She tried to catch herself, but the reverse momentum was too much. She fell onto her kneepads and slid down the wall on her hands and knees, eventually landing on the padded mat below with an indelicate grunt.

She slapped the mat. "Damn."

"Seven feet," Shaw said as he stepped up next to the wall and made a note on his clipboard. "Great. Now we know your starting point."

"Is it good or bad?" she asked, sitting up on her knees.

He glanced over at her. "It's neither. It's your personal day one. Next time you try, you'll be able to gauge whether you improved or not."

She hated that answer. Her competitive side wanted to know if she was worse, average, or better than other people on day one. She got to her feet and stared the obstacle down, irritated with it for existing. "I want to try again."

Lucas's lips twitched at the corners, but he didn't look up from his clipboard. He shrugged. "Go for it."

Taryn backed up and took a breath. She tried to channel the frustration she was feeling into energy to help her get farther up the wall. *One, two, three...* She took off in a sprint, her arms pumping. Two steps up the wall and gravity laughed at her again, yanking her backward with even less grace than the first time. She slid down, losing her balance and planting onto her ass. She hit the mat with a gasp. "Ugh! This wall sucks."

Lucas snorted. "Patience not a virtue of yours, songbird?"

"I have a doctorate," she said grumpily. "I spent almost a decade in college and graduate school. I'm familiar with patience."

"I can tell."

"Hush." She stood and dusted herself off like she'd fallen into mud instead of onto a mat. "Can *you* make it up the wall?"

"Yep," he said without hesitation. "But I couldn't on the first day."

She straightened her crooked top, trying to find some of her dignity. "Show me."

He looked her way, unmoved. "This is your training session, not a competition. What does it matter to you if I can make it up the wall?"

She crossed her arms. "Because I'm not convinced anyone can do it. Maybe this is a marketing ploy to keep people coming back and trying."

He huffed a laugh. "A marketing ploy?"

"Yes." She nodded resolutely.

Lucas gave her a patient look, tossed aside the clipboard, and strode past her. Before she could even track his technique, he took off in a run and scaled the monster wall in a few strides. Instead of grabbing the rope, he gripped the top edge of the wall and hung from it. The muscles in his arms flexed in full relief, and his track pants hung low on his hips, exposing a tan strip of lower back. Taryn had to stop herself from gawking because *hell*, it wasn't fair for anyone to look that good doing something as ridiculous as hanging from a wall.

Then, instead of dropping back down, Lucas pulled

himself all the way up to the platform at the top, turned around, and sat on the edge of the wall. He looked down at her, hands gripping the edge and feet dangling. "Satisfied, professor?"

Taryn harrumphed. "Show-off."

He stood and climbed down the ladder on the side of the wall and then hopped down, skipping the last few rungs. "You asked me to show off."

"Well, you didn't have to do such a good job of it," she said petulantly.

He laughed and handed her the bottle of water she'd set down earlier. "I have high hopes for you. This is a good sign."

"That I fell on my ass?"

"No." He picked her towel off the floor and looped it around her neck, not touching her exactly, but getting in her space enough to call her body to attention. "That you're pissed about it." He released the towel and stepped back, his eyes meeting hers. "It means you'll keep trying. It means you have fight."

She held his gaze for a moment, absorbed the words. "Right. You say that like you didn't think I would."

He considered her. "Honestly, I didn't know. It takes fight to start this kind of workout right after the scare you had on Sunday. But the night I met you…"

She rolled her eyes. "I ran off the stage like a big chicken."

"It wasn't the running off the stage I was thinking about but more the fact that you said you'd never been onstage at all. You have a great voice. You play guitar. But you've never performed?"

"No," she said. "That's not about fight. That's about

practicality. Music was something I enjoyed, but I had more important things to do with my life than writing a few songs or performing. The dive bars don't need another name in their lineup. My time is better spent on my research."

Lucas frowned at her.

She sighed. "What?"

"I don't know." He shrugged. "Maybe sometimes it's okay to do something just for fun. Just because it feels good, you know?"

"Yeah? What would you do just because it feels good?" The words were out before she could evaluate how they could be construed.

His eyes drifted over her, his expression darkening and making her all too aware of each part of her body. Her skin tingled as if his hand had just caressed her instead of his gaze. His jaw flexed and he looked away. "Never mind. We're wasting time you paid for. Let's work on some balance stuff for the last few minutes."

He turned to walk toward the other end of the obstacle course, and she hurried to keep up. Only exercise. She was only here for exercise.

And stress relief.

Ha.

When Lucas had looked at her the way he had, she wasn't sure she'd ever felt quite so keyed up. If she was here for stress relief, this professor was earning a big, fat F.

chapter
NINE

LUCAS DIRECTED HER UP ONE OF THE LADDERS ON THE far side of the main obstacle course and then joined her on the platform. Ahead of them was a thick cylinder that crossed over a wide foam pit like a bridge. Lightning flashed above through the skylights, illuminating the brightly colored foam blocks below. The pit looked very far down, and Taryn's nerves ratcheted up. "Um, this seems kind of advanced, Lucas."

"It can be, but there are some adjustments for beginners. Balance is a big part of this course, and it's important for building core strength." He squatted down and turned a few knobs and flipped a switch. A whirring noise filled the air, and two trapeze bars descended from a contraption above, revealing a narrow track that the trapeze could move along while you walked the cylinder, He dragged one trapeze bar toward her and then toed off his shoes. "We're both going to go out there on the cylinder and hold on to these. There's a button on the right side of the bar to control tension. Hold it down and it will lock into the track above, keeping the wire taut, and you'll get more support. If you release it, it'll give you more slack, and you can practice your balance. The goal right now is to get you used to the feel of standing on the cylinder and being this high in the air. Take off your shoes and socks. Try to use these muscles." He put a gentle palm over her abdomen, and she sucked in a breath at the heat of his touch. "Keep your focus there."

Oh, her focus was there. Very, very there. "Got it."

He moved his hand away, and she took the trapeze bar in her hand. He grabbed his own bar and stepped out in front of her onto the cylinder, walking backward and facing her. Looking entirely too comfortable with being so high up.

He stopped close to the middle of the cylinder bridge and then demonstrated how to lock it in place. He took one hand off the bar to beckon her to him. "Come on, songbird. You've got this."

She took a deep breath. "Is now the time to admit I may have a teeny, tiny fear of heights?"

"Just keep your eyes on me," he said calmly. "Don't look down. You're safe."

Taryn wasn't sure she'd be able to resist looking down, but she took off her shoes and socks and grabbed the horizontal bar above her head again. After one more deep breath, she took the first step onto the cylinder. She immediately pressed the button to lock the tension, testing the feel. The foam was firm beneath her feet but rough enough to give her a sense of grip. She kept her gaze on Lucas, and then she released the button, her hands tightly gripping the bar as she managed a few more steps out. The air-conditioning blew over her, chilling her skin even as her heart picked up speed.

"Good," Lucas said in a soothing voice. "Now I want you to get your footing without locking the bar. Try to find your balance without its help. It's just there for backup."

Taryn swallowed hard, the urge to look down tugging at her, but she adjusted her feet and did as she was told. She could feel every leg and stomach muscle working hard as she lifted her arms higher and released more tension in the bar. After a few wobbles, she felt when her body took over and was doing most of the balancing work. She lifted her face to Lucas, who was a few feet farther down the cylinder, and smiled. "Hey, I'm doing it."

He grinned. "You are. Before you know it, you'll be ready for it to roll."

"Roll?"

He pointed down at the cylinder. "Yep. This baby spins."

"Holy shit," she said with a laugh. "Yeah, let's not do that yet. I'm barely keeping steady."

"No worries. I flipped the switch to secure it in place. Try to take a few steps forward. Keep your abs tight and supporting you. Don't lock your knees. The goal tonight is for you to reach me."

Taryn's confidence was building, and she took a small step. It wouldn't require too many more to get to Lucas, but before she could take another, a loud crash of thunder rattled the building and the bright overhead lights blinked. Taryn made a startled sound, and she lost her focus, wobbling. She gripped the bar hard and managed not to slip off, but then the telltale *whoosh* of electricity going off filled her ears. All the lights clicked off. The cavernous space went pitch-black.

"Lucas!"

"Hell," Lucas said from somewhere in front of her. "Hold on. Just give me a second. I'll come and get you."

Lightning flashed, illuminating Lucas and his tense face briefly. Taryn's blood was rushing in her ears, and she tried to take a step backward toward the platform, but the trapeze was locked in place. "The bar is stuck."

"I know. They automatically lock when the power's turned off," he said, sounding closer. "I'll help you back. The emergency lights should come on."

But nothing happened. The only light was the intermittent flash of lightning through the skylights. Taryn glanced back during one of the flashes and realized how far she'd gotten from the platform, but she could feel the vibration in the cylinder. Lucas was moving toward her.

Soon, a hand landed next to hers on her trapeze bar, and the heat of Lucas's body brushed against her. The shift caused her to wobble, and he quickly wrapped his arm around her waist. "Easy. I've got you."

His chest was pressing against hers, warm, solid, steady. She wet her lips, somehow feeling both calmed and completely freaked out by his presence. "Thanks."

"Now I need you to listen to me," he said, his breath tickling her hair. "There's only one way to get off this thing safely right now, and you're not going to like it."

"You need to go ahead of me?" She was picturing some maneuver where he crossed over her and then guided her back or something.

"No," he said, his arm firm around her. "We can't risk walking back to the platform. You would have to let go of the bar, and it's too dark. If either of us stumble and fall too close to the platform, we could hit the equipment and get hurt."

She heard the words but didn't quite process what he was getting at. "What do you mean?"

"I mean the only safe way is down."

"*Down?*" She wobbled with the force of the word. "Oh, hell no."

"Listen." His tone was gentle. "It's a big pit of soft foam blocks meant to catch us. I've fallen in them many times. The only thing we need to make sure of is that we don't fall on top of each other. We're going to have to hold hands side by side and fall backward together."

"You've got to be kidding me."

"'Fraid not."

She groaned. "I'm going to freaking *kill* Kincaid. Why couldn't she drag me to Pilates or Zumba or something? No, no, that'd be too boring. We have to do goddamned acrobatics. In the air."

She could almost see Lucas's smile in the dark. "We've got this. Just don't think too hard about it. I'm going to release you, and you need to take one hand off the bar to hold mine. Side by side, okay?"

This was definitely not the stress relief Taryn had been seeking, but she gritted her teeth and forced herself to deal. "Okay."

"Good. Here goes." Lucas made sure she was steady and then released her. Keeping one hand on the bar, he tapped her arm with his other. She got the best footing she could, turning sideways and then let her right hand release the bar. Lucas clasped her hand in his, the grip reassuring. "All right. On the count of three, let go of the trapeze and just fall backward with me. We'll land side by side safely."

The thunder rolled outside, matching the rumble in Taryn's nervous stomach. She *did not* want to think about the trajectory of things if she lost her dinner up here. "Let's just get this over with."

"You got it. One. Two…" On three, she let her fingers slip from the bar, closed her eyes tight, and gripped Lucas's hand so tightly that her bones hurt. And then there was nothing beneath her feet. She screamed and air rushed past her ears as she and Lucas fell backward into the darkness. Her back hit the foam, stealing her breath as the pit absorbed them. She sank into the softness. Everything was still pitch-black, and the feel of the foam around her was disorienting. She'd lost her grip on Lucas when they'd hit.

"Lucas!" She flailed her arms trying to find purchase, panic going through her at feeling buried, foam blocks hitting her face. Which way was up? "Lucas!"

Finally, two strong hands gripped her upper arms and pulled her up, but she was still writhing around like a caught rabbit, and her momentum knocked him backward. She landed on top of him in the sea of foam blocks.

She was about to scramble up, but his hands went to her face, stilling her. "You okay? Are you hurt?"

"I-I'm fine." His hands were so gentle and he was so warm and solid beneath her that she couldn't think straight, much less move. "Are you? Okay?"

"I'm… Yeah."

"Good. That's good."

Their faces were inches apart, her hands splayed on his chest, the nearness making her brain go off-line. She could see the storm in his eyes as the lightning flashed, the blue irises gone gray in the dark.

She swallowed past her parched throat, her heart still pumping from the adrenaline but her blood pulsing with something altogether new. "We should probably figure out how to get up now."

"Right," he said, his gaze not leaving hers. "Good idea. We should do that."

But neither of them moved. Her fingers curled into his chest. His hand stayed on her face. His body stirred beneath hers, a very particular pressure growing against her belly. She sucked in a breath at the feel of his arousal, and a deep ache rushed through her. Bravery surged.

"Or maybe not."

"No?" he asked, voice gruff.

"Maybe sometimes it's okay to just do something for fun," she said quietly, repeating his words back to him.

His jaw flexed. "Just because it feels good?"

"Yeah."

Lucas's thumb traced her cheekbone, and she knew what was about to happen, knew it was a bad idea, but right now, she didn't care. She let him close the distance and groaned in relief when his mouth pressed against hers.

The kiss was soft at first, tentative and seeking, like a gentle slide into a warm bath, but when she let her hand track up his chest and shifted her hips against where he'd grown hard, Lucas made a strangled, needy sound. Their lips parted, and his tongue dipped into her mouth, tangling with hers. A floodgate of need broke open in her, the thin material of her leggings giving her an indecent preview of what Lucas could give her. The kiss turned deep and hungry, and her bare toes curled against the foam blocks. One of his hands slid to her neck, the other to her hip, kneading the flesh there, almost as if he were fighting not to flip her over and put her on her back.

In that moment in the dark, she would've let him. She wasn't one to sleep with guys she didn't know well, but she couldn't remember ever feeling this desperate to be skin to skin with someone. Lucas sat up, lifting her with him, and wrapped her legs around his hips.

He whispered her name and broke the kiss long enough to tug the loose bandanna from her hair. He tossed it somewhere into the pit, and then he was kissing her again, their chests pressing against each other with only a thin layer of cotton and Lycra between them. Taryn's nipples tightened at the contact, and heat gathered low and fast.

She tipped her head back, Lucas trailing kisses down her neck.

"Please," she whispered.

"Tell me to stop," he said against the curve of her shoulder, his hand tracking up her waist, precariously close to taking this to another level.

"Don't," she said without thought. "Please don't stop."

He groaned against her skin and let his hand travel up her ribs until he was cupping her breast in his big, warm hand. "You feel so goddamned good."

The heat of his palm through the thin material was setting every nerve alight, making her body respond with a full-throated chorus of *hell yes*.

"Want you," he said between kisses. "Wanted you from the moment I saw you on that stage singing your fucking heart out."

She gasped at the words and at the feel of his erection pressing against her. *Want you.*

Yes, please was all she could think. *Yes, I'll take a double order of that.* She put her hand over the one he had cupping her breast, encouraging him, rocking her hips without thought. Her brain was spinning, her body burning. She needed this. God, did she need this.

The doctor had ordered stress relief. This would be a helluva prescription.

She tipped her head back when he dragged his teeth along her collarbone, and she moaned. "Lucas…"

His name was a plea, a permission, a *Yes, let's do this right now.* But the second the word passed her lips, Lucas froze, his lips still pressed against her, his body going stiff.

Her thoughts stuttered at the pause, and her eyes popped open. "Lucas?"

He groaned, a painful sound, as he lifted his head and his hands slid away from her body. "I'm sorry."

She blinked in the darkness, trying to get a read on his expression. "What? What's wrong?"

He grabbed her waist and gently hoisted her off of him. "We can't. I can't… I'm sorry. This is messed up. I'm…"

"You're what?"

"Your trainer," he said after a beat. "I told you that you'd be safe with me tonight, and here I am, mauling you like a goddamned animal."

She stiffened at that. "Last I checked, what was happening was mutual. I didn't tell you no."

"That's not the point."

"What is the point, then? I don't know what to think when you—"

A loud whirring sound filled the gym, interrupting her words, and the overhead lights blinked on in a wave of blinding brightness. Taryn winced at the sudden change, the world going fluorescent white for a moment, but when her vision cleared, Lucas was climbing out of the foam pit, a dark scowl on his face.

She awkwardly made her way to the side of the pit, which was like trudging through hip-deep mud, and grabbed the edge. Lucas stepped over and put his hand out to help pull her up. As soon as she was on her feet, he released her hand as if it'd burned him.

"Lucas…"

He grimaced and raked his fingers through his hair before lifting his gaze to her. "I'm sorry."

"For what?" she challenged.

He waved a hand toward the pit. "For all of that. I can't begin to explain how out of line I was." He pinched the bridge of his nose, looking to be in actual physical pain. "I don't know what I was thinking."

The anguish on his face snapped her out of her own irritation. The guy was clearly beating himself up. Maybe she shouldn't take it personally. Maybe he had an ironclad code of ethics, and he'd just violated them.

"Hey," she said, trying to put lightness in her voice. "It's not a big deal, okay? I'm a grown woman who makes her own choices. I kissed you back. I was saying yes. We both just got caught up in the moment. It happens."

Though she couldn't remember it ever happening to her. Not like that. Usually if she decided to sleep with someone, the decision was very well thought out. Debates had been had. Pros and cons had been itemized. She was not a get-swept-away-in-the-moment kind of girl.

Lucas clasped his hands behind his head and let out a long breath. "I can move your training sessions to Rivers or someone else. And obviously give you a refund for tonight and—"

"Don't," she said firmly.

He looked up.

"I don't need my money back. You gave me a full workout before all that, and I like training with you," she said, going for honesty. "Even with the sadistic streak."

He smirked, a glimmer of humor breaking through his grim expression.

She stepped closer. "How about we chalk up what just happened to late-night thunderstorm madness? Our adrenaline was running high after that fall, and we let it bleed into…other things. I can move on if you can. We can pretend this never happened."

His brows lifted. "Yeah, 'cause that'll be easy."

She grinned, glad to hear she wasn't that forgettable. "You know what I mean. I don't want to quit this new thing just because… I don't even know how to label it. Because we're attracted to each other and you don't want to get involved with anyone?"

He exhaled and shook his head. "That sounds so lame."

"No," she assured him. "I mean, it's your right to have whatever reasons you have. Plus, I told you my life is busy, too. This was probably a bad idea on both sides. I have the biggest presentation of my life on Thursday night, and if all goes as it should, I'm going to be launching a program that will suck up even more of my limited free time. If what we were doing had continued, I'd probably be the one looking like a jerk because I'm going to be buried by the end of this week and won't be calling anyone for a chat or going out for a date. Just getting in these workouts is going to be enough of a challenge."

"Right." Some of the tension left his face. "What kind of program are you launching?"

Her shoulders relaxed, glad to be back on familiar footing. Work she could talk about. That was much easier than discussing the kissing and the touching and the way she'd wanted to be naked with him immediately. "It's a school-violence prevention program that I want to implement in the local districts."

His gaze jumped up to meet hers. "School violence?"

"Yeah." She grabbed her sweatshirt from where she'd left it. "That's my research specialty. I'm a forensic psychologist, so I've spent years on the why's, the causes. Now it's time to put it all together and hopefully use the information for prevention."

"Prevention."

"Yes. That's my ultimate goal. I was a Long Acre survivor, and I lost my sister in the attack, so it's basically what I've dedicated my career to so far." She pulled the hoodie over her head, her excitement about finally getting this program ready to launch making her ramble. "My program would focus on the isolation and insecurity risk factors and use a three-pronged approach to connect students to at least one mentor in the school or community, one older student with similar interests, and one extracurricular activity that focused on the individual's strengths. Based on all the research I've done, I really think this could be a game changer."

She turned back to Lucas, expecting that he'd checked out of her long explanation, but instead, he had gone pale and was staring at her. "You lost your sister at Long Acre?"

Her enthusiasm flattened at the catch in his voice. She was used to all varieties of reactions when people found out about her history, but Lucas looked downright shaken. "Yeah, I'm sorry. I say it so often now when I'm presenting my research that I forget how it can sound when I say it offhandedly like that."

Lucas was still staring at her, stricken, but he managed to finally say, "I'm so sorry."

She took a deep breath. "Me too, but I can't change what happened." The old memory flashed, a sliver of the moon shining, black metal, the sound *click-clack* echoing. She shoved the scene away. "All I can do is work my ass off to prevent things like that from continuing to happen. I need this presentation to go off without a hitch and then I can do that."

"Right." His stance had gone wooden, his fingers tightly balled into fists at his sides. "That's…admirable."

Admirable. She hated that word. "Thanks." She'd made them both uncomfortable with the serious talk. Time to free them from this conversation and this confusing night. "Well, I better get going. I have to drive back to Long Acre, and it's going to take a while with all this rain."

"You still live there?" he asked, his voice hoarse.

"Yeah. My parents wanted me to stay close, so I did, but on nights like this, I wish I lived here in town." She cocked her head toward the locker rooms. "I'm going to get changed."

He nodded. "I'll grab your shoes off the platform."

"Thanks." She stepped forward and reached for his arm, giving it a squeeze. "And thanks for tonight. I know it got weird, but before that, it was fun."

Lucas's throat worked and his arm muscles were stiff beneath her fingers. "Drive safe."

She was going to say more when she came back to retrieve her shoes from him, clear the now-foggy air between them so that the next workout session wouldn't be awkward, but he was nowhere to be found. When she headed to the main entrance, her shoes and socks were by the door with an umbrella that wasn't broken. Frowning, she grabbed everything and headed out alone.

When she got to her car and plugged her phone into the charger, the rain still pattering against her windshield, her phone dinged with a text message. She'd already messaged her parents before arriving so it wouldn't be them, but when she turned over the phone, she wasn't surprised to see Kincaid's name.

How'd it go?

Wasn't that the question of the hour? Taryn leaned her head against the steering wheel, replaying all that had happened tonight. How the hell was she supposed to answer that? Difficult. Fun. Scary. Sexy. Awkward. In that order.

After a few seconds, she lifted her head and typed the only thing she could think of that described it all.

Not boring.

chapter
TEN

SHAW POUNDED HIS FIST AGAINST THE APARTMENT DOOR, his heart beating so hard that his ribs were hurting. "Rivers, it's me. Open up."

He'd tried to call Rivers on the way home, but his friend hadn't answered his phone. He could be sleeping, but there was no way Shaw could go downstairs to his own apartment right now. He'd end up packing all his shit and driving away tonight. He couldn't do that to Rivers, not with the business just opening, but right now, that felt like the only goddamned solution. Panic was crawling over his skin like an army of termites eating away at him.

When he knocked on the door again, it swung open, revealing his friend wearing a scowl and bedhead. "Dude, what the hell? Are you on fire? Because if you're banging on my door like this for any other—"

Shaw didn't let him finish. "You didn't answer your phone," he growled as he shouldered past his friend, making Rivers turn sideways to grant him entry. He headed into the living room, which was dimly lit by the TV, and switched on a lamp. "Shut the door. We need to talk."

Rivers opened his mouth as if he were going to tell Shaw to fuck off, but something in Shaw's expression must've tipped him off that this was serious. He scrubbed a hand over his face, probably clearing the cobwebs of sleep, and shut the door. "What's going on?"

"Taryn."

Rivers sank onto the bright-blue armchair next to his couch and turned off the TV. "Taryn. Things didn't go well tonight?"

Shaw scoffed at the understatement. "I kissed her."

Rivers's face lit up. "Holy shit. That's fantastic!"

"No." Shaw began to pace like a caged animal, his mind going too fast for him to stand still. "No, it's not. It's a complete fucking disaster."

Rivers looked unmoved. "Are we really freaking out about a kiss right now? Come on, Shaw, it's about time—"

"She's a Long Acre survivor," he spat out, the words like glass cutting his tongue.

Rivers stared at him as if he hadn't heard the words. "Wait. *What?*"

"Oh, it gets worse." Taryn's words kept running around in his head on a hyperspeed loop. "She lost her sister in the attack. *Her sister*, man. Probably at the hand of my fucking brother. And I kissed her. Did more than that." He pressed the heels of his hands to his eyes. "*Jesus.*"

When Shaw lowered his hands, Rivers's face reflected Shaw's shock. "You didn't recognize her name? I thought you had them memorized."

Shaw grimaced. After the attack, he'd forced himself to memorize the names of his brother's victims as a kind of penance. It was the only way he could make himself accept the reality of what had happened, that those lives were gone. He'd used the rest of his college fund to make anonymous donations in each of their names. "I didn't learn the names of the survivors, and I haven't watched any coverage of it since the day it happened. I didn't even catch Taryn's last name."

Rivers reached out and grabbed his phone off the side table, opening something and reading it. After a second, he said, "It's Landry."

Shaw's mind scrolled through the long list of names that were forever imprinted on his psyche—an alphabetical line of tombstones. *Landry*. The name was right there. "Nia Landry. That was her sister." Shaw raked his hands through his hair, the panic trying to fully take over. "I'm going to be sick."

"Shaw."

"If she figures out who I am…" And that he'd kissed her and joked with her and almost *slept with her*. "I need to leave."

"No, you don't." Rivers blew out a breath, his gaze wary. "I'm not gonna lie. This is horrible, but if she hasn't figured out who you are already, she probably won't. We just have to get you out of the situation immediately. We'll come up with something. I'll assign her to another trainer or I'll take her on. I'll schedule you opposite her sessions. Avoid contact completely."

Shaw laced his hands behind his head, squeezing his skull, trying to breathe. Taryn had lost her sister. Taryn, that soulful singer up onstage singing her heart out, the woman who'd teased and joked with him tonight, was once a high school girl who had watched her friends and sibling be gunned down in front of her. She was dedicating her life to finding ways to prevent others from going through that. She was an amazing woman. And he had let her kiss the man partly responsible for all that heartbreak in her life.

That last fact wouldn't hurt her if she didn't know. He couldn't cause her additional pain and let her figure out who she'd spent the evening with. "She can't know."

"She won't," Rivers said, sounding more confident than he looked. "I'll make sure of it."

Shaw leaned against the wall and closed his eyes.

Rivers was quiet for a long moment and then said, "Thank God you didn't sleep with her."

"Yeah." Thank God. Because he had been well on the way there. They'd been riding a bullet train leading straight to the couch in his office, but when she'd called out the name Lucas with such pleading, his entire libido had flattened like roadkill. *Lucas*. She didn't even know his name. He didn't have the right to touch her, to hear those sounds from her, to make her feel good. He was a liar.

No. Now he was so much more than that.

He was her nightmare.

Early Thursday evening, Taryn's whole body was humming as though she'd been plugged into an electrical outlet. Her mind was running through her presentation, her lips moving with the unspoken words, and her feet paced along the perimeter of the building where the school board held its meetings. The floor would be hers in a few minutes. Her presentation equipment was being set up inside.

You've got this. The mini pep talk kept playing through her head. She had no problem speaking in front of people. She did it every day teaching her classes, but she'd never had so much riding on one talk. All her work, all that research, the years she'd spent buried in this topic had come down to this. Information without action was just words on a page.

She'd already laid the groundwork. She'd built a relationship with the school-board vice president and had communicated regularly with two of the trustees. The details of her program had already been sent to all the board members. She'd been told how much they loved the idea of her program. She'd only exchanged one email with the president, but he'd seemed really positive about it, too. Money had been allocated for school-violence prevention this year, and they were just waiting to award it. This meeting was going to be a formality.

Still, she wanted to nail it. The board meetings were broadcast live on the web, and she wanted the community to support the program, too, to know where their tax dollars were going. She wanted this to be a movement, something they could pilot here in Austin and then spread to the rest of the country. She wanted this to be the spark that would light the fires.

You've got this.

She closed her eyes, stopping her pacing, and went through the list of her most compelling statistics in her head. Mental health numbers about teens and mood disorders. Warning signs that had been present before the majority of school shootings. The compelling research on social connections and self-esteem. The effects of adult mentors.

Someone tapped her shoulder and she yelped, her eyes popping open. She whirled around. "What the heck?"

Kincaid smiled, Liv and Rebecca standing there with her. "Someone call the doctor. The professor is talking to herself."

Taryn put her hand over her beating heart, then she grinned. "What are y'all doing here?"

Liv tilted her head, her dark ponytail swishing behind her. "As if we'd miss this." She stepped forward and gave Taryn a tight hug. "This is your big moment, *chica*!"

Taryn hugged her friend back, and then Rebecca and Kincaid came in for their own quick embraces. Taryn laughed. "I can't believe y'all are going to subject yourselves to a school-board meeting. I have to warn you. They're about as exciting as watching C-SPAN."

Kincaid nodded, expression solemn. "This should prove how much we love you because I'm missing *The Real Housewives* for this."

Taryn laughed. "I'm truly honored."

"Are you ready?" Rebecca asked. She was still in her lawyer gear, a tailored gray suit and a crisp black blouse, but she'd pulled her red hair down from the twist or bun it'd been in, and it was curling around her shoulders. "Do you need us to be a practice audience?"

"Thanks, I think I'm good." Taryn patted the bag looped over her shoulder. "And if I get lost, I have all my notes in here. Most of this stuff is burned into my brain at this point."

Rebecca reached out and squeezed Taryn's hand.

"You're going to rock this. I read through your program last week, and it's amazing, Taryn. Really. This will save lives."

Taryn took a deep breath, the words sinking into her. "God, I hope so." Her phone buzzed, the reminder alarm warning her it was time to go inside. "That's my cue."

Her friends all gave her one last quick hug and then let her go ahead so she could get set up inside. She hadn't asked or expected them to come, but knowing they were going to be sitting behind her in that room, supporting her, believing in her... Well, it meant a lot. She took one more steadying breath as she made her way through the entry hall, then pulled her shoulders back and strolled into the large room with confidence.

The members of the school board were on a raised stage at a curved table. This was the building usually used for school theater productions so the acoustics provided a steady murmur from the voices of the people in the room. The board members were talking among themselves, the microphones turned off, and a thin guy with glasses was hooking up Taryn's laptop, which she'd dropped off earlier, to a podium at the front of the center aisle so her presentation would project onto the screen. There were some people in the audience but not many. These meetings didn't attract a lot of attention unless something newsworthy had happened.

Taryn wasn't newsworthy at this point. For that, she was actually thankful.

She made her way down the main aisle to the podium, facing the board members as if she were presenting to a court, and pulled her notes out. She set everything up the way she wanted it and then took a seat in the first row to wait for her name to be called. She tried to make eye contact with the vice president, Regina, a petite Hispanic woman with shoulder-length hair and a bright-purple blouse, but no one was looking her way. They were all too busy whispering.

Once the meeting was called into session, the group got through the formalities quickly and then introduced Taryn. There were a few light claps from the audience, and Taryn didn't have to look back to know they were courtesy of her friends. She stood, pasted on a confident smile, and made her way to the podium.

A shiver of nerves went through her as all the board members' eyes turned toward her, but she rolled her shoulders back and pushed her nerves away. This was it. This was what she'd been waiting for.

All right, Nia, here we go. This one's for you, baby girl.

Taryn started off strong, citing her memorized statistics and the findings of her research. Her passion for the topic was making her heart pound and her words come out with an urgency she hadn't planned. Emotion was beating beneath each word, but she kept it on a leash. This was about facts. Research. Proof. If she cried, they might dismiss her, discount her. She needed to be the professor today, not the victim.

She got to her last slide, which was a beautiful chart she'd put together with all the risk factors and how they connected to each other. Damn, she loved a chart. She used a laser pointer to walk them through it, proud of how ironclad her numbers were. When she was done, she smiled, pleased with the fact that she hadn't teared up, her voice hadn't cracked, and she'd gotten all the vital points across.

I did it.

But when Taryn turned from the screen to look at the board members and no one said anything, that burst of confidence faltered, a runner stumbling along the path. She took a sip from the water bottle someone had put on the podium for her and cleared her throat. "I can take questions now if any of you have them. I also have plans for how to best do the rollout and the breakdown of costs if you'd like to see those."

"That's not necessary. We saw those in the document you submitted, Dr. Landry," the president said, his voice loud and hollow in the microphone. He gave her a tight, brief, pat-her-on-the-head smile.

Taryn forced her own smile to stay in place even though she felt dismissed. "Right. Well, are there any questions? I'm prepared to have this roll out quickly, so as soon as I get the go-ahead, I could have this in a few area schools by the fall, and then bring more on by next spring. Or we could—"

"Dr. Landry," the president said, slipping into what she thought of as his politician voice—a slick tone that matched all the gel in his salt-and-pepper hair, "we really appreciate you presenting all of this information to us. You've obviously worked very hard and have done thorough research. The issue of school violence is a top priority for us, as I'm sure you know."

"Yes, sir," she said, some of the restriction in her chest easing. It was okay. This was important to them. She was freaking out over nothing.

"But—" he continued.

Her world came to a halt at the one word.

"We've evaluated the cost of your program, and with

our budgetary restrictions, this is just not going to be feasible," he finished.

Taryn's hands gripped the sides of the podium, her fingers going bloodless, but she forced herself to keep her voice steady. "Sir, I understand where you're coming from, but I was very aware of the funds allocated for this type of program, and I made sure to work it so it would fit within those parameters."

"Well, that's probably our fault," the vice president said, speaking up, her voice apologetic. She finally made eye contact with Taryn. "The figures you were sent have since been updated to reflect...other measures we're instituting to address this issue."

"Other measures?" Taryn asked woodenly.

"Yes," the president said, sitting up taller in his chair. "We've decided to place armed guards in each of the area high schools, and that has a pretty high price tag. After what happened at Blue Heights High up north, we don't want to take any chances."

Taryn's lips parted, all the words wanting to come out, but none forming. They were saying no. *They were saying no*. She fought to gather her composure. "Sir, with all due respect, I don't think this needs to be an either-or situation. However, we need to go further back to solve this problem—a systematic approach—not a stopgap measure. We need to help kids before they turn into killers. Trying to stop them after is important, too, but...then we still have killers. The research shows—"

The president lifted a hand, cutting her off. "You've explained what the research shows, Dr. Landry. And believe me, I find it very commendable that you're working on this, considering what you've been through. I think your program has a lot of merit, but I'm responsible for using citizens' tax dollars in the most efficient and effective way possible. I've talked to a number of our community members, and they feel better about armed guards. That's a visible action and presence. This program is…complicated to explain and expensive. I'm sorry, but we can't implement it at this time."

"We are really sorry," the vice president added, looking sympathetic but obviously unable to change anything.

"An armed guard wouldn't have saved us," Taryn blurted. "That wouldn't have saved any of us. We had a security guy at prom. He was killed because those boys didn't care if they died. I know *why* they didn't care. They could've been helped. We need to intervene before these kids get to that point, or this is going to keep happening."

One of the trustees frowned and looked away. "Shall we vote?"

"No," Taryn protested. "You can't… *No*." She knew she was out of order, but she couldn't help her reaction. She wanted to run up there and plead for them to listen, to clap her hands in front of their faces and tell them to wake the hell up and *hear* her. But her feet were rooted to the floor, her entire body trembling.

Taryn felt a presence behind her. She looked back and found her three friends standing there. They stepped up next to her. She expected them to gather her up and lead her away before she embarrassed herself further, but instead, they surrounded her, a united front facing the board. Kincaid put her arm around Taryn's waist and said loud enough for the microphone to pick it up,

"Let them say no to us all. My name is Kincaid Breslin. Survivor. Long Acre."

Liv shifted, tipping her chin up. "My name is Olivia Arias. Survivor. Long Acre."

Rebecca moved to Taryn's other side and took her hand, squeezing it. "My name is Rebecca Lindt. Wounded survivor. Long Acre."

Taryn's vision went cloudy with tears. The board members shifted their gazes downward or away. The vice president was the only one left watching the four of them. After a moment, she looked down in defeat. She couldn't help.

The vote started. It was like a tiny stab to Taryn's gut every time a vote was cast.

Taryn got one yes vote from the VP. Everyone else was a nay.

Her program, a decade of work, was dead on arrival. She closed her eyes.

I'm sorry, Nia. I'm so sorry.

chapter

ELEVEN

SHAW SAT IN HIS OFFICE FRIDAY AFTER A SESSION, drinking water and staring at his open laptop, debating. He didn't need to look. It wasn't his business. His fingers hovered over the trackpad. *Shut it down.* Instead, he clicked onto the local school-board site.

Rivers had moved Taryn's next session to one of the female trainers they'd recently hired and had an excuse all lined up for when she arrived tonight. Shaw now had the night off and would be leaving before Taryn arrived, but he couldn't stop wondering how things had turned out for Taryn with her presentation. He found his way to the recordings of the school-board meetings and clicked. The first part of the meeting was pretty dry, and he skimmed past all of that until he saw Taryn's face on the screen.

He hated how his body instantly responded to the sight of her—like a crackle of static electricity over his nerve endings. She looked so different from how she'd looked in his arms the other night when she was sweaty and undone and hungry with need. Now she was back to being the proper professor—pale-gray suit with a dark-blue blouse, black-rimmed glasses, and confident eyes. Dr. Landry. A woman on a mission. Hot as hell, still. His fingers ached to undo every button on that blouse and work his way down her body nice and slow until he made her toes curl.

Fuck.

Stop.

When it came to Taryn, his mind was like a determined dog who kept breaking off leash and running into traffic, completely oblivious to the danger. He reeled in his baser thoughts and shoved them down. He needed to remember who this woman was, what she'd suffered because of his family, and why he was watching this in the first place. Because he would never see her again and wouldn't get to ask.

Taryn was talking, so he turned up the volume. He could barely watch her presentation, the grim statistics, and the references to Long Acre. He almost stopped the video when his brother's face flashed on the screen along with a row of other killers. Seeing Joseph's photo, particularly the yearbook one all the news outlets had latched on to, was like having two knives stab him at once—the pain of losing the brother he once knew and loved and the devastation of knowing what Joseph had become. The only thing that kept Shaw watching was the compelling way Taryn was presenting her program. He'd already sensed it from being around her, but this confirmed his impression. The woman was brilliant. And driven. And fucking brave.

He couldn't see the members of the board because the camera was trained on Taryn, but he could only imagine the intent expressions they had to be wearing. However, when the presentation ended, Shaw didn't hear the applause he expected.

Instead, there was silence in the room and growing tension in Taryn's stance. Shaw watched in shock as Taryn was shut down with just a few words. Watched the disbelief in her gaze. Then her anger came out, her voice like a flaming arrow shot across the bow.

"That wouldn't have saved any of us. We had a security guy at prom. He was killed because those boys didn't care if they died. I know why *they didn't care. They could've been helped."*

Shaw's heartbeat picked up speed at the words. *I know why. I know why.*

No.

Taryn thought she knew why Joseph had done what he'd done, but that was impossible. Shaw had never talked to anyone. He'd only talked to the police. She couldn't know the real truth. No one did. No one could.

Shaw lifted his hand to slam the laptop closed, but he stilled, watching Taryn's eyes go shiny but not spill over with tears as the votes came in one by one. She'd told him she'd dedicated her whole life to developing the program. The board had taken five minutes to crumple it up and toss it in the trash. They'd dismissed her.

Her expertise. Her work. Her pain.

They'd broken her damn heart.

Shaw hissed out a breath, and a surge of anger rushed through him like lightning across a dark sky—a powerful, destructive force that filled his veins and squashed his self-control, making his muscles twitch and burn. He wanted to punch that smarmy school-board president, tell him he had no idea what the fuck he was talking about. Shaw tried to breathe through the urge, but before he knew it, he'd picked up his metal water bottle and had thrown it hard enough against the wall to leave a dent in the new drywall.

The bottle clattered loudly to the floor, cracking. The second he saw the water puddling on the floor, reality crashed back in and he put his head in his hands, his heart pounding in his ears, the anger inside him like a caged lion trying to break free. "Shit."

Dangerous.

The word whispered through him with warning. That was what his brother had been. That was what Shaw was, too. He needed to remember that and stay far away from Taryn Landry, her friends, and anything having to do with his past.

He couldn't help.

He'd only make things worse.

Taryn sat in front of the wall of names in the memorial garden at the high school, the setting sun throwing swaths of orange light over half the names carved into the stone. Millbourne High, the new name for Long Acre High, had let out hours ago, but somewhere in the distance, the sounds of a pickup baseball game drifted on the breeze and mixed in with the bubbling sound of the fountain in the corner of the garden. Taryn pulled her feet up onto the bench and set her chin on her knees, reading the long list of names, all those lost in the tragedy, with a hollow feeling in her stomach.

She had rubbed her fingers over Nia's name often

enough to know exactly where her sister was on the list, but Taryn let her eyes linger on each of the other names, too—former classmates, friends, strangers. She'd let every one of them down last night at the school-board meeting. She'd blown it. Even though she'd been blindsided by the board's reaction, she never should've lost her cool. Her outburst had undermined her authority and knowledge of her subject and had turned her into a victim in other people's eyes yet again, someone to feel sorry for and then dismiss as being too *fill-in-the-blank*— affected, emotional, involved, damaged. She was sure those words and many more had been murmured among the board members after she'd stormed out.

Taryn closed her eyes, gravity feeling heavier today. She hadn't been able to tell her parents yet. Her research was the rope her mom held on to, giving all this grief some glimmer of hope and purpose. She couldn't bear to tell her mother she'd failed. Spectacularly. And she had no idea how to fix it.

Even if she could figure out how to further shave the budget or water down some of the components of the program, how was she supposed to go back in front of the board and be taken seriously? They'd made up their minds. Without research, without years of data behind them, without a working knowledge of the brain, they'd made a decision. Based on gut feel, on politics, on whim. Based on bullshit as far as she was concerned.

She took a deep breath, letting the anger and grief rumble through her, a herd of buffalo destroying the path she'd laid out for herself. Trampled. That was exactly how she felt. As if she'd built a very intricate house, piece by piece over the last four years, and then in one stampede, all of it had been crushed and deemed useless. *So sorry, dear. Ditch that years-long research and start again on something new. On something different. This wasn't good enough.* You *weren't good enough.*

It didn't matter that she knew in the deepest part of her that she was *right*. That not just her gut but a stack of studies and research and many professionals in a number of fields agreed her program could be a game changer. That lives could truly be saved. None of it mattered because she couldn't do it alone. She'd gone as far as she could solo. Now she needed others to believe in the program, to put money into it, to care.

Last night, she'd gone home and had stared at her wall of research—all the photos and data and connections she'd built into this complex matrix. Part of her had wanted to rip every bit of it off the wall. Throw it in the fireplace and light a match. What did it matter what she'd determined if no one would listen? But when she'd put her hands along the pages to tear them down, she hadn't been able to do it. Instead, she'd sunk onto the floor and spent the night trying to figure out another way, another path to get the program off the ground.

The most obvious option was to continue to apply for grants, but so far, her success with that had been slow going. The competition for grants in her area of study was fierce, and the private money was dwindling. It could take forever to get what she needed.

Maybe she could apply to a new university in a different state, where other school districts would be an option, maybe somewhere that had a bigger budget or was open to a more comprehensive approach. She'd lose all the time she'd built toward tenure at her current university, though. She'd have to move away from her family, her friends. The losses would be big, and the idea made her stomach hurt, but she'd do it if it meant getting the program tested somewhere.

Maybe private schools? But they were smaller with a more specific population, and results would be harder to generalize to the public school system. *Maybe figure out a way to implement the program online?* No, too much of the program was built on face-to-face connections. *Maybe...*

She laced her fingers in her hair and gripped, a frustrated sound escaping her lips.

"You know, you keep doing that, and it's going to give you a headache and bald spots," said a familiar voice from behind her.

Taryn startled, her head popping up, and turned to find Kincaid standing at the edge of the memorial garden. She had her hands wrapped around her elbows, and she was studiously avoiding looking at the wall of names. Taryn put her feet to the ground and spun to face her fully. "Hey, what are you doing here?"

Kincaid took a few steps closer and shrugged. "I called you, but you didn't answer, so I stopped by your house to pick you up for your workout. When you weren't there, I chatted up your neighbor, and he said he saw you leave with a bouquet of flowers. I figured you were headed to one of two places. I got it right on the first try." She smirked. "Who said blonds are dumb?"

Taryn sighed. "I'm sorry you went through all that trouble. I totally forgot about the gym session."

"No worries. We still have time to make it."

Taryn shook her head. "I can't work out today. I

won't be able to concentrate on anything but figuring out how to get this program out of the trash can. This can't be the end, right?"

Kincaid frowned. "Knowing you? No. You're stubborn in the best way possible." She sat next to Taryn on the bench. "But maybe give yourself a minute to process this loss. Last night…sucked."

Taryn snorted. "Ya think?"

"I know, but honestly, I was thinking about this on the way home last night. Any school district you go to is probably going to bring up similar issues. Tight budgets. Politics. They'll make knee-jerk decisions based on minimal information, and they want to give people something they can see. Having a guard at school is immediate gratification. Your program works in a behind-the-scenes, get-to-the-root kind of way. People aren't patient, and they're angry. They want something now."

"So basically I'm screwed," Taryn said flatly.

"I'm not saying that. All I'm saying is that I understand how it happened. You know how hot-button this issue is." She glanced around the garden and then looked back to Taryn. "To us, this is our history. Our lives. We saw horrors those board members can never truly imagine or understand. I know it's small in comparison, but it's like when I'm trying to negotiate a deal on a house. I see a house with a set of features that is worth a certain amount. Cut and dried. But the owners of that house see the hallway where their kids took their first steps and the backyard where they had barbecues with their dad who's now passed. I can't feel the house like they do, and I never will.

"That's how it is with this times a million," she

continued. "School violence is just another topic on a list of controversial issues the board has to make decisions on. It's not something that has changed the course of their lives. It's not this potent grief that lives inside them every day. So I think before you jump into the next phase, you need to take a step back and evaluate the game plan. Come up with a different strategy. I have no doubt you have brilliant ideas buried in there. But you can't access them when you're this stressed and upset. You'll end up back in the hospital."

Kincaid was so rarely serious that it took Taryn a few moments to process all she'd said, but she heard the truth in her friend's words. This felt so big and monumental to Taryn and her friends. It was impossible to imagine how the fact that kids were regularly shooting up schools and killing other children didn't keep every single person up *every damn night*. But Kincaid was right. Those board members had a hundred other issues to tackle, many that were equally important, and this was just another one. Something they cared about but didn't feel down to their marrow. They thought they'd figured out a quicker, cheaper solution, and now "address school violence" was one more item they could check off their to-do list.

Taryn bowed her head and rubbed her eyes, emotionally exhausted. "I don't know where to go from here."

Kincaid wrapped her arm around Taryn's shoulders. "I do. We go straight to the hot guys who are getting us in shape. Your beautiful, busy brain is in serious need of a break. If you spend the night at home, you're just going to drive yourself up the wall. Let's go find some distraction. And after the workout, we'll go have cake."

Taryn laughed and lifted her head. "Cake? Doesn't that ruin the point of the workout?"

Kincaid scrunched her nose. "What is the point of working out if you can't have cake for your efforts? I work out for dessert, sugar. Let's go."

Taryn allowed Kincaid to take her hand and pull her up from the bench. Kincaid's gaze jumped to the wall behind her, and her smile faltered. Taryn squeezed her hand and turned to face the wall with her. "You okay?"

Kincaid's attention hovered on the same spot—maybe a group of names or a particular one. A little breath escaped her, making her blond bangs flutter. "Yeah, I'm all right. I just hate coming here. I see the names, and I can't help but hear roll call from grade school, all the names I knew for so long. And I just... I don't know. I think my mind sometimes tricks me into thinking these people are just living somewhere else, grown-up now and doing whatever they were supposed to do in this world. Like we're supposed to be distant Facebook friends with these people by now and rolling our eyes over their constant pictures of their kids or cyberstalking our former crushes to prove that we are way hotter than the person they married."

Taryn smiled, the sadness familiar. "Guessing who got their boobs done."

"Yes!" Kincaid said, pressing the corners of her eyes before tears escaped. "I'm pissed that they're not here."

Taryn bumped her shoulder into Kincaid's. "Me too."

Kincaid brushed her hair away from her face and rolled her shoulders, obviously trying to regain her bright attitude. "All right, enough of this. Let's get going. We both need to empty our minds for a while."

"With exercise and hot guys."

"Obviously. That is clearly the best course of treatment."

Taryn grabbed her purse off the bench. "You missed your calling as a therapist."

Kincaid put her hand to her chest with an exaggerated expression. "I know, right? Girl, I would've nailed that job. I've got *all* the advice."

Taryn laughed as they walked out, picturing Kincaid as a therapist—bossing clients around in sessions, hand on hip, finger wagging at them like a proper Southern momma. It was enough to get her mind focused on something else for at least a few minutes. That was the beauty of her wonderful friend.

Kincaid could make her smile, even with all this going on. Maybe the woman really had missed her calling in therapy.

chapter

TWELVE

"THIS DOES NOT LOOK LIKE AN ESTABLISHMENT THAT serves cake," Kincaid said as Taryn stopped in front of the Tipsy Hound bar. "And if it did, I wouldn't want to eat their cake."

"After that workout, I need something stronger than cake," Taryn said, feeling grumpy after the grueling session that Kaya, the perky female trainer who was definitely *not* Lucas, had put her through. Taryn had not been feeling in the mood for a workout already, but when she'd found out Lucas was no longer going to be her trainer because he'd decided to take some night classes, her attitude had plummeted further. Kaya's unending enthusiasm had not helped. If she'd said *You can do it!* one more damn time, Taryn might've pushed her in the pool.

Kincaid glanced at the chipped paint on the sign by the door. "This place looks like a dive."

"It is," Taryn agreed. "It's perfect."

Kincaid gave her a skeptical look. "And it's eighties

open mic night. Are we really going to subject ourselves to that?"

"You signed me up for something that involved trapeze and falling into swimming pools. I have earned the right to choose the next activity."

Kincaid relented and waved a hand. "Yep, you're right. Lead on, and I shall follow."

"Thank you." Taryn pushed open the door and was hit with the smell of beer and the sound of a Phil Collins song being murdered mercilessly by the woman onstage. "I've been here before. It's got…some charm."

Honestly, Taryn had no idea why she'd decided to come back to the Tipsy Hound. There were plenty of other places in Austin where she and Kincaid could've grabbed a drink. Better lit places. Places where their shoes wouldn't stick to the floor. But something about this bar had called to her again when they'd driven past. Maybe after watching her life's work get flushed down the toilet the night before, she needed to remind herself that at least she hadn't taken the path she'd originally planned and tried to be a songwriter. This would've probably been her future. Sticky-floored dive bars. She was still doing better than that, right?

Kincaid fluffed her hair, somehow managing to look completely put together with just a five-minute gym shower and some quickly applied makeup. Taryn had done her best to look presentable, but all she'd packed in her gym bag were hair products, lipstick, and some mascara. Maybe it was good the place was dark.

"Let's grab a table and see if this joint can make a decent margarita," Kincaid said, eyeing the possible places to sit.

Taryn pointed. "The one in the back over there looks good. And it won't be as loud."

"Hey, Jamez with a z!" a voice called from somewhere off to Taryn's left.

Taryn winced. She hadn't considered that someone might remember her from the other night. This place seemed to do open mics every evening. She was just one of many who'd gotten on that stage, but the owner apparently had a good memory. She gave Kaleb a discreet wave, hoping Kincaid didn't notice.

But he didn't take the hint. He stepped closer and flicked his bar towel over his shoulder. "Hey, do you do eighties, too? I hope so because, goddamn, we could use a good song tonight. The offerings have been bleak. This has been worse than karaoke night. And karaoke night makes me want to drink the hard stuff."

Kincaid turned around at that, doubling back. "Excuse me?"

Kaleb smiled affably. "Oh, you brought a friend. Right on." He put out his hand to Kincaid. "I'm Kaleb, co-owner of the place. I was just telling Jamez here that we could use her onstage tonight."

Kincaid cocked her head as she shook his hand, no doubt remembering the name Lucas had first called her at the race. Kincaid didn't forget anything. "Right. Jamez. Onstage."

"Have you seen her play?" he asked, jabbing a thumb toward the front. The singer ended her torturous rendition of "Sussudio," and a smattering of lackluster applause followed.

Taryn put her hands up as if there were a way to stuff that cat back into the bag, but of course, there wasn't.

Kincaid's attention flicked to Taryn, her eyebrows arching. "Play. Like an instrument. On a stage?"

"Yeah, man. Good guitar player and has some pipes on her, too." Kaleb grabbed his phone out of his back pocket. "What song you wanna do, Jamez? You can pick anything that hasn't already been sung tonight."

"Oh, no, no," Taryn said, waving her hand. "I'm just here to listen and have a drink tonight. I'm not up for performing."

Kaleb's face fell. "Really? You sure? Could I entice you with free drinks for both of you in exchange for a song?"

Kincaid perked up. "Yes, do you have marg—"

"No," Taryn said quickly. "Not tonight. Eighties really aren't in my wheelhouse. But thanks."

Kaleb shrugged and his affable smile returned. "Ah, nineties to the end… I get it. Well, let me know if y'all need anything. And first drink's on me anyway."

Kincaid put her hand to her chest. "Well, thanks, sweet thing." She waited until he walked off and then looked at Taryn with a wicked light in her eyes. "For the drink *and* the information. *Jamez with a z.*"

"Don't look at me like that," Taryn warned.

"Like what?" Kincaid asked innocently.

"Like I'm now the cake you were looking for. Can we just ignore that this conversation happened?" Taryn asked, stepping past her friend and heading to the table.

"Um, no, we cannot, missy," Kincaid replied, following closely behind, her high heels clicking on the floor. She waited until Taryn had taken her seat and then slid into the chair next to her. "That is not a conversation I can just forget. You *play guitar and sing*? Since when?"

Taryn ignored her for a moment and ordered two

margaritas on the rocks from the waitress. When they were alone again, she relented. "Since middle school, but I don't do it anymore. The other night—the night after that bad date—I had a lapse in judgment, gave Kaleb a fake name, and ended up getting onstage here."

Kincaid's lips parted on a gasp. "That's why Lucas called you Jamez! You met him here? He saw you sing?"

She shrugged. "He saw me freak out onstage and bail. Yeah."

Kincaid set her chin in her hand, a look of wonder and delight on her face. "It's like I don't know you at all. I need to see this singing Taryn. I need that in my life right this minute."

"Not happening. I'm retired." Taryn accepted a complimentary bowl of homemade barbecue chips and her drink from the waitress and took a long sip, the sweet and salty liquid cooling her dry throat. "It was a stupid thing to do that night. It brings back…too much crap. That was the person I was in high school, before everything. It just brought back painful memories."

Kincaid frowned. "Oh, I'm sorry, honey. Is that why you freaked out onstage?"

"Pretty much."

"Ugh," Kincaid said, leaning back in her chair and grabbing a few of the chips. "Trauma sucks."

"I'll drink to that," Taryn said wryly. "But at least we can sit here and listen to a sure-to-be-stellar rendition of 'Billie Jean' by that guy."

Kincaid looked to the stage where a very paunchy white dude with a biker vest was gearing up for some Michael Jackson. She groaned. "Oh Lordy, I'm going to need a lot of liquor for this."

However, to their surprise, when the biker actually started singing, he turned out to be pretty damn good. Good voice and much higher-pitched than anyone could've guessed. He was hitting every *hee-hee* with perfect pitch. Taryn found herself bopping her head to the music and enjoying the performance. But when he turned to the side, beer belly on full display beneath his T-shirt, and busted out his moonwalk, she and Kincaid almost lost it. Taryn put her hand over her mouth to stanch her laugh. "Oh my God, he's so nailing it."

"I take everything I said back. I love this place," Kincaid said, clapping and letting out a whoop. "It's my new favorite."

They listened to the biker do a few more songs and enjoyed another round of drinks, but when the audience demanded yet another encore, Taryn had to excuse herself to go to the restroom. Kincaid waved her off, her attention still riveted to the stage.

Taryn did what she needed to do, and when she stood in front of the warped mirror in the tiny bathroom to wash her hands, she found she had a smile on her face. The margaritas had given her a pleasant buzz, making her feel warm all over but not drunk, and the performance had made her forget about her crappy week for a little while. Just what she needed. This idea had definitely been better than cake.

After reapplying her lipstick, she stepped out into the dark, narrow hallway to return to her table and not miss more of the performance, but before her eyes could adjust to the low light, she bumped into a wall of a person. An *oof* escaped her, and she raised her palms in apology. "I'm sorry. I wasn't—"

But when she looked up, familiar eyes were staring back at her, looking just as surprised as she felt. Lucas blinked. "*Taryn?*"

"Lucas." She frowned, taking in the full view of the man in front of her, her brain verifying that she wasn't imagining things. "What are you doing here? I thought Rivers said you were taking night classes."

His wince was slight, but she caught it before he could cover it. He cleared his throat. "I am. They're done for the night. I was just stopping in for a drink before I went home." He jabbed a thumb in the direction of the main entrance of the bar. "My apartment is across the street. I'm kind of a regular here."

"Oh." She chewed on that for a moment, her gut telling her there was more to the story. "Cool."

He tucked his hands in the pockets of his well-worn jeans, making his pale-blue T-shirt pull tight against his chest. "Uh, how was your workout?"

"My what?" Seeing him was making her thoughts scramble.

He made a motion with his arms, mimicking lifting weights, which only distracted her more because it made his biceps flex. "The workout. Did you go?"

"Oh. The gym. Yes. I did. It was brutal. And… enthusiastic."

"Yeah, Kaya's got a lot of energy." He shifted on his feet and glanced past her shoulder, obviously uncomfortable. "I'm sorry I couldn't be there."

"Right. I'm sure you are."

His gaze jumped back to hers, obviously catching her tone. "What?"

"Sorry." She sighed, his behavior confirming her

suspicions. "I'm not good at talking around things. Can we not do this?"

He frowned. "Do what?"

"Play pretend." She pointed to herself. "Don't forget I'm a psychologist…in forensics. You're kind of terrible at this lying thing."

"I—"

"Look, I was hoping we could get past the awkwardness of what happened the other night because I liked training with you, but clearly it's still freaking you out. I don't know if you actually have night classes or you just didn't want to be my trainer anymore, but either way, it's fine. You don't need to lie about it or make a thing out of it. It's not that big of a deal."

He looked down at the floor and ran a hand over the back of his head, his hair falling forward. "Taryn…"

"To be straight up with you," she continued, the alcohol making her even more frank than normal, "I have enough drama going on in my life. I don't need to create more of it. We made out. You weren't a fan. Let's move on."

His attention flicked up. "Not a fan?"

She crossed her arms and shrugged. "I call it like I see it, and it's fine. My ego isn't that fragile."

"Not a fan," he muttered, looking away. "Right. That's why I can't stop thinking about you."

The words were low and almost to himself, but she heard him well enough. "Wait, what?"

He looked at her and squeezed the back of his neck as if he were trying to choke back his words. "It's not… Never mind. I've had too much to drink. I need to get home."

She lifted a hand and put it to his chest when he tried

to move past her. "Whoa, whoa, whoa. Hold up. You can't say that to a woman and then bolt. No way." She looked to his face, trying to catch his eye. "*You can't stop thinking about me?* What is that, Lucas? What the hell am I supposed to do with that?"

"Nothing," he insisted, not looking at her. "Ignore me. I shouldn't have said that. I've been drinking."

I shouldn't have said that. Not *I didn't meant it.* And his excuse rang false, her truth meter buzzing. He wasn't drunk. That much she could tell. *I can't stop thinking about you.* The words and the pained way he'd said them wrapped around her and infiltrated her mind like a spell, eating through her good sense. Without evaluating the cost-benefit analysis of her next move, she pushed up on her toes and kissed him full on the mouth, shocking herself as much as him. Lucas stiffened, his shoulders like bricks beneath her palms, and he gripped her upper arms. She braced for him to push her away. Out of line didn't even begin to describe her actions.

But instead of moving her back, after a second, he groaned and dragged her closer, her breasts pressing into his chest and his lips opening to hers. Everything inside her went off like a string of firecrackers as his tongue grazed hers and his hands tightened on her arms like he was afraid she would escape or disappear into thin air.

She melted into the kiss, and her muscles went liquid as he took over. He turned them, pressing her against a wall covered with concert flyers and moving a hand to the back of her neck as he deepened the kiss, his mouth and lips seeking more, taking more. Never before had she been kissed with such urgency. Her fingers curled into his T-shirt, and the warmth from the alcohol was replaced with hot liquid need. She moaned and lost track of where they were for a few moments, falling into the sensation of it all. *Lucas. Lucas. Lucas.* She wanted to wrap her legs around him, have him carry her off somewhere, anywhere they could be horizontal instead of vertical.

But a loud *thwack* cut through the erotic haze a few seconds later. Lucas straightened, instantly yanking his head away from the kiss, and cursed. "What the hell?" Another *thwack*. "Ow."

Taryn's eyes popped open just in time to see Kincaid swing her heavy handbag at Lucas's shoulder again. "Get your hands off her right now, or I swear to God I will Mace your ass!"

"Kincaid!" Taryn said in shock.

Kincaid gave her a look like *Don't worry, I've got this, honey* and continued to hit him.

Lucas lifted his hands as if the cops had found him and turned around, a scowl on his face. "What is happening?"

Kincaid's eyes went round when she saw Lucas's face and obviously registered whom she was hitting. Her arm fell to her side. "Oh shit. *Lucas?*"

"Yes." Lucas rubbed his shoulder. "Good Lord, woman, what do you have in there? Bricks?"

Kincaid looked back and forth between the two of them, her righteous expression turning sheepish. "I'm sorry. I had no idea it was you. I thought you were some rando who accosted drunk women in bar hallways."

Taryn closed her eyes for a moment, trying to right her spinning brain and focus on her friend. She opened her eyes and gave Kincaid a tight smile. "Nope. Just Lucas. But I appreciate you trying to defend my honor."

Kincaid looked back and forth between the two of them again and broke into a bright grin. "Always. So... this is a thing you two do now? Was this like a secret meet-up or something?"

"*No*," Taryn said, her face getting hot. "It's... We just ran into each other."

"Right. Lips first. I see how that could happen." Kincaid nodded seriously. "Well, sorry for the misunderstanding." She leaned forward and patted Lucas lightly on the shoulder where she'd beaten him. "Sorry about that, big guy. I would've felt really bad if I'd Maced you."

Lucas simply stared at her as if she were some exotic creature he didn't understand.

"Taryn, honey, I'm gonna head home if you're okay to drive," Kincaid continued. "I was coming to find you because I got a call that I need to be in to work really early tomorrow, and I have to get back home."

Taryn narrowed her eyes. "Really. You just got a work call this late."

"Yep. Duty calls." Kincaid gave a dramatic sigh. "So good night to you both." She stepped over and gave Taryn a quick hug. "You can get back to what you were doing. Have lots of fun. Use protection."

Taryn groaned. "Kincaid."

Her friend stepped back, smile still in place. "You kids have fun now, ya hear?"

With that, Kincaid was heading back down the hallway, hips swaying, a spring in her step. She'd found her cake.

Lucas looked to the ceiling and seemed to be gathering himself back together. Or maybe pleading for God to beam him up.

"Sorry about that," Taryn said, coming to stand next to him. "She's…protective."

"I can tell." He looked over at Taryn. "Would she really have Maced me?"

"Without a doubt," Taryn said, meaning it. "But maybe she should've been aiming at me instead. I was the one accosting the drunk. I'm sorry."

"Accosting." He made a dismissive sound in the back of his throat. "You know I'm not drunk. I could've stopped you at any time."

"But you didn't."

He frowned. "I didn't."

"And you're unhappy about that. You're confusing the hell out of me," she said, honesty spilling out of her.

"Taryn…"

A horrible thought hit her. "Wait. Are you *married*?"

His gaze widened. "What?"

"Oh hell." She took a step back. "Is that what this is about? You say you're not interested and then kiss me like the place is burning down and we need each other for air. You can't stop thinking about me, but you don't want to be around me. It makes sense. Oh God, you're married. You're someone's husband."

Panic moved through her as her stomach knotted.

"No," he said, looking horrified. "That's not it at all. Damn. I wouldn't… No. Not married. Very not married."

"Girlfriend? Boyfriend?"

"*No.* I'm not an asshole. There's no one."

She let out a breath, relieved she hadn't been kissing someone's man. "Then what is going on?"

"This. We can't…" Lucas opened his mouth and then shut it again. He stared at her, some indefinable combination of emotions crossing his face, a debate raging. He took a breath, glanced over his shoulder toward the bar, and then looked as if he'd made some kind of decision. "Look, we need to talk, but we can't do it here."

"Okay."

He gave her a look, tense lines around his mouth. "Would you feel okay going to my place? Not much is open around here at this hour besides bars."

Maybe she should worry he was trying to get her alone in a private place, but frankly, he'd had more than ample opportunity to take advantage of her if he was that kind of guy. "Yeah, that's fine."

He nodded. She let him lead her out of the dark bar, and he didn't say another word as they crossed the street and made their way to his apartment building. His shoulders were hunched, his whole body tense, and his jaw flexing. He definitely wasn't inviting her over for a good time. The closer they got to his apartment, the more she had a sinking feeling that she was not going to like what he was going to tell her.

Maybe for once in her life, she should just walk away, not ask the question, not investigate. But the researcher in her wouldn't let her stop. For better or worse, she needed to know why the guy she'd shared two of the hottest kisses of her life with couldn't ask her out on a date, why he'd actively avoided her tonight.

Theories ran through her head on a loop.

Nothing logical came to mind.

She had no idea what she was walking into, but dread filled her.

Whatever it was, it wouldn't be good.

chapter

THIRTEEN

SHAW'S HEART WAS KNOCKING AGAINST HIS RIBS LIKE it was trying to break out of his chest and run back out into the street. He couldn't believe what he was about to do. He was already mentally packing all his belongings as he led Taryn up the stairs to his apartment. He'd thought he'd have longer here in Austin. He'd thought he could simply avoid people and stay under the radar. It was a big town. Fourteen years had passed. He could disappear into a new life for a little while. But karma had other ideas. He had a feeling that no matter where he went in town, he'd end up face-to-face with Taryn Landry.

Maybe this was part of his penance. To find a woman he wanted to get to know, who made him feel like he was the guy he used to be, who made him nervous and made him laugh, and made him *want* with a ferocity he hadn't felt in longer than he could remember. And then to have that woman be someone he could never touch or even be friendly with without feeling like a complete scumbag.

He couldn't keep doing this. He owed Taryn the

truth. Then he had to leave town. Because she was going to freak out—legitimately so—and be angry and feel betrayed. She'd have no reason to keep his secret. Instead, she'd have every reason in the world to out him. Why did he deserve a normal life after what his family had taken from hers?

He didn't. That was all there was to it.

This was the end here in Austin. Rivers was going to kill him, but Shaw had no choice. He couldn't keep lying to Taryn. He unlocked the door to his apartment, flipped on the light, and let Taryn walk in first. "It's not much."

She glanced around at his simple furniture and absent decor, hands hugging her elbows. "It's nice. Modern minimalist."

He smirked. "Is that what you call 'haven't had time to shop yet'?"

A half smile touched her lips. "Yep."

"Got it." But now he wouldn't need to shop. He'd be gone. "You want something to drink? I have water and iced tea."

"Tea's good."

He went into the kitchen and busied himself with pouring her a glass. He ran through scenarios in his head, trying to come up with a gentle way to tell her who he was, but he knew there was no such thing. This was going to be fucking traumatizing. They'd kissed. He'd had his hands on her. More than once. The first time, he hadn't known who she was. Maybe she could forgive him for that, but tonight, he had no excuses. He'd let himself get wrapped up in the moment and had kissed her with full knowledge of who she was and who he was to her.

Unforgivable.

He returned to the living room, finding Taryn on his couch, her hands wrapped around her crossed knees, her leg bouncing as she looked out his window toward the bar. For a second, he let himself imagine what it would be like to have no history, to wipe the slate completely clean and start fresh, to simply be bringing a drink to a woman he'd invited over to get to know better. To be the kind of man who could take her out to dinner and not be paranoid about who looked his way.

But he could never be that man, *especially* not with her.

He cleared his throat and she turned his way, offering him a look of open curiosity, of trust, which made him feel even worse. God, she was so damn pretty that it made his bones hurt. She didn't wear much makeup, but she didn't need to. Her brown skin seemed to have an inner glow, and her smile alone could knock a guy on his ass. And that was all before she opened her mouth and revealed how freaking smart she was.

"I bet it's not sweet tea," she teased. "That wouldn't be gym-approved."

He handed her the glass. "You'd lose that bet, professor. Everyone deserves a splurge sometimes, and my grandmother would roll in her grave if I was serving a guest unsweetened tea. I even make my own simple syrup for it."

"Wow." She took the glass and sipped, giving it a nod of approval. "Mmm. That's good. Color me impressed... and surprised." She cocked an eyebrow at him. "You don't seem like you indulge in much."

He sank into the armchair catty-corner from her. "I'm guessing we're not talking about sweet tea anymore."

She shrugged but kept her eyes on him as she took another sip. "Just calling it like I see it. The Lucas..." She paused, lips parted, and frowned. "I was going to say the Lucas Whoever I've met seems pretty strict with himself, but I just realized I don't know your last name."

His mouth went dry, and he suddenly wished he'd poured himself a glass of tea—or something much stronger. He wet his lips. Now or never. "Shaw. It's Shaw."

"Oh, okay. Lucas Shaw," she said resolutely. "The Lucas Shaw I know—"

"No." He shook his head, cutting her off. Words tumbled around in his head and wrecked any chance at coherence.

"No?" She frowned and set aside her drink. "Am I pronouncing it wrong?"

Sweat gathered along his back, blood pounding like a waterfall in his ears. He stared down at his hands, which were clasped loosely between his spread knees. "It's not Lucas. It's Shaw."

She gave a small, nervous laugh. "Uh, maybe it's the two margaritas, but I'm confused."

Shaw looked up, meeting her eyes, gathering every ounce of courage he had as armor. "That's why we needed to talk. That's why I stopped things that night at the gym. You called me Lucas. That's not my real name."

A deep line wedged itself between her brows, and her relaxed posture tensed up. Her gaze darted quickly toward the door as if she was noting her escape routes. She was probably checking off boxes in her head on the list of Signs Your Date Is a Serial Killer. "Your name's not Lucas."

He adjusted in the chair, uncomfortable in a way that couldn't be fixed. "No. And please don't be scared. I'm not… You're not in danger, but I need you to know who I am. And I need you to know that I had no idea who you were until after that kiss at the gym. This was…not on purpose. In any way. I would've never…"

"Luc—" She bit off the rest of the fake name, and her hand gripped the arm of the couch as though she was ready to launch to her feet and race out the door. "*What* was not on purpose? Who the hell are you? You're freaking me out here."

He rubbed his damp palms on his thighs and braced himself. "Taryn, I've been using a different name here in Austin because I wanted to disappear and hide from the press. And the past."

Her expression pinched into further confusion. "The press?"

"Yes." He held her gaze. "My real name is Shaw. Shaw Miller."

"Shaw Miller," she repeated as though the name didn't mean anything to her, as though she was testing out the sound. But the moment the name sank in and the connection registered, her face went slack and then horrified, her eyes going wide and her body jerking back as if he'd raised a hand to hit her. She jolted to her feet. "*Shaw Miller.*"

"Yes," he said hoarsely.

"As in *Joseph Miller's brother*?" Her voice roared through him.

He stood, palms raised. "I'm so sorry. I had no idea who you—"

Fury filled her eyes, making the soft brown go black. "You *sick fuck.*"

The words were like bullets hitting his flesh, tearing into him.

"Oh my God. Are you kidding me right now?" she demanded. "What *is* this? Was this some sort of *game*?"

"Jesus, Taryn. No, of course not. That's why I tried to stay away. That's why I left the gym tonight. Once I knew—"

She put her hands in her hair, an anguished look on her face, as if the thoughts were too big and violent to hold in her head. "I can't believe I kissed you." She looked up. "And you let me. You *knew* who I was tonight."

He shook his head, shame moving through him in a wave and dragging him under. "I know. I'm sorry. I have no excuses. I'm just...*so sorry*. For the kiss. For Joseph. For everything you've been through. You deserve...the world. You didn't deserve this. I would never want to add any more hurt to your life."

She stared at him, her gaze jumping around his face, like she was trying to figure something out. *No*, he realized. She was looking for Joseph in his face.

"You have the same eyes." Horror tinged the words.

"I'm sorry." He would apologize for anything at this point. The color of his eyes. The blood that ran through his veins. He could never say sorry enough.

"God, I can't believe this. How did I not see it? I read about you," she said, frustration and disbelief there. "You were going for the Olympics." She cringed. "In gymnastics. *Shit*. I saw you tumbling the other day, and it never crossed my mind."

"Taryn..." He wanted to tell her not to blame herself. She'd had no context to place him then. But she was still talking.

"Then you got in trouble," she said, looking up. "The

news stories said you were violent like him. It's in my notes somewhere."

"I attacked a reporter." He wasn't going to sugarcoat it for her. "I hurt him."

Taryn's arms crossed tightly in front her, her stance defensive, her body visibly trembling. "I can't believe I was this *blind*. I should've recognized you. You're in my goddamned research file on Joseph's family history."

He hated the thought of that. Her knowing his past, the ugly parts. The illusion of Lucas shattered around them both. No clean slates. Only the truth. "I've worked hard for no one to be able to easily recognize me. I've changed my look. And I broke my nose in that fight. It healed crooked. I don't look anything like I used to." He almost stepped closer to her but then realized he was a threat in her eyes now, a danger. "But I never meant it to cause anything like this. I was here to lie low and help Rivers get the gym off the ground. I just…needed to not be Shaw Miller for a while."

She stared at him for a long moment, the tense line of her jaw softening a little. "Does Rivers know?"

"Yes. He's been my best friend since freshman year of college. He knows everything. Saw all the stages before, after, and during. Me moving back down here to open the gym was his idea." Shaw let out a tired breath and shook his head. "I'm sorry you got caught up in it. I knew better. I broke my rules."

"Your rules?"

"To not get involved with anyone—friendship, relationship, or otherwise," he explained. "That stuff is off-limits for me."

She frowned.

"I knew it would be too big of a risk," he continued. "I just thought the risk was all mine. I didn't realize I could hurt someone like you in the process."

She considered him. "You stopped things that night at the gym before you knew who I was. I didn't tell you about my research until after. That was because of your rules?"

"The rules were the last thing on my mind in that moment. I forgot them the minute we kissed, but you called me Lucas." He rubbed the back of his neck, finding it damp. "That snapped me out of it. I've done some really shitty things in my life, but I'm not going to take a woman to bed when she doesn't even know my real name."

Taryn stepped back and sat on the arm of the couch as if her body was suddenly too heavy to hold up. "My head is spinning. I can't believe this. Of all the bars to lose my shoe in…"

He wanted to tell her it was his fault. That fate was punishing him, deservedly so. If he hadn't found her shoe and followed her, he would've seen her at the race. She would've signed up for sessions at the gym anyway. He was supposed to be tortured. But fate had gotten it wrong because it wasn't supposed to drag someone like Taryn down with him. "Believe me, I know. I lost my shit when I figured out who you were. I'll never be able to express how sorry I am."

She looked up at him. "Your brother killed my sister."

The words were like a jagged knife twisting into his gut. He lost his air for a second. He nodded. "I know. I'm…so sorry, Taryn."

She pressed her lips together, but then a determined look came into those brown eyes. "Don't say you're sorry for that. You didn't do it."

He closed his eyes, a familiar pain racing through him like lightning. "He was my little brother. I wasn't there to stop him."

"That doesn't mean you killed anyone."

He opened his eyes to find her staring at him.

"You can say you're sorry for lying to me. You can say you're sorry for kissing me back tonight. You can say you're sorry for my loss. But don't take blame for things that aren't yours to own. I've seen what that can do to a person. Joseph, by all indications, was a sociopath who knew exactly what he was doing. A lot of things had to go wrong to make that happen." Her throat worked as she swallowed. "I don't know you, Shaw. Not really. I just know this person you've presented to me as Lucas. And I'm angry you lied to me, but I can't imagine you wanted the shooting to happen or for your brother to become who he became. And I can't imagine what you've been through." She met his gaze. "So...I'm sorry for your loss, too."

He blinked. "My loss?"

"Yeah. You lost a sibling, too. And it sounds like you've lost a lot more than that." She glanced around the apartment. "Long Acre had more victims than I realized."

Shaw simply stared at her, marveling. This woman, this woman who had been traumatized and who had lost her sister and friends, who'd had her whole life turned inside out because of his brother, was offering him condolences? Sympathy? "Do you..."

When he didn't finish, she tilted her head. "What?"

He flexed his jaw, his emotions trying to push to the surface. *Do you have any idea how amazing you are?*

That was what he wanted to say, but instead, he said, "Please don't waste sympathy on me. I'm okay."

She gave him a sad smile. "Cutting yourself off from any possibility of new friendships or relationships and living under a different name, looking over your shoulder every moment? That's not a life, Shaw. That's jail."

His jaw flexed. "Maybe I deserve the sentence."

She blew out a long breath, looking exhausted all of a sudden. "I have a hard time believing that. Not if you're anything like the Lucas I met."

He didn't respond.

"So that's your plan?" she asked in what he would guess was her professor voice—slightly chastising but edged with concern. "Run the gym and just pretend to be someone else for the rest of your life?"

"No. After tonight, I won't be running the gym. I'll need to leave."

"Leave?" Lines bracketed her mouth, her distaste for that idea apparent. "Why?"

He put his hands out to his sides. "Because you know who I am. You'll tell someone. The press will find me again."

She gave him an offended look and put her hand to her chest. "You think I'm going to *run to the press*? You think I like that kind of attention? I was in that media circus, too. I could barely stand to have the cameras pointed at me during the school-board meeting the other night."

He grimaced, realizing how self-centered and accusatory he'd sounded. "Maybe not the press, but if you tell someone, then they tell someone…"

She let out a harsh breath. "I'm angry at you, but I'm

not going to out you, Luc…Shaw. I have nothing to gain by doing that. I have no desire to screw up your life."

"But—"

She lifted a palm. "Your secret is yours to keep."

His shoulders sagged, relief a living, blooming thing inside him. "Thank you. I can't begin to tell you how much that means to me."

"Of course. I don't wish anything bad for you. We've all been through our own version of hell. I hope the gym is successful, and you can find some peace there." She grabbed her purse off the couch.

Peace. Right. That was an impossible goal, but he'd settle for a few months in Austin working with Rivers at the gym so he could buy the RV and set up the next phase of his life. Time was the biggest gift he could receive. "Thank you."

When she turned back to him, her expression had gone somber. "Just tell me one thing."

He tucked his hands in his pockets, feeling more vulnerable than he had in a long time. She knew who he was—the horrible parts. It was like standing naked in front of her. "What's that?"

Her grip on her purse strap flexed as if she were having trouble choosing her words. "Was the person I've been spending time with the real you? Or was the Lucas thing an act?"

The question caught him off guard. He searched her face, trying to figure out why she was asking, but her expression was frustratingly stoic. All he could offer her was the truth. "It was the person I wish I could be."

A flicker of disappointment moved over her face and, after a second, she nodded. "Goodbye, Shaw."

Goodbye. The word burned into his skin, leaving a tattoo of what-ifs behind. What if he had a different life? What if he'd never left home to pursue the Olympics? What if he'd never said those things to his brother? What if Long Acre had never happened?

But he didn't. He had. And Long Acre could never be undone.

"Goodbye, Taryn."

chapter
FOURTEEN

THE PINK FINGERS OF SUNRISE CREPT ALONG TARYN'S worn floorboards Saturday morning as she sat curled up on the couch with her laptop. She'd managed to sleep all of about two hours after leaving Shaw's place. She'd walked out feeling so many emotions that she barely remembered the long drive home. Anger that she'd been lied to. Embarrassment that she'd been so clueless. And then just deep, deep sadness. The kind of sadness that settled into her bones and made her feel tired in a way that had nothing to do with sleep.

One night. Two people with guns. The violence of that one moment in time stretched out like cracks in glass—always splintering, reaching out further, touching lives in ways no one but the people affected ever thought about. To be honest, *she* had never truly thought about what it must be like to be a family member of one of the shooters. She'd considered the families through the academic lens—their history, mental illness in their genetics, known traumas, all the things that could give her a better picture of the shooter so she could design her program. But she'd never tried to step into their shoes.

What would it be like for a parent to see their child turn into a monster? What would it be like to be that monster's brother? To know that someone you shared blood and history with had done something so horrible? Seeing Shaw last night, the anguish on his face, hearing how he'd basically shut down his life, she'd realized how shortsighted she'd been.

She recognized that despite her training and research, she'd dismissed the shooters' families the same way the public had, her personal feelings coloring their image. Why should she waste sympathy on the people who had produced murderers? It was a sweeping and unfair assessment. She was a psychologist, dammit. This was what she studied. She knew that so many different factors went into creating a situation like Long Acre. Her entire program was based on the fact.

She knew killers could come from good families, that the parents weren't always the ones to blame, that brain chemistry, environment, resources, social connections, other traumas, and so many factors played a part. The puzzle was both complex and complicated. She also knew Shaw didn't believe any of that. She'd seen it in his face last night. The blame. *He was my little brother*.

For whatever reason, he believed he was at least partially at fault. Maybe he was. Taryn couldn't rule that out. She didn't really know him. But what if he wasn't? That was what had kept her from falling back asleep this morning. That was what was twisting up her thoughts and making her head hurt. She'd learned in her life that her gut could usually be trusted, and everything was telling her that the man she'd met as Lucas wasn't a bad guy.

However, she needed to separate out the positive feelings she'd developed for Lucas from the fake and be real about this. She needed to do her research. So after a long sip of coffee to rally her resolve, she forced herself to type a name into the search box. *Shaw Miller*.

The page immediately populated with hits. Not a Facebook or LinkedIn profile, not a blog or a personal website, but hit after hit of news stories and video clips. She felt a strange kinship seeing that. She and Shaw shared that internet reality. Even after all these years, even with her research credits and career, the search results on her own name wouldn't be about her job. To the rest of the world, her life hadn't gone on. She was a person frozen in time in a news story. A tragic character. An anguished face in a still shot. A flat picture on a page or screen.

Her eyes skimmed down the results. At the top were the story and video of the incident Shaw had mentioned—him attacking a reporter. The headlines were ugly: *Killer's Brother Explodes in Violence. Former Olympic Hopeful Thrown in Jail. Like Brother, Like Brother.*

Taryn's heart thumped a little harder. Her finger hovered over the mouse, but she couldn't click yet. Instead, she chose one from a competition he'd been in to qualify for the World Championships. The video wasn't high definition, so the images were a little fuzzy, but she picked out Shaw quickly enough. His hair was military short, his nose straight and narrow, his face boyish but serious as he conversed with a coach. Shaw hadn't been lying. He looked so different from this fresh-faced kid, one who had the whole world rolling out a red carpet in front of him. Beyond age, trauma wrote lines onto people that altered their appearance in subtle but significant ways. Tiny markers that said *I've seen things I can't unsee*. She could almost believe the boy in the video and today's Shaw were completely different people, if not for the eyes.

Shaw's name was displayed on the screen along with the event he was about to do—pommel horse. Taryn watched in thrall as he walked over to the platform and strapped on the wrist supports, preparing. He was even more muscular then, youth and what had to be constant training making him look like human art. His expression was focused and intense as he stepped up to the pommel horse. After a visible breath, he reached out and grabbed the handles, swinging himself up and separating his legs to rock along the horse before twisting into an effortless handstand. Taryn held her breath in awe as she watched the routine, Shaw swinging his legs around and around at a speed that made her dizzy and moving himself over the apparatus like it was nothing. Strong. Elegant. Obviously gifted.

The announcers were commenting the whole way through. How good Shaw was. How talented. How he would be the favorite going into the Olympic trials if he did this well at the World Championships. During the routine, the screen split, showing Shaw's parents in the stands. His mom, a petite woman with short brown hair and the pretty blue eyes she'd passed to her sons, was clasping her hands tightly to her chest, obviously nervous. His father, a big man with a shiny bald head, was gripping a little American flag but not waving it, his gaze focused on his son's performance.

So much anticipation. So much hope. Looking like every other pair of parents who wanted the best for their kid.

Taryn's eyes skimmed down to the date of the competition. A few months before the Long Acre shooting. The air left her lungs as if someone had pressed on her stomach. The people in the video had no idea what awaited them. This was what their Before looked like. Taryn had one of those, too—a Before.

She blinked, her eyes going misty for herself and the people in the video. She quickly swiped at the unfallen tears and closed the video. She didn't want to see Shaw receive his medal, didn't want to see the face of someone who thought he was going to the World Championships and then the Olympic trials, knowing he'd never get to either.

Plus, this wasn't the whole story. She couldn't just watch the Shaw who was shiny.

She sat up taller on the couch, bracing herself, and opened the video with the most hits, the one Shaw was more known for now. She'd seen a version of it years ago when the story had broken, but she'd never watched it closely. It'd blended together with all the other horrible Long Acre news stories out there.

Sound blasted from her computer—shouts, cursing, and the heavy thud of punches landing on flesh. She winced and quickly lowered the volume, but the images on the screen played out in front of her. The camera was jumpy, someone running toward the fray, filming on their phone probably. Two men, one bigger than the other, were in a tangle. The person filming stopped enough distance away that Taryn couldn't get a clear shot of the men's faces, but it was obviously an all-out brawl.

A professional video camera was in pieces on the sidewalk. The smaller man was shouting and trying to defend himself against Shaw. Shaw clearly had the advantage—bigger, stronger, madder. He grabbed the guy by the collar as if he was going to shove him, but the reporter swung out wildly, landing a punch in the center of Shaw's face. Shaw's hand went briefly to his nose. If the video had been better, Taryn had no doubt that blood would be visible, but the broken nose didn't slow Shaw down. He cursed and shoved the other guy hard. The reporter tumbled to the pavement and Shaw followed him, kicking. The sounds of pain and begging were clear even over the street noise.

"Stop! I can't…breathe. You're going to kill me."

"You think I fucking care!" Shaw kicked him again. *"I told you to stay away from her!"*

Taryn had to look away and stop the video, the violence of it making her stomach turn. She couldn't wrap her head around the idea that the raging, violent man could be the man she'd gotten to know over the last week, that the funny, flirty guy who'd teased her about running up the wall was capable of this.

But maybe she hadn't known him at all. After all, he had been Lucas with her. Not Shaw. He'd said so himself. *It was the person I wish I could be.*

Not the person he was. That person was the brother of a killer. That person was capable of this kind of violence.

A chill chased over her skin, and she pulled her robe tighter around her. But the two sides she'd seen in the videos wouldn't join together in her head. She'd studied Joseph so thoroughly. He had all the markers of a sociopath. That disorder could have a genetic link in some cases, but she didn't see those traits in Shaw.

If Shaw was a sociopath, he never would've told her who he was. He would've gotten pleasure out of lying to her, taking her to bed without her knowing a thing. He wouldn't have felt compelled to tell her the truth. He wouldn't have said goodbye last night and apologized so much. He would've charmed or manipulated her into thinking he was a good guy. He'd done the opposite. He'd sent her away. So he could live his life in hiding. Almost completely alone.

Taryn clicked back to the gymnastics video, the freeze frame on Shaw's face as he grinned at the camera, receiving his high scores for his performance. He was just a college kid back then. A few months later, that smile, his family as he knew it, and his Olympic dream would be gone. His whole life would be irrevocably changed.

She wanted to step inside that video and go back in time and warn everyone. Tell Shaw's parents to go home and get Joseph some help. Even if curing sociopaths was next to impossible once they'd escalated to that level, someone could've at least caught the warning signs in Joseph, kept him away from guns, and intervened in his relationship with Trevor, the other shooter. Done *something. Anything.*

A few pulled dominos could've stopped the chain of them from falling. All of their lives would look different.

And she couldn't help but think of the questions that had haunted her all through her career: *How many dominos are being lined up right now in places around the country? How many Josephs and Trevors are making plans? How many families are blindly walking around in the Before?*

Taryn shut her laptop, an overwhelming resolve moving through her. She suddenly had two things she knew she had to do.

One intimidated the hell out of her.

The other just flat-out scared her.

Too bad.

She had to do both.

———————

"I've decided I can't give up on this program." It was late Sunday morning, and Taryn had just finished her first slice of spinach artichoke quiche at Bitching Brunch with the girls. She'd needed a little fuel before making her announcement and had wanted to let her friends catch up with one another first, but now she needed to get it off her chest.

Rebecca, who was pouring mimosas for them at the outdoor table in the food-truck park, looked up from her task. "Of course you can't."

"We knew you wouldn't." Liv dumped more hot sauce on her quiche and passed the bottle to Kincaid. Knight, Rebecca's big, fluffy black mutt, tried to nose his way to Liv's plate. Liv patted his head and gently pushed him away from her food. She looked to Taryn. "So have you come up with a new plan to present to the school board?"

"Fuck the school board," Taryn said, the bitterness slipping out.

"Damn, girl," Kincaid said, peeking over her shoulder

as if someone could overhear them, but of course, it was empty except for the birds pecking the ground for last night's crumbs. The food-truck park didn't officially open until lunchtime today. Rebecca's husband, Wes, had offered to make them a private breakfast, so they could have the place to themselves. "You're pissed. I like it."

"I'm pissed, too," Rebecca said, taking her seat and pouring herself straight juice instead of a mimosa. Knight plopped down by her feet with a huff. "They had their minds made up before you even spoke. And that superintendent was so dismissive. He was one step shy of patting you on the head and saying, *Now, now, don't get your panties in a wad, little lady*." Rebecca harrumphed. "Asshole."

"Well, thanks, babe. I love you, too," Wes said, sauntering up to the table with a bandanna around his blond hair and a tray of bacon in his hands.

Rebecca patted his arm and smiled. "Not you, honey. You're not an asshole. Especially after bringing me bacon."

"Excellent," he said. "I'll make sure to bring you a tray if we ever get into a fight."

Rebecca rolled her eyes, but when Wes took out a pair of tongs and put a slice on her plate, she recoiled and put her fingers to her lips. "Oh yuck. I think the bacon's gone bad."

Wes frowned. "What?" He lifted the tray close to his face and sniffed. "No, I just bought this. Brown-sugar crust. Smoked locally. It smells great."

Kincaid plucked a piece off the platter, examined it, and then bit. "Mmm, yep. That's a winner. Pile it on, chef."

Rebecca shook her head and put her piece onto Kincaid's plate instead. "Sorry. That just smells off to me."

Wes looked down at his wife, concern in his eyes. He cupped her cheek, examining her. "You sure you're okay, Bec? You look a little pale. Maybe you're getting a stomach bug. Xavier had it earlier this week. I sent him home, but he worked for a few hours in the truck."

Rebecca shook her head. "No, I'm okay. I'm just... I'll stick with quiche today."

Wes didn't look convinced, but he kissed the top of Rebecca's head, which made Taryn smile. Seeing her friend so happy and in love gave her a warm and fuzzy feeling. If Rebecca could find that kind of happiness after all she'd been through, maybe there was hope for them all.

Wes dished out bacon to those who wanted it, then disappeared into the big, yellow school bus he and Rebecca had converted into a food truck, leaving them to their girl talk.

"You sure you're okay, Bec?" Taryn asked after he'd walked away.

"I'm fine. Probably just spring allergies throwing my sense of smell off." She flicked her hand toward Taryn. "Go on with what you were saying. How are you going to get around the school board?"

Taryn smoothed her napkin, a ripple of anxiety going through her. "I need to take it to the public, to the media."

Liv's dark eyebrows disappeared beneath her bangs. "Like call out the school board for saying no?"

"No, I considered that, but it would get ugly and political. The message would get lost in the mix," Taryn explained. "I mean bypass them altogether and go to people directly."

"I'm listening," Rebecca said, her business face on.

Taryn took a sip of her mimosa, trying to organize

her thoughts. "I'd thought about writing a piece for the newspaper or a website, but then I was watching some videos yesterday, and I was struck by how powerful they were, how much they affected me. I think that's the better path. We live in a world of visual media and viral videos. That's what gets my students' attention. Plus, we live in a time where grassroots stuff can turn into a big deal. Think of how many marches and movements are started on social media now."

"Right," Kincaid said, her attention fully on Taryn. "But what exactly are you suggesting?"

Taryn looked to each of her friends. "I'm thinking I should raise money and put together a video campaign about the befores and afters of a school shooting. I love hard data because it's solid and I can see proof, but statistics are just numbers to most people. My whole presentation is full of facts and figures, but you saw what happened the other night. It didn't move anybody. It should, but that's not how humans work. We don't feel numbers. We feel people's stories.

"It's not enough to say, 'This many people died.' It's more effective to show '*This* person died. This person who was going to be a scientist or an actress or who loved her dog and wanted a family.' Or 'This life was changed in this way. This person will never be the same because he's been through this.' Or even with the killers, showing 'This is what could've been if someone had stepped in to help them.' I need to stop *talking* about intervention and instead *show* exactly what difference it could've made."

Rebecca was leaning forward now, her food abandoned. "Like if Trevor's depression had been caught early and he'd gotten help."

Taryn nodded. Rebecca had been secret friends with Trevor in a therapy group before the shooting, but Trevor had been deeply suicidal by then. Rebecca still carried the guilt that she could've done more. "Exactly."

"But how would you do that?" Liv asked. "Get those messages across?"

Taryn pushed her food around with her fork, the plan crystalizing inside her but overwhelming her a little. She'd never relished cameras being turned on her. "First, I'd need to raise money to make high-quality videos. Then, I get victims and their families to volunteer their stories, talk about the befores and afters, the what-ifs, and have them provide photos and home videos. Then we put the testimonials out there, explain how my program could help keep future tragedies like this from happening, and then ask for donations to fund my program independently. If we could get enough traction, I think that would also put pressure on school boards and lawmakers to consider more comprehensive programs. Even if that doesn't turn their heads, if I can get enough money to try the program in one school district, I could do a trial run to demonstrate the model, show how it helps and how it can be affordable. Go in with tried-and-true results next time."

Rebecca sat back and shook her head. "Wow, that sounds amazing."

"It does, but it also sounds like a really, really huge project," Liv said with a little frown.

"Yeah, sugar," Kincaid said, her voice gentle. "I love the idea, but the doctor told you to take on less stuff, not more. Planning fund-raisers. Producing and directing high-quality videos. Getting people to participate and arranging all that. Talking with victims and stirring up all that stuff. Then handling the press? That's…a lot."

"It's a full-time job," Rebecca agreed.

"I know." Taryn took a long sip of her drink, wishing it was more champagne than orange juice. "There's no way I can pull all of that off while continuing my research and teaching my classes."

Her friends all frowned in unison.

"Which is why," she continued, "I'm going to take a leave of absence from my job."

Kincaid's eyes went wide.

Liv sat up straighter. "Can you do that? Like a sabbatical?"

Taryn shook her head, her knee bouncing beneath the table. "No, I'm not eligible for a sabbatical yet. And they may not grant me a leave of absence at all. They could just let me go. It will for sure mess up my road to tenure. But…I have money saved up to get by for a while, if need be. And what else am I supposed to do?" she asked. "I can't go back and start a new research project and forget this one. I can't just file this away as 'Oh well, that one didn't work.' This is the only reason I went into this field. Maybe this attempt will fail spectacularly, but I have to try."

Her friends were quiet for what seemed like an interminable length of time. Taryn expected Rebecca, the most practical of the four of them, to tell her she could absolutely not risk losing her job. Or Liv to encourage her to take more time to think about it. She was half hoping they would talk her out of it because she was freaking out a little. What did she have if she wasn't a professor? That was her life. But her friends said none of those things.

Instead, Kincaid slapped the table, rattling the cups. "Well, hot damn. We've got ourselves a project, ladies."

The break in the quiet startled Taryn, and she turned to Kincaid. "Oh no, that's not why I'm telling y'all. You don't—"

"Oh, the hell we don't," Liv said, waving her fork at her. "If you're doing this, we're in, too. Your program needs to be in schools. Someone needs to freaking listen to the people who've actually been through this shit for a change. We aren't going to make you carry that torch alone. I can help with the filming and photography. After being part of that documentary, I've been itching to branch out into short films anyway."

"And we can all help with the initial fund-raiser," Rebecca said. "The costume run was a big success. I can show you how I structured everything, got sponsors, and advertised for it. We could do something similar to get some seed money."

"I have contacts who could get the word spreading," Kincaid offered. "Plus, with my blog, I'm dialed into a pretty big internet community. They would help us share online once we have the videos."

Taryn's nose burned, and the view blurred in front of her. "Y'all are killing me."

She shouldn't have been surprised—not that her friends wanted to help and not that they hadn't batted an eye when she said she was about to leave her job. That was what they did for one another. No-strings-attached support.

They believed in her idea. Even though it was crazy. And risky.

No, they believed in *her*.

In that moment, it was all she needed.

She stood up and forced them all to their feet to give them hugs. They ended up in a weird four-person formation. Their heads next to each other and shoulders at odd angles.

"I love you guys," Taryn said.

"We love you back," Rebecca said, giving another squeeze.

They stayed that way for a second longer until Kincaid burst out with, "Yes, we love each other and this project is going to kick ass, but am I the only one who's going to bring up the fact that Rebecca is so obviously pregnant and no one is discussing this amazing piece of information?"

"Kincaid!" Rebecca shrieked, jerking upward and breaking the group hug. Taryn almost stumbled backward at the sudden shift, and Knight started barking.

"Dude," Liv said, giving Kincaid a shocked look.

Kincaid put her hands up, the picture of innocence. "I'm just saying. Not drinking champagne. Meat making you nauseous. Superhot husband who obviously can't keep his hands off you. Could you *be* more knocked up?"

"I'm not—" Rebecca's eyes went wide. "Oh shit."

Before they could process that Kincaid had just broken news to Rebecca instead of the other way around, Rebecca was rushing off to the food truck.

Kincaid turned around and gave Taryn and Liv an *oops* look. "So...more quiche?"

chapter

FIFTEEN

SHAW WAS KNEELING BY A WEIGHT BENCH, WIPING down the equipment after his last training session Thursday evening while music blasted through his earbuds. His muscles were sapped, and the music was too loud to let him think. Mission accomplished. He was about to finish up when he caught a shadow moving across the wall in front of him.

"Riv?" he called out, turning down the music and wiping the last spot he'd sprayed down. Rivers had said he was heading out a while ago to have drinks with a friend, but maybe he'd forgotten something. However, when Rivers didn't answer, Shaw turned around, finding himself face-to-face with the woman he thought he'd never see again.

"Oh." He yanked the earbuds out of his ears and got to his feet, the sudden silence almost as jarring as the sight of her. "Taryn."

She was in casual clothes tonight—tight jeans, knee-high boots, and a pink sweater that fell lower on one side, giving him an enticing view of her bare shoulder and a bra strap that blended with her skin tone.

She gave him an apologetic smile and adjusted her glasses. "Hi. Sorry if I scared you. Rivers let me in."

Shaw set down the bottle of cleaner and the towel. "He let you in after hours?"

He really wanted to say, *He let you in, knowing who you are? What the fuck?*

"I may have had to do a little convincing," she admitted, holding up her thumb and forefinger and pinching air. "He's pretty protective of you. Good thing to have in a friend."

Shaw tilted his head, confused. "Why are you here?"

His mind raced through the possibilities. Maybe she was here to yell at him now that it'd sunk in that he'd lied to her. Maybe she'd changed her mind about outing him. Maybe she'd told people…

Taryn bit her lip, contemplating, as if she were nervous. "Well, there are a few reasons, but the first is that I need your help."

That was the last thing he'd expected her to say. "Help."

She tucked her hands in her back pockets, which only made that sweater look more spectacular on her, and stepped a little closer. "Yeah. I wanted to talk to you about it and not just go through Rivers."

Rivers? Shaw wasn't tracking at all. Maybe because she was so close and smelled so good, his thoughts were scrambling. "Talk about what?"

She cocked her head toward the set of weight benches he'd been cleaning. "Can we sit?"

He nodded. "Yeah, sure."

He sat on the bench he was closest to, and she took a spot on the one across from him, their knees only a few inches apart. Her scent drifted toward him, cutting through the astringent tang of cleaner and filling the space between them with the smell of orange and vanilla.

She braced her hands on her thighs and looked at him, something vulnerable there. "All right, I'll just get straight to the point. I know I told you the night of the workout that I had a big presentation with the school board coming up."

He had to hold back a frown, remembering the video he'd watched. "Right."

"Well, it didn't go well," she said flatly, her focus sliding to some spot over his shoulder as though she was seeing the terrible meeting play out again. "It went pretty much the opposite of well. It was—"

"I saw." The words slipped out.

Her gaze flicked back to his. "What?"

Shut up. You sound like a damn creeper. But it was too late. She'd heard him loud and clear. "Yeah. The night you told me about it, I saw how much it meant to you, that it was a big deal. I wanted to know how it went, so I looked up the video."

Her nose wrinkled like she smelled something bad. "So you saw me fail spectacularly."

"No, I saw a bunch of people who had already made up their minds and weren't listening to you," he said, unable to hide his irritation. "I'm sorry it didn't go well."

"Thanks. It sucked, and you're right. They didn't listen, but I'm tired of walking around complaining about it," she said, a line of steel running through her tone, hardening the words. "My parents always told me that you can't wait around for other people to do something. You want action, you be the action. That's why I need your help."

For a moment, he didn't respond. He was too captivated, seeing the strength and resolve rise in Taryn. He'd seen her softer side, her vulnerable side when she'd run off the stage at the bar and when she'd fallen at the race. This woman before him was different. This was the woman who'd walked through tragedy and fought her way to this point. This was the professor who'd spent her life busting her ass to get answers. This woman was tough. But then the rest of her words registered. "My help?"

"Yes." She gripped the edge of the bench and leaned forward. "I stepped down from my position at the university this week."

"You did *what*? Why?"

"Because I need to get this program into schools, Shaw. If the school board can't help, then I need to do it on my own. The university is granting me leave through the summer to try to get my program funded myself, but that's hardly any time at all. I need to act fast if I want to be able to go back to my job after this launches." She met his gaze. "That's where you and Rivers come in."

"I don't understand," Shaw said, his pulse picking up speed. He didn't want to come into anything involving Long Acre. He could feel himself leaning back.

Hell. No.

"I'm going to make a series of videos to promote the program and raise funds, but I need to have a fund-raiser to get seed money to start the project. Some kind of event that I can put together quickly, that doesn't cost too much, and that would appeal to a lot of people." She turned her head, looking at all the equipment and obstacles around them. "I need your gym, Shaw. For one day. One big event. It will be like the costume run, but people can compete here instead. Maybe some kind of team event. I was thinking maybe people could sponsor high school athletes—ones who'd have a good shot at completing the course. That'd get their parents and families to come, too. We could offer prizes."

Horror worked its way through him. "Taryn—"

"It would promote the gym, too," she said, rushing past his interruption. "It would get a bunch of people in here to see what y'all have put together. People will probably put videos on YouTube of the event. It's a win-win."

"A win-win?" he repeated in disbelief. "Taryn, I get what you're trying to do and damn, it's admirable as hell, but you know that'd be putting me in a situation I can't be in. I can't have something here, sponsor something, about Long Acre. I might as well put a big target on my back and invite the press here myself."

"I know. I knew you would say that," she said, putting a gentling hand up between them as if she were calming a skittish horse. "I've already thought of that. You would only have to help behind the scenes. I'd just need you to be my contact person so we can get everything organized. During the event, I'll bring in my friends and volunteers to run it. Rivers can help if he's willing. You don't even have to be here."

Shaw ran a hand through his hair, his head suddenly pounding. A school-violence charity event. Here. With high school kids. Welcome to his nightmare. "Look, I feel like a dick saying no, but you've got to understand. I can't, Taryn. I just *can't*."

"Please." Her eyes pleaded with him. "Before you say no, at least hear me out. The last thing I want to do is expose you. I absolutely will not let that happen. You need to know that I get it."

"You get it," he repeated, not sure where she was going with that.

"Yes. I get why you lied to me. I get why you wouldn't want to help with this. I get what you're trying to do here. Start fresh. Not have a past. Not be reminded of Long Acre." She took a breath. "To be honest, I get it probably more than you know."

Right. She probably thought she did. But being a victim and being the brother of the one who created the victims were two totally different things. People didn't hate her. People didn't want her thrown into a mental hospital or jail because *like brother, like brother.* He nodded. "If you get it, then you understand why I have to say no."

"No, I'm saying I get why you would think that, why you're hiding. But I also think your plan kind of sucks," she said bluntly.

He lifted his brows. "Excuse me?"

"You'd be much better off coming out to the press…in your own way. Do an exclusive interview or something. Control the information. Reset the image people have of you. It will be hard up front, but then after…after, you could live your life."

Live his life? He stared at her like she was crazy. That plan was so nuts, he could spread it on bread and serve it with jelly. "No fucking way. Don't you see what that would do? They would tear me apart piece by piece again. They'll compare me to Joseph. The video of me and the reporter would be shown over and over again. I can't change that the attack happened. I can't change who my brother is. There's no pretty spin on assaulting someone."

"Why'd you attack him?" she asked point-blank.

"Taryn." He shook his head. "No."

But she kept talking. "In the video, you said, 'Stay away from her.' Who's 'her'? The article said you'd never say. What made you so angry?"

He grimaced, his stomach turning. She'd watched the video. She'd seen that ugly, out-of-control version of him. He pushed to his feet, cold anxiety crawling over his skin. "We're not doing this."

"Tell me," she pleaded, the words soft, beseeching. "I'm not going to tell anyone. We've all got things we wish we could take back."

He had his back to her. "Oh, right. Sure we do. That's easy for you to say."

"No, it's not," she said, somewhere close behind him now, her voice quiet. "I'm not without my own mistakes."

"We're not talking about missing a deadline, Taryn. Or being mean to a friend. Or breaking a rule at work." His fists flexed. "I beat someone bad enough to break bones. I would've done worse if someone hadn't stepped in. It's not the same thing."

"Don't pretend to know everything about me. You don't."

"I know you're a good person."

"And you're not?" she challenged.

He didn't answer.

"You want one of my secrets?" she asked. "Something only the police know?"

He didn't want to look at her. He didn't want to do this. He couldn't go back to any of those memories. Still, he found himself saying, "What?"

She was quiet a long moment. "I opened the door."

He frowned, and when she didn't say anything else, he turned. "The door."

She was standing now and cupping her elbows, her arms held tight across her middle. "The news reports always said that Joseph and Trevor broke into a side door off the main hallway in the school. That's not what happened." Her throat flexed. "I was in the hallway because I wasn't enjoying prom. I didn't have a date, and I was annoyed that my sister—who was younger, prettier, and more popular than me—was there with a senior and having the time of her life at *my* prom." She looked down and took a breath. "I thought Joseph and Trevor were there to do a prank that would derail the dance. They got me to unlock the door. I realized too late what they were really there for."

Shaw's heart plummeted into his gut. *She'd let them in?* "Taryn—"

She met his stare, her eyes shiny. "I think that's the only reason they didn't shoot me. Because I helped." She rolled her lips together, obviously trying to keep herself from crying. "I helped them kill my sister and all those people."

"No," he said instantly, stepping closer and putting his hands on her upper arms, rubbing them as if she was cold. "No, you didn't. Don't do that to yourself. That's… They tricked you. They would've gotten in some other way."

She shook her head. "You don't know that. Maybe they would've gone to another door and gotten caught. Maybe the security guard at the main door would've seen something. Maybe. Maybe. Maybe. Believe me, I've considered all the scenarios."

Shaw stared at her, hurting for her. She was carrying around guilt she didn't deserve. How much weight must that be for her to bear? Only the police knew. She'd held it inside. No one had assured her it wasn't her fault. Something clicked. "This is why you're so determined to set things right. You think you owe something to everyone."

"Of course I do," she said as if that wasn't even debatable. "I owe a debt I could never, ever repay. But I'm also doing it because I don't want anyone else to go through what I've been though, what my friends have been through." She shook her head. "So I get not wanting the press in your face. The cops kept this information sealed once they cleared me of being an accomplice because they knew how people would attack me. To imagine anyone knowing this about me sends me into a cold sweat. I've never even told my parents. I mean, how could I tell them that I helped Nia get…"

"You *didn't* help," Shaw repeated, giving her arms a gentle squeeze. "But if you've told no one, why are you telling me?"

"Because I want you to know I understand wanting to hide, but if this information stood between me being able to live my life, I'd tell. The price is too high. There are other options."

"Other options? I appreciate you trusting me enough to tell me, but it's not the same." He let his hands fall to his sides. "People would forgive you. You were a kid who made a mistake with zero bad intent. People aren't going to change their mind about me. No matter what reason I give for why I attacked that reporter. That paired with my family history is a damning sentence. I can't help you."

She looked down, the strong woman looking suddenly fragile as a bird. Defeated.

He released a breath, not wanting to say what he was about to but feeling like he owed her honesty in return for hers. "My girlfriend. That was the 'her' in the video. The reporter, this sleazy guy who worked for a gossip website, was always following me and hounding me. I'd learned to deal with it mostly, but that day…he'd yelled out that he knew my girlfriend was pregnant."

Taryn's head snapped up.

Shaw's lips wanted to clamp down and cut off the words, but he forced them out anyway. "I knew if he had that information, he'd been stalking her outside of doctor's appointments or something because we hadn't told anyone yet. I was a mess back then and on edge. The unexpected pregnancy had me freaked out. So I was already pissed he had this news and let him know it. Then he asked me if I was worried the baby would be a killer like my brother."

Taryn's face went slack. "Oh my God."

"Yeah. I just…lost it." Shaw looked toward the other side of the gym, trying to keep the old feelings from welling up. "The girl and I were already on shaky ground, but after the assault charge and the video made the news, she ended the pregnancy without telling me." Saying the words out loud made his chest hurt. "Turns out, she was worried about exactly that, that she was carrying damaged goods. Me attacking the reporter and getting diagnosed with an anger disorder sealed the deal."

Taryn's face shifted into stunned disbelief. She put her hand over her mouth.

"So, yeah. I'm not going to the press with that," he said. "Besides, there's nothing to say to change people's minds. The circumstances still didn't give me the right to hurt that guy like I did."

"Maybe not the right, but a damn good reason," Taryn said, some fire coming back into her voice. "That's a disgusting thing to say to someone. And I'm so sorry, Shaw. That she… I'm sorry. I can't imagine."

"Yeah."

She stared at him for a long moment. He had to look away. He didn't want to see pity there. He didn't want to feel what those memories brought up. He didn't want to admit that losing a child that way had been like someone cutting out his heart. He also didn't want to admit he'd had the same worries as his girlfriend about the baby. What if his genes *were* damaged? What if *he* was so damaged that he'd mess up a child's life?

"Thank you for telling me," Taryn said, a sad edge to her voice. "I'm sorry I suggested the press. I won't push you like that again without knowing the whole story."

He nodded, relieved she was seeing logic and that the matter was settled. "Thanks."

She took an audible breath. "But I'm going to stand by the fact that isolating yourself like this is not healthy."

"Not healthy?" He smirked, trying to get this conversation far, far away from where they'd wandered. "Now you know my story and that I have an anger disorder, so you're gonna give me a therapy session, doc?"

"Oh, don't give me that shit," she said, quiet sass entering her tone. "I'm just being straight with you. And I hope they used more evidence than one attack to diagnose you. You were provoked in a vicious way at a vulnerable time. That's a one-off, not a pattern of behavior."

He looked away.

"But what I was going to say is that even if you don't come out publicly, you can't keep living like this."

He grunted. "Believe me, I can."

"Nope." She pursed her lips. "I can prove it's not healthy or sustainable, that it is a doomed plan."

"Oh really," he said, annoyance returning.

"Yes. Case in point. The night in the foam pit." She tipped her chin up as though her point had proven everything.

He glanced over at the pit in question, trying not to remember how it'd felt to have his arms around her, her soft mouth against his, to feel that heat surge between them. "That night was a temporary lapse in judgment."

"No. It was you being human." She crossed her arms like a lawyer ready to make her closing arguments. "Humans need people. They need to socialize. To have friends. To touch and be touched. To have people in their lives who they can be themselves around. Even though that's not part of your plan, you're still going to want that on some level—even if it's a subconscious need. That's why you couldn't help but take the risk with me that night."

He snorted. "That's why I kissed you? Because of my humanness?"

She nodded resolutely. "Yes."

He leaned in, letting himself indulge in the up-close view of her for one selfish moment. "I can assure you, professor. My humanness had nothing to do with why I couldn't keep my hands off you."

She straightened at that, her cheeks darkening. "Oh...I..."

"And I appreciate you worrying about my mental

health, but I'm fine. I'm much better off living like this than how things were before. I've got what I need. I need to protect that." He stepped back and crossed his arms to match her stance. "So I'm sorry it's not the answer you want, and I respect what you're trying to do, but I can't be involved with your event."

He turned his back, needing to get away from her. This conversation had cut too deeply, and he could feel the blood pooling at his feet. He didn't open up like this, flayed open, all his ugly secrets on display. He needed to stitch up and put that Lucas armor back on. But right as he was about to walk away, her voice hit him in the back. "Do you still want to kiss me?"

His muscles locked up midstep. He refused to look back.

"Taryn," he warned.

"No." Her heeled boots clicked against the concrete floor as she stepped closer. "Answer the question."

He forced himself to turn around and face her again. "That's an unfair question."

Her eyes held challenge as she planted a fist on the curve of her hip. "Why?"

"Because the answer doesn't matter."

"It does to me," she said, not backing down.

"Fine. You want the truth?" he said, going on the offensive, hoping to scare her right out the door. "Yes. And it has nothing to do with my damn subconscious. You're sexy as fuck. Smart. Interesting. And when I kiss you, your whole body responds like you're starved for something only I can give you. You know what that feels like?"

She blinked, clearly taken aback.

"Like a goddamned drug, Taryn," he said, frustration

burning through him. "Powerful and addictive and so tempting, it makes me crazy. *Crazy*. Do you know how long it's been since I've felt something like that? I can barely manage to share air with you and not completely lose my cool. It took everything I had that first night to stop and not take you right there on the gym floor. It takes everything I have *every time* I'm around you not to touch you."

Taryn was staring at him with wide eyes, her lips parted.

"So yes, I still think about kissing you. I think about doing more than that. I think about dirty, depraved things you should probably slap me for. But that doesn't matter." His voice echoed in the empty gym. "Because I am who I am and you are who you are."

Taryn's pulse was visible in her throat as she stared back at him. "Dirty, depraved things?"

His fingers flexed as his mind raced through all the fantasies that had invaded his mind since he'd met her. Some involving the equipment around them. "Yes. You should probably hit me and then knee me in the groin for good measure."

She stepped closer to him, and for a second, he thought she was going to take him up on that suggestion, but she didn't raise a hand or a knee. "That first night here, you said you stopped kissing me because I didn't know your name."

He clenched his jaw. Why was she so close? Why wasn't she running? Why did she look *so fucking beautiful all the damn time*?

She lifted her face to him. "I know your name now, Shaw."

All his ire left him in a hard gust of air, as if she really had punched him. He gave her a desperate look. "What are you trying to do here, Taryn? I don't have the energy to play mind games."

Taryn shook her head. "Not a game. I just need you to know that I know who you are. I know why this is a bad idea. And I still want to kiss you, too."

The words tumbled between them and then snaked through Shaw's blood like a dangerous potion. He closed his eyes and inhaled through his nose, trying to find his good sense, and then looked down at her. "Taryn, I know how bad you want this program to happen, but you don't have to do this to get me to agree."

Her brows popped up at that and then she laughed—actually *laughed* at him. "Hold up. Are you seriously suggesting I'd offer myself in exchange for that? In exchange for anything?"

"No, I—"

"Good Lord. Yes, I want this program to work so badly, it keeps me up at night. I'd sacrifice a lot to make it happen. I *have* sacrificed a lot. But I do have my limits." She gave him an exasperated look. "This is not about the program. What I'm saying to you is that maybe there's a way we can both get what we want."

The words washed over him with heat. What he wanted? What he wanted was her lips on him again. What he wanted was her calling his name and begging for him to taste her, touch her, be inside her. He pushed past the lump in his throat. "And what is it that I want, professor?"

"Besides depraved things?" she teased. "A clean slate."

"A clean slate," he said, voice flat.

"Yes. Maybe not from the world yet. But from me. What your brother did was…what your brother did," she said, the words hitching a little. "I'm not going to pin my feelings about that on you. That's not fair. And I know you have Rivers, but maybe…you could use someone else you can be yourself with. A friend. Maybe a friend you kiss."

He watched her lips move, processed the words, but couldn't believe what he was hearing. Surely, he was dozing in his office and this was some twisted dream. "Friends who kiss."

She adjusted her crooked glasses and wet her lips, distracting the hell out of him. "Yes. And maybe more than kiss, if that's where things go. Let's be real. We have a linked history we can't change. It's ugly and horrible, and I hate that it's there. But I like you, and I think you like me. Plus, physical chemistry is a real thing. A scientific thing, by the way."

He couldn't help but smirk. She probably had charts about hormones and pheromones she could bust out to show him. He'd never found science sexy, but he bet she could sway his opinion.

"Based on my previous experiences, such an intense attraction is not something that's all that common," she continued. "At least not for me. I don't normally want to rip some dude's clothes off the minute I kiss him."

His eyebrows shot up. "You want to rip my clothes off?"

She gave him a patient look, as if he were a kindergartner who just wasn't quite getting what two plus two equaled. "Was my memo not clear enough the night in the foam pit? Believe me, you haven't cornered the market on filthy thoughts."

"Uh…" His brain had stopped functioning. His libido had wrestled away the reins and was galloping off into the sunset.

"All I'm saying is that yes, our pasts are intertwined, but by no fault of our own," she said matter-of-factly. "Why should we let what happened take away yet another thing? Thinking about that… Well, it pisses me off." Her lips pursed. "I've been through hell. You've been through hell. If we want to kiss each other, why shouldn't we be able to do that? We're grown people. We're attracted to each other. We're both lonely."

He frowned. "You're lonely?"

She let out a resigned sigh. "I have fantastic friends, but my work is my life. I'm busy and am going to get busier. I'm not in a place to go out and find people to date. And when I've tried, it's usually been a disaster. You saw me after one of those disastrous dates the night at the bar. I'm an epically boring date, it seems."

"That's bullshit."

She shrugged. "Maybe. Maybe not. But being with you… I don't know. It feels easy."

Easy. He'd never heard that word sound quite so complimentary. No one described him that way. But this woman, this woman who had every reason to hate him, was asking to spend more time with him. To be a friend. To be more than that.

"You're serious about this," he said carefully.

"I am."

He couldn't stop himself. He reached out and cupped her chin with his hand, examining her expression, trying to read her. "You're telling me all this even when I said no, that I wouldn't help you?"

Her lips kicked up at the corners. "Oh, I'm not worried. You're going to change your mind about that whether we kiss or not."

He cocked his head, amused at her confidence. "Oh, is that right, professor?"

She stepped close enough that her breasts grazed his chest, which sent a zip of awareness straight downward. "Yes. Because you watched a boring school-board video, which means you care about what happens to this program."

He traced his thumb along her cheekbone, marveling at the fact that he was allowed to touch her again. "Maybe I just cared about what happened to you."

She leaned into his hand, a warm look crossing her face. "That works, too."

He stared down at her, his heart beating in his throat and much lower. *Damn.* This woman. How could he ever say no to her? He let out a breath, a white flag zooming up the flagpole. He closed his eyes briefly. "No one can know who I am. I can't be on camera or present for any press. And I won't be here for the day of the event."

When he opened his eyes again, her lips were curved into a sexy, triumphant smile, one that made her whole face glow, and she looped her arms around his neck. "You've got my word. Thank you."

"You're welcome," he said, his gaze searching hers. "'Depraved' didn't scare you off, huh?"

She laughed under her breath. "When you've been celibate for a long time, I think depraved thoughts are par for the course. Did I mention all the bad dates?"

He lifted a brow. "Oh, so the professor has her own mental file. How depraved are we talking?"

She gave him a saucy grin. "You worried?"

"Terrified."

"I can tell."

He pushed her hair away from her face. "I think I need

to kiss you now. You know, to see if this agreement is a good idea. Gotta make sure the chemistry wasn't a fluke."

"Good plan." She lifted her face to him, dark lashes at half-mast. "Kiss me, Shaw Miller."

Shaw Miller. Hearing his real name on her lips did more than it should to him. He couldn't wait any longer. He brought his other hand to her neck, feeling the heat of her skin, the flutter of her pulse. The second their lips touched, all the anxiety about agreeing to the event dissolved into the background. He couldn't worry about such things when Taryn's mouth was so soft and pliant against his, when her body was so warm and lush. She melted into the kiss as if she wanted to be nowhere else, as if she was relieved it was finally *now*. He knew the feeling.

He also knew this was fucked up. He was kissing one of his brother's victims. There was no way around that. And he couldn't offer Taryn more than this. His time here was limited. There was no future for this to grow into something. She wouldn't even be able to call him by his name around anyone else. He didn't deserve this. He didn't deserve a clean slate with anyone, much less this amazing woman, but right now, he didn't care. Right now, for the first time in years, he was kissing a woman as Shaw Miller.

And she was kissing him back.

She knew who he was and she wanted him anyway.

chapter
SIXTEEN

TARYN STOOD IN FRONT OF THE CURVED WALL, EYEING the thing as if it were a hated ex-boyfriend. She didn't know how a wall could be laughing at her, but it totally was. She felt its silent mocking. She should've gone out to the lobby to wait for Shaw while he showered and changed clothes, but her mind had been racing and restless energy had been coursing through her. After the heavy conversation they'd had, the agreement they'd made, and then that kiss, she needed distraction. So she'd decided to walk around the gym to shake off the nervous energy and to get ideas for the event. However, after one lap around the place, she found herself staring at that beast of a wall instead.

Even though she was in skinny jeans and not workout clothes, she unzipped her boots and took off her socks. Just one try. Her jeans had good stretch in them—as all respectable jeans should. She'd be fine. Probably.

She backed up on the runway and braced one leg in front of her. *One, two, three…*

She shot forward, using every ounce of power she had, and her feet hit the surface of the wall with a slap. She got three steps up, felt the lift, got excited, and then gravity smacked her right in the face again. *Not today, lady*. She stumbled backward awkwardly, but at least managed to stay on her feet this time and not land on her butt.

A grunt of frustration escaped her, and she hit her fist against the wall. "Ugh, you big, ugly piece of junk."

A chuckle echoed behind her. "You're going to hurt Wally's feelings."

Taryn peered over her shoulder. Shaw was heading her way, dressed in jeans and a dark-blue Henley that brought out his eyes. His hair was loose with a little wave to it, the ends still damp above his shoulders. *Good God*. A hard kick of arousal hit her low and fast. She loved a good man bun but had thought of tugging Shaw's hair free more than once. Seeing Shaw fresh from a shower with his hair down and his skin a little flushed from the heat of the water? Not fair.

She cleared her throat and tried to look unaffected at the sheer male beauty of him. She smiled to convey *See, totally handling this. Don't I look chill?* "Wally doesn't have feelings. He's inherently evil."

Shaw nodded toward the wall. "So he's still pissing you off, huh?"

She reached down for her socks. "No," she said haughtily. "I was just killing time."

"Uh-huh." He watched as she sat on the edge of the platform and pulled her sock on. "I think we should add to this agreement of ours that you'll still come for your workouts."

She gave him a look of warning as she zipped up her

boot. "Shaw, if you're telling a girl on your very first date with her that she needs to work out, you really need some lessons on Things Not to Say to a Woman."

His smile went sly. "Oh, don't give me that, professor. I've made it perfectly clear how I feel about your body. I'm literally doing everything I can right now not to ogle you."

"I'm putting on a boot."

"The collar of your sweater is gaping." He nodded toward her. "I can see the lacy edge of your bra and the curves of your breasts. If I don't stop looking, I'm gonna embarrass myself with an obvious sign of how much of a fan I am."

A curl of need moved through her at the heat in his voice, at the reference that she could make him hard with one little peek. That made her feel sexy…and powerful…and really hot under her light sweater. This Shaw was different. She didn't know exactly what to pinpoint, but she felt it. He wasn't the closed-off, tense man she'd talked with earlier tonight. A new confidence was there. He looked comfortable in his skin for the first time since she'd laid eyes on him at the bar. He could be himself. "Oh…well…"

He crouched down in front of her and took her other boot. He flicked his fingers, indicating she should give him her foot. "Here, sit up. I'll save myself the temptation of looking."

She sat up and lifted her foot to him.

"All I'm saying is that you came here to work out for a reason." He took her ankle in his big hand and gently slid her boot on. She had no idea why the simple move was so erotic, but her pulse had turned into a hammer at the base of her throat. "Obviously, the challenge of it is still calling to you. You should keep trying. I can train you and make sure you conquer Wally. Plus, it would be helpful to be familiar with all the obstacles for your fund-raising event."

"Right," she said distractedly as he took his time zipping up the long zipper, her skin electric with tingles even through her jeans.

He set her foot down and rocked back on his heels, still crouched in front of her. "Maybe you should participate in the event. Show those teenagers that us old folks can do it, too?"

That snapped her back into reality. "Ha. Correction: *You* can still do this stuff. I proved the other night that I definitely cannot."

"Yet."

She groaned. "Why are you pushing my challenge buttons? I'm that girl who could never turn down a dare. This is why I can't accept the school board's no. I don't like no. I have enough on my plate without worrying about if I can get up this damn wall."

His lips curled into a wicked smile as he reached out and took her hands to pull her to her feet. He leaned down close to her ear. "Taryn Landry, I dare you."

A hot shiver ran down her neck, his breath ghosting against her skin. "Mean trainer. Mean, hateful trainer."

He laughed softly. "I'll put you on the schedule. I'm a very good trainer. Very hands-on. You'll get up that wall."

He was still holding her hands, and she guided them around her waist, dragging him closer. "Hands-on, huh?"

He hooked his arms around her and tucked his fingers

in her back pockets, the heat of his palms against her ass making a flash of arousal go through her. "Very."

She could feel him, the hint of hardness growing against her making promises. She swallowed past her dry throat. "Well, that's all you had to say."

He held her there for a moment, his freshly showered scent surrounding her. She absorbed the feeling of simply being against him, feeling the whispers of arousal and his steady heartbeat, relishing the tease they were both giving each other. They'd agreed to take things slowly tonight and go on a date, but the delicious anticipation of what could happen in the near future was pushing all of her buttons.

After a few seconds, he lowered his head, touching his forehead to hers. "If I haven't said it yet, thank you."

She let her hands slide to his waist below his shirt, feeling the heat of his skin, holding him there. "For what?"

"For the chance to just…be how I want to be with you. I know a clean slate can't exist, but it feels really good to know that tonight, I can take you to dinner and not have to watch that I don't slip up and reveal my past, not have to worry that I'm lying to you. I can just…be myself for better or worse. That feels like a special kind of freedom."

Her heart broke a little for him. She wished he could be that way in the world and not just with her, but she didn't let it show on her face. She pushed up on her toes and brushed her lips over his. "I'm looking forward to getting to know the real you."

He kissed her back gently and then smiled. "Let's see if I remember who that even is."

"I bet it will come back to you quicker than you think." She stepped back and took his hand, forcing herself not to look at the fly of his jeans, not to move too fast despite her galloping libido. "How about you start by telling me what you feel like eating? And if you tell me salad and a protein shake, I'm kicking your trainer ass to the curb right now. I have no time for that nonsense."

He laughed and pulled her by the hand toward the front door. "Never. How about pasta?"

She nodded. "Mmm-hmm. I like."

He walked backward, leading her along and somehow maneuvering around the equipment behind him without looking. "And a little wine?"

"For sure."

They reached the main lobby, and he grabbed keys from a drawer behind the counter. "And maybe something with whipped cream at the end?"

She smiled, picturing *him* as the something with whipped cream on it, but they'd decided before he'd hit the showers that they needed to get to know each other a little better before getting carried away like they had that night in the foam pit. They had time.

Even though a big part of her wanted to just drag him home now. She'd waited this long to get in bed with a guy. She could wait longer. It was better to make sure they were both comfortable with this agreement before they took things to another level.

The naked level.

Shaw, naked.

She rubbed her lips together. "Whipped cream is good."

His gaze went hot for a moment, and she knew his mind had gone exactly to where hers had. She smiled. "Take me to dinner, Shaw."

He swept an arm in front of her. "As you wish."

—〰—

Taryn was full and a little buzzed after a leisurely meal
at a quaint little Italian restaurant not too far from the
gym. She and Shaw had fallen into easy conversation
about everything that didn't involve the past. Why Shaw
and Rivers had chosen that type of gym to open. What
kind of event she could plan to raise money. What books
they liked to read. What bands. Favorite movies.

At first, she was acutely aware of all the things they
were avoiding—talk of family, of careers, of college—
but after a while and two glasses of wine, they fell into
a comfortable rhythm. Also, she realized this meant she
wasn't talking about the things that usually infiltrated
her dates—details about her research or that she was a
Long Acre survivor. In a lot of ways, it was a relief. No
heavy talk. No sympathetic looks or darkly fascinated
ones. No glazed-over eyes.

On the other hand, it was disconcerting. She felt a bit
unmoored, a ship that had drifted away from the dock.
Who was she if not the research professor and Long
Acre survivor? What made her interesting to someone
else besides that? Shaw didn't seem to be bored, but
the thought stuck with her like a little thorn in her foot,
sticking, sticking.

Shaw paid the check after they shared a few bites of
tiramisu, and then he asked her if she wanted to take a
walk. Taryn wasn't ready for the night to end, and after
the wine, she needed to walk off the buzz a little. "Yeah,
sure. It's nice out."

He smiled, his face warm in the glow of the candle-
light coming from the little red votive jar at the center

of the table, and she got the distinct impression that he'd thought she was going to say no and was pleased she hadn't. That gave her a whole other kind of buzz that had nothing on the wine.

"Great." He pushed his chair back and offered his hand to help her up. "We can get our heart rates up and burn off some of these calories."

She made an affronted noise and hit him on the arm with her purse.

He laughed, the flickering light dancing in his eyes. "Depraved she doesn't hit me for. I mention calories and I'm getting abused. I'm *kidding*, professor."

He led her outside, the night air cool but almost a relief after the heavy, garlic-scented air inside, and let go of her hand. She missed the connection as soon as it was gone. "I can't believe you brought up calories after tiramisu. That's just cruel to do to a curvy girl."

"Curvy?" He gave her a raised-eyebrow look as they started to amble down the quiet street. "Is that what we're calling hot as fuck these days? Because that's really the only thing you could mean right now."

She gave him a look, though his blunt words sent a little shiver through her. "Well, for some, it can mean a good thing, but I'm a little more self-conscious when you're, you know"—she flicked her hand between them—"you."

He stopped on the sidewalk. "Me?"

She cocked a brow. "Yes. An athlete with probably less body fat than a carton of yogurt."

He frowned and stepped in front of her, putting his hands on her shoulders. "You're beautiful. Not because I say so. It just is. If I stopped ten people on this sidewalk, nine out of ten would agree and the other one would just be drunk."

She bit her lip, charmed by his vehemence.

"My body is my job," he said simply. "It's not some big accomplishment. It's just the only thing I know how to do well. Don't be too impressed. One-trick pony."

She shook her head. "I don't believe that for a minute."

"Believe it." He took her hand and they continued walking. "And to be honest, I'm not all that strict about what I eat. All those years of Olympic training and watching every calorie, focusing on food only as fuel, kind of killed my desire to ever go back to that. I try to be healthy, but I also let myself enjoy food. It's one of life's few pleasures."

Taryn kept walking alongside him, but when he said *Olympic*, her breath caught. He'd gone there, to the past. She didn't know if that was a slipup or if he actually felt comfortable enough to talk to her more openly. Maybe it was the wine. "I can't imagine the pressure that must've involved."

"If you'd asked me back then, I would've told you there's nothing tougher than being an athlete at that level." He glanced over at her before focusing back on the sidewalk in front of them. "But I learned pretty quickly that I had no idea what I was talking about. That was a cakewalk compared to what came after."

She nodded, their steps echoing along an empty alley on their right. "I know what you mean on some level. I thought things were so hard in high school. No one realized I was so angsty because I was a good student and ran track and looked to be doing everything right. But man, inside, I was kind of a disaster. Everything felt so huge at the time. Then once everything happened…I realized they were just the little problems of a little girl."

He squeezed her hand "What were you angsting about? Typical teenage stuff? Not that I'd know what that is, really. I spent most of high school with private tutors."

She peeked over at him, finding him watching her, and she gave him an embarrassed smile. "It's going to sound silly now, but I thought I was destined to be a singer-songwriter. That was my life. I was an *artiste*, thank you very much." She laughed under her breath. "I was very internally dramatic."

Shaw didn't laugh with her. "Why couldn't you be a songwriter?"

She gave him a come-on-now look. "Because only, like, the tiniest percentage of people can actually make that their job and because my parents were not going to be on board with something so flighty. My mom was a journalism professor and came from a family of doctors and lawyers. My dad is military and very old school about getting a job with a steady paycheck and benefits. I was supposed to get a scholarship, go to a good school, and get a well-respected, well-paying job. End of story."

"So you did."

She shrugged. "I wasn't going to, though they'll never know. I was feeling pretty rebellious by the end of high school. I was secretly applying to schools that focused on the arts. I was going to move to New York and just deal with the fallout. But after we lost Nia, it all seemed really silly and dumb. Selfish, you know? And I for sure couldn't leave town."

He frowned.

"Plus, I didn't want to write or sing anymore anyway. What was there to sing about? I was devastated and angry and needed action. Going into research made sense. It gave me an outlet for all that emotion. It was the right decision." She said it with such fervor that it sounded as if she was trying to convince him even though he hadn't passed judgment.

He pulled her hand up to his mouth and kissed their joined knuckles, a lock of hair falling over his eyes. "The world will be a better place because of your research. That's something to be proud of."

Her breath sagged out of her. "Yeah. It is. If I can get anyone to listen to me."

They walked a few more steps in silence. She thought the subject was done, but then Shaw spoke again, casually. "That doesn't mean you shouldn't let yourself indulge the other side of your personality sometimes."

She'd been lost in her thoughts, and it took a second for her to catch what he'd said. "The other side?"

They came to a corner with a crosswalk, and he pressed the button for the walk sign before turning to her and tucking his hair behind his ear. "I heard you sing, Taryn. You have a fantastic voice, and you were...I don't know, captivating onstage. I couldn't stop watching you. The way you sang that song made me... It made me feel shit because I could tell *you* were feeling it. It made me want to follow you out and *talk to you*." He gave her a wry look. "I don't want to talk to anyone."

Her skin felt too warm, the compliments both pleasing her and making her feel awkward. "Thank you, but that was just one random incident. I sang it with all that emotion because a memory of my sister hit me while I was up there. Which also made me panic and run off the stage, so not exactly a stellar performance."

The walk light blinked, and he tugged her hand, leading her across the street. "I think you should sing anyway. You don't have to make it your job, but it doesn't hurt to feed that side of yourself, too."

She frowned. "Shaw—"

"I know I'm the last person anyone should be taking life advice from, but I can tell you that when I stopped gymnastics, when I let that part of me slip away, it was bad. I had this hole I kept trying to fill…with drinking, with anger, with a bad relationship. You can't just shut down a big part of who you are without consequences." He turned to her when they reached the curb. "Starting the gym, being back in that environment, even in an anonymous way, has made a huge difference. No, I'm not training for the Olympics anymore. That ship has sailed, been lit on fire, and sunk to the bottom of the ocean. But I can still do gymnastics. I can train other people on how to push themselves physically. I can tap into that vein of who I used to be even if I can't actually be him." He glanced past her. "You could do that, too. On the side. Write songs. Sing. Just for yourself. Just because it feels good."

Taryn stared at him, hearing the fervor in his tone, appreciating the concern, but he didn't understand. He'd seen what happened. "I can't."

"You can." He guided her along the sidewalk, walking backward in front of her, a devilish, almost boyish look in his eye. "Taryn Landry, I dare you."

He stopped on the sidewalk so suddenly that she almost stumbled into him, but when she heard the music and turned her head, she already knew what she'd see. The Tipsy Hound. She groaned. "You have got to be kidding me. You did not just set a trap. On our first date, no less."

He laughed and lifted his palms. "I did no such thing. I was leading us toward my place because my car is there. I was going to drive you back to the gym. But I'm not ready for tonight to be over yet, and if I take you to my place, I'm not sure I'll be able to keep our agreement to take things slow because"—he pointed to his chest—"depraved. So here's the perfect solution. One more drink. And a song."

"This is not…" Taryn was about to protest some more, to shut this down, but then her eyes landed on the little chalkboard announcing tonight's theme. She read the title twice. *Oh, hell yes.* She bit her lip so she wouldn't smile and give herself away. She schooled her expression into one of haughty confidence. "Fine. You win."

His eyebrows arched. "Really?"

"If"—she raised a finger—"you agree to help me out if I need it."

He smiled. "Of course. If you get freaked out again, I'll be right there to get you off the stage. But I don't think that's going to happen."

He wasn't getting her point. Good. She grabbed his hand, keeping his back to the sign. "All right. Let's get this over with."

Shaw followed her into the dark interior, and the scent of the place—beer and barbecue potato chips—was becoming oddly familiar to her, something she maybe should be worried about. No one was onstage yet, and music from an old jukebox was playing. Shaw grabbed a table and ordered drinks for both of them.

Taryn went off in search of Kaleb. When she found him, his face brightened. "Hey, you're becoming a regular."

"Seems so," she said. "Good chips."

"Family recipe. You gonna sing?" he asked. "It's only karaoke tonight, but we're trying out a new theme. You'll need—"

"Yeah, I know. I saw. I thought it'd be fun. But I was wondering if you could help me with something first…"

Kaleb didn't hesitate. "Sure, what'd you have in mind?"

A few minutes later, Taryn returned to the table to find Shaw sipping his beer, the bowl of potato chips half-empty. He looked up. "All set?"

"Yep." She revealed what she'd been holding behind her back and plopped the cowboy hat on his head. "We're all set."

Shaw looked up at the brim of the hat. "Uh…what's this? Undisclosed cowboy fantasies?"

"You do look good in a hat." She slid into her chair. "But no. Since you were so eager to participate tonight, I figured you were aware of what was required."

"Required?" His gaze turned wary.

She smiled sweetly, victoriously. "It's country-duets karaoke. We'll be singing 'Islands in the Stream.' I'll be Dolly, and you can be Kenny. We're up first."

Shaw's posture stiffened as if he'd sat on a hot stove. "A duet? Oh, hell no. I didn't realize that was the theme. That was not the deal. I don't sing. And I can't…I can't be onstage in front of people."

"I can barely see you under that big-ass hat. Plus, I signed you up as Lucas. If you're not up for it, we can go because I'm not singing solo on duet night. It's not allowed."

He narrowed his eyes. "You're getting around the dare."

Yes. Yes, she was. *Winning*.

"I am a professor. Don't take a smart woman out on a date if you don't want to risk being outsmarted." She smiled and patted his hand, digging deep and finding a Dolly accent. "Better luck next time, darlin'."

He watched her, a look of challenge coming into his eyes as she picked up her beer and took a long, victorious sip. *I am woman, watch me gloat*.

"Ready to go?" she asked.

Kaleb went to the stage. "Please welcome our first singers tonight. Lucas and Jamez!"

One lady applauded. Everyone else ignored the announcement. Taryn pulled out her wallet and left money for the drinks so they could bail, but Shaw's hand covered hers, pinning the bills to the table. "No way. You're not wiggling out of this on a technicality. Come on, Dolly. We've got a song to sing."

Her eyes widened. "No, come on. You know you don't want to do this. Admit you lost."

Shaw took her hand and pulled her to her feet. "Nope. This is happening. You're a professor. Well, I'm a former champion athlete. I don't like to lose."

No, no, no. He wasn't supposed to say yes. Taryn had to move her feet quickly to keep up. She suspected she'd pushed the man too far, and with a few drinks in him, he wasn't thinking logically. They couldn't do this.

But they were still walking. She'd played poker with him, and he'd called her bluff.

He led her onto the stage and then let go of her to step out of the main spotlight. He faced her, angling himself to be able to see the screen behind her that would play the lyrics.

Taryn wanted to run, but the opening bars of the song were already starting. Shaw eyed the scrolling lyrics and put the microphone near his mouth. "Baby, when I met you…"

Oh no.

This was happening.

She froze for a moment, the screen behind him flashing her upcoming lyrics, but hearing Shaw's singing voice threw her for a loop. Her attention was locked on him. He looked unsure of himself, but he wasn't half bad, and somehow the cowboy hat didn't look out of place, even though he'd told her at dinner he was a fan of rock. He finished his opening lyrics and looked at her, something sweet in his eyes. A nudge. A vote of confidence.

That was when it hit her. He was doing this for her. The last thing Shaw wanted to do was be onstage in front of people, but he'd gotten up there *for her*. Not because of the dare. Not to win.

Her heart squeezed at the thought, and a surge of bravery swelled in her. She was being ridiculous. This was a nowhere bar with people who were barely paying attention. It was karaoke. No one cared if she messed up. In fact, they probably hoped she would. This was supposed to be fun. Everything didn't have to be so damn serious all the time. She'd forgotten that part.

She lifted the microphone and didn't bother looking at the screen. The words came to her without her reaching for them, written on her childhood memory wall and forever imprinted. Her dad loved country-western music and used to play it around the house all the time, driving her classical-music-loving mother crazy. Dolly was one of her daddy's favorites. The words tumbled off Taryn's lips with a faux country accent. This song was so wrong for her raspy voice, it was comical, but she found herself getting into it.

The beaming smile that appeared on Shaw's face when she started singing almost made her knees go out from under her. He tipped his hat to her and sang along, messing up some of the lyrics when he forgot to look at the screen, but he didn't seem to care. They got to the chorus, and she found she'd crossed the stage to get closer to him. The audience disappeared. She and Shaw held eye contact and sang about sailing away together to another world.

In that moment, that was what it felt like. Being in another world, one untouched by her current drama and their complicated past. They were just two people on a date, singing a ridiculous song and having fun.

Her tight muscles loosened, her throat opened up. Soon, she was singing and doing Dolly some justice. Shaw pulled her to the edge of the spotlight onstage and tugged her close, his smile mischievous as he sang. He'd won the bet. She didn't care. When the line about making love with each other came around again, her skin heated and his eyes darkened.

They sang their way through the chorus on autopilot, their gazes locked. And when the song ended and they didn't move, it startled her to hear actual applause. Some guy in the audience called out, "You gonna kiss her or what?"

Taryn laughed, but Shaw set the microphone aside and caught her chin in his hand. He dipped down and kissed her like no one was watching, nearly knocking his borrowed hat off his head.

A whistle of appreciation came from the audience, and Kaleb came back on the stage. "Well, folks. I'm not sure who's going to top that. Let's hear it for Lucas and Jamez!"

Shaw was still looking at her with hunger in his eyes, and she had to take a breath before she could speak. She lowered her microphone. "You should probably let me go now."

"I...cannot at this moment. We need to wait for the lights to go off."

Her lips parted, and she forced herself not to look down. Man, she wanted to look down. But her body was at least safely blocking him from the crowd. "You realize I will never ever let you live it down that you got turned on by a Dolly song."

The hand on her waist flexed. "Professor, this has nothing to do with Dolly."

The spotlights dimmed and she stepped closer, gasping when the steel length of his erection brushed against her thigh. She wet her lips. "Sha...Lucas."

"Yes."

"This whole plan about taking it slow..."

"Yeah?"

"Is really overrated."

"Epically."

They hurried down the steps on the side of the darkened stage, almost tripping over each other in their haste. Shaw pulled off the cowboy hat and tossed it on a nearby table. They were out the door in a flash. This time when they crossed the street, they didn't bother waiting for the walk signal.

chapter

SEVENTEEN

TARYN'S BACK HIT SHAW'S FRONT DOOR WITH enough force to rattle it. Now that they'd decided to do this, it was as if neither of them could tolerate one more millisecond of not touching each other. Shaw kissed the curve of her neck, his hand cradling the back of her head, as the other hand fumbled for his keys.

The hallway was empty, but the security camera tucked into the corner stared back at Taryn, silently judging her lack of decorum. Someone would get quite a show if they watched any of the footage. Right now, she couldn't find it in herself to care. She groaned as Shaw's teeth grazed her collarbone, and her nipples hardened in anticipation of him moving lower. Her fingers threaded in his hair, that thick, silky hair. She closed her eyes. "We need to get inside."

"Yes. Inside," he said between kisses. "Inside is good."

He finally got hold of the key and jammed it into the lock next to her hip. The door released behind her, making her stumble backward, but he banded an arm around her, keeping her upright. Once they'd crossed the threshold, Shaw kicked the door shut behind them. The apartment was cool and dark, but Taryn's skin was burning all over. Never before had she felt so desperate to get naked with someone. It felt like end-of-the-world urgency. Like this was the last sex she'd ever get to have, and the clock was ticking. Aliens were descending. Killer viruses had been released. *Go! Go! Go!*

"Shaw," she panted, the plea in her voice borderline embarrassing.

"Light. We need light. I want to see you," he said, breaking away briefly. He hit some switches, making the lamps come on. Her chest heaved with urgent breaths as her eyes adjusted to the sudden light. When he turned back to her, the need on his face made every female part of her light up and report for duty. His gaze tracked over her without shame. "God, you're gorgeous."

She smiled, basking in that look of pure want he was sending her way. "Back at you, cowboy."

He laughed and gathered her to him. "Now, *that* is something I've definitely never been called."

He slid his hands down to her backside, pulling her against him, letting her feel the hard heat of him and how much he wanted her. Her inner muscles tightened, aching. But Shaw didn't go back to kissing her. His gaze searched her eyes. "Tell me you want this. Tell me I'm not rushing you. Tell me you're not drunk."

"Want it. Not rushing. Not drunk. Have wanted this since I met you."

"But now you know who I am. I need to know you're really okay with this," he said, holding her close. "Tell me you're okay, Taryn. When you wake up tomorrow, it's going to be with me. Not Lucas. Not your trainer. Not a random date. Me."

She cupped his jaw, the words pinging through her. "I know. I'm okay. I want this, and I want you."

He closed his eyes and released a breath. "Thank God."

With that, he slid his hands to her waist and pulled her sweater over her head. When he looked down at her lace-edged bra, he made a guttural sound deep in his throat. "Fuck. Look at you. I want to taste every sweet part of you and then go back for seconds."

He cupped her through her bra, drawing a thumb over the sensitive bud, and she let her forehead fall to his shoulder as sensation raced over her skin. "I'm not that sweet."

He laughed as his hand slid beneath her bra strap and lowered it down her shoulder. "Good. I like that about you." He reached around and unhooked her bra, the cool air kissing her skin. "I like a whole lot of things about you, professor."

The words wound through her as he walked her deeper into the living room and guided her onto the couch. The leather was cool against her body, her internal furnace dialed to max. He lowered to his knees on the floor beside her. His head dipped down, his tongue tracing over her sensitive nipple, making it tight and achy. The move was simple, but the sensations were so decadent that it was like unlocking a door she hadn't known she'd sealed. Her neck arched, and she let out an embarrassing shriek.

She closed her eyes, suddenly self-conscious of the noise. All that shrieking and yelling was only supposed to happen in movie sex, not real life. And all he'd done was put his mouth on her. "Sorry. It's been a while. I'm…wound up."

"Shh. Don't you dare apologize, baby." He kissed her breast with featherlight touches, his hand following the tracks. "You have no idea what hearing you does to me."

Baby. The endearment made her warm inside because she could tell it'd just slipped out. He wasn't being so careful with his words anymore. Her eyes stayed closed as he traced a hand up her ribs and palmed her other breast. "Tell me what it does to you."

She wanted to hear. She needed to know.

He shifted and took her wrist in his hand. He guided her palm down and pressed it against him, letting her feel the steely length of his cock behind the fly of his jeans. "It makes me crazy for you. It makes me want to hear you lose it completely. It makes me *so fucking hard*."

The word *hard* had never sounded quite so illicit, and it sent a rush of liquid heat straight downward. She let her hand map his erection, stroking him just enough to make him grunt. He eased her hand away. "Easy, professor. You said it's been a while for you. Last time I was doing this, dinosaurs roamed the earth."

She snorted and opened her eyes. He was smiling down at her, a flush high on his cheeks. She traced her hands up his chest, taking his shirt with her. He helped her pull the shirt over his head and then tossed it toward the coffee table, giving her an eyeful of that body she'd been drooling over since the day she'd met him. Her tongue ran over her teeth as she let her fingers explore his bare skin. "I'll go easy on you."

"Don't. We have all night." He dragged his fingertips down her sternum, making her shiver. "The first time will be like the bread we had on the table tonight." He leaned down to kiss her. "Delicious but just the appetizer."

He shifted down her body and removed her boots and socks. Then his hands were gliding up her thighs, his thumbs brushing precariously close to where she ached the most. She arched her hips and moaned, no longer worried about the sounds she made. He unfastened her jeans.

He peeled them off as though he were opening a present he wanted to savor. After he tossed them aside, she was left naked except for her simple black panties. Kneeling between her legs, he stared at her with a look of delicious intent. He traced the edge of her panties, making goose bumps race over her skin. Self-consciousness tried to edge in again. Normally, she felt pretty comfortable with her body, but this Olympic athlete thing was messing with her head.

Her body wasn't perfectly honed like his or the women he'd see walking through his gym. She had curves and swells. She was soft in places meant to be hard. But when she looked up at Shaw's face and saw the rapture there, all the ugly, useless thoughts scattered like scared mice. He hadn't been lying to her out on the street.

"You are so goddamned sexy, it's making me hurt," he said, an actual look of pain on his face. His hand tracked over her and slipped inside her panties, finding the wet, tender place that was pulsing with her heartbeat. She gasped. He groaned. "Fuck, baby. I apologize in advance. I'm going to break land-speed records when I get inside you."

She laughed, a hot tremor moving through her. "We've got all night, remember?"

Dark satisfaction crossed his face. "Yes. Yes, we do."

He yanked down her panties as if they were now offending him, and he shifted further down the couch.

He pressed his hands to the back of her thighs, opening her like a book, leaving her as exposed as one could be. Before she could process what was about to happen, he leaned down and kissed the very center of her with his hot, wet tongue. Her eyes tried to roll right out of her head. She gripped his hair, afraid she might just levitate off the couch, and he grazed her clit. Electricity shot up her spine and fanned out to all her best parts, tightening everything in its wake. She let out a choked sound. "Oh God."

He made a satisfied noise, the vibration of it moving along her skin like a mini-earthquake as he continued to taste her, sucking and licking and kissing, his tongue far more skilled than that of any lover she'd had before. Her feet flexed, her muscles tensing involuntarily as the pure, sharp pleasure moved through her. She cried out—too loud for an apartment.

But that revved up Shaw more. "Yes, baby, let me hear you. Let me hear you come for me."

"Too loud," she gasped. "Neighbors."

"Don't care," he said, easing a thick, callused finger inside her and making dots of light appear behind her eyelids. "I don't care if Rivers hears you upstairs. I don't care about anything right now besides making you feel good."

He put his mouth back on her, sensation enveloping her, drowning her. His name came out as a prayer. "*Shaw*."

He eased another finger inside, slowly and skillfully stroking her until he found the place she craved. Her mind went blank. Thoughts gone. Her fingers curled into his hair, gripping so tightly that she was afraid she'd leave him with a bald spot. But she couldn't stop. She had to hold on to something because it felt like she was about to break apart into a million pieces, just shatter into dust on his couch.

Then the rush rolled through her like a thunderclap, sharp and breath-stealing and nothing like the orgasms she gave herself. There was nothing quick and to the point about this. She screamed, literally *screamed*, and couldn't find it in her to give a damn that she was being too loud or too much or too whatever. A sound rumbled through Shaw, and his grip on her thighs tightened, letting her know he was getting off on it, her abandon, and that just set her off more.

When she collapsed back into the couch pillows, gasping and sweating, her mind in a blender, he finally eased away and lifted his head. He looked like a devil, his now-messy hair hanging in his face and curling at the ends, his eyes burning with sordid intentions, and his lips slick and swollen. He braced himself over her body and looked down at her as if he were going to devour her bite by scrumptious bite.

She reached up and grabbed him around the neck, pulling him down to kiss her. He tensed in surprise at first and then sank into the kiss, climbing fully over her and pressing his still-clothed bottom half to her nakedness. She dragged her fingers up the nape of his neck and into his hair, gripping the locks and holding on.

"Need you," he said between kisses. "Now."

"Yes." She kissed him back, writhing beneath him, urgency pulsing through her.

"Shit," he groaned and pulled back. "Protection. I didn't—"

She quickly pressed her fingers over his mouth. "Condom. In my purse."

Relief descended over his features. "Bless you. Because I don't know where the hell mine are. And they might've dry-rotted."

She laughed, silly with pleasure. "I was a Girl Scout. Taught me two things. You can never have too many cookies. And always be prepared."

He grinned. "Of course you were a Girl Scout."

She shoved his shoulder playfully. "What is that supposed to mean?"

"Nothing bad." He bent and kissed her again. "Always trying to make the world a better place. The do-gooder, my warrior princess. Be right back."

She watched him as he headed toward the front door where she'd dropped her purse somewhere along the way. The do-gooder. She didn't know how to feel about that opinion, but she was too lust-drunk to dissect it. Plus, Shaw shirtless and heading back her way with a condom was far too distracting for her to think straight.

Shaw returned with lightning-quick speed, and she plucked the foil packet from his fingers. "Take off your jeans. I'll take care of this."

He smirked and unbuttoned his jeans. "I can put it on. I haven't forgotten *that* much."

"I know," she said, reaching out for him. "But give a girl one of her dirty fantasies."

His gaze went hooded. "You've had fantasies about rolling a condom on me?"

But she couldn't answer because at that very moment, he shoved his pants and underwear down, leaving her with a view that had her body revving like a muscle-car engine. *Hot damn*. Shaw's body was enough of a wonder that she wanted to stare at all the things, but following the v-shape of his pelvis and finding herself with an unencumbered view of his cock, hard and thick in his hand, was enough for her to lose her power of speech for a second.

The tip was glistening, and she wet her lips as he stepped closer. Shaw rubbed his thumb along the head, almost an absentminded move, as if this was how he touched himself in private. That image struck Taryn as unbearably erotic. After all these years without a woman, Shaw had probably become quite an expert at giving himself pleasure. She could imagine him in the shower, fist around himself, muscles straining as he stroked his cock and fantasized. Had he thought about her in the past two weeks when he did it? The image was almost too much for her to take. She reached for his hand and brought it to her mouth, sucking the salty fluid off his thumb and looking up at him.

He groaned, the muscles in his jaw flexing with restraint. "Taryn. Please…"

She knew he was asking for the condom, knew he was already on the brink, but she couldn't help herself. She scooted to the edge of the couch, and instead of rolling on the condom, she set it aside and took off her glasses. She could feel Shaw watching her, sense the tension rolling off him. She reached out and wrapped her hand around his erection.

He let out a long, hissing breath but didn't move away. His fingers flexed at his sides. A man on the verge. She loved it—all that leashed need pulsing between them. She wanted him to feel as good as he'd made her feel. So she did what she'd only done a few times in her life, always as a favor to the guy. This time, it wasn't about favors. She craved him, his taste, his desire. She put her lips over the head of his cock and took him into her mouth.

Shaw made a strangled sound, and his hands went to her hair, his fingers pressing against her scalp. "*Taryn*."

She closed her eyes, waiting for him to tell her to stop, that it was too much. When he didn't, she took her fill, sliding her mouth and tongue along his length, tasting his heat, the salt of him, the velvet skin. Rolling the condom on hadn't been her fantasy. This was. Making this strong, beautiful man weak in the knees. Giving him pleasure, feeling her own feminine power.

"Baby." His voice was cracked, ragged. "Won't last like this. Too…good."

She heard the ache in his voice, the warning. He was trying so hard to not be that guy who couldn't hold it together, but she loved that he was so undone, loved hearing the strained sounds he was making. He'd waited a long time for some pleasure. They had all night for more.

She slid her hands up his thighs, massaging, as she gave herself over to the art of making him feel every bit of her tongue and lips, providing pressure and easing back, teasing and torturing. But when she trailed her hand higher and cupped his balls, letting her nails gently track over the delicate skin there, a hard tremor rumbled through him. His grip went punishing against her head, and the gritty sound he made rivaled her own level of noise. He moaned her name and then he was lost to her, his body pulsing and filling her, letting her have every last drop of him.

When he finally released his grip, she collapsed back onto the couch, her own heart pounding hard. He touched her face with reverence and slid her glasses back on with care. When her vision sharpened, she caught him looking down at her in wonder. A look that made her breath stall. A man had never looked at her like that. As if she held his world in her hand. She knew not to read anything into how a guy looked at her after she gave him head, but the effect still made her blood go fizzy in her veins. Shaw dropped to his knees, parking himself between hers, and kissed her hard. Kissed like he was afraid she would dissipate and this had all been just a dream.

He pulled back, his thumbs stroking her cheeks. "You didn't have to do that."

"I'm aware." She smiled and put her hands to his shoulders. "I wanted to. Plus, we only have one condom. I couldn't have you breaking that land-speed record our first ride out. I need a little more time with you than that. It was a calculated plan to extend the pleasure. Perfectly executed, I might add."

He blinked, and then he laughed big and loud. "I always knew I liked smart women."

"That wasn't about being smart. This is about being greedy."

He kissed her again. "I like greedy even more. Or maybe I just like *you*."

The simple words warmed her.

This could get complicated. This could get messy. He made her feel greedy for more than sex. But right now, those words were what she had to focus on. They liked each other. They were now friends who kissed. That would have to be enough.

Because that was all this could be.

She smiled up at him. "Take me to bed, Shaw."

chapter
EIGHTEEN

SHAW'S HEARTBEAT WAS STILL THUMPING HARD IN his ears as he led Taryn into his bedroom. They'd gone from zero to a hundred since walking through the door, and he hoped their night would continue, but he could tell the second Taryn walked into his room that something had shifted in her. Her brow was slightly furrowed, and she was biting her lip. The buzz of her orgasm had worn off and now she was thinking, thinking, thinking.

On instinct, he walked over to his dresser and pulled out one of his T-shirts. He held it out to her. "It's a little cold in here. Wanna borrow this while we take a little breather?"

She gave him a grateful look and smiled, some of the pensiveness leaving her face. "Thanks."

He grabbed a soft pair of sweatpants for himself and watched Taryn tug his old T-shirt over her naked body. Something about seeing her there in his bedroom, bare-legged, mussed from orgasm, and wearing his clothes made him want to freeze-frame the moment. Hold it in his vision longer than time would allow. How had he gotten here? He still wasn't convinced he wouldn't wake up from a dream soon.

Taryn glanced up from beneath her lashes, catching him staring. She smiled, and he was happy to see the flirtatious glint back in her eye. "Guess Rivers didn't hear us. No knock on the door wondering if someone was injured."

Shaw chuckled and took her hand, leading her to his bed. "No. I doubt he's even home. He told me he was going out tonight." He folded back the covers, and she slipped beneath. "But I wouldn't care if we disturbed him. We were college roommates. I had to listen to his nighttime escapades more than any friend should. He owes me a few."

She laughed as Shaw climbed into bed next to her. "He'd bring dates over with you in the same room?"

"Nah, not that bad. Athletes got the good dorms. We had a suite that had two small bedrooms and a shared living room. But the walls were thin, and apparently Rivers is a rock star in bed."

"Ha." She rolled onto her side and propped her head up on her hand, an amused expression on her face. "That must've been awkward. My college roommate just listened to a lot of death metal without headphones and always reeked of pot. I thought that was bad enough."

Shaw settled back on his pillows, liking the feel of her warmth next to him. "Nah, it wasn't a big deal. It became sort of a joke between us. I think at first he was testing me."

"Testing you?"

He frowned. "Yeah, making sure I wasn't lying about not caring that he was gay. He'd had a shitty roommate situation before me. Guy who wanted the nice suite but turned out to be a serious homophobic douche bag."

Her nose wrinkled. "Ugh."

"So yeah, probably testing me at first, but he eventually opened up to me when he realized he could trust me. He'd had a rough go before college. Had come from a small town and was closeted during high school. He was a swimmer, so a student athlete, and all the locker-room situations that go along with that made him feel like he had to hide who he was. He couldn't be himself." Shaw looked over at her. "So I figured he'd earned some loud, don't-have-to-hide-it sex, you know?"

Taryn's eyes went soft. "You're good friends to each other. He was very protective of you tonight. He really didn't want to let me in. Made me work pretty hard for it."

Something tightened in Shaw's chest. "He's the best person I know. No one else stood by me when everything happened. My family didn't rally together. We fell apart. My so-called friends abandoned me like I was contagious. But Rivers never flinched. He was there for me in a way that probably saved my life. I'm not sure what I would've done if I'd been left alone during all of that and what followed."

Taryn frowned and reached out to put her hand on his chest. "It's everything to have a friend like that."

Shaw blew out a breath and lifted his arm to gather her in. She settled into the crook of his arm, her hair tickling his chin. He traced his fingers along her arm. "It is. Seems like you have a few of those, too."

He could feel her smile against him. "I do. Now."

"Now?" he asked.

"Yeah. The four of us lost touch for over a decade.

I think we all needed space away from everything that had happened. Well, they did. I never left Long Acre, so I didn't get space. But Liv, Rebecca, and Kincaid were there for me right after the shooting when I needed it most. And I think the universe brought us back together now because we were all feeling a little lost in the world. We're compasses for one another."

Shaw stared up at the ceiling, her words falling over him like cold rain. He didn't want to imagine Taryn and her friends running for their lives, his brother turning a gun on them. He didn't want to picture what she'd been through in losing her sister. He swallowed past the burning in his throat. "How are you lost?"

She exhaled slowly. "I don't know. I didn't think I was. We all wrote time capsule letters that summer after Long Acre. We dug them back up and read them when we got together for the documentary. My friends all had things in those letters they hadn't done, paths they hadn't followed, action plans they could use to improve how they were feeling now. Like Liv changing her career. And Rebecca leaving divorce law and focusing on at-risk youth. But mine...I'd pretty much stuck to what I'd planned. Be a researcher. Find answers. Make it better."

"But?" he asked when she didn't continue.

"But have I really? I haven't made any difference at all yet. And I feel like I've been in this holding pattern. Like I put my life up on a shelf so I could get this other stuff done first. I need to get what I set out to do done, but"—she nuzzled closer—"I shouldn't be in my thirties and in the hospital with chest pains. I shouldn't have a guy think that I'd sleep with him just to get a charity event locked down."

He grimaced. "Taryn, I didn't—"

"No, why wouldn't you think that? I'm the do-gooder, like you said. The mission first, always. At all costs."

"That's not a bug, though. That's a feature. It's an amazing thing about you, your dedication," he said gently. "That's not something to be ashamed of."

She propped herself up on his chest to look at him. "I'm not ashamed. I'm just, I don't know, mad."

His brows lifted. "Mad?"

"Yes. Mad that I've let my life become so narrow. Mad that I shrieked so loudly out there because..." She glanced away.

He put a finger below her chin and drew her gaze back to him. "Because why?"

She rubbed her lips together. "Because I've been with so few guys that I didn't even know it could feel like that, not just physically, but that I could want and be wanted that way. That I could feel that level of desire. I thought that just happened in books or movies. I shouldn't be thirty-one and not have felt those things."

He pushed her hair away from her face. "You're right. That is a travesty." And it was. He couldn't imagine a woman with this much passion never having let it run free. "But that's not your fault. You can't help it if those other guys weren't as awesome in bed as I am."

She snort-laughed and he smiled, happy to see his joke take away the melancholy look on her face. She shook her head. "You're ridiculous."

"I know. But seriously, don't be so hard on yourself. You're still young. You've got time to do all those things you want. Launching your program. Changing the world. Getting really, really hot sex and loud orgasms with me. And I bet I can even last at least three minutes now."

She laughed again, and he wanted to bottle the sound and keep it in his closet for when she was gone and he had bad days. "You better not be making promises you can't keep, mister."

He pulled her all the way on top of him. "Well, you're a researcher, so you must know there's only one way to find out."

Her lips curved as she straddled him, T-shirt bunched up around her hips. "Of course. Run lots and lots of trials."

Shaw stared up at her, the lamplight making the edges of her hair glow like a halo. In that moment, he could believe it really was one. This woman had earned her wings, but he could hear it in her words and see it on her face. The do-gooder warrior needed a damn break from her life. She needed to be selfish, to feel good, to have fun. He couldn't give her much, but he could give her that.

In fact, he'd never wanted to give anyone anything more.

He reached for her T-shirt and lifted it up and off, taking his fill of the view. Lush curves and a sexy smile. He'd never seen anyone more beautiful in his life. He let his fingertips track over her body, watching the goose bumps rise on her skin in his wake, her nipples going tight, her breath quickening. She was so very hungry—like him. Starved for touch. Starved for pleasure. Starved for a few moments where they didn't have to be anything but in their own skin. He wanted to feed them both, gorge on everything they were offering each other tonight.

He moved his hands down her body, his thumb finding the swollen, slick nub between her thighs. He'd grown hard the moment she'd straddled him, but at the sound she made, his body revved like he hadn't just had an orgasm a little while ago. "Those other guys must've had no clue what they were doing. You're so sensitive and responsive. It's beyond hot."

She splayed her hands on his chest, leaning forward and smiling. "Those other guys weren't you."

The words hit him in a way that took his breath for a second. She'd probably meant that she was simply more physically attracted to him, but something inside him unfurled. She wanted *him*. He wasn't sure he'd ever had that. In college, girls wanted the popular, on-his-way-to-the-Olympics athlete. After Long Acre, Deidra, his girlfriend, had liked the drama and infamy of his background, how the press still followed him. That seemed exciting to her—until it didn't anymore. But Taryn had no angle. If anything, she should want nothing to do with him. Still, she hadn't been able to stay away, even knowing it was the best thing. She wanted him badly enough to be with him despite their shared horrible history. She knew him and was still here.

She doesn't know everything.

Taryn draped her body over him. "Ready for trial number one?"

He pushed the ugly thought away and smiled up at the woman above him. "I'm ready for you."

―∽∾―

I'm ready for you.

The words wound around Taryn, wrapping her up in

a blanket of contentment. She'd found herself heading into a melancholy zone, lying there with him, thinking of all the things she'd missed along the way in her life. But Shaw had a knack for bringing her back, for making her laugh, and for taking her mind right back to where it needed to be. Enjoying this moment. Enjoying him. All her worries and stress could wait outside tonight.

She leaned down to kiss him, and Shaw rolled them over, putting him above her. He braced his arms beside her as she tugged down his pants. His erection sprang free, landing heavy and hot against her thigh, making tingly heat spread up her belly. So much of her wanted to just part her legs and feel him inside her, no barrier, just skin to skin, heat on heat. But she wasn't on any backup birth-control method and couldn't take the risk.

She gazed up at Shaw. "Don't like a woman on top, huh?"

His grin went sly. "Baby, I could look up at that view all damn night. Just thinking about your hips rocking and your breasts bouncing as you rode me makes me want to roll you right back over."

She wet her lips, his talk making her flush all over.

"But after what you told me, I want to make you feel every part of this. You have to trust me, though."

"Trust you?"

"Yes." His gaze tracked down her body before meeting her eyes again. "I'm a good student, professor. I paid attention when I was touching you out there. I'm learning your favorite spots. Taking notes."

The thought made her shiver. "Are you going for an A plus?"

His lips curved, dark promise there. "With extra

credit." He touched her hip. "I want you on your knees and elbows. Put a pillow under yourself if you want extra support. Your arms may give out on you."

"Elbows and knees?" she asked, feeling suddenly shy. She'd never done that position with anyone. That wasn't get-to-know-each-other sex. And she'd only had get-to-know-each-other sex with guys.

"It's not the most romantic position." His eyes flickered with heat as his erection brushed against her belly, leaving a trail of damp arousal along her skin, marking her. "But it will let me touch you. It will let me angle my cock to rub just where I rubbed you with my fingers." He leaned down, his lips against her ear and his body pressed against hers. "It will let me fuck you so good and deep that I bet I can make you scream loud enough for Rivers to hear even if he isn't home."

Her body went awash with need, and a gasp escaped her. She'd never considered whether or not she liked dirty talk. No one had really gone there with her, but she wouldn't have to run an experiment now. She had her answer. She liked it. She liked it a whole helluva lot. She swallowed hard. "I better get on my knees then."

"That's my girl," he said, a growly rumble in his voice.

My girl. She liked the sound of that, even though it wasn't true.

He lifted up so she could roll over and get settled. He tucked a pillow beneath her, and she heard the unspoken promise. *This is going to be so good you won't be able to hold yourself up.* She indulged in the mental image of him rising up behind her, cock in hand, her body spread before him like an offering. Liquid heat rushed between her legs.

Now would probably be the time to feel self-conscious. She was about to put her ass in the air, but she was too turned on to care. She wanted exactly what Shaw was offering. *A hot fuck*. The word still made her want to bite her lip like she was twelve and shouldn't be thinking such a thing. She had always thought of sex in more clinical terms, but hearing the crude words directed at her did things to her body she hadn't expected but liked.

Maybe this was what had been wrong with all her other encounters. Sex wasn't polite. Or clinical. Sex was inherently raw and crude. Naked bodies. Sweating. Begging. Urges as base and animalistic as they could get. She took a breath and settled herself in the position.

Shaw made a sound that seemed to come from somewhere deep in his chest. She peeked back over her shoulder, finding him staring down at her with a ravenous look. His gaze flicked to hers. "You gonna watch me fuck you, gorgeous?"

She gathered the boldness that was coursing through her and gave him a salacious smile. "Maybe I will."

Shaw ran his fist over his erection, keeping his eyes on her, and then rolled the condom on. "If you can keep eye contact, you win."

"And if I can't?"

He ran his hands over her hips. "You still win."

She didn't know exactly what he meant, but she watched. Watched him settle on his knees behind her, watched him take in the view, lick his lips, caress her. Felt him run his fingers over her slick flesh, sending sparks of sensation up her spine.

"You're so wet for me," he said, almost to himself. "So sexy."

Then his gaze came back to hers as he positioned himself at her entrance and pressed the head of his cock against her. He took it slow, agonizingly slow, as he slid in inch by inch, stretching her, waking up dormant nerve endings, and setting off a cascade of new sensations. A groan slipped past her lips, the feeling of the invasion like sweet torture, the slow ride up the highest peak of the roller coaster. All the while, they held eye contact— the intensity of that connection making the physical awareness more amplified. She could see the tense lines appear around his mouth, the muscles in his neck flex when he seated himself fully inside her.

He took a slow, deep breath as if talking himself into not rushing, and then he reached around her hip and slid his fingertips over the place he'd so thoroughly worshipped with his mouth earlier. A sharp breath cut through her at the blissful feel of that rough skin over her most sensitive spot, and she broke the eye contact for a moment. Feeling filled by him and then having his fingers teasing her was almost too much. She tried to breathe through the rolling sparks and find his gaze again, but then he started to move. Pumping into her slowly at first and then grabbing her hip with more purpose and angling deeper, rubbing across that electric place inside her. All hope of looking at him went down in flames. She moaned and her face planted into the bed, her elbows already quivering.

"That's it, baby." His voice was almost soothing, but it was edged with sharp, male determination. "You feel so damn good. I can feel you gripping me every time I go deep." He angled again and every part of her body clenched. "Yes. Right there. Take what you need, gorgeous. Use me."

She couldn't hold back then. She rocked her body toward him, helping him get to that secret place that felt like heaven wrapped in lightning dipped in *oh my God*. Over and over just where she needed, his fingers still working her like magic. Her sounds got louder, and her fingers gripped the comforter as if it were a lifeline. He went faster, his movements sure and confident, but she could feel him unraveling along with her, could hear the hitch in his breath. How long had it been for him?

Right now, it didn't matter because the man sure as hell knew what he was doing. Sex had never felt like this for her. Ever. Not even close. He'd paid attention to her. Taken mental notes. Was figuring out exactly what made her lose it. He didn't just want her. He wanted to please her, to make it amazing for her. To make it perfect. For some reason, that made her want to cry.

But she didn't have time for tears. Shaw got more urgent, his hips slapping her backside and making the most delicious, erotic skin-to-skin sound. His grunts became louder, feral. Her inner muscles flexed, her nerve endings alive with every beautiful sensation the female body was capable of. It felt like a wonder. Like a gift.

Her breaths became loud and sharp, the bed squeaking beneath them with the force of their joining. Rough. Desperate. Perfect. Her arms collapsed beneath her, putting her at a more severe angle, surrendering to all of it. And that was when it happened. His cock rubbed against her inner wall at the same time his fingers touched just the right spot. Fireworks exploded through her system, wrecking her.

She cried out with a scream that made the one on the couch sound like a whisper, and her body jerked with the force of the orgasm. Her fingers flexed in the sheets and her muscles spasmed as if the energy had to escape but had nowhere to go, so it just kept looping through her, sending hard waves of pleasure through her again and again. Shaw was cursing and groaning and finally lost the fight to hold off. He buried himself deep, holding her against him, and cried out with guttural relief as he came loud and long.

The neighbors were probably calling nine-one-one.

She didn't care.

There *was* a fire. *She* was on fire.

But she wasn't going to let anyone come in and put it out. *Burn, baby, burn.*

Shaw collapsed on top of her, bracing his weight with one arm, but his face buried in her hair. His heart beat hard against her back, and she pressed her cheek to the sheets. Her glasses had fallen off at some point, so everything was a little blurry, but she had a feeling that even if she had her glasses on, her vision would be cloudy.

Shaw let out a long, satisfied breath. "I win."

She laughed beneath him. "Oh, no. I think I really, *really* won. Someone needs to bring in a trophy."

He made a happy grunting sound, his chest still rising and falling with panted breaths. "Let's call it a tie. We'll definitely need a rematch."

"Definitely." She felt as though she were spreading out and melting into the bed, her muscles made of warm honey. "But maybe not tonight. I'm not sure I'll ever be able to move again."

He laughed. "Ditto. Hope you like me because I think we're stuck like this in this bed forever now. We'll have to have food delivered."

"I—"

A loud knock sounded from the living room, startling them both.

"Uh-oh," Taryn said, trying not to laugh. "May have bothered the roommate after all."

Another pounding knock.

"Shit," Shaw said, pulling out and rolling away from her as if she'd burned him. "Give me a second," he called out, but she couldn't imagine anyone outside could hear him from all the way in here. "Get some clothes on, baby."

Taryn forced her limbs into action and flipped over lazily. Shaw disposed of the condom, his movements a little frantic as he searched for his sweatpants. She indulged in the view as he bent over and grabbed them. "I don't even know where my clothes are. It's probably just Rivers. Can't he wait?"

"No, he—"

Taryn heard the click.

"Has a key," Shaw finished.

Her eyes went wide, and she yanked the covers up to her neck. "Crap."

"One second!" he called out. "Don't come in here."

Shaw was just yanking up his sweatpants when Rivers poked his head in the bedroom. "Dude, what is—"

"Out!" Shaw demanded.

Rivers stared at Taryn like he'd never seen a woman in his life, his lips parting. "Oh shit. I… Hi."

Taryn cringed, her cheeks burning. He'd come over because she'd screamed so loud. Now he knew exactly what the noise had been. She barely resisted pulling the blanket over her head. "Um, hello."

Shaw hurried over and herded Rivers out the door. "Get the hell out of here, man. Privacy. Damn."

Poor Shaw looked so harassed and Rivers so shocked that Taryn couldn't help it. A laugh bubbled up as they exited the room. It was all so ridiculous. Was this what college sex would've been like? Nosy roommates showing up when they weren't supposed to. She had no idea. She'd barely had any sex in college.

Shaw had shut the door, but she could hear the boys talking in low, tense tones out in the living room. She should probably get dressed or be more concerned, but she couldn't find the energy to worry right now. So she just lay back in bed, too blissed out on sex to give a damn about much of anything.

She grinned up at the ceiling. Guess Shaw had finally gotten revenge on his loud roommate.

chapter
NINETEEN

"RIV, WHAT *THE FUCK*?" SHAW DEMANDED, TYING THE drawstring on his pants and glancing over his shoulder to make sure the bedroom door had shut behind him. "You can't just walk in like that. I told you to give me a sec."

Rivers stared at Shaw, his expression horrified. "I always walk in here. You woke me out of a dead sleep. I thought you were having a stroke or something."

Shaw raked a hand through his hair. "Maybe assume the 'or something' first and call me instead."

"Right. I should assume you have a woman over because *you never have anyone over ever and have sworn off sex*. So yeah, I should just assume that shit." He swept his hand toward the bedroom door. "And don't 'what the fuck' me. I'm the one who gets to say that. Dude. *What. The. Fuck?*"

Shaw flinched and motioned for Rivers to lower his voice. "Can we talk about this tomorrow? I have a guest."

"No shit. Have you lost your mind? Are you drunk? High?" Rivers looked around, noticing the discarded clothing near the couch, which apparently he'd missed when he'd first come in. He continued in a whisper-yell. "Are you aware you have Taryn in your bed? *Long Acre Taryn*. The woman you were in a panic over. The woman you moved your entire schedule to avoid."

Shaw ran a hand over his face, his head beginning to hurt. "Yes, I'm aware. You're the one who told me to get back out there and sleep with someone."

He gave Shaw an are-you-kidding-me look. "Yes. Someone. Not...not *her*. She's—"

"I know who she is, man, believe me," Shaw said grimly.

"And you don't think that's messed up? You don't think this could be a major problem?" Rivers linked his fingers behind his neck and squeezed—a stress habit he'd had since college. "I didn't want to let her in the gym tonight because I didn't want you guilted into this charity thing. I didn't want you anywhere near this type of situation. But it never crossed my mind that you'd freaking sleep with her. After all this work to keep you hidden? And what if she finds out who you are? Do you have any idea how that will make her feel?"

Shaw took a deep breath, trying to rein in the anger that wanted to lash out. "She knows."

Rivers's eyes went round. "She... *What?*"

Shaw held the eye contact. "I told you I wouldn't sleep with anyone who didn't know my real name. She knows. I told her."

Rivers lowered his head as if this information was too much to take. "Jesus Christ. All this work to get things set up here, and you're going to blow it all up before we even get started."

Shaw's jaw flexed. "She's not going to tell anyone who I am."

Rivers scoffed, his head snapping up. "Not right now, but what about when you end things? What about if you mess something up? Piss her off? What then?"

Worry tried to creep into Shaw's mind, but he shoved it down. "She's not like that. She knows this is just…a temporary thing. She's not looking for something more. She knows I'm in hiding and plan to stay that way."

Rivers shook his head, a sad look in his eyes. "Damn, brother. I know you're lonely and that this woman looks like a good solution. But this is a really bad idea."

"Riv—"

"No, I'm not trying to be a dick, but there are millions of other women in the world. You shouldn't mess with this one. It's like playing with matches while sitting on a gas tank." He sat on the back of the couch as though he was suddenly too tired to stand up. "What do you think her friends would think if they knew who you were? Her family? You think they'd be fine with her bringing you home to Sunday dinner?"

A sick feeling twisted Shaw's gut. "Of course they wouldn't. But what they don't know won't hurt them. This isn't a get-invited-to-Sunday-dinner situation. It's just…a hookup."

Even as he said the words, he felt like a Grade A asshole. This didn't feel like a hookup. Not at all.

Rivers shook his head. "A hookup is simple. A good time with a clean exit. No one gets hurt." He glanced toward the closed bedroom door. "There is nothing close to simple about what you've gotten yourself into. You said yes to the charity thing, didn't you?"

Shaw didn't answer.

"Of course you fucking did," he said with a scoff. "That's how you got her into bed."

Shaw's fists clenched. "Watch it, Riv. You ever imply again that I tricked someone into my bed, we're going to have a problem. And if you make Taryn sound like someone who would fuck me because I did her a favor, you're gonna get punched."

Rivers stared at him for a long moment and then let out a breath. "Right. I'm sorry. That was out of line, but you gotta realize this terrifies me, man." He braced his hands on the edge of the couch, his knuckles flexing. "I haven't forgotten how things were before. I worried I'd get a call one day that you were dead. Because I didn't trust that you would care enough not to drive too fast or drink too much or watch your back on a dark night."

Shaw looked down, the words like little pieces of glass in his skin. He hated that he'd made his best friend worry with those kinds of thoughts. Hated that he couldn't say those worries had been unfounded.

"I know things aren't ideal in this situation," Rivers continued. "But it's a whole lot better than what it was. I've seen glimpses of the guy I used to know. I've caught you smiling with your clients and sneaking in morning gymnastics routines. You've made jokes. Bad ones but jokes, Shaw."

Shaw smirked.

"I don't want this to blow that up. One bad move, and she's going to tell someone who you are. Or she'll slip up by accident. Everything we've worked for here will be gone." Rivers snapped his fingers. "Like that."

The last words punched Shaw right in the gut.

Everything we've worked for. Meaning he'd ruin Rivers's dream in the process. If word got out about who Shaw was and that he was part owner, no one would want to spend their money there. It'd be over.

Shaw could handle a lot, but he couldn't bear the thought of taking Rivers down with him. He nodded. "I won't let that happen. I've got this handled."

Rivers gave him a pointed look but finally a nod of acquiescence. "Fine. I'm not going to tell you how to live your life."

Shaw snorted. "Right. You would never ever do such a thing."

"Never." A quirk of a smile played at the corners of Rivers's mouth. "Just be careful. Please."

Shaw put a hand on Riv's shoulder and gave it a squeeze. "I will. Thanks for trying to save me from a stroke...and for everything. But right now, it's time to get the hell out."

"Your hospitality skills are sorely lacking."

Shaw flipped him off.

Rivers pushed to his feet and let Shaw lead him to the door, but a real smile finally broke out on his friend's face when he turned to face Shaw. "And may I just say...dude."

"What?" Shaw asked.

"You are fucking *loud*. Tell that woman to ball gag you if y'all are going to have round two. A guy needs his beauty rest."

Shaw laughed. "Don't even give me that shit, McGowan. Let's not forget I was around for your kinky experimentation phase junior year. I've heard things I cannot unhear, *Daddy*."

Rivers bit his lip at that, a slight tinge of pink chasing up his neck. "Yeah. Okay. We're even."

"Not even close. But I assure you a quiet night for the rest of the evening."

Rivers stepped out into the hall. "Tell Taryn I'm sorry for barging in. It just never crossed my mind that you'd have a woman in there."

"Will do. Good night." Shaw shut the door on his best friend and then leaned against it, his heart beating too fast and Rivers's words chasing around in his head like angry dogs.

This *was* a bad idea. Shaw knew it. Had known it going in. Knew it now.

He opened his eyes and looked to his bedroom door, imagining Taryn in there, sleepy and soft and tucked under his sheets.

He knew it. Right now, he didn't care.

Being with her felt good. It'd been a long, long time since he could say that about anything. He pushed away from the door, turned out the lights, and headed back to the bedroom.

—⁂—

The sound of the door woke Taryn from her dozing. She turned her head, sleep making her thoughts slow. Shaw's expression was unreadable when he slipped back inside. "Sorry, didn't mean to wake you."

"S'okay." She sat up, dragging the blanket up with her to cover her breasts. "Everything all right?"

Shaw ran a hand over the back of his head, making

his messy hair messier, tension wafting off him. "Yeah. Riv said to tell you he's sorry for bursting in here. He's not used to worrying about me having…company."

"It's fine. A little embarrassing but no major harm done. We're all grown-ups."

Shaw walked over to the side of the bed and stared down at her, hands in the pockets of his sweatpants, expression pensive.

She suddenly felt like Baby Bear being found in a bed she wasn't supposed to be sleeping in. This was a first date. Yes, they'd had sex, but sleeping over was a whole other thing. She'd never actually slept at a guy's place before. "Um, I better get going. It's late."

Shaw's face shifted into one of displeasure. "It's the middle of the night. Your car is at the gym."

"I can take an Uber back to it."

"The hell you can." He sat on the edge of the bed beside her. "If you want to leave, I'll drive you." He put his hand on her knee on top of the blanket. "Do you want to leave?"

She sat up taller, the question feeling loaded. "We agreed to keep this casual."

"Right, but casual is whatever we decide we want it to be. I'm tired. You're tired. I don't want you driving all the way to Long Acre this late. It makes more sense for you to stay. But if sleeping here with me tonight feels like too much, I can crash on the couch."

She put her hand over her face and shook her head, smiling. "We sound ridiculous. Sleep on the couch? You were just inside my actual body a little while ago."

"I'm very aware of that. Acutely aware, actually."

"I'm naked right now."

"Yep. Very aware on that count, too." She could hear the amusement in his voice.

She looked up at him. "Here I am, worrying that sharing a bed with you tonight might be crossing a line, and you're sitting there offering to sleep on the couch in your own place. What is that?"

"What do you mean?" he asked.

"I just don't understand why everyone puts these labels on everything. It makes it more complicated than it needs to be. A kiss on the mouth means this. Sleeping over means that. Your penis was *in my mouth*, Shaw."

His eyelids went half-mast. "Keep reminding me, professor, and neither of us may be getting any sleep at all."

She smirked. "All I'm saying is that I shouldn't feel weird sleeping beside you tonight, right? We should get some rest…next to each other…in the same bed. And not make a thing of it."

He leaned over and cupped her cheek. "There is no thing to be made. I want you to sleep here. You want to stay. End of story. I'm going to take a shower, if you want to join me in there, and I'll dig out a spare toothbrush because it's not gentlemanly to leave a lady with penis breath."

She laughed and touched her fingers to her lips. "I have no such thing."

"Better let me double-check." He caught her wrist, dragging her close to kiss her. The kiss was one that didn't ask for more, just a simple, sweet I'm-glad-you're-here kiss. All her worries softened around the edges.

This didn't have to be a big deal. They'd just be sleeping.

After a little naked time in the shower.

No. Big. Thing.

chapter

TWENTY

EARLY THE NEXT MORNING, TARYN BLINKED IN THE golden light peeking through the blinds and, for a moment, didn't know where she was. A shot of disoriented panic went through her, but when she heard soft snoring next to her and felt the heat of the man behind her, her mind came back online, the night replaying in quick, colorful highlights. *Shaw. Singing. Sex. Shower. Sleeping.*

She relaxed back into the pillow, relishing the soft bed and cozy warmth of having Shaw next to her. The pillow smelled of him, whatever shampoo or deodorant he used—masculine and fresh. It was the scent that had perfumed the steamy air of the shower last night when they'd touched and kissed and soaped each other until the water ran cool. She had a silly urge to bury her face in the pillow and inhale. She squinted at the clock on the bedside table to check the time, her vision blurry without her glasses. She didn't have anywhere to be this morning—her usual Friday class had been taken over by another professor— which felt strange, but also a little decadent.

Shaw must've felt her movement because he reached out with that long arm of his and gathered her against him. "Not time yet," he mumbled into her neck. "Early."

She snuggled into him, letting his body spoon around her. He'd ditched the sweatpants for a pair of soft boxer shorts, and she was still wearing his T-shirt, but there was nothing else between them. Just sleep-warm skin and soft breaths. Her backside was pressed up against his crotch, and she felt the firmness there, the morning or her presence arousing him. But it wasn't an urgent nudge or an invitation. He nestled her closer like he just enjoyed feeling her against him.

So this was what she'd been missing out on those times she'd left a guy's house or sent one home from hers after sex. Maybe this was why people put labels on things. In a lot of ways, this felt so much more intimate than when they'd had sex last night. Now she knew what he wore to bed. What he smelled like after a shower. What brand of toothpaste he used. That he liked to cuddle and sleep late. He now knew that she wrapped her hair in a silk scarf at night to save her curls from becoming a flattened-out disaster. He knew she needed two pillows or she'd never fall asleep. She'd learned that he snored and liked to keep a hand on her while he slept, never completely disconnecting.

She knew she was the only woman who'd slept in this bed.

And was the only one who knew his real name.

That thought sent a ripple of anxiety through her, making her belly dip. That felt like a lot of pressure. On one hand, she could feel special. He wasn't inviting anyone else to his bed. On the other hand, was he so interested in her because she was the only woman who was an actual possibility right now? If he was able to live openly as himself and not Lucas, would she factor in so high on his radar? She'd basically propositioned the guy. What if it was a "yeah, this one will do" situation?

Ugh. Second-guessing was the worst, but her brain was prone to analyzing things to death, a researcher's cross to bear. Maybe she shouldn't have slept over. Maybe they should make some rules. Maybe they'd moved too fast too soon. Maybe…

Soft lips pressed against her shoulder, yanking her from her panicky thoughts. "You smell good," he mumbled.

She smirked. "I smell like you."

"Mmm." His hand traced over her thigh with feather-light touches. "That's the best way to smell. Means I got to rub all over you."

"Ha. Like a dog marking his territory?" she teased.

His hand cupped her behind the knee, bending her leg so he could fit his knee behind hers, bringing her in even better contact with his hardening erection. "You're not territory, but marking you with my scent? I'm not going to lie. That's kind of hot."

She laughed, but the sound caught halfway in her throat because his fingers slid down and touched the increasingly aware spot between her legs. He groaned when he discovered her warm and slick.

"You are so damn sexy," he said against her ear as he expertly teased her with lazy strokes, making her fingers dig into her pillow. "Thanks for staying. It's a helluva way to wake up."

"Yeah?"

"Yeah. I'm glad you're here."

With those words, the anxieties she'd awoken with melted away. *I'm glad you're here.* Maybe she shouldn't pick everything apart so much. Maybe she should try simple for once, accepting things at face value. They enjoyed each other. He'd wanted her to stay. She'd wanted to stay. Now they could have a little more time to indulge.

He rocked against her slowly, rubbing his cock against her, only the thin layer of his boxers between them as he used his fingers to drive her to the brink and then easing her back before she could go over. Up and down. Back and forth. Tiptoeing on the edge. She was writhing against him by a few minutes in, desperate for more of him.

"Shaw, please…"

"Please what?" he asked, his voice full of gravel, his own arousal evident.

"I want you. Now." But then a mood-killing thought hit her. "Hell."

"What?"

"No condoms."

He groaned. "I am such a stupid, stupid man."

"Where are the ones you had? We could check the expiration date. I think they have pretty long lives."

He moved his hand away from her. "The drawer beside you."

Taryn pushed up on her elbow and reached over, yanking the thing open. She had to squint without her glasses but could see enough to determine what things were. There were remote controls, ink pens, extra batteries. *Come on.* She kept digging. A big, black bottle of something rolled forward. The label had bold red letters on it, easy to see even without her glasses on. Lubricant.

She couldn't help it. She snorted like a kid who'd found something naughty.

"What?" Shaw asked warily.

"Nothing." Her voice was innocent. "That's just...a lot of lube, my friend."

Shaw groaned dramatically and rolled onto his back. "Mental note: Don't ask anyone to dig through your bedside drawers. I'll just lie here in my humiliation now."

She laughed and peered back over her shoulder at him. "Don't worry. I've got my own secrets in my bedside drawer. Plus, now I'm picturing your really dirty alone time and am even more turned on."

He smirked and ran a hand over the erection tenting his shorts. She found it unbearably sexy, the way he handled himself, lazy and confident. "You might be watching that show live and in person in a minute if we can't find a condom."

That wasn't a totally unappealing idea. Shaw sliding his hand over his cock, getting it slick and shiny, watching her watch him give himself pleasure. *Hot.* But right now, her body was aching for him. She needed that condom. She went back to rifling through the drawer and finally found the crinkled box in the back of the drawer. *Hallelujah.* She pulled a foil square out of the half-full box and lifted it to her face to read the date. "November. We're good!"

Shaw pumped a fist in the air. "Praise the gods of prophylactics!"

She laughed and tossed the packet his way. Then they were naked again, laughing this time, playfully tussling and getting each other hotter without being in a rush. Because there was no rush. The whole morning was theirs.

She could be his. He could be hers.

For these few hours, there was no outside world.

For once, she wasn't going to overanalyze it.

"Are you *singing* to yourself?" Kincaid asked as she followed Taryn into Gym Xtreme Sunday morning.

"Hmm?" Taryn asked distractedly as she held open the door for Kincaid, Liv, and Rebecca. The scent of barbecue followed them in.

They'd decided to forgo their usual leisurely Sunday brunch so they could work on the fund-raiser. Bec had picked up a bag of breakfast barbecue tacos on the way instead.

"Singing," Kincaid repeated. "You were singing."

"Was I?" Taryn shrugged. "Guess I'm in a good mood. Friends and tacos. That inspires song."

As does spending a really hot, sexy weekend in a certain man's bed. She'd barely seen the sun since Friday night. She and Shaw had taken turns not wanting to end the date. First, it was *Let's get some breakfast* after they'd slept together Saturday morning. Then, *It's such a nice day, maybe we should take a walk in Zilker Park*. Then *Maybe we should stop by the store and pick up something to cook*. Then they'd ended up back at his place for lunch and dessert.

He'd had a few clients to train on Saturday afternoon, so Taryn had told him she'd head home when he went into work. Instead, he suggested she go home and pack a bag, and then come back so they could go out to dinner and she could stay over again. She knew it was too much. They were overdosing on each other, both starved after being solo for so long, but even knowing that, she'd found herself packing a bag and humming a tune.

She hadn't stopped singing since. She could still feel Shaw coming up behind her at the sink this morning while she brushed her teeth. He'd planted a kiss on her shoulder and then lifted his head. She'd caught his gaze in the mirror. She'd never had a guy look at her like that. Like he couldn't believe how lucky he was to have permission to touch her. The feeling was heady. Addictive.

In one weekend, she'd become a goddamned junkie for him.

Kincaid put a hand to her hip, skeptical look on full throttle. "Friends and tacos."

Taryn smiled brightly. "Yep."

"So this has nothing to do with being at the gym where the hot trainer who I caught you kissing works?" she asked.

Liv's head whipped around, her dark ponytail swinging like a weapon. "Kissing?"

"The hot trainer?" Rebecca said at the same time. "The guy who helped you at the race?"

"That's the one," Kincaid said with a knowing nod. "Full-on lip-lock at a bar."

"Oh my God," Taryn said, glancing around the lobby of the gym as a few members walked by. "Could we not do this right now?"

She'd told Kincaid after that night in the bar that nothing had happened with Shaw. Because it hadn't. Except that she'd found out he was Shaw Miller. She'd shut the conversation down cold so Kincaid would leave the topic alone, but Taryn should've known that wasn't the end of it. A scandalous kiss for Kincaid was like waving shiny ribbons in front of a cat.

Kincaid lifted her palms. "Fine. Fine."

On cue, Shaw stepped through the doorway that led to the main part of the gym. His face lit with a smile when he saw her, his hidden dimple appearing. "Taryn."

She bit her lip. He was in black workout pants and one of those sweat-wicking T-shirts that clung to everything. She got a secret thrill knowing what he looked like beneath all those clothes. She'd licked that body this morning. "Hey there."

The words came out like she should've tilted her head and twirled her hair along with them. *Lord. Get it together, girl.*

Liv looked back and forth between the two of them, eyebrows climbing upward. Kincaid made a barely there scoff just loud enough for Taryn to hear.

Taryn cleared her throat, trying to regain some semblance of professional composure. "Lucas, I'm not sure if you've officially met Liv and Rebecca. These ladies will be helping, too."

Shaw stepped forward, introducing himself as Lucas, his gaze a little wary. Taryn had warned him that her three friends were also Long Acre survivors. He hadn't been happy to discover that fact. He stepped back, his expression schooled into an unreadable mask. "We've got a table set up in the corner for y'all to work at and have your breakfast. If you have any questions about the equipment, both Rivers and I will be around. I think if you're going to have high school students compete, you may want to focus on the main obstacle course with the biggest foam pit. That one is the most fun and interesting for spectators to watch. Plus, there are a lot of modifications we can do to make it beginner friendly without looking too easy."

"And it doesn't involve that horrible Wall of Death," Taryn pointed out.

Shaw laughed, a warm sound that filled the space between them. "Taryn is not a fan of Wally. She thinks our wall has a personal vendetta against her."

Taryn crossed her arms. "It does. Let's not argue. You know I'm right."

He gave her a playful look and a wink. "Okay, professor. Whatever you say."

God, she was in so much damn trouble. He was just a guy. *A guy.* No big deal. And she was a grown-ass woman who did not get silly around men. But she felt like a schoolgirl when she was around him like this. She must be lust-drunk or something because she wanted to walk right over there and plant a kiss on those smirking lips.

"Well, let me know if y'all need anything," he said, schooling his attention back to her friends. "I'll be with clients, but I can step away for a minute if need be."

"Thanks, Lucas," Kincaid said with a little too much enthusiasm. "You've been an *enormous* help."

Shaw gave Taryn a quick look and then walked back into the gym, leaving them behind in the lobby. As soon as he was out of earshot, Kincaid turned on Taryn, eyes sparkling. "*Girrrrl.*"

"What?" Taryn said, shifting her gaze away.

"What? You slept with him," Kincaid declared, glee in her voice. "I'm so proud of you!"

"Oh my God, *Kincaid*—" Taryn started, but her friends didn't let her finish.

Liv grinned wide. "Oh, you so did. I'm sorry. It's not my business, but it was super obvious. Y'all bantered."

"No banter was had," Taryn said, hands on hips.

Liv laughed. "And he was totally giving you that *Hey, girl* look."

"He was not." Taryn could feel her face getting hot.

"Oh, he was. That was freaking adorable," Rebecca said, laughing. "And you've good taste. He seems sweet…and you know, mega, underwear-model hot."

Kincaid laughed. "Bec, I'm telling the father of your child that you're calling other men mega-hot."

Rebecca rolled her eyes, but Taryn's mouth fell open, and she whirled toward Rebecca. "Hold up, *father of your child*? Like for real?"

Rebecca chewed her lip and then broke into a grin and nodded. "For real."

"Oh my God!" Taryn put her hands to her face like a scream emoji, but she couldn't help it. Bec was *pregnant*? "How did I not know this was officially official?"

"Because you didn't answer your phone *all* weekend. I nearly died holding on to this news," Kincaid said with an eye roll. "And I was not leaving that in a message."

Taryn spread her arms out, happiness for her friend fluttering like a hummingbird in her chest, and pulled Rebecca into a hug, the bag of tacos swinging in an arc around them. "Oh, Bec, that is fantastic news. Congratulations!" Then another thought hit. She leaned back, examining her friend's face. "Wait, this is good news, right? Y'all wanted this to happen?"

Rebecca laughed, her eyes a little teary. "Yeah. I know it's fast, but we're married, we love each other, and biological clocks and all. We thought it would take a lot longer, so it was still kind of a surprise."

Yeah, biological clocks sucked. Taryn could almost hear that *tick, tick, tick* in her own head. Growing up, she'd always assumed she'd have kids, but she'd accepted a while ago that it wasn't going to be part of her journey. She was too busy to put in time to plant seeds of what could become a family. And she was way too busy to even consider attempting single parenthood. Hell, she didn't even trust herself with a pet.

Taryn gave Rebecca another hug. "I am so happy for you, girl. You'll be a fantastic momma."

"Thank you. I'm going to do my best. I'll be learning on the fly since my mom didn't stick around long enough to show me how it's done," she said wryly as Taryn released her from the hug. "But I know how it shouldn't be done. So there's that."

"You're going to be fine," Liv said, putting her arm around Rebecca's waist and giving her a side hug. "You and Wes will be amazing parents. And this kid is going to have three aunts who are going to smother him or her with love and presents and annoying advice. You're all set."

Rebecca's eyes watered. "Oh, you guys. Don't make the pregnant lady cry. I'm a disaster right now. I sobbed at a toilet paper commercial the other day."

Taryn laughed, but the word *aunt* hit her in a tender place. It was a word she never thought would apply to her now that Nia was gone, but Liv was right. These three women were her sisters in every way but blood. They were more than friends. They were family.

Taryn swiped at her eyes before tears could escape.

"All right, my sisters. Before we all completely lose it, let's get to work. Rebecca is officially not allowed on any of the equipment."

Kincaid clapped her hands together, a sunny look on her face. "What a fantastic morning. Rebecca's baking a bun with the hot chef. And Taryn is playing hide the sausage with the hot trainer."

"Girl," Taryn said on a laugh. "You are relentless."

"Am I supposed to apologize for that?" Kincaid asked. "I am invested in knowing what is making my friends so happy. Some would call that being an excellent friend."

Taryn smirked. "Fine. Let's just get this over with then. Yes. I spent the weekend at Sh...Lucas's place. It...did not suck."

All three of her friends grinned simultaneously. Three damn Cheshire cats.

"The whole weekend," Liv teased. "*Nice*."

"It was," Taryn confirmed and looked to Kincaid. "Happy? Can we get to work now?"

Kincaid let out a little celebratory squee as they walked toward the doors. "Yes. I'm happy. My matchmaking streak continues!"

Liv gave her a look. "I met Finn in high school. You did not match us."

"And I met Wes during a robbery," Rebecca said. "You had nothing to do with that."

"And technically, you didn't even introduce me to Lucas. I met him the night before the zombie race," Taryn pointed out.

Kincaid shrugged. "Details. I laid the foundation."

Taryn shook her head with amusement as she fell into

step beside Kincaid. "And who's going to find a match for you, oh Wise One?"

Kincaid's lip curled. "Sugar, there ain't no match for me. I'm like really expensive, extra-potent liquor. Best in small doses."

She said it like a joke, but Taryn caught the flash of truth in her friend's eyes, and it took her aback when she realized Kincaid actually believed that. Despite her unending interest in the love lives of her friends, she didn't have the same hope for herself? *Best in small doses*. Kincaid dated around and was a shameless flirt but never got involved in anything serious. Maybe this explained why. She thought she was too much for one guy long term.

Taryn reached out and squeezed her friend's hand. "You're worth getting drunk on, girlie. Don't let anyone make you believe any different."

Kincaid gave Taryn's hand a squeeze back but didn't say anything else, the signal clear. She wasn't going to talk about it.

Once they got settled at the table and had their breakfast, all talk of their personal lives ended and they dove into the work. For the next few hours, the four of them went over the game plan for the fund-raiser. In between his sessions, Shaw helped them design a beginner-level course that would still be interesting to watch. Despite his initial protest about getting involved, he was engaged and seemed excited when they landed on the final course structure. Rivers joined in, too, offering his engineering expertise to shift around some of the components and sketch out the course.

"I think this is gonna work," Taryn said finally, her

eyes skimming over Rivers's sketches. "I would've loved to do something like this when I was in high school. Plus, it should be fun for families and classmates to watch." Her mind was clicking through all the possibilities and potential. "Hopefully, we get a lot of interest. We have an outside chance of hitting our funding goal in one day if we can do this right."

"And the money will go to the school program?" Rivers asked, standing behind Kincaid's chair. Somehow she'd talked him into rubbing her shoulders. The woman was a sorceress. Even gay men couldn't resist a request.

"Not directly," Taryn explained. "The program is going to require a lot of money. This event will give us the seed funds to create a video campaign that we can use to promote the cause and, hopefully, garner public support and attract big donors. We'll make a short video that can easily be run as a commercial and shared on social media. We might even be able to get the documentary producer to include it with his film. We'll also have a longer version for people who want to get more in-depth information about the program and why it's important."

"Yeah, we'll need something catchy for the short one," Rebecca said. "Attention spans are short these days. Maybe we could put a song in the background. Something people will remember. I can check on the legalities of doing that."

"Or Taryn could sing something," Shaw said from behind her. "She's got an amazing voice."

"What?" Taryn turned, shooting him a look. "No, that's not…"

"No, that's a great idea," Kincaid said, leaning forward on her forearms, her business face on. "That would add a personal element to it. The only way people are going to give us money is if we effectively tug their heartstrings and make them feel something. Like what you said about dry statistics, Taryn. We need to put faces on the issue for people. A survivor singing a poignant song could be really memorable. We'd need to find the right song for you to cover."

"Or she could write one," Shaw suggested.

"Wait, you write songs, too?" Liv asked, turning her way. "That's amazing. How did we not know this about you?"

"Because I don't anymore," Taryn said, her tone clipped. "I think we're getting off track here…"

"But what if you tried?" Liv continued. "I mean, I know that's a lot to ask, but it could be amazing."

"My songwriting is not amazing. I haven't done it since I was seventeen."

"But the ability might still be there," Liv pushed. "I mean, I get the fear. When I decided to pursue photography again, it was kind of terrifying. Like, what if I wasn't good at it anymore? What if I'd lost my creative spark? But it was still there, waiting for me to get my head out of my ass and come back to it. Maybe your spark would still be there for you, too."

Taryn frowned. "Did you just tell me to get my head out of my ass, Olivia Arias?"

"Of course not," Rebecca interjected, ever the level-headed lawyer. "I think what Liv is trying to say is that it can't hurt to try. I think Kincaid's right. It could be a really effective tool. Like those ASPCA commercials with the break-your-heart photos of animals in need and that Sarah McLachlan song."

"Oh *gawd*," Kincaid groaned, collapsing back in her chair as if she were going to melt out of it. "Those are *the worst*." She dragged her fingers down her cheeks. "Tears down my face every damn time. Here, just take all of my money, ASPCA." She motioned throwing money. "All of it."

Rivers chuckled behind her. "Yep. I've totally donated. Most depressing but most effective charity commercial ever. I've heard it earned like thirty million dollars in the first two years."

Everyone turned to look at Taryn.

She was sweating in front of all the expectant gazes. Normally, she didn't mind taking on big responsibilities, doing whatever was necessary, but they had no idea what they were asking. *Write a song?* She hadn't written one note or lyric since she was seventeen. That creativity wasn't hiding. It was gunned down. "Y'all…"

"Maybe just try?" Rebecca said gently. "If it doesn't work, it doesn't work."

Taryn glanced back at Shaw, who'd remained silent after his original suggestion. He shrugged. "You don't have to do anything you don't want to do. I just know you have the voice for it."

Taryn sighed, her shoulders sagging. "Fine. I will agree to *consider it*." She lifted a finger. "*But* we need to have a solid, quickly executable backup plan for when all I come up with is 'Mary Had a Little Lamb and It Was Awesome.'"

Her friends beamed at her as if she were Oprah and

had just told them they were all getting new puppies. *You get a puppy! You get a puppy!*

Taryn shook her head, but her lips twitched with a smile. "You bitches are pushy."

Kincaid reached across the table and patted her hand. "We love you, too, sugar. Now...let's talk marketing plan for this event."

Her friends rolled on to the next topic, even though Taryn was busy having an internal hair-on-fire panic at the thought of attempting a song. Not just a song but an emotional one about the hardest thing she'd gone through in her life. *Yeah, okay, no problem. I'll just whip that right up.* She took a long sip from her water bottle and decided right there that she wasn't going to do it. She wanted to make her friends happy and for the video to be successful, but there were better ways to do it. There were amazing songs already out there. Her friends were giving her juvenile songwriting skills more credit than they deserved.

They were asking more than she was capable of.

She wasn't that person anymore. She couldn't be.

chapter
TWENTY-ONE

A FEW WEEKS LATER, SHAW SAT ON THE TOP OF WALLY, his feet hanging off the platform as Taryn faced him from the bottom. She'd been working out of an office at the gym that they were letting her use to coordinate the fund-raiser, but after work each day, she dutifully put on her workout clothes and had been tackling the obstacles with him.

She complained about it most of the time, giving him a hard time about being the most sadistic trainer ever, but he could see the look of satisfaction on her face with each notch of progress she made. This gave her relief from the intense work she was doing to coordinate so many things on her own. All that responsibility took a toll on a person, but Shaw could tell she was determined to both keep going and not to end up in the hospital again. So every night, she stopped working around five and often spent the night with him, at the gym for a little while and then back at his place for much longer.

They were developing a routine that felt oddly

domestic even though it'd only been a few weeks since the first night she'd slept over. Something about their shared history and the circumstances had made the relationship deepen at a staggering rate. There were no games, no should-I-call-her-today-or-wait-a-day bullshit. It was as if they both sensed that this relationship had a definite time limit and they were determined to eke out every drop of enjoyment while they had each other around.

He probably should've been more worried about how much time they were spending together and how easily they'd fallen into a relationship, but he couldn't help how much he enjoyed having her there every day. Everything inside him felt lighter. His life felt shockingly…normal. He had a girlfriend, even though they hadn't put names on their relationship. He laughed during the day and got to do a job he loved. Rivers got to tease him about never getting any sleep anymore because his neighbors were so loud.

With all that going on, Shaw could ignore the stuff he didn't want to think about—that he'd never gone to her place because he couldn't bear the thought of going to Long Acre, that she kept canceling dinner plans with her parents because she couldn't invite him along, and that he was putting her in a position to lie to the people she cared about most.

Those things would keep him up at night. He shoved the thoughts away and peered over the edge of the wall. "You gonna get up here, Landry, or just admire the view from down there?"

She stepped forward, giving him an unencumbered view of her cleavage, and looked up. "I think maybe I need to accept that this wall is just not for me. Maybe I'm anatomically unable to do this."

"Maybe," he said, not buying that for a minute. "Or maybe you're overthinking it."

"Overthinking it?" she asked, affronted. "What's there to overthink? It's a twelve-foot wall and I am not an elite athlete."

"Be careful. Do you want me to throw annoying inspirational quotes I found on the internet at you?" He grinned, swinging his legs and gripping the edge of the platform. "Because you sound like you need them."

"Oh Lord, please don't."

"'If you think you can't, you're right.' Henry Ford."

She flipped him the bird. "I hate you."

He pulled a serious face and put a hand over his heart. "'Believe you can and you're halfway there.' Theodore Roosevelt."

She put her hands over her ears. "La-la-la, not listening."

He laughed, his chest filling with affection for her. She looked so damn cute sending him petulant looks and singing *la-la-la* in perfect pitch.

He cupped his hands around his mouth to call out, "'You must do the thing you think you cannot do.' Eleanor Roosevelt."

"Doe, a deer," Taryn sang, getting louder and moving into *Sound of Music* territory.

He smiled and watched her as she continued the song, looking both determined and playful at the same time. He had the bizarre urge to go down there, grab her hands, and join in. Another quote came to him unbidden, one that had been on the wall in his college English class but had nothing to do with motivation. "'Beauty surrounds us, but usually we need to be walking in a garden to know it.' Rumi."

A wrinkle appeared in Taryn's brow, and she lowered her hands, her song cutting off. "What was that?"

Shaw swallowed hard, a feeling he didn't want to think about pushing at the edges of his mind. "Nothing. Just that I think you could sing the phone book and I'd want to listen."

She smiled.

"Speaking of which, how's your song coming?" he asked. "Am I going to get to hear it?"

Her smile instantly fell. "It's not. I'm not doing it."

He frowned. "Why?"

She looked up at him. "Because that's a much bigger wall than this. And I don't want to talk about it."

The words weren't angry, but they were like a gavel falling. Conversation closed. He could tell by her shift in stance that she wasn't going to open up to him about whatever was stopping her. That stung a little, reminding him what this was. A brief affair. An intense one but still one with a time limit for her because he couldn't give her what she needed. He had no doubt she meant more to him than he did to her, and he had to stay aware of that. He wasn't someone she was going to open up to fully. That was their unspoken agreement. They didn't talk about the past. They lived only in the present moment. They were living in an imaginary bubble that would eventually pop.

"All right. Enough talking. Get your ass up here, professor," he said, trying to shake the unwelcome sensations moving through him and focus on just this moment, trying to enjoy it for what it was. "I promise I'll greatly reward you later if you can reach me."

She put her hands on her hips. "Baiting me with sexual favors is just dirty pool, man."

"I never said I'd play fair."

She gave him a perturbed look, but he could tell by the way she wet her lips that he'd gotten to her. That was what they had. Chemistry. He needed to focus on that. He loved that she found him so tempting. The feeling was more than mutual. It had to be enough.

He tapped the top of the wall, beckoning her. "Come on, gorgeous. You're tough. This is just a dumb wall. You've got this."

A determined look crossed her face, and she pulled up her kneepads. "All right. Let's do this."

She backed up, keeping her eyes focused on the spot in front of her, and then got into her runner's stance. After a silent count, she shot forward.

Shaw called out words of encouragement, and then her feet hit the curve. He knew from watching so many people attempt the wall that her momentum was good. She made it four steps up and her gaze collided with his, shock there. She'd made it farther than ever. But the power behind her was fading. Without thinking, he reached down and caught her hands. She grabbed on tight, and he helped her on the last stride, pulling her up and falling back with the momentum. She landed on top of him, straddling him and panting.

He grinned up at her wide eyes. "You did it!"

She smacked his chest. "I did not. You helped. You—"

"Stop." He brought her hands to his mouth and kissed her knuckles. "You made it farther than any other woman I've seen attempt it yet. You were perfect."

"You helped," she complained. "Doesn't count."

He pushed up on his elbows, examining her frustrated

expression. "Something only counts if you do it absolutely alone?"

"Yes."

"I'm not sure that's true," he said. "Isn't making it most of the way there with a little help from others how most people find success in this world?"

She groaned. "Oh my God, are you inspirationalizing me again?"

He smiled and sat up, wrapping his arms around her. "No. But I once had a very wise woman tell me humans need other humans and that we can't do it all on our own. I'm finding the advice pretty helpful, so maybe it's something to consider."

She huffed and looped her arms around his neck. "I can't believe you're using my own words against me."

"Dirty pool is my favorite game."

She sagged in his hold and touched her forehead to his. "I never tried to write the song. I gave up before I even tried. I lied to my friends."

The words caught him off guard, the confession hitting him right in the center of his chest. He rubbed a hand down her back, afraid to spook her and have her shut him out again.

She lifted her head, her eyes searching his. "I'm afraid it's going to open up a door to stuff I can't handle."

He smoothed a stray hair away from her face. "Okay."

She frowned. "You're not supposed to say okay. You're supposed to say that I'm tough and I've done all this research and this could help and I shouldn't be such a baby about one stupid song, that I should at least try because I promised I would."

He studied her, the storm in her eyes. "Baby, all of

those things are things you think you owe other people. You don't owe anyone a damn thing. Not the world. Not your friends. Not your parents. You've given so much of yourself already, even when there was no debt to be paid in the first place."

"But you suggested the song. You're the one—"

"I suggested the song *for you*. Because I've listened to you sing, and I've heard you talk about your songwriting dreams. I've seen your face when you get lost in a song. I saw it the other night when we were getting ready for bed. I don't even think you realized you were singing, but you were transformed for those few minutes…like the world was lifted off your shoulders and you were free of it. It was a beautiful thing to watch."

"Shaw…" she said softly, her eyes getting shiny.

"I never meant to put any pressure on you. I thought maybe you'd want to write a song because it would give you a chance to take back a part of you that was stolen," he said. "I would never want you to do it for any other reason. So if your heart isn't in it or you think it will hurt you, please don't do it."

She blinked and lifted her hands to cup his jaw. "You… You're a beautiful person, Shaw Miller."

The words hit him, cutting deep and stirring guilt. He looked down. "Taryn…"

"No, I'm serious. I don't know how anyone could ever know you and think anything else. Maybe if you gave people a chance to know—"

"Please. Stop." He eased her off his lap so he could stand. "Let's not do this. Don't give me that much credit. The situation hasn't changed. I can't…be anything but Lucas in front of anyone else."

She stood. "Shaw—"

"No. People aren't going to see me like you do. You see the best parts of me because that's what you bring out in me. That doesn't mean the other parts aren't still there."

Taryn's lips pressed together in frustration. "Which other parts, Shaw? What are these scary other sides I see no evidence of?"

He ran a hand over the back of his head and tightened the rubber band holding his hair back, wishing he could just slide down the wall and escape this conversation. "I have an anger problem. Diagnosed and everything. Intermittent explosive disorder."

She grimaced like she'd bit into something sour. "IED? To get that diagnosis, you'd have to be having aggressive outbursts consistently two or three times a week. Or you would've needed more brushes with the law in the years since you attacked the reporter. I've been around you for weeks. I've seen no signs of an out-of-control temper at all," she said flatly. "I think they let your brother's history influence them."

She was so ready to see the good in him. But she had no idea.

"You need a sign?" he said, his stomach hurting. "That wasn't the first incident. The first time I lost my temper like that was with Joseph."

She stared back at him. "What do you mean?"

He didn't want to say it. He'd never said it. But he couldn't bear to let her stand here and tell him what a wonderful person he was. She didn't deserve to be fed that bullshit. His fingers curled into his palms, and he forced the words out. "A few months before the shooting, I visited home. Joseph was bitching about the fact that my parents bought me a car at sixteen and he still didn't have one because they'd used the money to pay for extra training for me. That I was the favorite. That it was unfair.

"I blew him off because the only reason I got a car so early was because I needed to get back and forth to practice. He didn't have anywhere to be. Well…" He looked away toward the windows, the story spilling out. "That night, Joseph and Trevor stole the newer car I'd traded up to in college. When I tracked them down a few hours later, they were in the park near the school in my car, smoking weed and getting everything filthy. Fast-food wrappers everywhere, a spilled drink and muddy footprints all over the floorboards."

Taryn gripped the railing of the platform but didn't say anything.

Shaw looked back at her. "I saw red. I yanked my brother out of the car like a goddamned lunatic and pushed him into the dirt. In front of his friend, I told him he was just a pathetic kid who was having a tantrum, trying to get everyone's attention." His jaw flexed, the memory still fresh in his mind. "I told him that if he wanted to be noticed so badly, then he should stop whining all the time and do something worth noticing." He met her gaze, knowing he was ruining this but unable to keep lying to her or letting her think he was some helpless victim in all this. "So he did."

Taryn's eyes were big, and her hand pressed over her mouth.

He looked down. "A few months later, the shooting happened. The world noticed him."

Shaw steeled himself for her reaction, braced himself

for her anger. He'd been the trigger for what had caused so much pain and loss in her life. He'd put the idea in Joseph's head. So when she took a step toward him, he almost wondered if she was going to push him off the platform. But instead, she stopped in front of him, heartbreak on her face, and wrapped her arms around him, putting her cheek to his chest. "Oh my God, Shaw."

He stood stiffly, not knowing what to do. He kept his arms at his sides and closed his eyes. "I'm so sorry. I should've told you the truth sooner. I should've…"

She squeezed him tighter. "I'm so sorry you've had to carry that with you."

He shook his head, tears burning his eyes. She didn't get it. "I set him off. I caused it. It was my fault."

She leaned back and looked up, her head already shaking. "Oh, Shaw. No. That's not…" She touched his face. "You didn't. Don't say that."

"It's the truth."

"No. This is just more of their crime, the other insidious way they victimized everyone," she said, ire in her voice. "Leaving behind a long list of people who are left to question themselves forever about what they could've done differently. I told you. I think about opening that door all the time. Rebecca embarrassed Trevor and blamed herself for what he did for years. Your parents probably question every parental move they ever made. And you, you reacted to something your brother did with the sole purpose of angering you. He was *trying* to provoke you. He was creating his own justifications that the world was against him." Her eyes flared with determination.

"Every indication shows that Joseph was already

past the point of no return in the year leading up to the shooting, the antisocial behavior cropping up in all these little ways. His destruction of your property? Just another sign. He'd planned for Long Acre a lot longer than a few months before. You didn't make it happen. No one thing made it happen. The wheels were already in motion by then."

Shaw stared at her, listening to her impassioned speech and not believing it. He'd told her what he'd told no one else in this world, not even Rivers, and she was absolving him. Just like that? No. He didn't deserve a pass. "I should've seen that he was in trouble. I shouldn't have been so damn full of myself."

"We all should've looked harder. That doesn't mean we're to blame," Taryn said fervently. "That's a big reason why I've worked so hard on my program. There are signs so many of us—parents, teachers, doctors, classmates—could've caught. But we didn't know what we didn't know back then. You can't blame yourself for that. How many brothers get in fights every day? You had no reason to think your fight with him was any different than any other run-of-the-mill sibling spat. You didn't know he was already a ticking bomb." She put her hand to his chest. "You were just a kid back then, too."

Shaw shook his head, tears finally escaping. "You can't do that. You can't just wipe that slate clean. I hurt him. I let him down. I let everyone down."

Empathy pinched her features, and she wrapped her hand around his neck, pulling him down to her. He laid his forehead against her shoulder, and the anguish washed through him in a flood. He hadn't sobbed in years and the sensation felt painful and foreign.

Taryn caressed his hair, pulling it loose from the rubber band, whispering soothing words as if he were a child and not a grown man who towered over her. "It's not your fault," she whispered. "Let it out and let it go."

He knew she was probably in therapist mode, but right now, he didn't care. Something about the way she was holding him, the whole-cloth acceptance of what he'd told her, broke something open inside him. The grief he'd walled up for so long was busting through the seams.

He lost track of how long they'd stood there, but eventually, he lifted his head, feeling emptied out and a little lost. He looked down at her, a surge of something powerful and pure rolling through him. This woman was…everything. "What am I supposed to do with you?"

Taryn had been crying, too, and she smiled through shiny eyes at him, wiping at his cheeks and then kissing him gently. "Just be you. I happen to really like that guy. Even with his cheesy inspirational quotes."

He smiled, some of his brain coming back online. She was giving him an out, a way to gracefully step away from the sobbing mess he'd just become. He probably should joke back, but the truth slipped out instead. He pulled her against him and sat his chin on her head. "I adore you."

She melted in his hold. "Shaw?"

"Yeah, baby?"

"After dinner, can we run by the guitar store?" Her voice was muffled against his shoulder.

He leaned back and looked down at her. "The guitar store?"

She gave him a tentative smile. "Yeah. It's time I try

to write that song. Just for me." She wet her lips. "I think it's time we both take back what's been stolen."

He stared down at her, so many scary feelings running through him that he was sweating. But for the first time in his adult life, he let himself feel everything fully and didn't feel guilty about it. "I agree. Let's do this."

———

Taryn's phone buzzed in her pocket as she scanned the acoustic guitar selection at the local music store. She pulled the phone from her back pocket and frowned when she saw the message appear. Her parents inviting her to dinner.

She hadn't stopped by their house since starting the preparations for the fund-raiser. Her life had gotten too busy. No, that wasn't the only reason. She'd also been spending almost every night at Shaw's place in the city. Driving to Long Acre just to grab dinner with her parents was too much of a hassle. A thread of guilt tried to wind its way through her, but she tamped it down. She was an adult who had a life. She loved seeing her parents, but they had to accept that she wouldn't always be visiting weekly and texting them each night. *Right?*

"Everything all right?" Shaw asked from his spot in front of the music books.

"Yeah, it's just my mom inviting me to dinner. She said she misses me and is worried I've been so quiet."

Shaw set down the sheet music he'd been looking at and turned to her. "Are you going to go?"

She shrugged. "I don't know."

He frowned. "Baby, if you want to go, you should go. Don't worry about me."

"That's the crappy thing," she admitted. "I *don't* want to go. I love them, but I feel like every conversation revolves around my research and program. I haven't told them yet that I went on leave from my job. I'm not in the mood to go into it and answer all their questions. And I don't want to explain where I've been or who I've been spending time with."

"Right," Shaw said softly. "That would get complicated."

She sighed. "It's just been kind of nice breaking away a little, living my own life. Which I know sounds ridiculous for someone my age to say but..."

"It doesn't sound ridiculous. They've put a lot of pressure on you to be that involved. You have the right to some breathing room. I know you worry about them, but they're grown-ups, too."

Her phone dinged again.

> **Mom:** I had a bad nightmare last night. I dreamt someone was trying to kidnap you. Are you being careful on campus at night? I know you've been working late.

Taryn groaned, guilt edging back in. "I should probably go."

Shaw stepped closer and put his hands on her shoulders, a dimpled smile on his face. "I thought we were both working on not giving in to 'shoulds.' Tonight, you wanted to buy a guitar, eat some Indian food, and then have ridiculously amazing sex with yours truly. If that's the plan you want, you should stick with it. Your parents are fine. If you're not up to it, they can survive without seeing you for dinner."

She stared at him, his charm hard to resist. She knew he'd have no problem with her going to her parents' house if that was what she wanted to do, but he knew she didn't. She shook her head and laughed. "You're a bad influence."

"That's the best kind."

She stepped back and texted her mom.

> I'm sorry. Working late tonight. Yes, I'm being safe. I'll stop by soon. Love you.

She looked up and smiled. "Done."

"Good. Now let's get you something to play with, rock star."

"I thought I was playing with you," she teased.

He grinned and pecked her on the lips. "Later. That is most definitely on the agenda."

He grabbed her hand and led her to the other wall with the fancier guitars. She tried too many to count, playing songs and laughing with Shaw when she forgot the notes.

They'd had a long, emotional day, but when she fell into bed with him that night, she wasn't thinking of his confession or that she had to write a song. She wasn't thinking about all the work still to be done or if her parents were angry at her for not coming over. All she could think was that finally, finally, she felt...happy.

chapter

TWENTY-TWO

SHAW CHECKED THE TIME AS HE MANEUVERED HIS vacuum into his bedroom to get the place cleaned up. Taryn had said she was going to be working until five and then planned to head over. He'd seen her at work this week, but she hadn't been over to his place in a few days because she was wrapping up the final details of the big event with her friends. But tonight they were going to celebrate, so he wanted the place to look nice. After weeks of hectic planning, Taryn had managed to get fifteen area high schools to sign up for the fund-raiser. Each school was offering two athletes—one girl and one boy—to represent their school. She'd also worked in a best friends/pairs event.

Shaw couldn't believe all that Taryn and her friends had accomplished in such a short time, but he knew it was mainly because Taryn had worked her ass off. She'd been at the gym every day. She'd made calls and had given her pitch hundreds of times. The woman was something to behold when she was doing her thing.

He had tried to help with what he could behind the scenes, but this was her show. Instead of getting in her way, he'd made sure she remembered to eat, take breaks, get her workouts in, and come over to his place for some relaxation in between. She'd spent more nights at his place than her own. Partly because it was easier than having her make the hour commute home every night, but really, he flat-out just loved having her there.

Even when they were tired and just shared a meal and watched something on TV together, it felt like breathing rare air. He'd been flying solo for so long that this was downright foreign. He couldn't remember ever feeling so…at ease. Even before everything had happened with Joseph, his life had always been at full speed. Endless training and practice. Traveling to competitions. Filtering everything through the frame of how it would affect his performance. What he ate. How he slept. Even whether or not he had sex if he was close to a competition. Then after the shooting, all of that had been swept away, leaving behind just chaos and grief—both in his world and in his head. He'd never felt truly calm or comfortable in any one place or time since.

But with Taryn around, the jagged edges inside him were smoothing out. She made him laugh. She didn't let him take himself too seriously. And she kept him on his toes. Then, at night when they crawled into bed, he lost himself completely to the sweet oblivion of her touch, her words, her body. She'd become a drug he couldn't get enough of.

It was dangerous territory to tread in.

He tried not to think about it, tried to just be in the moment and enjoy it. He'd learned long ago how fleeting good moments were. Reality had a bad way of crashing a perfectly good party. They were on a fantastic ride, but that train ultimately had nowhere to go but dead ends. He was leaving before the end of the year. And even if he changed that plan and figured out a way to stay, he'd still be living under a false name. He'd still be who he was.

Taryn deserved more than that. She couldn't introduce him to her family. She couldn't tell her friends who he was. He would blow up her life and risk her relationships. There was no path forward for them. Plus, if word got out they were together, the media would pounce on it and milk it for every sensational ounce.

His stomach turned.

He was letting this go too far, getting too selfish. No matter how good it felt to have Taryn in his life, the risk was always there, pressing at the back of his mind like a bad headache. He could ruin the calm, successful life she'd worked so hard for. Or, at the very least, make a living hell out of it again. He could not—*would* not—do that to her.

They needed to talk. Soon. He needed to tell her about his plan and when he'd be leaving. Go forth with eyes wide open. Because if this kept on like it was, he could do something really terrible. He could forget this had an end and fall in love with her.

Maybe he already had.

Shoving the thought away, he flipped on the vacuum and pushed it forward with more force than necessary. He couldn't go there.

He stepped around the bed, putting vacuum lines in the carpet in a methodical way. The sound and the motion soothed his frayed nerves. He started to make a list in his head to get his mind on anything else. He wanted to clean a few more things and then jump in the shower since he hadn't rinsed off after work today. He and Taryn could go out, or they could pick up some steaks and borrow Rivers's grill.

A loud crackling sound broke Shaw from his train of thought. The vacuum was trying to suck up something too big. He switched off the power and squatted down. He was famous for sucking up random socks that had fallen under the bed. But when he flipped the machine over and looked, he saw the culprit immediately and smirked. A condom wrapper.

Not a surprise. He should probably buy stock in the company that made them, based on how quickly he and Taryn went through them. But this wrapper was a different color from the brand they'd recently been using. He frowned and pulled it out of the vacuum's roller. Half of it was gone, but he could still read the label.

It took him a second to realize it was from the box they'd found that first night when Taryn had dug through his drawer. He smiled at the memory of her teasing him about his lube and then her true cheer of victory when she'd found the condoms. He loved that about her, her complete lack of awkwardness or shyness about sex. She was a straight talker. Maybe it was the psychologist in her, but she had no qualms about telling him what she liked and wanted and what she didn't. Shaw flipped the wrapper over, trying to remember when he'd even bought that box, but then his eyes caught on the small stamped writing at the bottom of the wrapper.

Exp. November—

Shaw blinked, trying to adjust his vision. Surely, that said *November 2019*. But when he looked again, his stomach dipped.

2016.

Sixteen. Not nineteen. It wasn't just expired, it was almost two and a half years past that date.

2016. 2016. Years. Past.

Oh shit.

His mind rushed back to that first night. Taryn leaning over and smiling at him. She had told him the condoms were good. They'd used the rest of the box over the next few weeks. She was always cautious about protection with him. But...*hell*. The vision was clear in his head now, her smiling. She hadn't had her glasses on. She'd misread it. Then they'd just assumed the condoms were okay every other time they'd plucked one from the economy-size box.

Shaw sat down on the edge of the bed, his heartbeat thumping behind his eyeballs and his mouth dry. *Expired*. Okay. He didn't need to panic. There were no diseases to worry about. He'd been tested since Deidra. And he didn't recall any problems with the condoms. None had fallen apart. But had he looked closely every time? Could any have had a tear?

He felt sick.

Flashbacks to Deidra raced through his head. The unexpected pregnancy. The panic. Then the acceptance that he was going to be a father. Then the utter, annihilating grief when he found out the baby was gone.

He could *not* get anyone pregnant.

He definitely could not get *Taryn* pregnant.

Suddenly, the specter of their shared past, always

looming in the background, became a full-out monster, snapping its jaws and threatening to consume him in one big chomp. He put his head in his hands and tried to get ahold of his runaway thoughts. He didn't need to freak out yet. The condoms had probably worked. He and Taryn hadn't had issues with them. Expiration didn't necessarily mean completely ineffective.

Everything was probably fine.

Please, God, let everything be fine.

―――∾∾――――

Taryn headed up to Shaw's apartment and stretched her neck as she climbed the stairs. After so many hours sitting at that desk and making phone calls, she felt as if her spine had fused to her shoulder blades. She'd almost been tempted to work out for a few minutes after to loosen things up. *Almost.* The gym had become a mental respite for her, but she was still a little sore from a full obstacle workout two nights ago.

She'd crossed the rolling cylinder with no help from the trapeze during the last session without falling or peeing herself with nerves. A win by all accounts. Her body was feeling stronger and more solid with each passing week. If she had to do the costume race again, she would make it to the end without gasping for breath. That felt like a victory.

She needed one badly because the songwriting attempts had been like falling into the foam pit over and over again. She'd spent hours plucking out notes on her guitar and trying to find something that inspired her. Nothing had come together. The vein of creativity she used to tap when she was a kid wasn't there. Or maybe it had never really been there. Her songs in high school had been performed for an audience of one—Nia. And it wasn't like her sister was going to tell her that her songs sucked.

Maybe she couldn't write. End of story.

She'd tell the group and Shaw soon. Right now, she just wanted to forget it all. The fund-raiser was ready to go. She'd celebrate that milestone tonight and not think about the rest. She wanted a nice, relaxing evening with Shaw.

That feeling of happy anticipation filled her as she reached Shaw's apartment and knocked. He opened the door, and an automatic smile curved her lips. "Hey there, handsome."

"Hey." Shaw's hair was damp from a shower, which was normal after a workday, but the drawn expression on his face was new.

Her smile faltered as he opened the door wider and let her walk inside. She waited until he closed it before speaking. "Is everything okay?"

He turned around and scrubbed a hand through his hair. He didn't look her in the eye. "Probably."

Her brows lifted. "Probably?" Her mind jumped to all the worst-case scenarios. Someone had found out who he was. The press knew. He was leaving. *Click-click-click* like dominos falling in her head, but she forced herself to slow down. "What's going on?"

Finally, he looked at her, lines creasing his forehead. He let out a breath. "I was going to wait until after dinner to talk, but I'm not sure I can."

"Talk?" A new bee of anxiety buzzed around her. "About what?"

A talk didn't sound like news had leaked out. It

sounded more personal. Maybe this was going to be it—the talk she'd been expecting. The talk where he realized they'd moved too fast and that things had gotten too intense. She didn't know why she was anticipating such a talk, but somehow she'd known from the beginning it would come at some point. They were a temporary thing for each other. A respite with a time limit.

She'd prepared herself for that, but still she found herself bracing for his answer.

Shaw reached out and took her hand, leading her to the couch. They both sat, facing each other. "Taryn, everything is probably fine, and I don't want to freak you out, but I also can't not tell you this."

She frowned. "What are you talking about?"

Shaw licked his lips, looking more nervous than she'd ever seen him, and pulled something from his pocket. At first, she had this bizarre thought that he was proposing, but her brain quickly gave her a *Girl, please* reality check. Propose? She wasn't sure what to be more *what the fuck* about—the fact that she'd thought a proposal was an actual possibility with this man or that part of her had thrilled at the thought.

That hopeless romantic inside her needed to take a seat in the corner and think about her life choices because she was getting delusional.

But when Taryn looked down at what was in his hand, her confusion deepened. Not a ring. Obviously. But a condom wrapper. She raised her gaze for an explanation.

"Taryn, this is from the box you found in my drawer that first night. I found it when I was cleaning."

"Okay…" she said, still not tracking. "You found a condom wrapper. Not a surprising discovery."

He wet his lips. "It's over two years expired. We read the date wrong."

"We…" Her stomach muscles tightened, and she looked down at the wrapper again, taking it from his hands. She held it up, reading the date. *November 2016.* "Crap." He'd said *we* but she knew who'd really read it wrong—her and her faulty eyesight. "Damn. I'm sorry. Guess we got lucky they held up, huh? How many of these did we use?"

She lifted her gaze to him, finding his worried. "I didn't keep track, but…enough. So, everything's good, then?"

She felt an awkward smile jump to her lips. "Uh, yeah, sure. What do you mean?"

He released a breath and rubbed his palms on his jeans. "I mean, I was looking back at the dates. I don't know how many we used or when we finished the box, but I feel like it's been at least a month and we haven't…paused for anything, so I was worried that maybe one didn't hold up. But are you on a pill or something or the shot or…"

His words went long and distorted in her ears, like someone had hit the slo-mo button on her eardrums. *It's been at least a month…A month.*

Had it been a month since she'd had a period?

Everything had been happening so fast and frantic, both with the fund-raiser and with Shaw, that the weeks were blending together. She never kept close watch on her period. She'd always had irregular cycles and weird hormonal patterns. It hadn't crossed her mind that she hadn't had one in a while. "I'm not on the pill or anything else. My body responds weird to hormones."

His lips parted, a snap of fear crossing his face. "Taryn…"

She shook her head, the possibility not even something she could process. "No, don't panic. It's fine. It's probably fine." The wrapper crinkled in her fist as she squeezed too tightly. "My cycles vary and can go long. It happens all the time."

"Yeah?" he asked, a hopeful note in his voice.

She nodded, trying to reassure herself along with him. "Yes."

Shaw ran a hand over the back of his neck, visibly shaken. "Right. Okay."

She reached out and gave his knee a squeeze. "None of the condoms broke. I'm sure we're fine."

But acid burned the back of her throat. *What if they weren't?*

He put his hand over hers, and she could feel a slight tremble in his. "I bought a test. I think you should take it, you know, just to ease our minds. I don't think I can... not know for sure. After..." He cleared his throat. "I'd just feel better with confirmation."

Her mind jumped back to what he'd told her about his past, the pregnant girlfriend, why she'd ended it. *Jesus.* This was a code red in Shaw's head. How could it not be? Her ribs cinched tight, her heart hurting for him. "Of course. I'd like to know for sure, too."

Shaw leaned forward and cupped the back of her neck to kiss her. "Thank you. I know I'm probably panicking for nothing but—"

"It's fine," she said, touching her forehead to his. "I understand. Let's get this done so we can eat some dinner, okay? I'm starving."

He gave her a tremulous smile. "Deal."

Taryn tried to remain one hundred percent calm as

Shaw went to the grocery bag on the counter and pulled out a pregnancy test. She took it from him, staring down at the bright-pink box, her hands beginning to shake. *Shit*. She was taking a *pregnancy test*.

Her mind wouldn't wrap around that fact. The self-talk ran rampant in her head. This didn't have to be a big deal. This was just a precaution. Paranoia. The condom hadn't broken. Expiration dates were just estimates. She'd once eaten a bag of Doritos that were a year expired. They were fine. She didn't need to freak out. She was just doing this to ease Shaw's mind.

Shaw followed her to his room and stopped at the bathroom door. "Can you come out when you're done so I can watch the results with you?"

"Sure," she said, the word coming out too high.

Taryn went inside and braced her hands on the edge of the sink for a moment, trying to get herself in check. She would not lose it. She was *fine*. Rebecca was the pregnant one. Not her. She could not be pregnant.

With a *baby*.

With *Shaw Miller's* baby.

Oh fuck. She couldn't go there. The thought was too twisted and screwed up to even consider. Soap opera screwed up. How the hell had she ended up here? This was just supposed to be a fun, no-pressure affair.

Taryn took a few deep breaths so as not to completely lose her shit and tried to read the instructions for the test. Then she did what she needed to do, which was surprisingly challenging—aiming for a stick held by a trembling hand. She washed her hands, set the test on the counter, and opened the door.

Shaw had paled three shades since she'd closed the

door. He stepped inside, his eyes going straight to the stick on the counter. "How long is it supposed to take?"

"Two minutes," she said. "In other words, forever."

He huffed. "No kidding."

She put a hand on his back, trying to give comfort, but really seeking it for herself as well. "One line means we're good."

"Right."

Neither of them dared mention that there was any other possibility but one line.

So they stood there and stared. Taryn's mind spun so fast that she felt like she was outside herself, watching the two of them watch the test. She had set a timer on her phone, and when it went off, they both startled.

Shaw's head dipped between his shoulders, his whole body sagging against the sink.

Taryn started laughing, an edge of hysteria to it, the relief palpable. She leaned back against the wall and closed her eyes. "One line. Good job, old-ass condoms."

Shaw spun toward her and swept her into a hug. His grip was bordering on desperate, squishing her breath from her. "I'm so sorry, Taryn. I'm so, *so* sorry to have put you in this position."

Taryn frowned at the vehemence in his voice. "Not your fault. I'm the one who read the date wrong."

"But you shouldn't even have to consider…" His voice caught.

"It's okay." She rubbed his back. "Anytime you sleep with someone, there's inherent risk. That's the price. I'm a big girl. I know that."

"No. You know it's more than that." He pulled back

and looked down at her, anguish in his eyes. "I would never ever want to inflict...myself on you. Or a child."

She swallowed, the words sharp and ugly to her ear. "Inflict."

"Come on. You know what I'm saying. My family name. My genes. My history." He released her. "I decided a long time ago that my family line ends with me. It's the least I can do for the world. Could you imagine a kid growing up with my past in his family tree? And what if there is something genetic there?"

Taryn's breath left her, his words breaking her heart with painful little fissures. For him, but also because she couldn't deny the panicked thoughts that had run through her head while she was taking the test. "Shaw, I understand what you're saying, and I'm glad there's only one line on the test, but it's not because I think you're damaged goods. You realize that's not how I see you, right? You are a different person from your brother. I wouldn't be here at all otherwise."

He rubbed a hand over his face and exhaled slowly. "I'm just sorry I put you through this."

"It worked out, all right? We're okay," she said gently. "We'll be more careful."

"Right."

She took his hand, leading him out of the bathroom. "Come on. Let's get some dinner and relax. This is enough panic for one day."

But as she curled up next to him that night after they'd made love, her heartbeat never slowed down. They'd dodged a major bullet, but now she couldn't keep her mind from going down the roads of what-if. None of those roads looked good.

She was right on one thing. There was inherent risk in any sexual relationship.

But Shaw was right on the other.

This was no ordinary hookup. Theirs suddenly felt like a ticking bomb, and they were tossing that bomb back and forth between each other. Carelessly. Capriciously. Not thinking of what this could do to the people around them. She could hear the clock counting down with each of Shaw's deep, sleeping breaths.

So many paths they could stumble upon had explosions waiting for them at the end.

What if her family or friends found out who Shaw was? *Boom*.

What if she *had* been pregnant? *Boom*.

What if she fell in love with him?

What if that was already happening?

BOOM! BOOM! BOOM!

She rolled over, facing away from him, the last thought blaring through her mind like a tornado siren. *What if you love him? What if you love him?*

The truth of it sank her like quicksand. There was no what-if. She'd gotten hit in the face with that reality tonight. She'd let it happen. Had walked right into this relationship and let the one thing she wasn't supposed to do happen. Tonight, that ludicrous flash of hope that he was proposing had proved it. Some part of her had wanted that, had wanted to get her romantic love story.

The handsome guy. The whirlwind romance. The happy ending.

She was finally the star in her own romantic movie. *Hurrah!*

But she wasn't. That was a fucking delusion. That

handsome guy was someone her family would never accept. This whirlwind romance was something that would horrify her friends and put the gossipy press into a feeding frenzy. And there was no happily-ever-after. Shaw was in hiding and planned to stay that way. They could never be together like a real couple.

She needed to get through the fund-raiser at Shaw's gym and then do what was necessary. Make a clean break. Save them both.

This was not sweet. This was not simple. This was as complicated as it got. They would have an ending. But not a happy one. Her falling in love with him didn't matter.

Taryn suddenly had new song lyrics in her head.

But they were all about goodbye.

chapter
TWENTY-THREE

TARYN'S PHONE VIBRATED ON THE SIDE TABLE, PULLING her out of the fitful sleep she'd fallen into in the middle of the night.

Shaw groaned from beside her. "Tell them to go away."

But her phone didn't stop. She extracted herself from his hold and sat up to grab her glasses and reach for it. The name on the screen made her cringe. Her mother.

She still hadn't managed to get over there to visit, but she doubted her mom would resort to early-morning calls to ask her about that. Something could be wrong. She put the phone to her ear and tried to ignore the fact that she was taking this call half-dressed in a man's bed. "Uh, good morning."

"Good morning, yourself," her mother said. "Where are you?"

Taryn quickly glanced at Shaw who had rolled onto his back, his chest bare and his sleepy eyes looking her way. God, she was going to miss that look. "I'm...in the city."

"In the city?" her mother repeated, as if she'd never heard of the word *city* before. "At this hour?"

"Yes. I had…an early appointment. Did you need something?" she asked, trying to keep her voice even. If there was no emergency, she needed to get off this call before her mother sniffed out the lie like a bloodhound. Plus, no one wanted to have a conversation with their mother when they were half-naked in bed next to a guy.

"I'm in your driveway," her mother said impatiently. "We're supposed to go to breakfast before we go to the cemetery."

"The…" The room flipped over in Taryn's vision for a second, and she put her hand on Shaw's arm as if she might tip over. It was the thirteenth. Nia's birthday. A day she always took off from work. A day she always spent with her family. A day she spent making sure her mother didn't fall apart.

She put her fingers to her temple. She'd *forgotten*. How *the hell* had she forgotten? Tears jumped to her eyes.

"Baby, are you okay?" Shaw asked, lifting up on his elbows, the concern on his face instant.

She tried to hush him but not quick enough.

"Who is that?" her mother asked, too sharp to miss the intrusion.

Taryn tried to find her voice even though her heart had crawled up her throat and lodged there. "Just a colleague, Momma. I needed to…meet with him about something this morning." About something? What the hell kind of lie was that? Awful. She could see her mother's eyes narrowing already. "I'm about to head back to town. I can meet you and Daddy at the cemetery. I'm sorry I forgot to mention I couldn't make it to breakfast."

"Your colleagues call you *baby*?" she asked in that mom tone, that you-better-rethink-what-you-just-said-young-lady tone Taryn remembered from her childhood.

The reprimand wasn't necessary. There was nothing her mother could say that would make Taryn feel worse than she already did. She'd forgotten her baby sister's birthday. Instead of being with her family, she was in bed with a guy—no, with *Shaw Miller*—worrying about her own petty dramas. *Poor Taryn, she's fallen for a guy she can't be with. Wah-wah. Boo-hoo*. She'd never felt more selfish.

"I'm sorry," she said finally. "I lost track of what day it was and slept at a friend's place in the city. I'll be there as soon as I can."

"Slept?" Her mother sucked in a breath. "What friend?"

"No one you know."

"You slept at some *strange man's house*?" She made it sound as if Taryn had walked into a dangerous part of town wearing diamond earrings and a sign that read *Rob Me*. "Taryn, do you know how many young women are murdered going home with men they don't know? Body parts found strewn somewhere months later! I cannot believe you would put yourself in that position. Is this what you've been doing when you've been ig—"

"Momma, I'm fine. You don't know him, but I do," Taryn said, feeling tired and terrible at the same time. "Look, I'll be there soon, okay?"

Her mom made a perturbed sound but didn't lecture her further. That would no doubt come later. "Remember to pick up flowers and eat something because now you won't make it in time for breakfast."

Taryn ended the call with her mom and put her face in her hands, the reality of what she'd forgotten pouring over her in a flood.

Shaw shifted to sit up and put his arm around her. "Hey, what's going on? You okay?"

"No, not really," she admitted. "But it's fine. I have to go. I'm sorry."

"What happened?"

She shoved the covers aside, slipping from his hold, and got out of the bed. Her stitched-together emotions felt as if they were unraveling thread by thread. "Nothing, all right? I just need to go."

He flinched at her tone. "Baby, if there's something I can do to help—"

She looked at him, feeling like she was about to crumble in front of him, just fall apart right there and dump a whole bunch of emotional shit at his doorstep. She could not let that happen right now. She needed to get out of there. "Thanks, but you can't help. No one can. I forgot it was my sister's birthday. We always spend the day as a family. And I forgot. And my mother is smart enough to know what kind of friend's house I was sleeping at. One who calls me 'baby.'"

Shaw grimaced. "I'm sorry about that. You looked so upset."

"Not your fault. This is completely mine." One hundred percent, totally hers. Being here. Getting so involved with someone that she'd lost sight of what was most important. How could she ever let herself forget? "I'll deal with it. I need to get dressed."

She left the bedroom and started searching around for her clothes, but Shaw followed her out soon after.

She'd managed to tug on her jeans and shirt, but before she could reach her socks, Shaw intercepted her, putting his hands on her biceps and halting her hectic search. "Hey, look at me."

She didn't want to, didn't know if she could keep from crying much longer, but she forced her gaze his way. "What? I need to get ready. I'm already late."

"Hey," he said, his tone softer. "Don't do this to yourself."

"Do what?" She jutted her chin out, trying to scare him off this track. "Go? I have to go."

"No. I mean, don't beat yourself up. It was an honest mistake. You have the right to not be perfect. You're going to forget things sometimes. You have a lot going on."

Her molars pressed hard against one another as she tried to keep tears from appearing. "You don't understand," she said finally. "I don't forget."

His gaze held hers. "Maybe you should sometimes."

His voice was gentle, but her spine went straight and stiff as if he'd yelled. "Maybe I should *forget*?"

He let out a breath. "You know what I mean. You'll never forget. Neither will I. But it's okay to tuck the painful stuff in a closet every now and then and take a damn breather. You've dedicated your life to this. Every day. Your whole career is focused on this. It's a beautiful, admirable thing, but when do you get a break?"

"A break? Are you kidding?" Her voice had risen in volume, but she couldn't help it. "That's what I've been doing for goddamned months. That's why I forgot."

"No, you haven't been on a break, Taryn," he said, frustration in his voice. "You've been working your ass off on a fund-raiser and in between trying to live a little bit of your life. That's not something to feel bad about."

"*I forgot*, Shaw."

"You lost track of time. Good. I know what remembering every damn second does to a person. I've been there. It's a dangerous house to live in," he said, his expression going grim. "You saw where my head went last night. Memories can fucking drown you if you let them."

"I can't change the memories, Shaw." She snatched up her socks and tugged them on.

"I know that. All I'm saying is that it's okay if you lost track for a minute. You haven't done anything wrong. So you've been spending time with a guy, enjoying yourself a little in between all your work. It's nothing to apologize for. You deserve your own life. Don't let your parents make you feel like that's not okay. Don't make yourself feel bad for wanting that."

The thought was ludicrous. "You don't get it. This is *not okay*. It's not okay that I forgot. It's not okay that I picked you to be with despite all the obvious risks. It's not okay that last night there was a very real possibility I could explode my entire life and destroy my parents in the process. It's all so very *not okay*. Don't you see how goddamned selfish all that is?"

He winced like she'd punched him. "Taryn…"

"I'm not blaming you. This is my doing, but don't act like you get it. I don't get to take on a new identity and pretend I'm someone else. This is it." She put her hand to her chest. "This is all I've got. I'm the sister. I'm the one who's going to fix things. I'm the one who keeps my parents going. I don't get a vacation from things like you do."

He scoffed and dropped his arms to his sides. "You think this is a *vacation*? Look around at my life. I'm in *hiding*, Taryn. My parents don't even speak to me anymore. I live my life looking over my shoulder. I can't even take you on a proper date without worrying who's watching. I can't be with you the way I want to be with you. I'm not asking for sympathy because it's my own fault, but damn."

She winced and shook her head. "I'm sorry. That wasn't fair. I know this isn't an easy life for you. But me forgetting like this, being so selfish, is a betrayal. To my family. To Nia."

A pained look crossed Shaw's face and he stepped closer. "Wanting to have your own happiness isn't a betrayal. That isn't selfish. You deserve that. Wouldn't Nia want that for you?"

Taryn went rigid. "Do not use her name against me like that."

"Use it ag— Come on, you know that's not what I'm doing." He ran a hand over his face. "Are you trying to pick a fight with me?"

She looked away, her fists balling.

"That's it, isn't it?" he said, backing off from her, his expression closing. "This is about last night."

"Shaw—"

"No, I get it. You want out, and this is an easy way." His jaw clenched. "For all your talk of acceptance and not judging and 'You're a different person from your family' speeches, you finally realized who you were sleeping with. It finally sank in, and now you want no part of it."

She pressed her lips together, breathing hard through her nose. She wanted to tell him no, that wasn't it at all.

That she loved him. That last night had ripped her open. That she wanted to be with him so badly, it made her bones hurt. But what was the point? This was an unfixable situation. There were no solutions. And she was losing sight of too many things, being wrapped up in him. The biggest favor she could do them both was to end it.

So as hard as it was, she said what she needed to say to make it clean. No questions. No gray area.

"If I deserve happiness, you think I can find it here with you? With your fake name and this half life? You gonna step out into the light of the world to be with me?"

His throat worked, and lines appeared around his eyes like her knife had landed deep. His voice was strained when he finally spoke. "You know I can't. You wouldn't want people to know who I am either. You wouldn't hurt your family like that."

"You're right. I wouldn't. So this life you say I deserve? You're not the one who can give it to me."

The comment was brutal. The truth. They both knew it. But it hurt like hell anyway.

Shaw dipped his head. "No. I can't."

His utter acceptance of her statement gutted her. Her eyes burned, but she forced herself not to cry. Her voice was softer when she spoke again. "We always knew this would end."

He lifted his head, meeting her eyes, resignation there. "It wasn't supposed to hurt like this."

"Guess we both fucked up then."

He raked a hand through his hair, grabbing the strands between his fingers as if he were going to pull it all out. "Taryn, maybe we could…"

"I can't," she said, cutting him off before he could

offer her some shred of something that could tempt her. She was too afraid she'd grab at it. "We can't. Today proved I've let this go too far. It's not fair to either of us to drag it out. When the fund-raiser is over this weekend, I...won't be coming back to the gym."

His eyes revealed pain, but he nodded. "Right."

She looked down at her feet. "I've really gotta go."

He tucked his hands in the pockets of his track pants and gave her a look devoid of all emotion. "So go."

The icy chill in the words stung, but she didn't want to extend that painful feeling in her chest any longer. Her parents were waiting for her. Her real life was waiting for her.

This had just been a road trip through some land that didn't actually exist. She and Shaw had created a fictional, protected world between them with pretend characters. Taryn, the carefree woman who could shack up with her trainer, and Lucas, the quiet athlete who was just looking for some companionship. It had been a wonderful escape. But it hadn't been real.

She packed up the rest of her things, slipped on her shoes, and walked out without a goodbye.

Their fictional story was over. Turn the page. The end.

———

Two hours later, Taryn was sitting in the grass next to her mother in front of her sister's grave, grief filling every empty space inside her. Selfish grief for what had happened this morning with Shaw. Familiar grief for what lay before her. But she'd cried enough on the way here to leave her eyes dry.

Bright gerbera daisies filled the permanent vases next to the headstone. They'd been Nia's favorite flower because they came in so many colors, but Taryn found herself wondering if they would've remained her sister's favorite or if she would've changed her opinion by now. If she would've picked something more sophisticated in her adult years. They'd never know. That made Taryn want to cry again, but she managed to take a deep breath and quell the urge.

Her father was standing alone under a nearby tree, doing his own version of visiting his daughter's grave site, which meant pulling up weeds he found around headstones and humming. Daddy had always preferred to keep busy when it came to the sad things, so he had to take out his grief and anger on plant species that hadn't earned the right to be there.

Her mother was next to her on the blanket, her legs tucked to the side as though she were seventeen instead of in her sixties, and her hands were clasped in prayer. The wind was gentle around them, rustling the leaves of the big trees that guarded the cemetery and blending with the chirping of the birds. Taryn tried to get in touch with the peacefulness of it all, but her thoughts and emotions were knotted inside her like thorny vines, and she couldn't get comfortable.

Her mother finished her prayer and turned to Taryn with a somber smile. "I'm glad you could finally make it today."

Taryn didn't miss the dig. "Me too. I'm sorry I was so late."

Her mom looked toward the headstone. "Sweetie, can you believe I called your sister this morning and she was at some strange man's house? You'd think I'd raised you girls to be more careful and discerning than that."

Taryn pinched the bridge of her nose. "Momma…"

Her mother ignored her. "I'm just saying. I've never heard your sister mention a new man. He can't have been around that long and already…sleeping over."

Taryn groaned. "Momma, I'm not a teenager. I know him. He's not dangerous. It was just a friendly thing. I'm not dating him."

Her mother glanced over with a cocked brow. "And what is this young man's name?"

"Sh—" Taryn caught herself, almost choking to keep the name from slipping out. "Lucas. He's a trainer at a gym I joined."

Her mother's brows crawled higher. "A trainer? Honey, you are a *doctor*."

Taryn took a page from her mother's book and looked toward Nia's headstone. "Girl, do you hear your mother? She's become a snob."

Her mother pursed her lips. "I've become someone who doesn't want her daughter being used."

Taryn snorted and picked at the grass. "Mom, I'm a professor, not an MD. No one is after me for my money. There's not that much of it. And I have even less now because I'm on unpaid leave."

Her mother stiffened. "Unpaid leave? What are you talking about?"

Taryn explained what had happened and about the fund-raiser and video campaign. The irritated look on her mother's face slowly morphed into a smile.

"You're going to put the program in schools yourself?" she asked, beaming.

Taryn shrugged and let the grass shavings fall from her fingertips. "If I can raise enough money."

Her mother clasped her hands together at her chest and then looked to the grave. "Nia, did you hear that, sweetie? Your big sister is not giving up. The board said no, and she's not taking it. She's going to make sure your program gets in schools. She's never going to give up on you." Her mother looked back to Taryn, taking her hands in hers, eyes glistening. "I'm not sure I've ever been prouder of you."

Taryn forced a smile, but her chest felt like an elephant had sat on it. "Thanks, Momma."

"Emmett!" her mom called out. "Did you hear what our baby is doing?"

As her parents surrounded her, hugging her in front of Nia's headstone, Taryn felt like she'd drifted out of her body and was watching from a perch in one of those trees. This was her life. This was what she'd told Shaw she needed to get back to. But suddenly, it didn't feel like hers at all.

When her parents decided it was time to leave, Taryn told them to go ahead without her, that she wanted some alone time. Her mother beamed at that and left her to it.

Taryn waited for them to depart and then knelt down, rubbing her fingers over her sister's birth date as if to memorize it anew. She wasn't sure if she believed in an afterlife, but she hoped one did exist. "I'm sorry I forgot your birthday this morning, baby girl. I'm so sorry." Her voice caught and she had to take a second to breathe through it. "I wish you were here so I could tease you about getting old. I'd take you out and get you drunk. You'd probably end up dancing on a table. I'd end up singing. We'd embarrass ourselves completely. We'd have a time."

The wind gusted, sweeping Taryn's hair away from her face, and a small bird landed off to her right. He hopped around, pecking the ground, almost looking as if he were dancing. Taryn smiled through fresh tears.

"I wish you were here so badly, I can barely stand it," she confessed. "I want my sister back. I want to hear your secrets and tell you mine. I want you to be the first to hear that I fell in love." She sniffled. "And totally messed it up. You'd be giving me quite a lecture right now." She sat back on her knees, feeling heavy and tired. "I want to talk about who you're dating and if you want kids. I want you to fight with me over who gets to host Christmas. I want to stand behind you at your wedding and have you stand behind me at mine. Not that I'll ever get married at this rate."

The bird squawked. Opinionated little sucker.

"I know we used to fight sometimes and that I was jealous of you that night, but I swear, I'd do anything in the world to have you back to argue with. I don't want to be an only child. I was never meant to be without you. I have no idea what I'm doing here."

Tears made slow tracks down her face, and the bird moved closer, seemingly curious about this unusual creature who was making strange noises. But when he hopped next to her hand, which was splayed in the grass, and jumped on top of her fingers, Taryn didn't move.

She blinked through her tears, and the little brown bird stared at her with serious eyes. In that moment, she didn't know how, but she knew her sister was there with her. Hearing her. Telling her not to give up.

Taryn's tears stopped, and she stayed still as stone until the little bird hopped away. A sense of peace came over her, and she felt that burn in her gut renew. As much as it had hurt, she'd made the right decision this morning. She didn't need to veer off the path again. "I've got you, Nia. I'm still fighting. Don't worry."

chapter
TWENTY-FOUR

TWO WEEKS LATER

SHAW SET DOWN HIS PHONE, FEELING SATISFIED IF not happy. He'd been scanning the online ads regularly for deals, and he'd finally found the RV he'd wanted. He'd gotten a great price because the couple who'd owned it was getting a divorce and selling off property as quickly as they could offload it. The bank had approved the transaction today, and they'd called to tell him it was officially his. He just had to get down to Galveston to sign some papers and get the keys.

He wasn't in a place where he could move into it yet. He really needed to stay longer to help Rivers and to sock away more money, but something inside him settled, knowing the RV was on the coast waiting for him. He'd go down this weekend and take a look, make a list of any repairs or remodeling he wanted to do, and then set up a plan.

He got up to pack a suitcase. For the first time in the

two weeks since Taryn had walked out, he felt some of the tension slip out of him. Distance would help. He needed a weekend away. Being in this apartment was too much—with her scent still lingering in the shower every time he turned the hot water on and memories of their time together haunting every room. He needed a change of scenery in a bad way.

The news droned on in the background as he packed, but his ears perked up when he heard her name. *Dr. Taryn Landry*. He'd been hearing it a lot lately, and it sliced through him every time, like a thousand little blades. He tried not to turn and look at the screen, but he couldn't help himself. They were rerunning clips of the fund-raiser. The event had been a big success and had garnered a lot of community attention, along with some national coverage.

Taryn was beaming on the screen as she announced that they'd surpassed their goal and hoped to have the wider campaign ready to go in a month or two. Clips of the competition flashed over the screen—kids having fun on all the obstacles, the boys showing off when they actually made it through one, the girls looking smug when some of them beat the boys. So much of him wished he had been there to see Taryn's project come to fruition, but for once, the news cameras had been the least of his worries.

He couldn't go to her. She'd said goodbye, and the kindest thing he could do was leave her alone. She'd laid out the bare truth for him, just like she'd always done. *You can't give me a happy life*. Straight shooter. It was something he loved about her, but it had hurt like acid in an open wound because he couldn't deny it. He wanted to be something for her that he wasn't capable of.

What the hell could he say? *Hey, wanna come live in an RV with me and drop out of your life? Leave all that hard work, your family, and friends behind because I love you and want to be with you?* Like he was some prize. Please.

He clicked off the television.

He'd always known he deserved penance for what he'd done to his brother. He thought he'd served it. He'd been wrong. This was it. This was what payback felt like. He'd gotten to experience what happiness was, what love felt like, only to have it dragged forever out of reach.

This is not for you.

Well played, universe.

He zipped up his roller bag and shoved it to the side, but a knock on the door had him lifting his head. Shaw headed to the living room, assuming Rivers must've forgotten his key. He'd promised to stop by today, but when Shaw swung open the door, an unfamiliar guy in a brown suit smiled an all-teeth smile his way.

Shaw frowned, not in the mood for Sammy Salesperson. "Sorry. Whatever you're selling, I'm not interested."

"Oh, I think you will be." The stranger stepped closer, putting his loafer-clad foot in the doorway, but holding the smile. "I won't take much of your time."

Shaw's patience, already thin, disappeared. He put his hand on the door. "I said I'm not interested. Please remove your foot from my doorway."

He pushed the door, ready to shut it, giving the guy a second to get his foot out of the way, but before Shaw could shut it, the guy said, "Mr. Miller, I just have a few questions."

The name shot up his spine like a spear of ice. *Miller*.

The shock gave the reporter the moment's hesitation he needed. He nudged the door a little more open again, his head poking in. "Mr. Miller, I just want to get a comment on the video that's come to light."

The video. Those were the same words from so many years ago. The room spun a little, and for a moment, Shaw wondered if he'd fallen asleep and was having a nightmare. There were no more videos. He hadn't done anything else.

His brain snapped back online. "I don't know who or what you're talking about, but this is private property. Get the hell out of my doorway."

He moved to close the door again.

"A video of you and one of the Long Acre survivors. Dr. Taryn Landry."

Shaw stilled, a sick feeling washing over him. *No*.

"Is it true that the two of you are in a relationship?" the reporter demanded. He turned his phone screen Shaw's way. A familiar country song blared from the speakers. A shaky video of their karaoke performance played in front of him. He stared, unable to look away. Whoever was filming kept zooming in on their faces. Shaw's cowboy hat shielded him until he accidentally stepped into the spotlight with Taryn and kissed her.

"How did you get this?" he asked, trying to keep his voice devoid of any emotion. He hadn't admitted he was Shaw Miller yet. Maybe the guy didn't really know for sure.

The reporter slipped inside as if Shaw had offered him an invitation. "Dr. Landry is quite the local celebrity right now. Someone posted the video online to show her singing, and a commenter recognized you. We face-searched you and traced you to your former college roommate." He smiled again, but there was a predatory edge to it. "Care to comment about why you're victimizing Dr. Landry? Your brother doing that wasn't enough?"

Anger surged. "What the hell are you talking about?"

"You're posing as someone else. Surely, you're not going to tell me that this woman, a victim who is spending all her time raising money for school shooting prevention, is willingly kissing the killer's brother?" He gave Shaw a lifted-eyebrow look.

What could he say to that? Saying yes threw Taryn to the wolves in front of everyone—her friends, her family. He couldn't. "Get out of my apartment. You can't be here. I didn't invite you."

"What, you gonna hit me?" the reporter goaded.

Shaw's fist balled. "*What?*"

The guy took a step back, knowing he'd crossed a line Shaw could legally call him out on. "I'm only the first, Mr. Miller. Give me an exclusive, and I'll be kinder than what the others are going to say. The story isn't going back in the bag."

Shaw felt like he was going to throw up. It was starting all over again. And he'd dragged Taryn into it. "She didn't know a thing. Leave her alone. Now get out."

He herded the guy out, careful not to touch him, and then slammed the door shut.

Sweat rolled down his back, and his heart felt like it was going to give out. He grabbed his cell phone and hit a number, stalking away from the door so no one could eavesdrop.

Taryn's voicemail answered. He hated leaving a

message, but he didn't have much choice. She might not answer any of his calls, and he needed to warn her. "Taryn, it's Shaw. I'm sorry to tell you like this, but a story got out about us. A video from karaoke. Don't answer your door or phone if you don't know who it is. I told the reporter you had no idea who I was. I'll be gone before they can get any more information out of me. Just deny everything. Say you never saw me again after that night. We met at the bar, sang, and that was it. Say you were drunk."

There was another knock on his door. *Fuck*. "And, Taryn, I'm so sorry for all of this. I never meant to drag you into my mess. I loved the time we spent together." He wet his lips. "No, I think I probably just straight-up love *you*. I know that coming from me, it could never be enough, but I thought you should know. Take care of yourself, songbird."

The confession slipped out, inappropriate as fuck, but he had to get the words out there. He needed her to know that she was more to him than just a hookup. That even if it was brief, their relationship had meant something and he'd forever be thankful for having known her.

He ended the call before he could say more shit to make it worse.

He punched another button on his phone.

Rivers answered. "What the hell, dude? My phone is ringing off the hook. What's going on?"

"A video of me and Taryn got leaked. Someone recognized us both. I told the reporter who came here that Taryn didn't know who I was. Stick to that story. I'm going to call building security to get the reporters out of the hallway, and then I'm leaving out the back.

I've got to get out of town. I'll call you from the road. I don't know if I'm going to be able to come back."

"What? You can't just leave permanently," Rivers protested. "Dude, they don't get to fucking chase you off. You didn't *do* anything."

Shaw scoffed. "I did enough. I'm sorry. I'm heading down to Galveston."

"*Galveston?* Why?"

"I bought an RV." Man, this was not how he wanted to tell Rivers, but he had no choice. "So don't worry. I'll have a place to stay. I'll touch base with you when I get there, so we can figure out what to do with my stuff. Thank you for everything, man."

"Shaw—"

But he ended the call. All this hurt too damn much. He just needed to get on the road and get the hell out of there. He wouldn't make it through the goodbyes this time.

"Whoa, what is going on?" Liv asked, breaking the silence in the room. "You have dog treats in your purse or something?"

Taryn looked up from the laptop they'd set up on Rebecca's dining room table, her eyes swimming with spreadsheets but the numbers still not making sense. She couldn't freaking concentrate. She hadn't been able to concentrate on anything since she'd walked out of Shaw's apartment. She'd managed to go through the motions, run the fund-raiser, do the press for the event, but her mind was always somewhere else—mainly, sitting in a room rocking back and forth and freaking the hell out. "Hmm?"

Kincaid, who was sitting next to her working on the new blog, cocked her head toward Rebecca's big, black dog. Knight was nosing Taryn's purse, which she'd left on the couch, and whining like he was being denied beef jerky.

Rebecca stepped out of the kitchen and frowned. "Knight, don't do that."

Knight barked and pulled the strap of Taryn's purse with his teeth.

"No," Rebecca said sharply as she plunked down a pitcher of iced tea on the table. "No, sir. You put her purse down."

At her firm tone, Knight hopped back and dropped the strap from his mouth, puppy-dog eyes in full effect. Rebecca groaned as she walked over. "You are the worst. I will not feel guilty." She grabbed the purse. "Oh, your phone's vibrating. Knight hates that noise."

"Aww," Kincaid said and made a cooing noise to call the dog over. "Does that hurt Mr. Knight's ears? You poor baby."

Knight's tail thumped on the hardwood floor and his tongue lolled out.

Rebecca handed Taryn her phone. Taryn looked down. "Holy crap. I have, like, ten new voice messages."

"Uh-oh." Rebecca glanced down at the screen with her. "That's not good. From who?"

Taryn scrolled through. "Lots of unknown numbers and—" The name that came up on the screen had her breath stalling for a moment. "And some other ones."

Kincaid peeked over. "Lucas. The bastard. How dare he call?"

Liv snorted. "How do you know he's a bastard? She's

never told us what happened. Maybe *she* broke *his* heart. Maybe he's a nice guy and they just didn't click."

"I know because of simple math," Kincaid said matter-of-factly. "Lucas in her life equaled happy, upbeat Taryn. Lucas out of her life equals won't-stop-working, grumpy Taryn. He broke up with her. Therefore, he is the bastard."

Taryn stared at her phone. Shaw had left a message. But so had a bunch of other numbers. She couldn't deal with the Shaw message yet. She hit the button to play one from an unknown number on speaker. "Hi, Dr. Landry, this is Casey Carrigan from Channel Four. We talked at your event a few weeks ago. I was hoping you could make a comment about your relationship with Shaw Miller."

Taryn's stomach flipped and she dropped the phone, trying to stop the message from playing. It clattered to the floor.

Kincaid blinked. "Wait, what?"

"Shaw Miller?" Rebecca asked, brow knitting. "What the hell is she talking about?"

The next message started automatically before Taryn could get her phone back in her hands. Another reporter from some website. "Dr. Landry, a video has surfaced. We understand you must be in shock, but we'd like to speak to you about how you're feeling about Shaw Miller conning you…"

With shaking hands, Taryn hit Pause, her fingers going numb. "Oh God."

All her friends had stopped what they were doing. Rebecca sat down next to her at the table, eyes wide. "Taryn, what's going on? What are they talking about? Conning?"

"Shaw Miller," Kincaid said sharply. "As in Joseph Miller's brother?"

Taryn put her hand to her forehead, her vision cartwheeling for a moment. They knew. Someone knew. Shaw had been outed. *Oh God.* That was why he was calling.

She closed her eyes. "No."

"Honey, you're scaring me," Kincaid said, her hand going to Taryn's shoulder. "What are they talking about?"

There was no denying it now. All these messages. Everyone knew. *What video?* She couldn't even begin to know. Them kissing somewhere? At the gym? At the bar?

She stood abruptly, the room tilting. "I need a minute."

Her friends backed up, giving her space. She put her phone to her ear to listen to Shaw's message. His words were rushed, tumbling over each other, frantic.

"Taryn, it's Shaw. I'm sorry to tell you like this, but a story got out about us. A video from karaoke. Don't answer your door or phone if you don't know who it is. I told the reporter you had no idea who I was. I'll be gone before they can get any more information out of me. Just deny everything. Say you never saw me again after that night. We met at the bar, sang, and that was it. Say you were drunk." There was a pause, a thumping in the background. *"And, Taryn, I'm so sorry for all of this. I never meant to drag you into my mess. I loved the time we spent together."* The phone went silent for a second. *"No, I think I probably just straight-up love you. I know that coming from me, it could never be enough, but I thought you should know. Take care of yourself, songbird."*

Taryn stared at her phone. Her heart was racing. Her

skin was damp. Someone had found out who he was and had linked him to her. That was enough of a shock. But Shaw's parting words had her knees going out from under her. She leaned against the wall and slid to the floor. He'd covered for her. He loved her.

Shaw *loved* her.

But it wasn't enough.

Her friends hurried to her side again, all crouching down around her. Liv pressed her hand on Taryn's knee. "Tell us what's going on. Please. You look like you're going to faint."

Taryn stared at their expectant faces. "Lucas is Shaw. Shaw Miller."

Three sets of eyes went wide. Rebecca made a horrified sound.

"Are you fucking *kidding me?*" Kincaid said, standing straight up with murder in her eyes. "Lucas… He pretended…to you…and he's… I'm going to disembowel the sonofabitch. What's his address?"

"I'm calling Finn," Liv said, rising and going into instant motion as well. "This is like…rape or something…something illegal. Oh my God, Taryn. I'm so sorry. What sick bastard would—"

Taryn lifted a hand. Shaw's words rang in her ear but she couldn't. She just couldn't. "I knew."

The quiet words halted her friends' ranting and moving about. They all stared at her.

Rebecca, forever the calm one, was still crouched in front of her and spoke first. "You knew who he was?"

Taryn nodded miserably. "Yeah. Not at first but early on, before anything got serious. He told me. I'm sorry I kept it from y'all."

Kincaid collapsed into her chair, looking down at Taryn on the floor, a helpless look on her face. "You've been dating Shaw Miller?"

"Yes," Taryn said softly.

"*Why?*" Kincaid asked, clearly dumbfounded. "Didn't he, like, go to jail or something? I heard he's like his brother."

"He's not and he didn't," Taryn said, maybe too sharply. "He had an assault charge on a reporter who verbally attacked him. He's…been through a lot."

Rebecca exchanged a worried look with the other two women.

Taryn smirked without humor. "Y'all think I'm crazy."

Kincaid pressed her lips together. "Can we go with misguided for now? Sugar, I get that he's cute, but the fact that he messed with you at all is…kinda screwed up. What his brother did to all of us…to your family. How could he even approach you?"

"He didn't know who I was either. The night we met, I gave him a fake name. Then things just…happened before we connected all the dots." Taryn rubbed a hand over her brow bone. "He's not his brother. He's sweet and funny and…kind of amazing. But we both knew it was doomed from the start. That's why I broke it off."

Liv groaned and plopped down on the floor in front of her. "*Girl*. We've all been hoping you'd get out there and date, but you went from zero to Romeo-and-Julieting this shit right out the gate."

Taryn laughed, even though tears flooded her eyes. "Do I get extra credit for that?"

Rebecca settled next to her and put her arm around her. "No extra credit but maybe extra hugs. And wine."

Wine.

Taryn started crying and leaned in to Bec. "I thought y'all were going to hate me for lying."

Kincaid's expression turned sympathetic. "It's not my favorite thing you've ever done, but I get why you did. And if you say he's a good guy, then he's a good guy. We've got your back."

"Of course we do. That's never a question," Liv chimed in.

Taryn's chest expanded with their easy acceptance and trust in her, their unconditional love. She knew even thinking about Joseph had to hurt them, but her friends weren't going to judge her or criticize her. Their only concern was that she was okay and safe. No matter what happened with this huge mess, Taryn found comfort in knowing that these women were there for her always, that she was never really alone. That she was part of this family and no one was going to kick her out.

Taryn swiped at her eyes, looking at all her friends. "Thank you. Y'all are the best people I know."

Kincaid smiled. "Of course we are. We're amazing. So are you. That's why you're in the club."

Taryn sniffed.

"But you've got a big decision to make," Liv said gently. Taryn turned her head and met her friend's worried gaze. "What do you want the public to know?"

"More than that," Rebecca said grimly, "what do you want your family to know? You know we'll back your decision no matter which way you choose, but you're going to have to decide."

Taryn closed her eyes. She didn't want to think about it. If she lied to the press, she threw Shaw under the bus and made him look like a sick manipulator. If she told the truth, her family would be devastated and she'd look like a traitor. The internet would eviscerate her and possibly threaten her fund-raising. *That chick is crazy. Who wants to give her money?* Normally, she wouldn't care about public opinion, but the momentum she had in the press for her program would be lost because everyone would be digging into her personal life and mental state instead.

Her phone rang again. Another unknown number.

She needed to talk to Shaw but wasn't sure she could. *I think I probably love you.*

What was she supposed to do with that? The words were everything she wanted to hear and the very thing that hurt her the most. Because he was right—sometimes love wasn't enough.

Sometimes the world took those choices from you. Or worse, it made you decide between different kinds of love.

In this case, only one could win.

She had to decide, and she knew there was only one choice.

She got to her feet and swiped at her eyes. "I need to go."

chapter
TWENTY-FIVE

SHAW TURNED OFF HIS PHONE AND LISTENED TO music on the way down to the coast. He'd had a little trouble slipping past the reporters at the apartment complex, but he'd learned a lot of tricks over the years and had lost the one who had followed him at a complicated interstate interchange. At the end of the day, this story would be a blip on real media, so reporters weren't going to hunt for long. But like last time, this would take on a life of its own on the internet. The public shaming would begin. People who knew nothing about his life or his family would deem themselves experts. He'd be diagnosed, torn apart, and called every disgusting name people could think of. His character, already shredded, would be murdered for good.

He needed to get far away if he wanted any kind of peace. The road seemed like the only choice at this point. He needed to do a little preparation once he got to Galveston Island and signed the papers because his new RV needed more supplies if he was going to take the thing on the road immediately, but he'd worry about that when he got there. He could get it ready quickly enough. He'd just have to suck it up and take out loans for living expenses to make it work until he could find a way to earn some money on the road. He wouldn't be working at the gym anymore now, which gave him a pang of loss, but he'd prepared himself for that. He'd always known it would be a temporary respite.

Just keep moving. That was what he told himself, but his mind kept looking back, the music not loud enough to drown out his thoughts. All he could think about was the mess he'd left behind for Taryn. He couldn't bear the image of those vultures going after her, but he hoped that the story he'd given her to tell would turn all the ugly light toward him and they'd leave her alone. Maybe she'd even be able to raise more for her foundation if people felt she'd been tricked by him. That was little comfort, though.

This was exactly why he should never have let himself get involved with anyone. He only brought drama into their lives. Rivers was going to be dealing with it, too. God, what a fucking disaster. When he got to his destination, he'd compose a statement, confess that he'd tricked Taryn and that she hadn't known any better. Let everyone think he was as sick as they suspected.

What did it matter anymore? The world already thought they knew him. There was no changing people's minds.

He'd known it from the start. He only messed things up for the people he cared about. First, his brother. Then, his best friend. Then, the girl he loved. He didn't belong here.

Or anywhere anymore.

He never should've tried.

—⁓—

Taryn stared at her phone before rolling forward when the light turned green. So much of her wanted to call Shaw back, to hear the words straight from him, to tell him everything was going to be okay. But she couldn't do that. Things were not okay.

All of this was not okay.

Love isn't enough.

It'd been a lesson she'd hoped wasn't true. She was a scientist by nature, but her heart had always held on to the hope that the stories were real, that love conquered all, that if you held on to that notion, things would turn out all right.

She loved her sister. She loved her family. She loved Shaw.

None of that love had been enough to keep them safe, to keep them happy.

She passed Long Acre High, now with a different name and look, but always the same in her memory. Her body tensed. She seized up almost every time she passed the high school, even though she'd lived in this town her whole life. The scars never went away. Her sister's blood was soaked into the sediment of that school, along with that of so many others. She couldn't change that, no matter how hard she tried. No matter what she did or how much research she completed or how many programs she created, the result was the same.

Her sister was gone. She couldn't bring her back.

Taryn pulled into her parents' driveway, and her

father was outside waiting for her. He'd already looked years older than his real age, and the new lines of worry made him look worse. He hurried to pull open her car door. "Thank God you're here, *cher*. A reporter called. Your momma is not taking this well. She needs to see you're okay. *Are* you okay?"

Taryn climbed out of the car and accepted her father's tight hug. "I'm okay."

"I can't believe… We'll deal with all of it," he said in that gruff, fatherly tone he used when he was trying to keep everyone calm. "We can bring charges against him. He impersonated—"

She lifted a hand. "Daddy, let's take care of Mom first, okay?"

He nodded grimly. "All right."

They walked inside, and Taryn could hear her mother's sobs the second she passed the threshold. Her mother shot to her feet when she saw them, her face streaked with tears, and came to Taryn. "Oh, baby." She put her arms around her, trembling. "I cannot believe this. Those horrible people. They took my baby, and now they're trying to hurt my other one. I don't think I can take it. Someone needs to do something. How is he walking the streets?"

"It's okay, Momma." Her mother was bordering on hysterical, and Taryn made soothing noises and hugged her back. She was well practiced at this part at least. The first few years after the shooting, her mom got into these states often, cycling between panic and grief. "Come on, let's sit down."

Her stomach was in knots, but Taryn managed to lead her mom to the living room with her dad in tow. Her mom sat right next to her and put her hands on Taryn's face. "What did he do to you? Have you called the police?"

"No."

"You need to call the police," she insisted.

"Momma," Taryn said, her voice betraying her with a quiver. "He didn't hurt me. I'm okay. Please calm down."

"I will not. How am I supposed to be calm about this?" Her eyes went wide. "Is this the man whose house you were at the other morning?"

"Mom—"

Alarm crossed her face. "Oh God, he raped you."

"Honey…" her father said, his voice tight. "Let her talk. This is very difficult for her."

Taryn felt nauseous. Her parents were staring at her, bracing for the horrible news, ready to comfort her. So much of her wanted to soothe them, to tell them that yes, she was the victim, that none of this was her fault. It was the same feeling she'd had when she'd decided not to tell them she'd opened the door prom night, not to tell them she'd been annoyed with Nia that night. It made it easier for her—but also for them. This time, she couldn't bring herself to do it. "He didn't hurt me. I… was there willingly."

"But he lied to you," her father cut in, hot anger in his voice. "That's rape, Taryn. I know it doesn't seem like it, but he lied and…toyed with you."

Taryn swallowed hard. She'd come here to do this, but now that it was the moment, she wanted to run. She didn't want to hurt them. They'd had so much hurt already for one lifetime. She looked down. "He didn't lie to me."

The words fell between them like a guillotine, cutting off her mom's sobs and replacing them with a sucked-in breath. Taryn lifted her head. They both stared at her as though she'd spoken in a different language.

"What do you mean?" her father asked carefully.

Taryn rubbed her damp palms over her thighs, smoothing invisible wrinkles out of her jeans, trying to find the right words. There were none. All the words were lined with sharp glass. "He didn't lie to me. I knew who he was. We've been seeing each other."

Understanding dawned on her mother's face like night falling over the plains, her expression going from sad to horrified. "Taryn, you are not telling me…"

"I am," she said, her tongue dry as a bone. "I knew who he was. He's not a bad person. He's—"

"The brother of a *murderer*," her mother shouted, getting to her feet. "*Taryn*."

Her dad had a shattered expression on his face.

Taryn pushed forward, trying to stay calm despite her heartbeat crashing in her chest. "I know it's hard to understand. And I'm sorry. I never wanted to upset you. I know how this sounds. He's Joseph's brother, but he's *not* Joseph."

"You study this," her mom said, anger like fire in her voice. "You know this runs in families. He was raised by the same people. He's been in trouble before. How could you do this to us? *To Nia?*"

Taryn got to her feet at that, tears streaming now. "Don't do that, Momma. Please. This is not about Nia. And I study this, but if I believed people were destined to be evil, then what would be the point of all my research and the program? He grew up in the same family, but so many things go into creating a murderer. That's why interventions can work."

Her mother was shaking her head, denying Taryn's words before she was finished saying them. "No. *No*. You are *never* to see this man again. You hear me? This is…ludicrous. I don't know what he put in your head, but—"

"He didn't put anything in my head. He's just a person. A regular person."

"He is not a regular person. He is a Miller. Joseph came from that family. He did not come from a vacuum." Her mother pointed at Taryn. "And you will not tell this to the press. You will not shame this family like that. Think of all the other victims and families," she said, voice shaking. "Think of how this will look. How selfish. You brought that family back into our lives. Just because what? You thought he was good-looking?"

Anger flared in Taryn then. "Think about the victims? The families? *My* family? When do I think about anything else? When?"

"Taryn—" her father warned.

"No. I love you guys with everything I have. I love Nia." She pressed her hand to her chest, her breathing labored now, grief choking her, but she forced the rest of the words out as tears streamed down her face. "I have spent every waking moment of my life since that horrible night fighting for her, for you, for all of us. *Every waking moment*."

"Apparently not all of them if you had time for this man," her mother snapped.

Taryn stared at her in disbelief. "I have given every-thing I have to this. I wanted to help. I wanted to make you proud. I never wanted to hurt you. You have to know that."

"You will never see him again," her mother reiterated. "And you will tell the press you didn't know who he was."

Her dad stepped closer and put his hand on her mother's shoulder. "She's right, *cher*. You know what people will say. You know how ugly this would get. I won't have you putting your mother through that. We've come so far."

Taryn straightened, the guilt spear hitting solid, right in the center of her chest. If this blew up and her mother fell apart again, it would be her fault. After all the work she and her father had done to get her mom stable. But... "I can't do that. It's not right to throw blame at Shaw for this. I won't lie."

"Because you suddenly have a problem with it?" her mom asked. "Didn't seem you had much trouble while you were sleeping in that man's bed."

The words and her mother's cold look burned like an electric shock. Taryn shook her head, staring at the parents she loved so much, and she felt the ground breaking beneath their feet. Nothing would ever be the same if she didn't do what they were asking. This would hurt them. They would never forgive her.

Taryn took a breath. "I don't know if I'll ever see him again. I don't even know where he is right now. But I'm not lying to the press. I won't do that. And I won't say he's a bad person because he's not. He's a victim, too."

Her mother scoffed. "He's brainwashed you. Sociopaths can do that."

"Please," Taryn pleaded. "Please understand. I never did this to hurt you. I love you both more than anything."

"We love you, too, but that's why you need to do what we're telling you to do," her father said gently.

"It's not just the best thing for us. It's the best for you. This man is not worth ruining your reputation over, your program. People will think you sympathize with the killers."

She met her daddy's gaze, her heart breaking. "I have to go."

When they didn't say anything else, her heart crumbled inside her. She turned and walked out the door.

She'd done everything in her life out of love for her family.

She'd hurt them anyway.

Sometimes love wasn't enough.

chapter

TWENTY-SIX

TARYN SAT DOWN IN THE DAMP GRASS, HER BODY feeling empty after the hard sobbing she'd done in the car. After leaving her parents' house, she'd planned to go home but found herself driving to this place instead. The cemetery was eerily quiet at this late hour, and if she believed in ghosts, she'd be nervous, but the only ghosts haunting her tonight were in her head.

She pulled her knees to her chest and looked at her sister's headstone. The daisies they'd brought were already drying out. She didn't know why she'd come here or what she wanted to say, but she'd just felt drawn to this place. Maybe because when she'd have arguments with her parents as a teenager, she'd retreat to her sister's room, knowing she still had at least one person on her side.

This time, she wasn't sure where Nia would stand. Maybe she'd think Taryn was nuts, too. Maybe she was yelling at her from wherever she was now. But as Taryn closed her eyes and pictured her sister, she had a hard time imagining Nia reacting that way. Nia had been popular and well-liked by a lot of social groups because she'd been a naturally openhearted and accepting person. She didn't judge people based on superficial information. Taryn couldn't imagine her labeling Shaw a bad guy without giving him a chance first.

She also couldn't imagine Nia being okay with Taryn doing something that was going to hurt their parents. If she told the truth, Taryn was going to lose that connection with them. Her parents loved her. She knew that wouldn't go away. But she also knew her mother could hold a grudge like a champion. When Taryn was in sixth grade, she'd watched her mom cut a longtime best friend from her life because the woman had said something rude about Taryn's dad. There was no opportunity for forgiveness or discussion. Her mom was just done with the woman.

Taryn didn't want her parents to be done with her. She wanted them to be happy, to find some peace. She'd spent so much of her life trying to give them that. She exhaled and rubbed her hands over her face, further smearing her already destroyed makeup. Could she really cut her parents out for the sake of a guy? That seemed so... messed up. She'd seen coworkers and friends in her life give up so much in the name of a man that it felt categorically against her life philosophy to do that. Anti-Taryn.

But was this really about a man? There was so much more on the line than that.

Taryn released a long breath. "I don't know what to do, baby girl. I've messed this all up."

This time, there were no birds to visit her or signs to guide her. She had to make the decision all on her own. No matter what she did, she was going to hurt someone.

Who was she going to protect?

The answer that whispered through her mind made her ache inside. She didn't want to do it, but she had to.

She pulled her cell phone from her pocket, found the number of one of the reporters who'd called her, and made the call.

———— ⁓ ————

Shaw had made it to the coast, and after spending a restless night in a hotel, he'd taken care of all the final paperwork this morning for the RV. It was his. He'd emailed Rivers to let him know he was okay, but had otherwise kept his phone off.

That afternoon, after grabbing something to eat, he sat on a bench, staring out at the stretch of beach and the Gulf of Mexico beyond. A family was playing along the sand, tossing a football back and forth. The last time Shaw had come here, he'd been eleven or twelve. His parents had promised Joseph a beach vacation during the summer. Joseph had been begging for Florida, hoping for a stop at Disney World, but his parents had chosen Galveston instead because it was cheaper and Shaw had a competition in Houston. All their family vacations once he'd started gymnastics had revolved around where he had a competition.

Shaw remembered Joseph being happy on that trip, though. He could picture the two of them on the stretch of beach before him, throwing "snowballs" at each other made of wet sand. It'd taken days to get all the sand out of their hair. And while Shaw had swum in the surf, Joe had been set on collecting every hermit crab he could find. He'd wanted to start a colony. Their mom had reluctantly agreed to let him bring one home. Joe had snuck home three. Shaw could still remember his little brother's tooth-missing grin when he'd pulled two shells from the pockets of his swim trunks when they'd gotten back to the hotel.

"Don't tell," Joe had whispered to Shaw. "I can't just bring one home. That's stupid. They need friends or they'll be lonely."

Lonely.

The word hit Shaw in the gut, and his hand flexed against the back of the bench. He didn't realize it then, but it was so clear now. Joseph had been alone a lot. Always being dragged to Shaw's events, left to occupy himself during long practices. Joseph had tried a few sports and even gymnastics, but he'd been gangly and had never grown out of the uncoordinated stage. Plus, he'd never been all that interested in sports and had preferred books and video games to keep himself busy—probably because he could do those by himself. Keeping friends had been a challenge. They'd moved a couple of times before settling in Long Acre, each time uprooting Joseph's world but keeping Shaw's relatively the same since he always had his friends at his gym.

Simple loneliness didn't create what Joseph had become, but Shaw couldn't pretend the seeds didn't grow from there. What would his brother have been like if Shaw had been just a regular kid, equal to his brother in his parents' eyes? What if he'd been more supportive of Joe instead of wrapped up in his own drive to get to the Olympics? The guilt was real and pervasive, but as he watched the family on the beach laugh and joke around with one another, so much more than that filled the corners of his heart. He felt the loss. The loss of what could've been.

Now they were all alone. Joseph was gone. His parents had separated. And he was here, back at the same beach, with no one to toss sand at. He would never have what that family in front of him had. No family trips. No marriage. No kids. There was no road to that. His experience in Austin had proved it. Maybe that was for the best. What did he know about marriage or kids? All he knew of them was how families looked when they fell apart, how they failed, how dangerous things could grow and fester right under the surface.

He glanced down at the laptop he'd set beside him. He'd written his statement to send to one of the reporters, explaining that he'd lied to Taryn and misled her, officially burning down what little normalcy he'd built in Austin. This was how it had to be.

But the selfish part of him refused to regret the time he'd spent there. He wouldn't trade his time with Rivers and working at the gym, and he wouldn't trade those two months with Taryn. He hated how things had turned out, but they'd given him a gift he could never repay. The anger that had pumped inside him for so damn long, the beast he'd fought so hard to keep tame, was quiet. He'd realized it when that reporter had pushed his way into his apartment. He'd been upset and angry, but he hadn't lashed out. He'd stayed in control and handled the situation. He'd chosen the better path. He'd changed.

Maybe Joseph could've done that, too. Yes, he was damaged. Yes, Shaw should've handled so much with him differently. His parents shouldn't have favored one child over the other, but in the end, Joseph had made a choice. He hadn't gone insane. He'd known what he was doing. He didn't ask for help. He didn't call someone. He very deliberately planned a massacre and executed it. Shaw wished that he could go back in time and intervene, not say what he'd said to his brother, but Joseph's choice had been his own.

Joseph's crime didn't mean Shaw was destined to go down some dangerous path, too. It didn't mean he was internally broken like he'd thought. Taryn had shown him that. She'd shown him that he was capable of happiness, of falling in love, of being a friend. He'd lean on those memories of her when he was out on the road. Once upon a time, he'd had the girl of his dreams and she'd found him worthy of her for a while. That would have to sustain him.

He'd find out-of-the-way places across the country and not bother anyone. He'd be alone. But at least he would go forward knowing he wasn't a terrible person and that he had earned the right to grieve all he'd lost, too. Maybe after a while, he could even let go of some of the blame he'd carried around so long. Make peace with those mistakes.

But first, he had to protect the woman who'd given him that gift. He lifted the laptop and hit Send. The computer made the sound like mail going through a chute. No turning back now. It was official. The world would think he was just like Joseph.

But Taryn would be safe.

Shaw took one last look at the family on the beach, shut his laptop, and got to his feet. His RV was waiting. He'd pick up the last of his supplies, and then he'd say goodbye to Texas for the last time.

It was time to go.

chapter
TWENTY-SEVEN

Late that evening, Shaw trudged through the sand at the beachside RV resort, arms weighed down with grocery bags. People were scattered around in little groups, some cooking on outdoor grills, others drinking around a fire even though it was too warm for fires. In this part of Texas, you had to take a cool breeze as cold enough. Shaw nodded if people glanced his way but otherwise avoided looking at anyone and inviting conversation.

Music drifted from somewhere in the distance, the melodic chords of a guitar wrapping into the crashing waves. He recognized the song as one his parents used to claim as "their song" when they still loved each other — "Danny's Song." Something about having a son and not having money and being so in love with you, honey.

A wash of loneliness went through him, the strumming making him think of that first night he'd met Taryn. It'd been a completely different place and atmosphere, but the mood felt similar. He'd gone into the bar that night to drink in the dark and forget who he was for a few minutes. Then she'd appeared onstage and flipped all his plans upside down—a light beaming right in his face and daring him to blink and miss it.

Tonight, though, it was just him, and he couldn't even have a drink because he planned to drive all night. His phone buzzed in his pocket and he groaned. The reporter he'd sent the confession to had emailed to say she needed verbal confirmation and wanted to call. Shaw had agreed, even though it was the last thing he wanted to do, but he needed to get it over with. One more call and he'd be done with this mess.

He shifted the bags to one arm and pulled out his phone. "Hello."

"Mr. Miller? This is Angelica Lopez," said a young, eager voice.

"Yes. Hi," he said without enthusiasm.

"I appreciate you taking my call," she said, rushing on. "First, I wanted to thank you for reaching out to me. I'm really pleased you chose me to tell the story."

He sniffed. He'd picked her because her approach had been the least annoying. Not a hard contest to win based on his phone messages. "Ms. Lopez, I'm sorry, but I only have a minute. What do you need from me to run the story?"

"Well, that's what I wanted to talk to you about," she said, some of the bounce in her voice flattening out. "I can't run the story."

He stopped walking. "What? Why?"

She cleared her throat. "Well, because Dr. Landry has made a statement, and it's contradictory. She said she knew who you were and was a willing participant in your relationship."

Shaw dropped the bags with a *thunk*. "She did *what*?"

"Yes, sir. She said that you're a good man who's been terrorized by the media and that the press needs to quote 'leave him the hell alone and let him live his life because he's a victim in all this, too.'"

"Shit." He looked up to the dark blanket of night sky, some weird combination of frustration and amazement washing over him. She'd told the truth. Taryn had stood up for him. She'd told the truth and made herself a target. Risked her friends' and family's trust. He let out a rough breath. *Dammit, professor.*

Why would she do that? Why would she put herself through that? He'd lined everything up to save her that pain. The wind off the ocean whipped around him, tugging his hair out of the rubber band he'd pulled it back with, blocking his view of the sky.

"So I was hoping you'd give me a statement?" Angelica asked, her voice rising at the end. "Confirm or deny?"

He pushed his hair out of his face, grabbed his bags, his fingers numb, and picked up speed to get back to the RV. He needed to see what kind of fallout Taryn was facing. Maybe he could still undo this. He could say he'd put her up to the statement or… God, he didn't know. *Something*. There had to be a way to undo it. "I can't make one right now."

"Mr. Miller—"

Shaw ended the call and caught sight of his RV. The music grew louder, and the smell of roasted hot dogs drifted on the air, but his stomach was churning. He'd set everything up for Taryn to be okay. He needed to figure out how to fix this.

But when he rushed around the rear corner of his RV to get to the door, he stopped cold. Sitting on a rock under the light of the moon was a girl with a guitar, her hair dancing in the ocean breeze like a wild thing and his parents' song drifting from her fingertips. His heart fell to his feet.

Taryn looked up from her guitar, and his breath froze in his chest. He was afraid to move, as if she were a butterfly who'd easily startle and flit off if he so much as breathed. She gave him a tentative smile, her fingers stilling against the strings. "Hey."

Her eyes looked puffy from crying, and there was a somberness to her, but he'd never seen anyone look more beautiful—the guitar cradled in her arms, a long, flowery skirt swirling around her legs, moonlight kissing her smooth skin. He set his bags down slowly, afraid he was having some kind of mental episode and hallucinating her presence. "Taryn."

She draped her arm over the top of her guitar, an unsure look on her face. "Surprised?"

And the winner of the Understatement of the Year Award goes to…

"What are you doing here?" He glanced around as if he expected the answer to pop up from behind the sand dunes. *"How* are you here?"

"How?" She smirked. "You do realize I'm a researcher, right? Stalking is in my wheelhouse. Your phone's on Rivers's account. He tracked your location."

He stared at her. "But why?"

"You weren't taking my calls, and I needed to talk to you." She wet her lips. "Because you can't tell a woman you think you probably love her in a voicemail and then disappear into the night. That is a chickenshit thing to do, Miller."

"A—" His lips parted, but he was having trouble finding words.

"I thought we should talk," she said finally. "You know, before you go."

He shook his head, still not believing she was right there in front of him. He'd thought he'd never see her again, and his head was spinning, but then the phone call he'd just received set in. "You told a reporter the truth. You weren't supposed to do that."

"Yeah." She looked down and ran her fingers over the strings. "I'm not real good at following orders."

"Taryn…" His ribs cinched. "Your family. Do they—"

"They know." Her shoulders rose and fell with a deep breath, and she set the guitar aside, leaning it against the rock. "I told them before the news could get out. They…did not take it well." She looked up at him. "But I wasn't going to lie about you. You don't deserve that."

He stepped closer, almost afraid to get within touching distance. He wanted to embrace her, to tell her he was sorry, to take away some of that hurt in her voice, but he forced his arms to stay at his sides. "You don't deserve to have your family upset with you. You didn't do anything wrong."

"Neither of us did. That's the point." She stood and pushed her hair away from her face, her skirt dancing like flames around her legs. "Believe me, I considered lying for the sake of my family, but shielding them from the truth meant harming you. Harming *us*. Long Acre has enough victims. We shouldn't have to apologize because we…like each other. Don't we both have the right to feel what we feel? Haven't we earned that?"

"Of course you have," he said without pause. "You deserve the world, Taryn. That's why I didn't want you dragged into any of this."

She took a step forward, her arms at her sides, palms facing him. "But what if I want that world to include you?"

His lungs compressed as if they'd forgotten how to draw air. "Taryn…"

"Don't leave," she said quietly, meeting his gaze. "Not if you really meant what you said on the phone. I can take whatever people want to throw at me. I don't need your protection or you falling on a sword for me. I'm not sure if you noticed, but I'm pretty fucking tough all on my own."

Tough? They'd need to come up with a stronger word than that to describe this woman.

"My family will have to handle this in their own way," she continued, a flash of pain in her eyes. "But my friends are in full support. Rivers supports you. We won't be alone in this. *You* don't have to be alone in this anymore. You can be you. With me. No more hiding."

Not alone. Not hiding. With Taryn. The concepts seemed so foreign that he almost couldn't grasp them and hold them in his mind. Taryn wasn't just offering herself but her friends, her world, inviting him in, even with all the heavy baggage that came along with him. It was everything he wanted. It was too much.

He closed the gap between them, unable to help himself. He had to touch her. He cupped her face in his palms, an ache deeper than he'd ever felt pinging through him. "Baby, I can't tell you what that means to me, but don't do this. You're too big-hearted. I don't want you to get hurt in this. You don't need to save me."

She smiled then, tears making her eyes shine. "What if I'm saving myself?"

He looked down at her, bewildered. "Taryn..."

"I love you back, Shaw."

The words hit him like a blow to the head, stunning him and making him feel dizzy. He held on to her, afraid he'd fall, his heart pounding.

"I know we didn't get that much time together," she continued. "But I think I knew almost right away. That night I met you outside the bar, I felt something different with you, something I'd never come close to before. Like the universe tapped me on the shoulder and said *this one*. I think that's why I refused to give up even when I found out who you were." She shook her head in his grasp. "And I'm not saying that to put pressure on you or to make you feel like you have to jump into something serious. You said you think you probably love me, but if that's not for sure, I understand. Either way, I thought you should know how I feel, and I didn't want you to leave without knowing and—"

She was rambling. And she loved him. And he couldn't take it anymore. He bent down and did what he'd been wanting to do since he'd seen her sitting on that rock. He kissed her, cutting off her words and giving himself over to the love that was coursing inside him, letting himself feel it fully for the first time. No fine print. No warning labels. He kissed her like a man who'd thought he'd never see his woman again. He poured every ounce of emotion he'd been holding inside since she'd walked out the door two weeks ago into it. And she kissed him back as if she hadn't been able to bear it either.

She loved him.

She *loved* him.

She loved *him*.

Every part of that was a damn miracle.

Eventually, he pulled back and brushed her tears away with his thumbs. She was so beautiful, it almost hurt to look at her. Like staring into the sun. "Baby, there is no *think* or *probably* about it. I love you. I love you so much that it's killing me to think any of this ugliness is gonna touch you."

She smiled. "You are not ugliness. You are Shaw Miller, the guy I love. You are worth the trouble."

"Taryn," he whispered.

She pressed her hands to his chest, her tears still slipping out. "I needed you to know all that first. But that's not all I'm here to say. Before we take this any further, there's something else you should know."

He frowned at the flash of wariness in her eyes. He swiped at her tears. "What is it, baby?"

Taryn's throat was trying to close. She'd never been so happy and terrified at the same time. She felt like there was just a pinprick of space to push words through, but she took a breath and straightened her spine. She'd spent the entire three-and-a-half-hour drive down here thinking of what she was going to say to Shaw. But now that the moment was here, she was panicking.

Shaw looked down with concern and pushed her

hair away from her face. "Tell me what's going on. Something with the press?"

She shook her head. *Do it. Do it.* She'd just given her speech about being tough, but now she felt like she was going to collapse into a pile of useless marshmallow fluff. The campers she'd passed could make a s'more out of her. *No.* She could do this. She took another breath and met his gaze. "So, before I drove down here, I did a thing."

His brows lifted. "A thing?"

She stepped back out of his embrace, wanting to give them both breathing room, and pulled her phone out of her skirt pocket with a shaky hand. She pulled up a photo, stared at it for a long moment, and then looked up at him. "Yeah. Turns out the first one was wrong."

After a steadying breath, she turned the phone to face him, and he took it from her. His eyes scanned the screen, his Adam's apple bobbing as he examined the photo, and then all expression washed off his face, along with the color in his cheeks.

"Two lines," he whispered.

Taryn's heartbeat was louder than the ocean waves, pounding against her temples. "Yeah. Two lines. We must've taken the other one too early. I did two more after the one in the photo to confirm. Two lines. Two hearts. And a yes."

Shaw looked up, a frightened-rabbit look on his face. "Oh God, Taryn. I'm…" He stepped past her and collapsed onto the rock where she'd been sitting. "I'm so sorry. This is…"

Her stomach dropped, his reaction not what she'd been hoping for. She could hear the unspoken words in the empty space. This is…*awful, terrible, bad news.* "Shaw."

He set her phone down and put his head in his hands, his hair hiding his face from her. "Jesus, no wonder you tracked me down. I'll help with whatever you need. I'll go with you."

"Go with me?"

He looked up, grief on his face. "To take care of it."

Her chest constricted, and she stepped forward, lowering herself to her knees in front of him. "Shaw, there is no taking care of it. I know this wasn't the plan. At all. But…I'm not ending this pregnancy. You can be part of that or not, but I'm keeping the baby."

Shaw's eyes rounded. "Keeping…but it's… My family… Why would you want…"

She couldn't bear the heartbreak in his eyes. She put her hands on his knees. "I'm not worried about your family. This baby was created from you and me. We are two amazing people, and though this wasn't planned, it was created out of love. This baby is going to kick ass."

Tears glittered in his eyes. "You want to have my baby?"

The hope in his voice nearly cracked her right open. She smiled through her own tears. "Yes. Have you seen how hot we are? This baby is going to be gorgeous."

A choked sound escaped him, some combo of a laugh and a sob.

"But if you're not ready to be a dad, I'm not going to force it on you. This is a huge, unexpected, life-altering thing. It's your choice to get involved or not," she said, trying to be mature but also freaking out on the inside. She could do this on her own. She could. But she didn't want to. She wanted Shaw in her life, not just as her baby's father, but as her guy. "I'm not going to stop you from leaving."

"Leaving?" he said in disbelief. "You think I would leave now?"

She looked away. "I don't want guilt or obligation to be the only thing that keeps you here."

"Taryn. This isn't—" Shaw slid down onto his knees, a look of wonder on his face. "Of course I'm not leaving. I wasn't leaving the minute you showed up here and told me you loved me back. This is…everything. I've never been so happy as the days I've spent with you. I felt it that first night, too. That this-is-special thing." He kissed her gently. "I love you. I wanted to be with you before this, but now…" He looked down at her belly, putting his hand there with a whisper-soft touch. "Now, you're never getting rid of me. I hope you realize that. You're stuck with me, songbird."

She grinned and swiped at her nose, on the edge of going into the ugly cry. "I think I can probably live with that."

"*Think* you can *probably?*" he teased.

She laughed. "I definitely can."

He cradled her face and shook his head in awe. "A baby. *Our* baby. Holy crap."

The words still made anxiety shimmer through her. This was all so much so fast. It was all so new. But another part of her felt the rightness of it all, the perfect combination sliding into the lock and opening a door she'd never thought she'd walk through. "Pretty crazy, huh? I think the universe had a plan."

He arched a brow. "An expired condom plan?"

"It works in mysterious ways."

"Yeah, it does." He kissed her again, a little more urgently this time. "How are you feeling?"

"Good. Excited," she confessed, meaning it. "And completely freaking terrified because...holy shit, a baby."

He laughed. "Glad we're on the same page. Because I have no idea what I'm doing."

She touched her forehead to his and wrapped her arms around his neck. "You think I do? How about we figure it out together? We'll climb the wall as a team."

"Together." He closed his eyes and held her. "That sounds perfect."

"Yeah," she whispered. "It kinda does, doesn't it?"

He lifted his head and looked at her, tenderness there. "Everyone is going to think we're batshit crazy."

"Let 'em. I'm really, *really* tired of worrying about what other people think."

He cocked his head. "And I'm going to need to sell this ridiculous RV."

She snorted and glanced over at the giant vehicle before looking back to him. "I don't know. It looks kinda cool. Maybe we can take family vacations in it."

"Family vacations." The look that crossed his face undid her completely. In that look, she saw everything she needed to know. All of her doubts and worries faded. He wanted this. All of it. Her. And this baby. A family.

They were going to be a family.

She didn't expect it to be easy. This was all new and scary and sudden. The world was going to have its opinions. Their child would one day learn about the past. Taryn's family may never forgive her. But for once, all that mattered was how she felt in this moment. She was happy. This was right. They loved each other.

She'd been wrong.

Sometimes love *was* enough.

Shaw stood and pulled her to her feet. "Want to see inside our new family RV?"

She squeezed his hands and rocked forward on her toes. "Of course. I think it's proper procedure to christen a new vehicle before travel...you know, for luck."

"Yes. Absolutely," he agreed, his tone serious. "Naked christening. I think that's a requirement."

She nodded. "Of course. We have to do it right."

He grinned and bent down, sweeping her off her feet and into his arms, grocery bags forgotten. "We will. Do it right. But I don't need the luck. I already have it."

She pulled at the collar of his shirt. "Because you're about to get lucky?"

He shook his head. "No, because I have you."

She put her hand over his heart, something restless settling inside her, and took a long-awaited deep breath. "You do. You had me right from the start."

He kissed her again and then carried her into the RV. "And I want you to the very end."

chapter

TWENTY-EIGHT

SHAW LAID TARYN ALONG THE BED IN THE BACK OF the RV, thankful that he'd taken the time to put new sheets on the mattress, and stared down at this woman in awe. No, not this woman, *his* woman. She smiled up at him, trusting, glowing with happiness.

With more than that. Not just happiness, but glowing with new life and love. He still couldn't believe it. When she'd told him she was keeping the pregnancy, every cell in his body had wanted to collapse—with relief, with love, with fear.

So much about this scared him. He didn't know how to be a dad. He didn't know if some dangerous gene ran through his blood. He didn't know how he would tell his son or daughter about their uncle Joseph and the pain he'd caused so many people. All of that flat-out terrified him. But the other picture of the future, the one where Taryn was holding a child who had her bright smile and her curly hair and maybe little pieces of him, too, one who was a blend of both of them, that image filled him with a joy he'd never experienced before. One that flooded every dark corner inside him with light. He was going to be a dad. Hopefully, a husband one day, if Taryn would have him. He would be part of a family. He would be part of love.

He knew this probably wasn't how Taryn had planned her future to turn out. She'd probably had a much more methodical, well-thought-out plan in mind, but right now, he chose to believe her when she said she was happy and excited. When she said she loved him. That was a miracle in and of itself. As was getting her pregnant because of a random box of condoms. He was done questioning unexpected gifts.

He wasn't sure if he believed in a higher power. He'd questioned the existence of any entity that would allow Long Acre to happen. But right now, gazing down at this woman he loved, for the first time, he believed the divine could exist. Somehow, the universe had brought Taryn to him. He couldn't deny the magic in that.

He lowered himself onto the bed, straddling her thighs and brushing the back of his hand over her cheek. "You are so epically beautiful."

A warm, full smile lifted her lips. "Back at ya, handsome."

He traced the edge of her jaw. "I'm sorry you had to give up so much to be here."

"Stop." A frown wrinkled her brow. Then she reached for his shirt and pulled him down to her, brushing her lips over his. "Don't you get it, Shaw? Letting you walk away would be giving up so much more. You are a gift. You're worth the price of admission."

He closed his eyes, letting her words move through him. "I love you, Taryn Landry."

"I love you, Shaw Miller."

His real name had never sounded so sweet to his

ears. He braced above her and let his gaze drift over her, wanting her so badly, he ached. "So is there anything I need to be careful about?"

She grinned and wiggled beneath him. "Yeah, make sure it's good."

He laughed, the sound loud in the small space. "You know what I mean."

She unfastened the buttons of his shirt. "I've researched."

"Of course you have," he said, warmth filling him. "And what have you discovered, professor?"

She dragged her fingernails over the exposed strip of his chest. "No special rules. Except one."

He tilted his head, loving the feel of her hands on him, his body growing hard and ready at the simple touch. "What's that?"

She let his shirt fall open and licked her lips. "I want it to be just you and me. No more condoms." She gave him a sly look. "I mean, it's not like you can get me pregnant."

"Ha."

She ran her fingertips over his abdomen, sending tendrils of sensation downward. "I want to feel all of you. Your skin. Your heat. No more barriers."

His blood went hot at the words. No more barriers. But more than that. No more walls. No more secrets. Naked in all the most important ways. "I can do that." He tugged off his shirt and tossed it somewhere behind him. "I hope this thing has insulated walls because I plan to make this road trip of yours worth it."

Her expression turned wicked. "You better. Houston traffic is a nightmare."

He laughed.

She dropped her hands to the waistband of his jeans. "Let's scandalize the park."

He reached over and cracked the window just enough so they could hear the crashing waves out on the beach. "Let's drown out that ocean."

He lay beside her and undressed her, taking his time and revealing each delectable inch of smooth, warm skin. He couldn't believe how lucky he'd gotten, finding this woman. He was fascinated by every inch of her—how her belly fluttered as her breaths quickened, the way her nipples tightened in anticipation of his touch, the way she kept licking her lips—but most of all, he loved how she looked at him. Like he meant something to her. The love and desire were drugs he could get used to.

He took his time stripping her bare and got rid of his own clothes. Then he pressed every part of him against her—skin to skin, heartbeat to heartbeat, soft against hard—taking her mouth in a kiss and letting all the worries and stress of the last fourteen days dissolve in the space between them. He'd made it to the other side of what he'd thought was an endless bridge. This was a new journey, and he couldn't wait to start.

Taryn sighed as Shaw's warmth and weight pressed against her, his cock hard and heavy already and his touch lighting her on fire. She could feel the difference in him. She'd thought she'd seen all of him, but this was new. There was an abandon in him, a laid-bare vulnerability. It took her a moment to realize what it was. *Trust.* He was trusting her to see him defenseless, his heart pinned on his proverbial sleeve, a core of sweetness and yearning he'd never let her see before.

He loved her, and he was showing her the full depth of his feeling. He kissed her as though she was his air, and she breathed him in, letting all that this meant wash over her. He was hers. She finally got the distinction between sex and making love. She'd always thought the latter would be significantly less hot, but she'd been so very wrong. This was the sexiest she'd ever felt in her life.

She let her hands travel down his back, feeling his muscles roll and flex with tension as he rubbed against her, lighting her nerve endings up with all the most delicious sensations. Her hands reached his backside and she gripped, loving the thick muscle and the feel of him hot in her hands. *Mine*.

She'd been so afraid driving down here, not knowing what to expect, preparing herself in case he still wanted to leave, but now she could let that fear go and simply enjoy him. There were still a lot of things they'd have to deal with when they got back home. But she felt confident in her decision.

She'd chosen the truth over living a lie. It was the right thing to do, not just for Shaw but for herself. She'd denied herself a lot of things in her life in the name of her research and fighting for her family. She didn't regret giving up singing or her dreams of living somewhere else. She was proud of the things she'd accomplished. But she would've regretted giving up the chance to love and be loved. She deserved happiness—even if there was so much loss and sadness in her past. She would've said that before if someone had asked, but she'd lived her life not really believing it, never making room for it, always putting her own needs on the back burner.

Sitting at Nia's grave had confirmed what was the right thing to do. Her sister would want her to fight and to keep fighting. Nia would want her to take care of their parents. But ultimately, Nia wouldn't want Taryn to give up her life to do it. Her sister would want her to be happy.

So Taryn was here, taking that leap. She was happy. And she would not feel guilty about it.

Shaw pulled back from the kiss and smiled. "Still with me, beautiful?"

"Always."

His smile made her insides melt. "Then let's get loud, baby."

"Hell yes."

Shaw worked his way down her body, kissing her breasts and teasing her with his tongue, marking a path down her sternum and her belly, and then he found her center, kissing her there with soft lips, a hot tongue, and the skill of a lover who'd paid attention and learned her favorite parts.

He was her favorite part.

His touch made everything inside her soar. She arched as he licked over her sweet spot and teased her with his fingers. Slowly, skillfully, and with the reverence of a guy who loved going down on a woman and making her moan. It hadn't been but a few weeks since she'd last been with him, but her body felt starved for him. She rocked against his mouth, shamelessly gripping his hair and murmuring nonsense. He was in full worship mode, and her body tightened so fast that she thought she might snap into pieces. She called his name in warning, but then he sucked her clit between his lips, and colors exploded behind her eyelids. Her orgasm rushed up like a rocket, taking her breath and then making her cry out. She made needy sounds she'd probably regret later, but right now, she didn't care who heard.

Shaw groaned, let loose a few expletives, and then crawled up her body, kissing his way back up like a starved man gorging on a buffet. When he made it back face-to-face, he took her by the hips and rolled her atop him.

She braced her hands on his chest, now damp with sweat, and her lips curved. "I get control tonight, huh?"

He dragged a ravenous gaze over her body. "You can have whatever you want, baby. I just want to watch you. I want to see your face when you come like that again."

Heat rolled through her and she shivered. Even though she'd just had an orgasm, her body ached for more of him, all of him. She lifted herself up and took his cock in her hand, rubbing her palm along the length of him and smoothing the drop of fluid at the tip with her thumb. The smooth velvet feel of his skin made her shiver with anticipation. He would be inside her just like this. Skin to skin. He was watching her with rapt attention as she brought her thumb to her mouth and licked the taste of him from it.

Shaw groaned, and his grip on her hips tightened. "You're going to kill me, professor. And I'm going to die a happy man."

"No dying. I've got plans for you, Miller. Lots of dirty, dirty plans."

He slid his hands along her thighs. "I'm here for you, gorgeous. I'm here."

Yes, he was. And so was she. In this moment. And for many, many more.

She positioned the head of his cock at her entrance,

teasing him a little and loving the look of erotic pain on his face, and then she lowered herself, welcoming him inside her body and taking her sweet time doing it. He was going to regret making her do all that exercise. She could hold herself in this torturous inch-by-inch descent for as long as she wanted, but eventually, her own needs gave way and she let herself go. The slick glide of him filling her completely made her teeth bite into her lip and her breath rattle out of her. She closed her eyes as he groaned along with her, letting herself enjoy all the sensations, feeling every bit of him inside her.

When she lifted her lids, he was giving her a look that said he was about to ruin her in the best way possible. "Remember that first night when I said I might not last long?"

She smirked and let her fingers trail down his abdomen before running her fingertip along the spot where they joined. "Yeah."

His cock twitched inside her, getting even harder. "You feel so good, I think I'm going to make this one last all night."

He dragged her down to him for a kiss and rocked into her deep, cupping her ass and moving her just how he wanted her, angling himself in a way that made her want to thank God she was a woman.

He'd said she had the control, but that was a lie. Because in that moment, with his body pumping into hers and his arms wrapped around her, she was lost to him. Her soul and her heart. She'd spent her whole life fighting. She would still fight.

But when it came to love, she'd learned that she didn't need to fight for it.

She needed to surrender.

Epilogue

THREE MONTHS LATER

TARYN TRIED NOT TO BITE HER NAILS AS THE SCREEN was set up in front of the auditorium. A small crowd of people, many of whom had attended the charity event at Gym Xtreme, sat in the audience, along with other supporters of the cause. She'd also caught sight of the vice president of the school board, the one who'd been apologetic the night of her initial presentation. She'd smiled and nodded Taryn's way when she'd come in but hadn't approached her. Taryn didn't want to get her hopes up that the school board members might be changing their minds, but it was nice to see someone still willing to listen.

Kincaid stepped up beside Taryn and gave her arm a pat. "This is a great turnout, lady. Way more than showed up for that school board meeting."

"I know, right?" Taryn smiled. "See, I can't take credit, though. I have this friend who's really good at spreading the word on social media and around town. She'll talk to anyone. I should introduce you to her. Oh wait, it's you."

Kincaid curtsied. "Who said a big mouth doesn't pay off?"

"Thank you for all your help. Also, I have to say, the appetizers are top-notch. Those mini biscuits were to die for. You should put them on your blog." Kincaid's side project was a blog where she re-created restaurant recipes for the home cook, and she was always coming up with delicious home-style food.

"Thanks. I tweaked a family recipe and added cheese, because cheese makes everything better. But I had help, too. I menu planned and provided recipes, but Wes executed it all. He's the real chef with the skills to cook for a crowd. My limit is dinner for eight. If I'd cooked for this many people, I would have flour in my hair, half the food would be burned, and I'd be on my second bottle of wine by now."

Taryn leaned into her friend to bump shoulders with her. "You're the best. I'll never be able to repay you for all this. Your real estate job keeps you busy enough. You didn't have to give me so much of your time on this. Neither did Liv and Rebecca."

"As if we'd do anything else," Kincaid said with an eye roll. "This is an amazing thing you're doing. We all want this to succeed. The world needs Dr. Taryn Landry's program in their schools." She eyed the stage. "I just hope I look cute in the video. I got all"—she waved a hand in front of her face—"tragic. My water-proof mascara barely held up."

"Aww, I'm sure it's fine. Liv made sure we all had great lighting when we filmed. Plus, when do you not look cute?"

Kincaid nodded with mock seriousness. "Valid point. Though with two pregnant ladies around me, I'm falling down the cuteness chain of command fast. I cannot compete with pregnancy glow. Maybe I should carry around a puppy or something."

Taryn laughed, automatically touching the little belly pooch that was rounding more and more every day. "You'll be back on top when we get to the grumpy, waddling walrus phase."

"Nah, y'all will be adorable then, too. Oh, which reminds me. I've found you and Shaw the perfect two-bedroom condo. It's right near where Shaw is now but has much more space, is on the top floor, and has a gorgeous view. Really close to a park, too. I set up a tour for tomorrow morning."

Taryn lit up. "Really? That's fantastic." She and Shaw had decided to move in together and let go of her house in Long Acre. It didn't make sense for her to be commuting so much, and she was always staying at Shaw's place anyway. The thought of living in the city thrilled her, even though a pang of sadness went through her that she wouldn't be near her parents anymore.

"Yeah, you won't be too far from Rebecca either, so your kiddos can grow up near each other."

The thought warmed Taryn. She scanned the room. "Where is Bec?"

"She's helping Wes keep the food trays refreshed, and Liv is backstage, making sure everything is perfect with the video. She was editing until late last night."

Taryn huffed and put a hand on her waist. "I told that woman to go to bed. The video looked perfect in the last round she sent me."

"She's a perfectionist." Kincaid gave her a look. "Plus, I think maybe she had a little more to add."

"More to add?" Taryn lifted an eyebrow.

Kincaid shrugged and had a little too innocent a look on her face. "You'll see."

Taryn didn't like the sound of that. She didn't need any surprises tonight. This event needed to go off without a hitch, but before she could comment, two big arms wrapped around her from behind. "It's almost time for your big show, songbird."

Shaw's fresh soap scent surrounded her, and she automatically melted into his hold, leaning her head back on his shoulder. "Hey, you. Where'd you disappear to?"

"I did a poison test on all the food and made you a plate for after you're done."

She snorted. "A poison test?"

"Yes. It was important to try each thing…you know, for the good of the crowd. Did you know they have tiny cheesy biscuits?"

She laughed. She'd learned quickly that Shaw could out-eat a pregnant lady. All those hours training people at the gym required a lot of fuel. She tried not to hate him for being able to eat whatever he wanted. "The biscuits are Kincaid's recipe."

"That's a keeper," he told Kincaid, who had turned to face them, a pleased smile on her lips.

"Thanks," she said. "And y'all are sickeningly cute together. I can barely stand it."

But the words were delivered with a sappy smile. Taryn stuck her tongue out at her friend. "You matched us. It's your fault."

"Yes, I totally did."

Behind Kincaid, Taryn caught audience members glancing her and Shaw's way, trying to hide their obvious curiosity. She ignored them. The story had broken on a local news website that a Long Acre survivor and the shooter's brother were a couple and were heading up a campaign to raise funds for a school program. Gossipy non-news sites and conspiracy-theory message boards had sensationalized the story and tried to stir up shit, but both she and Shaw had learned it was best to ignore idiots on the internet. They'd also gotten phone calls and emails from the press for a few weeks, but the attention had blessedly slacked off. There was always new news, fresh scandals.

The only thing that still hurt was the strained situation with her parents.

They'd gone radio silent, and that saddened Taryn every time she thought about it. She'd spent her whole adulthood seeing them at least weekly and having a close relationship with them both. Now there was a huge blank space in her world. One of the biggest things in her life had happened—she was going to have a baby— and she couldn't talk to the person she wanted to talk about it with most, her mother. Her mom and dad had no idea they were going to be grandparents.

Beyond her desire to have a relationship with them, Taryn was worried about her mother, but she couldn't do anything about it if they weren't ready to talk to her. She wasn't going to push them. She'd left a voice message telling them she was always willing to talk. That was all she could do. Be open to them. Still, their lack of response had hurt.

Shaw gave her a squeeze. "You ready for this?"

Taryn nodded. "Yep. I'm proud of what we've put together. We've done the best we know how to do. We're swinging for the fences."

"Seriously," Kincaid said, crossing her arms. "If this doesn't bring the money in, then people have no hearts. We kicked that Sarah McLachlan animal video's ass. And that was a tough ass to kick." She pointed to the crowd. "I expect tears. Hand-wringing. And wallet-emptying. Anything less and these people will have to deal with me."

Shaw chuckled softly against Taryn's ear. "Sometimes your friends scare me."

Kincaid put a hand to her hip. "You better be scared, big guy. Top-notch treatment for this one, or you're going to have to face all of us. Be afraid."

Taryn snorted. "She is small but mighty."

Shaw lifted his palms. "If I treat her like anything less than a queen, you have the right to throat-punch me."

"Throat-punch?" Kincaid smirked and cocked a brow. "I aim lower, honey, just so you know."

Shaw hid behind Taryn. "Ouch."

Taryn laughed. "Yeah, don't wrong this one. Remind me to tell you about a certain guy in high school, a wandering eye, and a car full of dog food."

"It was more than his eye that wandered," Kincaid said flippantly. "Now, get yourself ready to inspire and amaze. You're on in three minutes." She gave a little wave and walked off to check on things.

Taryn turned in Shaw's arms. "You sure you want to stay for this? It may be…hard."

In the longer video, they'd had survivors do testimonials. Even knowing the stories, Taryn had sobbed watching the rough cuts Liv had sent her. She'd had to fight not to lose it when she gave her own testimonial. She couldn't imagine what it was going to be like for Shaw to see all these people talk about losses his brother had caused.

He looked down at her and kissed the tip of her nose. "It's supposed to be hard. That's okay. I avoided anything having to do with Long Acre for a long time, but I need to be here for this. Seeing this program get into schools is important and personal to me, too."

She let out a breath, still worried for him but also relieved to have him there with her. "Okay, then let's do this. Save me a spot in the front row."

Shaw gave her a quick kiss and then left her to go find their seats. She smoothed her suit jacket and then took her note cards out of her pocket. But after glancing at them briefly, she put them away just as quickly. She didn't need this to be rehearsed. That was the mistake she'd made with the school board, speaking from an intellectual, scientific place—the safe place where she was just a professor reciting statistics, the place where she didn't have to feel every bit of her grief. Tonight, she needed to be Taryn, not Dr. Landry. She knew what she wanted to say, and she needed to say it from her heart.

When the lights dimmed, Liv stepped out from backstage and up to the microphone to introduce her. Taryn turned, smiled, and walked up to the stage with her heart firmly attached to her sleeve. For so long, she'd protected that thing like it was the Hope diamond. Safe. Guarded. Lonely. She'd first started to unlock that vault when Liv, Rebecca, and Kincaid had come back into her life, but Shaw had helped put in the final numbers to that code. They'd taught her something she never would've believed before—that vulnerability was a superpower. Tonight, she had to wield that superpower with all her might.

She stepped behind the podium, took a deep breath, and looked out to the audience. "Thank you for coming.

It means a lot to me to see so many of you here. Maybe you already know I'm a professor and that I've spent years studying this topic, but tonight, I'm standing in front of you not as the expert but as a survivor, pleading for your help. It's been many years since I walked the halls of Long Acre High and a long time since that horrible night, but something like that never leaves you. The *loss* never leaves you. The news cycle moves on, but we are the ones left behind to deal with it."

The audience was quiet, all eyes trained on her. She took a breath and went on.

"It changes who you are. The pain is always there. The people we lost never come back." Her throat tightened. "Every day, I think of my younger sister, Nia. Every day, I miss her. I miss who she was, and I mourn who she could've become. That was stolen from her. It was stolen from me and my family. All of us who were there that night or who are connected to someone who was there walk around with holes inside ourselves, wounds that can never be healed. And I'd like to say it was a freak incident, that it was a one-time thing, that we were just unlucky, that no one else will have to walk around with these gashes ripped into them, but I can't. I can't because we are not alone in this grief. Since Long Acre, there have been so many more tragedies just like it that most of us have lost count. Every few weeks, another group of kids and teachers gets membership in a club no one wants to be in—the victims, the survivors, the traumatized, the grieving. Or worse, the perpetrators."

She took another breath and caught Shaw's gaze in the audience. "It's time not just to say 'enough' but to *do something*. Not after the next tragedy. Not during it. Now.

Before it happens again. Kids are hurting. Growing up is tough. But these tragedies don't happen in a vacuum. Kids may be born with certain vulnerabilities, but they aren't born killers. We are not helpless. We need programs in our schools and community that don't just step in when it's too late. We need all children to have access to supportive mentors, to mental health services, to their community, to each other. We need to connect them to activities that will give them confidence and a sense of pride and belonging.

"We are most at risk when we are alone. Isolation breeds dark and dangerous things. Love and connection combat that." She swallowed hard. "Love goes a long way. So I hope you'll watch these stories and help me and the other survivors spread the information so that we can do something now. Doing nothing is no longer an option. Doing nothing is saying that we think this is okay. It's not okay. We have to fight." She put her hand to her belly without thinking.

"I don't want my children to walk into school wondering if they're going to make it home that day or if they're going to become an only child overnight. I don't want my children to ever feel what I and the people in these videos have felt. I hope you'll join me in writing an ending to this story because none of us wants to see a repeat of it ever again. We have seen it far too many times already. Thank you."

Taryn gripped the edge of the podium, feeling emptied out and laid bare, but when the applause started, she let herself breathe. She looked to Shaw and her friends, and they had the proudest looks on their faces, which just made her want to cry. Luckily, before she could lose it onstage, the lights went dark and the videos started. The opening guitar chords of the first song she'd written since she was a teenager filled the auditorium as the short video played.

She'd written "Nia's Song" in the RV on the way back to Austin. After all the failed attempts at writing something before then, the words to the song had come to her unbidden on the road trip home, the lyrics coming from a place of healing, not a place of grief. *Hope you like it, baby girl.* She made her way back to her seat, took Shaw's hand, and let the tears fall.

The intro video finished and the testimonials started. At some point, Taryn closed her eyes, listening to her classmates' stories and leaning on Shaw. But after the first three survivors' segments, the sound of a familiar voice had her eyes popping wide. She sat up straight as Shaw's image filled the screen. She glanced at him, but he was looking straight ahead, his jaw tight.

She looked back to the screen, listening as Shaw's segment began.

"My name is Shaw Miller, and fourteen years ago, my younger brother, Joseph, walked into senior prom with his friend Trevor and opened fire. I'm not here as a survivor, but I am here to tell you that I don't believe my brother was born a murderer. When we were growing up, he was just a regular kid. He could be funny and annoying and sweet and smart. He could be all the things we all are sometimes. He could beat all my family at Monopoly. He loved the beach. He could win all the hardest video games." On-screen, Shaw looked down at his hands, gathering himself.

"He also had things going on that we didn't see because we weren't paying close enough attention. Because we weren't there enough. I realize now that he felt ignored.

He felt slighted. He felt less than. I was not an involved big brother because I was too wrapped up in my own dreams. When he accused my parents of favoring me, I told him, 'Maybe you should do something worth noticing.'" Shaw looked right at the camera, pain in his eyes. "Then, he did."

The audience gasped, and Taryn's chest squeezed tight. Shaw had confided in her the words that had haunted him for so long, but she never imagined he'd ever go public with them. She gripped his hand harder.

"Every day since then, I've blamed myself for what I said, for what I contributed to Joseph's state. But I realize now that it was one small piece in a very big puzzle that created the monster Joseph became. If something like Dr. Landry's program had existed back then, maybe Joseph would've had more of a chance, more people in his life to help. Families fail sometimes. Brothers let down brothers. Sometimes a dangerous turn in a person is so quiet that no one notices. We need to put as many safety nets as we can in place so that kids don't fall through the cracks. Please join us in our fight. Don't let there be another Joseph."

The segment ended and Taryn looked to Shaw, her heart filling with so much love for him that she thought it might burst. His darkest secret, the one he'd protected most preciously, was now on display because he thought it would help sway people. He'd done this for her and for the program. He'd given her everything he had to give. She leaned over and pressed a kiss to his cheek, breathing him in. "Thank you. I love you so much."

"I love you, too, baby." He gave her a soft smile. "Thank you for giving me the courage to say it. I needed to do that. I feel…better."

She understood. Secrets smothered. They were both ready to breathe some fresh air.

"You're amazing," she whispered.

"You're my favorite," he whispered back.

She leaned back in her seat and watched the rest of the fantastic presentation Liv had edited. Everyone sitting around Taryn had tears in their eyes. But Taryn didn't feel that sadness. All she felt was hope. And when the audience exploded with applause at the end, she felt...complete. For the first time since she'd started this journey, the ever-present anxiety smoothed out. She'd done it. This was going to work. She didn't know how she knew, but suddenly, she had no doubt.

She'd kept her promise to her sister and her family.

This program would happen.

A few people came over to talk to her, congratulate her, and offer donations, but when Shaw ushered her toward the exit to give her a break and a chance to eat, two familiar faces were standing at the back of the room.

Taryn's steps stuttered, and Shaw froze next to her, reacting to her sudden shift in mood. Both her parents had tissues in their fists and wet cheeks. How long had they been there? "My parents," she whispered.

Shaw tensed. "Oh, I—"

Before he could say more, Taryn felt her feet moving forward, and she dragged Shaw with her until she was standing in front of them. "Mom. Dad," she said, dumbfounded. "What are you doing here?"

"Hi, Taryn," her father said, voice thick. He looked like he'd aged another five years since she'd seen him last.

Taryn smiled tentatively. "Hi, Daddy."

Shaw was still at her side, his hand on the small of her

back. He cleared his throat. "I'll give y'all a minute." He turned to Taryn, his eyes saying a lot. "I'll be outside if you need me."

But before Shaw could step away, her mother's hand shot out and landed on his arm. "Stay, young man."

Shaw glanced at Taryn, and when she gave a little nod, he stayed put.

"What are y'all doing here?" Taryn asked again, overwhelmed by the sight of them.

Her mother, who was wearing a pretty flowered dress but a drawn expression, took a visible breath. "Your father heard that you were giving this presentation, and he thought we should come. For Nia."

Taryn looked down, the words cutting her hope down. Her mom didn't want to be here. "Right. For Nia."

Her mom let out a heavy sigh. "And for you," she said finally. "Your father is smart. He knew how I would feel if I saw this, saw you, speaking. Singing."

Taryn's attention flicked to her mother's face.

"You did an amazing job," her father said quietly. "You...you have made us so proud, *cher*."

Tears pricked her eyes. "Daddy..."

Her mom's stern expression finally broke. "Your presentation was amazing. And that song... I didn't know you could write something so beautiful. It was...just right. I'm so sorry I accused you of not caring about Nia."

Taryn rolled her lips together, emotions welling up.

"I know how hard you've worked for this, how much you've given up." Her mother's gaze flicked to Shaw briefly. "And maybe that's why I was so angry that you were risking all of that for a man."

Taryn laced her fingers with Shaw's.

"But we miss you, honey," her mother admitted. "And your father... Well, he reminded me that he wasn't exactly my parents' favorite choice either."

"That's putting it mildly, love," Taryn's father said. "They thought I was a goofy coonass from the bayou looking to use your mother for her smarts and her money. Plus, I was about a hundred shades paler than they were hoping."

Her mother smacked her father's arm. "Emmett, please. You know it was not about you being white. The accent did scare them, though. I think they pictured me moving to the swamps and raising gators for a living."

Her father snorted derisively and turned back to Taryn. "The point is, hearing that you were with this young man was difficult, but we both realized that we're judging someone without knowing him. I wouldn't want to be compared to my brother. We're nothing alike." He put his hand on her shoulder. "And we have raised you to be a strong, intelligent woman. I can't imagine you're easily tricked." He eyed Shaw. "So if this man means something to you, then there must be something to him."

Joy was swelling in Taryn's chest.

"And after seeing that video, young man," her mother said, looking at Shaw, "I think we jumped to conclusions that we shouldn't have. That was a very brave thing for you to do."

"Thank you, ma'am," Shaw said, voice gruff. He quickly glanced at Taryn before looking back to her parents. "And I know this is complicated, but I love your daughter and plan to do everything in my power to make sure she's happy." His throat worked as he swallowed. "I'm sorry for all the pain my family has caused yours."

Her mother stared at him for a long moment and then she straightened, rising to her full diminutive height. She put her hands out and took one of Shaw's between hers.

A rush of nerves went through Taryn.

But her mother gave his hand a squeeze and said, "I'm sorry for your loss as well."

Shaw blinked, clearly shocked, and then dipped his head. "Thank you."

Taryn couldn't take it any longer. She stepped forward and threw her arms around both her parents, something cracked inside her gluing back together. "I've missed you guys so much."

Her parents embraced her and cried along with her. When they finally pulled back and looked at each other, Taryn smiled, everything feeling right in her world.

"I love y'all," she said, the words spilling out of her.

"We love you too, honey," her mother said, "and we'll leave you to it now. I know you probably still have things to do here."

"No way." Taryn shook her head. "I can handle anything that's left tomorrow. We have to go to dinner."

"Oh, we have to, huh?" her father teased.

"Yes. Work can wait this time." Taryn looked over at Shaw and smiled, her heart full. "I have so much to tell you."

"We can't wait to hear." Her father put his hand out to Shaw and shook it. "I guess we're all going to dinner. Ready to meet the parents, son?"

Shaw smiled. "I'm ready for all of it, sir."

And so was Taryn. So. Very. Ready.

The life she was meant for had finally begun.

Acknowledgments

To my husband, Donnie, for loving me, for always being there, and for having the confidence that I will be able to find the right story even when I'm doubting myself at every turn.

To Marsh, for being so lovable, sweet, and amazing. You're my favorite.

To my parents, for being my cheerleading squad and an endless well of support and love.

To Dawn and Genny, for the laughs, the support, and for helping me get through "Dark January" without throwing my computer into a ditch.

To my editor, Cat Clyne, for her wise input, her enthusiasm for these characters, and for not freaking out when I had to ditch thirty-thousand words and start over with a new story line because I was telling the wrong story.

To my agent, Sara Megibow, for always being in my corner and for her ongoing enthusiasm for the stories want to write.

And, to you, dear readers, thank you, thank you, thank you for continuing to read my books and joining me on this journey. I hope we're together for a really long time. :